THE HALLS OF VALHALLA

1

GABRIELLA DENNANY

Contents

Pronunciation Guide

Milo
(MAL-oh)

Astrid
(AS-trihd)

Thalia
(THAH-all-ee-uh)

Silas
(SIAL-uhz)

Kali
(KAHL-ee)

Loki
(LOH-uh-kee)

Sigyn
(SIH-jihn)

Odin
(OH-dihn)

Thor
(THAW)

Heimdall
(HA-ihm-dal)

Rundi
(RUUN-dee)

Aegir
(A-ehg–ihr)

Hrvaesvelgr
(HER-ace-vel-gar)

Skadi
(SKA-dee)

Ullr
(ULL-er)

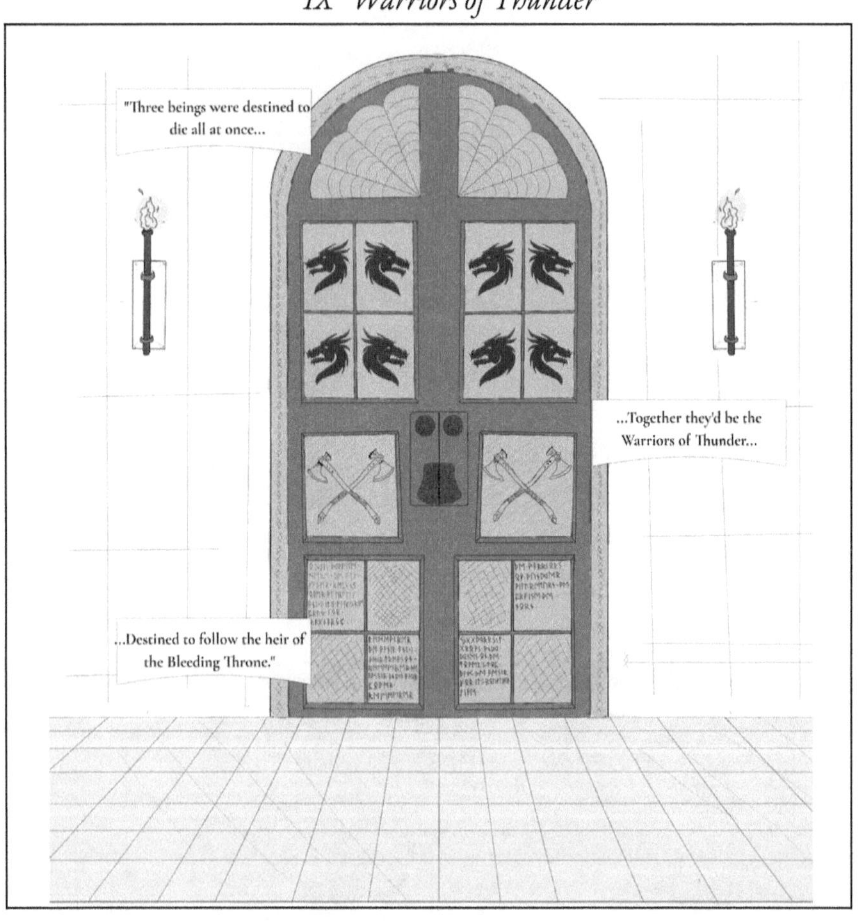
"Three beings were destined to die all at once...
...Together they'd be the Warriors of Thunder...
...Destined to follow the heir of the Bleeding Throne."

Wake and Funeral and Reception

I. The Day We Die

It was midnight, stifling, the bruise forming on his lip throbbing, and Milo Bohr might've been slightly high on painkillers, but that girl - that girl right over there - was her. *The* her.

She was as familiar as a recurring dream. He would know - most nights, he'd wake drenched in sweat with her face faint behind his eyelids. But there, in the shadowy room, she looked perfect: shoulders rounded down, head cocked to the right, nose an inch from her pen. Her fingers were nimble and slender; even from his distance, Milo could see the deep callouses lining her skin, grooves, and bumps along her fingertips. Chestnut hair fell from her shoulder. Absolutely one hundred percent absorbed. Milo's chest swelled with a painful euphoria. She was close, down the bar, and silent at her high top.

Reality lurched up his throat like a toad. There he sat, feigning drunkenness in the crowd to blend in, mesmerized by a nameless woman, a spun and threaded face stripped from his memory—an ethereal being plaguing his nightmares, suddenly alive, as physically apparent as he. The dreams on their own proved ridiculous: a limitless tower catching flames, ashen snow surrounding a frozen lake, and hands stained with blood. She remained the only constant: beautiful and haunting and earth-shattering. He ripped his gaze away.

The bar, known as *Carson's* to the locals and sleazy nightclub to the tourists, was home to none other than high school graduates. Loaded with fake IDs and unwarranted enthusiasm, young adults entering the real world swarmed to Carson's after the morning's cheery commencement ceremony, leaving behind the chattering and crying family members. Cheap booze and blaring EDM was the prize for twelve grueling years, only for it all to begin again at sunrise.

"Me-low!" Oba, the only person alive who could pronounce Milo's name wrong, clobbered up to the bar. The Nigerian native slapped his hand against the wood, flashing a pearly grin towards the bartender. His shout was incoherent, jumbled, and muffled against the music. The bartender, sour-faced and tired, responded with water. Oba shrugged. "What do you think?" He motioned to his clothes, the second outfit from his newly adopted 90s fashion phase: wide-legged jeans and a baggy muscle tank top. Against his Abraham Lincoln beard, piercings galore, and blemish-free skin, nothing stopped Oba from being the most enthralling person in the room. "Too much?"

"Never too much." Milo winked. "Not *enough*."

Oba jumped onto the stool beside him, clumsily knocking his elbow into a beer glass. The bartender, once again too relaxed to care, ignored the spill. "Where's your drink?"

"Designated driver."

His friend grinned, reached over the counter, and waved his hand frantically in the air to grab the bartender's attention. "Whiskey." Oba's voice was faint. "Calm the nerves."

He nodded. The anxiety medication he took this morning wore off hours ago, between graduates tossing their caps to the sky and his mother crying as her camera flashed. He eyed the glass, liquid glistening a bronze cream. "How'd you know?"

"You've got the look," said Oba.

Milo smiled. "The look."

"Like the world's fallin' on your shoulders." He motioned for Milo to drink.

He swallowed a mouthful, the heat spreading to his stomach. "What if it was?"

"Don't go existential on me, Bohr."

He sunk to the counter, its wood soothingly cool against his cheek. He saw the nameless girl's distorted figure through the whiskey glass, rippling like she was made of the ocean. A heaviness settled upon his side as he lay there, staring at her and intensely aware of Oba's steady gaze. His lips parted, breath fogging up the glass, and she disappeared. "I think I'm going crazy," he whispered.

"You had one sip, man."

"I'm not drunk."

Oba's lips pressed together. "Are you sure?"

"Do me a favor," his hand snapped over, latching onto Oba's wrist, "is she really there?"

"Who?"

"*Her.*"

Oba swiveled around. "The brunette?"

He nodded.

"She's there, buddy." He swung back. "And totally out of your league, by the way."

Milo lifted his head above the glass. "Is it possible to know someone before knowing them?"

"You mean, like, fate?"

"Is it possible?"

Oba looked away. "Does it matter?"

He fixed his gaze on her. Alarm bells reverberated against his temples, a headache boisterously growing within his skull. No matter how much it hurt, he could not turn away or make any decision that was not already written out before him. Her eyes scored his dreams, now real and there, waiting. He wasn't quite sure what he said to Oba, but it left his friend patting him on the shoulder, an encouraging look in his dark eyes.

Standing from the seat, Milo staggered across the room, the whiskey glass loose between his fingertips. He glanced at his reflection: black curls pulled behind his ears, sharp angles protruding from his face, giving off a hauntingly gaunt look. Stormy gray eyes stared back at him, squared glasses smudged and dirty, and the massive bruise formed on his bottom lip discolored a deep purple over tanned skin. *Good enough*, he thought. *And if not, it'll have to do.*

She was oblivious to his arrival, still staring at her paper, dragging the pen silently.

The glass rattled when he set it down. Her head jolted. He sunk into the seat, moving slowly and clumsily. She stared. People bumped into his back as they squeezed into the bar, laughing while he lurched forward. Heat, like the alcohol's burn, erupted in his throat, spreading across his collar and assaulting his neck. He sipped whiskey, hoping to find relief. The girl sat her pen down. Milo's heart banged against his chest. A shaking hand reached to his collar, pulling it aside as sweat trickled down his back.

"Damn you, pills," he muttered, touching the painkillers sitting so guilty in his pocket.

She turned. "Sorry?"

He cleared his throat. "Nothing from me." He glanced at her, quickly investigating how her lips curved as her eyebrows bunched together. He peeled his gaze away.

"Okay, then." Her Scottish accent rolled off the tongue like syrup.

He watched as she moved back to the paper. She scored the page with unusual marks. Considering starting a conversation, Milo contemplated his next words, suddenly realizing the lack of things he had to say. Either way, he kept getting the increasingly alarming notion that he would have something to regret if he spoke.

The pen slammed against the table. "I'm sorry, but do I know you?"

He shook his head. "If you knew me, we probably wouldn't be talking right now."

"Who said we were talking?"

He smirked. "Is this not talking, or do you have a different definition than I do?"

"Are you one of those creep guys waiting to slip something in my drink?"

His eyebrows lifted. The only glass on the table was his own. "No," he said, "thought you could use the company."

"I'm plenty involved in my work."

Milo looked at the paper. "Scribbles?" His fingers traced the same lines on the table.

"If that's what you want to call it." Her eyes gravitate towards his fingers, watching with a firm frown.

He chewed on his mouth, twirling the glass around absentmindedly. Condensation trickled down his fingers. He tapped the table, wondering how long it would take him to burst, rambling with crazy questions about dreams and her existence. As the glass teetered around, threatening to spill across the wood, her eyes following his movements, he realized he didn't want to know it. He didn't want the truth or reality, the tainted danger lying behind her eyes, the mystery in her appearance, and her role within his life. He steadied the glass, eyes snapping to meet her own. He wanted the lie. "Do you believe in fate?"

Her frown deepened. "That's what you're going with? Got my attention in a smelly bar filled with rowdy kids, and you go with that?"

"Still got your attention," he said, "don't I?"

Her mouth gaped open, but she quickly shut it. Her expression softened. "Something's there," she said, "*out* there. Watching our moves and planning what happens next. Whether we follow it or not is on us."

Milo watched her.

"And you?"

He sighed, settling into the creaking wooden chair. "I think there's this selfish thing trying to be a god. But instead, it fucks up every single thing on this planet."

"Right," she drawled, "you're a nihilist."

"I prefer the term 'hopeful nihilist'." He leaned forward. "Nothing has meaning, right? We go day by day; thousands die, and thousands are born. Nature moves through time in this cycle, a pattern of order. No matter what, the pattern continues. We, pieces of this natural order, believe we have this sense of free will, despite seeing the loop everything else is played on, despite knowing nothing we do changes that."

"I hope this gets hopeful at some point."

He grinned. "The key to surviving the inevitable is passion."

"Passion."

"What's the biggest f– you that you can give to a primordial being called fate? Having a passionate life with passionate people." He fell back against his seat. "My high school graduation was this morning, and I tripped over the gown to fall on my face in front of the whole student body." He reached up, poking at the bruise on his bottom lip. "I'm taking all these meds cause my Mom freaked out, but my mouth is still sore." He shrugged. "This shit would've happened whether my shoes were tied or not. It's how fate works. But you know what? It didn't bother me 'cause I am sitting here, feeling like my soul is on fire."

When he looked at her, her smile lit up the room. Air poured into his lungs, a strong awareness of being there in that moment seeping into him. The sudden surge of being alive, realizing one exists within reality, shocked him, rattling him as though he was only made of bones. She smiled at him, and his vision became sharp, the heavy weight of exhaustion raised from his shoulders. He returned it as much as he could. "What?"

"Nothing," she said. "Just interesting. Unusual."

"I'll take that as a compliment."

"Good. That's what I meant."

He wanted to scream with glee.

"Did you plan on introducing yourself sometime tonight?"

"That was my next line," he said. "Milo Bohr."

She frowned. Seeing the sudden unhappiness triggered something dark within him. He pinched himself so hard blood stained his nails. *How could I have made her stop smiling?* He nervously popped the bones in his hand, opening his mouth to let the sarcasm tumble between them. "Sorry, does my name not fit your standards?"

"Look," she began while packing her things, "you're tipsy, high, and infuriating, so go home."

"Infuriating?"

Her hand twitched. "Go home, Milo."

The mystery girl from his dreams was gone. His head fell onto the bar counter with a loud *thud.* Pain throbbed through his forehead. *"Ouch."*

"That was harsh."

Milo struggled to lift his head. Oba took over the girl's seat, lingering booze faint on his breath. "Thought I was doing good."

"You were," he said. "I *think* you were."

He covered his face. There was an annoying smudge on his glasses, but his hands weighed a million pounds, and he had no urge to clean them. Let them be dirty. He aimed for full dramatics. It was one of those nights.

"I should take you home, then." Oba jumped down from the stool.

"You're drunk!"

"No more than you, my friend. Come on."

With Oba's arm holding him up, Milo let his friend guide him out of the crowded bar as their classmates screamed and shouted excitedly. The normal Manhattan rush common during the day had no place that night. His senses were on high alert. He wanted the silence to become noise and noise to be silent. *It's just the pills*, he thought, *just the pills.*

A sharp ring came from his pocket. Oba retrieved his phone for him, glancing at the screen to see who called. He furrowed his brow and passed the phone to Milo. "It's your mother," Oba said.

Milo raised it to his ear, suddenly terrified of sounding drunk. He doubted his mother, Natalie Bohr, would mind much if he had a few drinks with friends after the commencement ceremony. But something in him reeked of shame, and an unbearable fear of making her frown overtook him. He regretted going out rather than staying home with her. That was the shame. It had only been the two of them, but he chose to venture out of his comfort zone and go to the bar. She never showed disappointment if she felt it. He bred his shame.

"Mom," he blurted.

"Honey?" Her sweet voice became muddled in the weather. The wind rushed around them, and droplets landed on his forehead. "It's storming here. Are you inside?"

"Yeah, Mom," he lied.

"Are you feeling okay?" Her voice sounded suspicious. "You sound off."

Milo dragged his hand across his mouth as though it would erase the whiskey he had. "I'm good, Mom, really. It-it's just been a long day."

She sighed lightly. "I know, honey. I thought you could get back soon, and we could talk."

"Sure, sure," he muttered, distracted at Oba, who was slowly walking into the empty street.

"Are you listening to me?"

"Mhm."

"Milo," she said sternly this time. "It's an important talk."

"I understand, Mom," he tried to peel his eyes away from Oba, but something about how he lurked through the shadows put him on edge. "I'll be there, okay? We'll talk."

She was silent for a moment. "Okay, Milo."

"I won't let you down, Mom."

"Okay," she whispered.

"I'll see you soon."

"I love you, Milo."

He smiled. "I love you more."

The phone clicked, and the call ended. A pit of dread grew in his stomach at the call for a reason he couldn't identify. He fumbled, searching the nighttime for his friend.

"It's raining." Oba sounded miles away.

Everything was numb and unreal, nothing and everything touching him all at once. His glasses clouded with steam. Swiping them quickly along his shirt, he replaced them to see wet smudges. He felt his clothes. *Drenched.* Looking at the sky, he saw the streetlights blur with pelting rain. He staggered. Oba's guiding presence disappeared. Like a hollow bullet casing, previously filled with destruction, he echoed with air.

Milo breathed deep, the rain and the city wafting over him like a wave. Calmness washed through him, and he looked towards the unrelenting rain. He extended his hand in the motion's blur, reaching for the foggy face that formed before him—the girl from the bar. The rain became sharper, and he looked away. Manhattan towers grew sharp in his eyesight, stark silhouettes like blocks in the moonlight. Darkness shaded over him.

The world became stagnant.

Milo shuddered. A stillness wrapped around him as though the world knew what was coming without telling him.

A hand grazed against his elbow. Milo lifted his rain-soaked face to Oba. His beard flattened against his chin, and his lips moved, but Milo couldn't make it out. He opened his mouth, only a sigh left.

"Do you understand?" Oba's voice strained.

Milo squinted at him. "*What?*"

Oba looked angry. He turned his head to stare at something across the empty street. Milo felt his eyes widen - something was wrong with Oba's head. Veins extruded from beneath his skin. Thickly with wood and stone, antlers had erupted from his buzzed hair, extending into the sky above him like arms. The veins were moving, growing, spreading across the thin skin along Oba's cheeks. Rain slid down his midnight body like paint, colors bouncing around his figure like a halo. Milo fought the urge to laugh.

Fear was far from his mind. He stepped back to see the man before him in full, and his jaw dropped. Wondrous colors exploded around them and into the air. The rain roared momentarily, pulling and pushing Milo around as though fists pelted into him. Oba's figure changed and warped as he moved, trying to steady himself in the rain's onslaught.

Three things, then, became frighteningly clear.

First, Milo's best friend - scratch that, his *only* friend - was a giant with deep oceanic skin, stark antlers, and swirling eyes that held galaxies.

Second, he found himself outrageously and incoherently falling for the girl from the bar.

And lastly, with a sudden awareness that chilled him to the bone, he was going to die.

"What's happening, Oba?"

The rain lightened, and Milo's senses came back, sharpening reality. Oba reached above nine feet, clothes shredded and piercings flung away. His giant form blocked out the moon like an eclipse. Everything settled in Milo's chest. Rationality took control: fear became his number one emotion, and nothing stopped him from doing what he did next.

Oba's words came to him like booms of thunder. "It's time to
_."

Milo ran.

Milo pelted by, the fallen rainwater splashing at his feet, cutting Oba's voice off. The ground shook and cracked as the giant pursued, sending tremors quaking through Milo's body. And, as though wings had sprouted from his shoulder blades, he wondered what flying would be like.

Milo, however, had an asthmatic history and was currently still getting over the fact he took too many painkillers earlier and didn't get very far. The ground shook, and Milo's legs faltered, sending him crashing down. Rolling onto his back, Milo squinted at the stars. Orion's constellation became clear, forming like a clay figure in his mind. His mother told him, once, during the early hours of the night, that his father could spend hours watching the stars; he held his hands over his eyes like binoculars. The stars looked closer for a second. He smiled. To be a star. Milo blinked - it was happening.

Oba's statuesque, giant form suddenly blocked out the stars. Everything about him looked the same, excluding the protruding veins and blue-tinted skin. Oba brought his face down towards Milo's, hot breath fanning him. "The Warriors of Thunder," he snarled, teeth ragged and sharp, "*where are they*?"

Milo considered crying. He read once that crying humanizes a person to danger's face. A shooter would be less likely to kill a girl who screams her name. Or how many fish she had. How bad her grades were. He frowned. *Why do I remember that?* It didn't matter - no tears were in stock to shed. There he was with an aching pain in his back, a wheeze escaping his lips now and then, his best friend - who *might've* been lying about who he was - standing over him, and all he could think about was two things. His mother sat in her rocking chair positioned by the front door, reading - but not *actually* reading - her latest Entertainment Weekly magazine, waiting nervously for her son to unlock the door.

And her, obviously - it always *had* to be her. He was thinking about her. Milo blinked and imagined her almond-shaped eyes staring back at him, glistening against the bar's dying lights as cheesy pop music played in the background. A girl he barely knew but had haunted his dreams for weeks was on his mind while death stood before him. He imagined it to be wonderful to reach out and touch his fingertips across her cheek's curve. Those chestnut curls would drop through his hands like honey. Milo was seconds from reaching out with his hand towards that foggy figment of his imagination.

"The Warriors of Thunder," Oba repeated. "Where are they?"

Milo thought about crying again but only felt empty as Oba raised his oversized fist. Was there a moment when life crossed that line between fiction and reality? He searched for it like a beggar, hands outstretched and wanting. And then he realized he stood with a foot on either side, waiting for something to rock him toward that inevitable ending. His heart pounded weakly against his rib cage as a monster held his thin, mundane life in his hands like a string.

He wondered what it would feel like. When he was little, he imagined thunderous wolves whisking away his father, which was why he was never around. On other days, he saw himself, older with white strands running through the curls, walking with wolves at his hips and a menacing raven hovering above his head. It didn't matter, though. There were no wolves or ravens. Instead, Oba's boulder-sized fist was hanging above like the moon, soaring down with an unstoppable force, down upon Milo Bohr.

Darkness overtook him, and death silenced his thoughts with a charismatic smile.

There was a whisper. A spring breeze washed across a field with blooming flowers, sending seeds soaring. It was soft, quiet, almost unintelligible, but at the same time, as clear as day. A singular note carried on the clouds. It crossed the dark chasm surrounding him, bounced, and echoed until it landed. He reached, but nothing moved. It echoed.

Milo.

He swore he heard a shout. It wasn't a cry, but loud and filled with rage. A horse's gallop followed it, clobbering footsteps ripping across a stone street. Another yell, a screeching war cry, erupts through his ears. The power it held echoed and burnt like a billowing fire.

Come back.

There was a lulling pull. In the darkness, Milo felt as though a rope was tied around his waist, and someone on the other end yanked, sending him jerking backward constantly. All that lay between him and beyond was the urge to remain within the darkness, sleep, and heal till he never wanted to get up again. He ignored the lull for a moment. He forgot about it. He wished to cut the rope.

And then he heard her.

Wake up.

Milo Bohr opened his eyes.

II. A Warrior's Voice

Astrid dangled in the darkness, sore shoulders aching, rusting chains digging into her wrists as she tried to sleep. The metal chains kept her upright. It could've been day outside, but it remained unknown to her. There was only the hunger for sleep, the lull beneath her eyelids calling for rest.

In the distance, screams echoed through twisting tunnels - unrestrained wails trying and failing to escape cruel punishment. The ear-splitting cries bounced off stone wall corridors. It was a recurring sound. Astrid, though, appreciated the screams, like forbidden music. It kept her awake and her heart beating as steady as possible. She tapped her fingertips against the chains to the chorus of screams.

Astrid knew her fellow prisoners' pain as much as hers. Even while fighting in the King's army, she never imagined experiencing such anguish. Her eyes closed. The shared pain within the war prisoners burnt like venom throughout, interlinked by a singular soul. Astrid breathed deeply, feeling a sting within her chest. She ignored it and willed it to grow dull in her mind. The man screamed again.

She straightened, toes barely touching the floor, releasing pressure off her burning wrists. After just a few more hours, Astrid was sure her shoulders would finally dislocate out of the sockets. For a moment, she wanted just that: a break from dull pains to taste something poignant enough to pull screams from her throat.

Her fingers twirled around a rusted pin. It was a lucky find during her rare excursions. Pushing it into the keyhole, Astrid worked the pin around, hoping to hear a particular click. The iron jingled in her ear. She kept her fingers moving, wiggling the pin's edge throughout.

The prisoner kept screaming.

The cell door creaked open. Astrid tensed, covering the pin with her hand as it sunk through the lock. *Stay quiet.* The pin poked her.

"Well, warrior," grumbled a voice, "you really are looking more like the devil's shit every day."

Astrid said nothing. More feet shuffled into the room, at least three sets. Her head remained downcast, avoiding eye contact. For a moment, before the heavy door closed, cool air rushed inside, pushing through her hair and her thin clothes like an invisible hand. She breathed it in. The door slammed shut, and the breeze was gone.

"But you're going to host a visitor!" He mockingly clapped and sneered. "Might as well clean you up then."

The pin snapped and dropped, clattering against the stone floor. She watched as men approached her on either side, unlocking the chains. The hands gripped onto her. They led her forward, down to her knees. The hands tore away the rags covering her flesh, leaving her bare and naked before them.

Astrid shuddered, keeping her eyes squeezed shut as coarse rags scrubbed her, harshly cleaning away the dried blood. Hands trimmed her long, knotted hair with sharpened razors, dragging scented perfumes against calloused skin. The men smelt like trash and iron. It was rare that Astrid was presented with a pathway towards escape. Her prayers to the gods went unheard, their attentions pulled elsewhere during such times. But then, the rusted blade yanking at her hair, she imagined Odin's hand upon her own, his divinity resting upon her shoulders.

Energy rolled down her body, and the ballistic urge to lash out in any way possible could not be held back any longer.

Her legs snapped out, knocking into their knees. They fell with a short shout. Astrid snatched at the razor, feeling its edge poke her fingertip. It sliced against her captor's skin, sending them gasping for relief as they fell to the floor. The other hurtled towards her, ripping a sword out of a leather sheath.

Astrid rolled across the floor, lashing out, the old razor cutting against his leg. She jumped, pressing her elbow against his neck, hearing the air leave his throat with a suction. The man dropped his sword and wrangled with her legs, trying to pull Astrid off his back. With a slash, the body became limp, falling from her arms. Her hand latched around his fallen sword. She approached the door, a slight limp in her step. It swung open again, knocking her to the floor, the sword sputtering away. Blood trickled from her nostrils, dripping to her mouth.

Another man, taller than the last, blocked the doorway. "And I thought you'd be docile today." His words were poisoned against her ears.

Magic.

His voice burrowed into her, slipping through her ears and whispering sleep to her brain. She became as heavy as iron. The fight and strength slipped from her, melting into the air. She groaned, staring up at the ceiling. Mortality laced her bones and trickled across her blood, binding her always to be the magic's lesser.

A woman entered the cell behind him, carrying simple trousers and a cotton shirt. With a quick snap, she helped pull the clothes over Astrid's body.

"Ready for a stroll?"

More armed guards entered the cell, hoisting Astrid up from either side. Deep dents littered their armor, weapons rusted and soiled at the backs. Astrid remained still and silent, watching feverishly before they stole her sight.

They covered her head with a wool bag, the outside concealed. Quickly, they escorted her from the cell, the door shut behind her. The screaming started again, bouncing off the walls with a piercing echo. An eerie closeness. Astrid took shuffling steps. Even though she was blind to the world around her, the warrior reached out, noting the direction and draft temperature, the corridors and their echoes, the pungent smells coming from rot and death.

Minutes passed, and another door opened. Astrid limped inside, the bag removed. A single guard remained as her other escort shut and locked the only exit. It was considerably comfortable compared to other cells. There was only a chair in the room's center. Astrid collapsed and, from the torches' dim light, examined her wounds. The magic from before faded slowly, and life drifted back into her limbs. To her left, beside her feet, was a thin puddle of liquid. She stared, dehydration clawing at her throat, and she fell towards it, her nose a hairs away from it. Before the animal in her took over and drank as much of the unknown liquid as she could handle, Astrid's reflection caught her eye.

Before the war, when she doned Royal Guard golden armor and walked the castle halls, she held a radiating glow like a halo, an angelic aura she never deserved. It was a glow that clung to her mortal figure, left over from moments spent wrapped up with the immortal. Their divinity made her seem ethereal for a day, till age crept back around ehr heart and the glow disappeared. She still recognized herself back then - round face, jutting chin, eyes like the midnight sky, curls falling down her shoulders. But then, looking at herself in the dimly lit reflection, Astrid saw an animal. Her face was stained with dirt and blood, knotted chestnut hair framing her guant skull. Those eyes stared back at her and didn't look like her own - no more were they filled with the radiant night sky; instead an emptiness, an everlasting darkness. There was no divinity left to cover her. She lifted herself onto the chair, ignoring the tempting water.

Hours passed before the cell door opened again.

A woman entered, and Astrid's eyes flickered with recognition. Standing six feet, she dressed in shimmering chain mail, a blade strapped to the hip. Her brown locks were buzzed to the scalp, golden jewelry hanging from her ears. Once the most respected general in the King's Guard, Ester committed treason and led the rebel invasion through the city.

"We meet again."

Astrid swallowed, gathering air in her stomach before pushing out a voice she no longer recognized. "What brings you down to the dungeons?"

Esther smirked. "And so the great warrior speaks! Odin would be disappointed."

"You dare say his name?" Astrid grimaced. "The All-Father would have your head if -"

"If he lived?" Every tap of her foot against the stone ground slammed through the small room, banging like drums. She walked with a limp, her left leg slightly dragging against the ground. "I suppose he would. Then again," she paused, standing directly before Astrid, "he got old over time, didn't he? Odin, the great Enemy of the Wolf, Lord of the Aesir, Havi the High One: slain by a rebellion." Her laugh sounded like blades clanging against steel. "How pitiful."

She stubbornly ground her teeth in silence.

A smile spread across the rogue soldiers' scarred lips. "Where were we?" Esther tapped her foot again. "Ah, yes, I am here to celebrate the end of my worries."

"Do you honestly believe you can conquer all of Asgard in a single year?"

"A keystone is a single entity," Esther said, "yet when it is removed, the structure collapses."

"Others remain, and others will rise."

"Is that hope I hear for the lost Prince? My friend," she said, her tone apathetic and mocking, "Thor is gone. It has been months since he disappeared, and there have been no sightings. The King is slain. The heir is gone. There is no one left to rise. Anyone who tries to fight against us has ended upon my blade. Astrid, you're a fine warrior who could do well at my side. What did the crown ever do for you except murder your family?"

Nausea gripped the warrior's chest. Memories flared through her brain: a blazing fire, agonizing screams, gods with soaring power riding through villages. A face: stark, blue eyes, golden curls framing sharp, tanned angles.

Astrid looked up at Esther. "You will never have my loyalty."

"I don't need it. There is nothing left for you to try and save. What good is your righteous adoration to the gods? It's over."

Astrid chewed on her lips. There was nothing inside her that was untouched by the gods. Her life centered around servitude. In battle, she shouted war cries for the gods. Before sleep overtook her, she prayed in thanks for surviving the day. There was nothing for her without them. She kept her head raised. "If you cannot bite, never show your teeth."

"How about this, warrior," Esther said, "hold your parables, join the rebellion, and I can offer you a place among the Aesir. Asgard's high society."

"What do you mean?"

"If you were to become a goddess, and Thor would miraculously return home, you could live a real life with your loved one." She dramatically placed a hand over her heart. "What an offer."

Astrid didn't speak. It would be foolish to lie and say the darkness tempted her. Nights tangled up beside the Prince, her hand running across his immortal skin, wondering how bright her skin might look as a god. Doing such dark magic was considered treason. Loving him was just as dangerous. She did not look Esther in the eyes. "I fight for the Bleeding Throne," she said. "Not a flawed rebellion with no meaning except to gain power."

"Open your eyes, Astrid, this war isn't meaningless."

Astrid lifted her head. Her eyes locked on to the blade strapped to Esther's belt.

"This is your last chance. Join the rebellion, or die with your King."

She smiled. "I would rather be tortured for all my life than to join you, scum."

Esther sighed. Removing her sword, she approached Astrid slowly. The blade glimmered underneath the cell's dim light. "Death is the only torture you will receive today, warrior," she said. Esther raised the blade, watching the light bounce off the sword. "Nifelheim awaits."

The sword shined against the firelight as it swung towards Astrid's neck. She rolled from the chair and underneath Esther's legs, tumbling out by the door. The guard lunged, a short blade aimed at her neck. Twisting away, Astrid snapped his wrist down, catching the blade before it fell, and dragged it across his neck. With scarlet blood painting her vision, all that remained was the warrior and Esther. Astrid rose. Fire and rage raced through her veins, her heartbeat hammering.

"Still have a fire in you," Esther commented as the lifeless guard fell.

Astrid pulled his long sword from the sheath, feeling its weight in her hand. "That's the thing, old friend," she said, "it never left."

Astrid rushed at Esther. She dipped and weaved as Esther slashed downwards. Their blades clashed, shrieking through the air, sparks showering down. It wasn't until then, that she realized Astrid remembered her unwavering love for battle, her yearning to be in war, the bloodlust beneath her fingertips. The adrenaline she used now was held deep inside during her imprisonment, a secret weapon meant to keep her alive. Now, it fueled her movement, and she quickly dipped and weaved. Her blade moved without effort, and after gripping onto Esther's chest guard, it slid under the steely carapace and against her mortal skin.

The general sank to the floor, blood escaping from her lips. Astrid placed her down gently, searching her pockets for a key.

Esther's stone-cold hand grabbed her, looking as pale as a ghost. "No god can protect you now, warrior."

Astrid ripped away, grabbing a bronze key. "I do not need one."

She unlocked the cell door, hearing the old metal clank as it opened. As she pushed the great door, the air was stolen from her throat. She could see the halls ahead, and she recognized the old tunnels. Her tattered clothes shuttered in the air, striking into her as though there was no skin. She was bones and nothing else. Odin's army used the tunnels to transport soldiers swiftly and take care of prisoners discreetly. Once decorated with paintings of Asgard's royalty, the halls stood stained by war and deceit. The art laid beneath brutish paint, words Astrid never wanted to repeat. There was no recognizing it now.

Clutching onto the blood-stained sword, Astrid left Esther inside the cell and ran through the tunnels. Astrid's bare feet padded softly against the stone floor, like a ghost trapped between the physical and the beyond.

Two guards came into view. She waited, hidden by a corner, her breathing quiet and slow. The two passed without noticing, keeping pace in the opposite direction. Astrid picked herself up and kept running. The exit ladder quickly came, the same as all those years before. If she remembered hard enough, she could see a young Thor. He was only a Prince, his short blonde locks curled against his ears. He would give her a playful look with crystal blue eyes, maybe throw a wink, and climb the ladder.

The steps grew louder, echoing down the hall as they approached. Carefully, trying not to stick herself with the sword, Astrid climbed the ladder. After a few nudges against the latch, the circular door popped open like a suction, sending warm wind. She reached and clutched the grass, pulling herself up and out of the trench tunnels. The dirt and grass were hot beneath her, the sun casting a heavenly glow against her body. She pulled herself into the outside world, the hatch snapping shut behind her.

It was a clear summer day without a cloud in the sky. Locking the latch, Astrid fell onto the ground, sucking in the sweet air she used to worship. Asgard once smelt like baked goods from the market or flowers blossoming near the castle doors. Even then, with the familiar scent gone, comfort still filled her chest. She willed herself to stay down, stay flat against the ground for as long as possible. The longer she lay there, the longer nothing else mattered. The devastation and ruin that riddled the realm didn't matter as long as she was there. Slowly, she peeled herself from the ground. She recoiled at her home. It smelt like fire and ash. Smoke arose everywhere, and some small houses lining the city's outskirts remained ablaze.

The skyscraping castle seemed the same, except for Odin's legendary statue, which was now deconstructed and crumbled before the golden city. It used to stand ominous in the castle courtyard, inviting all citizens to see the power and charity the great All-Father provided. It was now torn down, and the debris splattered like bodily remains around the cracked ground. She chewed her dry lips and held her fists tight to her sides. A scream lodged in her throat.

Astrid raised her left hand and pressed her index finger into her palm. She could feel her hand, the pressure from her finger, cold stiffness taking over the muscle. She breathed slowly. When night terrors shook her awake as a child, her mother taught her to touch her hand and ask a question: *am I dreaming?* She looked down.

"No," she said, "I am awake."

"Warrior."

Stunned, her heart dropping to the floor, Astrid flipped around at the stranger. A man stood behind her, beside the hatch where she escaped the underground prison. Rags and tattered cloth hung over his shoulders, a mismatched cloak mended with patches of cotton draped over his head. Only his face was exposed: a strong chin with pursed lips and a furrowed brow, and from the shadow of his cloak came an ethereal glow. He had an aura of golden light, and his eyes seemed to hold the sun.

Astrid staggered; whether it be from the exhaustion of imprisonment or shock, she could not tell. The being before her brought her to her knees without saying a word.

He grunted with annoyance. "Do not bow."

"It is respect," she said, voice muffled by the ground. Her nose dragged against the dirt.

"Do you know who I am?"

Chills ran down her spine. "You are Heimdall," she said, "the Watcher, the One who Sees." Curiosity nipped at her fingertips. Astrid stole a glance up at him. The god stared down at her, his golden eyes projecting a heat she had never felt. She had seen a handful of gods gather for council in Asgard's castle but never Heimdall. He remained at the Bifrost most days, his blade being the key to opening the Rainbow Bridge's portal. Since the war, no living soul entered or left the realm without him knowing.

"And what I see is a Kingdom without gods. Without it's King. My people have fled Asgard. We are no longer your Royals."

Astrid struggled to stand under his stare. "Does that mean he is truly dead?"

"The All-Father perished long ago." Heimdall's eyes eerily glowed.

"And his son?"

He looked down at her. "His son?"

"Thor!"

"You know as much as I."

"But you," the hope dripped from her hands, "you see all."

"Then that is your answer." Heimdall walked past her, standing at the cliff's edge to overlook the city. Strapped to his back was Hofond, the brilliant greatsword used to open the Bifrost. It glimmered in the sunlight. "Do you know who sits on the throne?"

"I am unsure," she replied. "The day we lost the castle is blurry in my mind." Astrid wrapped her arms across her chest, feeling a sudden chill. The attack was unexpected. It was a day free of work for her, and she spent it with Thor. He had felt the invasion within him as though every god bore the same soul. Astrid only saw the infiltrating army from the Prince's window: unmistakable even from a distance, mortals led by something entirely immortal. Though she never saw the army's leader, she remembered the war upon her doorstep, alighting the castle with rusted red and lost souls and a low-hanging miasma of death. Astrid ran with Thor from the castle's eastern wing to it's most southern point, avoidng the clanging shields and screaming gods. Spirits roamed the castle, enemy and friend alike, watching as the empty shells they once belonged to rot and melt and stain.

Astrid grew woozy in the bright sunlight. A heaviness overtook her eyelids as they fluttered close, a memory overtaking her before the watching guardian god.

It was a moment she relived every day within her cell, remembering fleeing through the castle's dim halls, avoiding the war at every turn. She had grabbed Thor, seeing his wildness in the torchlight, and screamed, "how can you run?"

Thor had pressed his hand against her chest, feeling her pounding heartbeat. "*This* is how." He touched her lips. "This." Her temples. "These." Her stomach's curve. Her fingers. The scar above her lip. The frail, stretched skin above her left eye, where one of her father's horses bashed her. She took his hand again and they ran. Her lack of guilt for the fallen left her nauseated.

Heimdall's heavy hand rested on her shoulder, ripping Astrid away from the haunted memory. "Sigyn the Sorceress," Heimdall said. "You once fought alongside her, yes?"

Her brow furrowed, her brain still foggy with ghosts. "Lady Sigyn was one of the All-Father's commanders. She was a goddess of war." Astrid stumbled over her words. "We were on many battlefields together before -"

"Before her exile," Heimdall interrupted. "She was banished."

"I remember."

"Sigyn led an army of rebels through the realm. The Aesir had been too preoccupied with the squabbling Vanir to notice a revolt brewing beneath their noses." Heimdall's fists clenched at his sides. "She used the unrest to enact her revenge."

Astrid opened her mouth and snapped it shut like a fish. The god was silent now as though he waited to hear her thoughts.

Speechlessness grasped at her throat. "She sits on the Bleeding Throne," she said stupidly.

"Sigyn has spent the last year overtaking the realm," he explained. "All that remains are the Stone Quarters. It is the way towards the Bifrost."

"I'm familiar with it."

Heimdall reached within his rags and presented her with an amulet. It was eight-sided, colored a dark purple, and hung at the end of a rusted silver chain. A glow sat at the jewel's center, pulsing rhythmically. Astrid gasped, snatching the jewelry from his grasp without thinking. Years ago, Thor surprised her with the necklace, pressing a kiss against her neck as he draped it over her head. It was enchanted to mirror Thor's heartbeat. There, in her hands on the cliffside, it had a beat similar to hers.

"Where did you find this?" Astrid said breathlessly.

"I see all," he said.

She narrowed her eyes at him. It was an easy phrase to get out of any pressing questions. She brushed it off. How he found it was no longer important. The moment she began her imprisonment was the last time she saw it. Astrid pulled it over her neck. "Why are you helping me?"

Heimdall looked back towards the castle. "Your journey has just begun, young warrior. The survival of our realm depends on you."

"Me?"

"You must live to save the throne." Heimdall reached over his head, retrieving Hofond from the sheath at his back. The blade glinted in the sun as he pointed the hilt towards her. "Take Hofond. Activate the Bifrost and find the lost Prince of Asgard. It is your destiny."

The amulet hummed against her skin. The sword radiated an enticing energy, almost like its glow beckoned for her to reach for it. She ran her fingertips over the steel. Astrid grasped the hilt, expecting it to be as heavy as a small dog, but she did not drop it. Instead, the sword was light in her palm, almost like an extension of her arm. Heimdall watched with a sadness she could not understand.

"Can you take me to the Stone Quarters?"

Heimdall smiled. "As you wish."

Astrid looked over the cliffside as Heimdall reached for her. Her home, the single realm she worshiped, was crumbling and dying. But Astrid swore an oath, a duty to her King. Even then, years after her induction into the army, Astrid would die for the gods. They could throw anything at her. Nothing would stand in her way.

The pair disappeared with a flash.

III. Pre-Pubescent Oily Chewbaccas

The ceiling was moving.

The ceiling was moving.

Milo blinked rapidly. Pinched his elbow. Rubbed his fingertips into his eyes till neon static laced his vision. He was awake, and the ceiling was moving.

It was high above him, painted a thousand different colors, shades Milo couldn't recognize or describe. The pastel clouds slid slowly across a dark blue backdrop, revealing sprinkled and glittering stars that blinked in and out. As the clouds moved, a chariot drawn by ghostly horses followed behind, a beautiful woman with long, silver hair holding the reins. A feathery cloak flew behind her, soaring through the painted sky. A massive tree constantly growing sliced through the painting, nine faint circles drawn like halos about its trunk.

Milo lifted his hand towards the painted ceiling. It might've looked far away, but it *felt* so close. It was disappointing to reach up and not grasp a handful of clouds. Milo shut his eyes. He had his fair share of odd dreams, and Oba murdering him with a skyscraper-sized fist fit into the mirage nicely. He rubbed his hands over his eyes and pinched the skin beside his elbow again. The dream remained. Pinch. Nothing faded.

Reality settled in.

He shot up, sending his stomach up into his chest. Everything came rushing through his head in flashes.

The girl.

Oba. Manhattan. Rain.

"Where are the Warriors of Thunder?"

Death.

"What the hell is going on?" he murmured, the quiet jarring amidst the silence. Pressing his hand against the itchy cloth on his chest, he felt for his heartbeat. He yanked his hand away. *No,* he thought. *I'm in a hospital, not dead.* Milo exhaled, snagging his glasses folded neatly on the nearby nightstand beside him.

Milo staggered across the wooden floor, trying to regain his balance. Everything in him felt wrong like his limbs were being pulled away from his torso, his skin burning with an invisible fire. An itch crawled up his back, and with every step he took, needles stabbed into his heel, the muscles lining his legs cramping.

Milo began to tumble, his hand shooting out to stop the fall. Breathing heavily, Milo pushed himself up. The entire wall was a mirror. He wiped the sweat from his forehead and met his reflection.

"My clothes," he said, gripping a logo stitched onto the shoulder. The intersecting triangles. The sweater was large on him, going past his waistline and over his fingers. The trousers were old and tattered with holes.

What kinda hospital is this?

Milo flinched as he remembered Oba's fist soaring through the air and towards his body. Lifting his sweater, he expected to see bandages. Wounds. Blood. Anything. He touched the skin. There was nothing, as though the events from last night never happened. Everything within him was stretching, pulling, and snapping. He suddenly feared that he wasn't in his own body, instead, his soul was snatched up and moved, placed into something unbeknownst to him. He clawed at his stomach. *Let me go.*

His heart raced - which resulted in a surprised laugh. His heart wasn't *actually* racing, was it? It rocked against his rib cage, slamming through him. His nerves kicked in, and everything told him to run. The feverish look in his reflection's eyes. The twitching in his muscles. He wasn't his own. "Put me back," he said to his reflection. "Take me back." He stared at himself. His fist slammed against the glass, a loud *thud* answering him. Milo backed away from the mirror and marched for the door. It opened without a sound, revealing an empty, narrow hallway.

Milo barely stepped when two people running side-by-side zipped by him, sending him flat against the wall. He watched as they ran by, laughing and shouting with heavy voices. He considered going back into the room. Milo walked down the curving hall, following in the running pair's footsteps.

"That there is the wrong hall, boy."

Milo shrunk in fear and prepared sarcasm like a shield against his thin skin. His mother used to twirl his hair around her fingers, pressing a motherly kiss on his forehead whenever his words whipped out like a scorpion tail. "It's a single hallway, buddy." He began to turn around. "Unless you've got a sign -"

He had seen many things in his life, but it normally narrowed down to oversized rats in the subway and two-headed cockroaches. He stepped up on crazy when Oba became a blue-antlered giant. But nothing would get crazier than the being before him.

"Aye, *buddy*, ye probably couldn't see the sign 'cause it was too high up yer arse."

He swallowed. The speaker was a woman who bore a rustic and flowing beard and grazed the high ceiling with her head. She was covered with classical Nordic armor Milo recognized from high school textbooks. She wore fur and leather, covering forged steel. The only thing rendered unusual was the blue bow tied through her messy curls. If anything, the first thing he felt was jealousy. He touched his bare chin. Two years ago, he got a single chin hair, only for his mother to yank it out, cackling as she joked about holding his manhood in her hand.

"What," she snapped, leaning down, "ain't ye ever seen a beard before?"

"Oh, well, I have," he stammered. "None as...as yours. I, for one, can't grow a singular hair!" The laughs that came out sounded more like a duck begging for food. He pinched himself.

She scoffed. "*This* is what I get," she muttered, obviously annoyed. The woman raised her eyes, turned to him, and pointedly stated, "All 'em from Svartalfheim got bushels ol beards, boy. It keeps the earth from our lungs, mining 'n such through the labyrinth." The woman chuckled, adding quietly, "Thank Nordri - he made it real 'n all before he left for the North."

Milo stared blankly at her. Nothing resonated in his brain; it pooled within him like he ate something bad. It made him unsettled and itchy in his clothes. He blinked, staring at her bloodshot eyes, scars that scrounged her fingers and face, a sword as tall as Milo's lanky legs hanging at a loop in her leather belt. Everything should've made her frightening to look at. But he glanced towards her beard, a bow shining out from the wild curls, and became content. The feeling was fleeting but like fresh air in the windowless hallway.

"I -" he cleared his throat, "Uhm, sorry." Milo looked up, trying to appear taller than he felt. "I think I'm in the wrong place," he muttered, pulling on his fingers as the bones let out sharp popping sounds - cracking his hands, a nervous tick his mother tried to prevent constantly.

Her nostrils flared. "Wrong place?" She looked him up and down, shook her head, and said, "I don't think so, lad."

"What?"

"You're dead, aren't ye?" she waved. "Follow me." She turned and went down the hallway, leaving Milo in shock.

Everything started to look blurry as his legs buckled. Her words echoed through him. *You're dead, aren't you?*

"Catch up, whelp!"

Milo looked up to see her turning down the hall. He ran after, sliding around the slippery corner in his bare feet. The turn revealed silver and sleek elevators like those in expensive hotels. *Who knew,* he thought, *that the afterlife has elevators?* Following her inside, she hit a button, and the doors slid closed. Cheery jazz music looped through the small compartment.

"I've been here since the binding of Fenrir," the bearded woman began, her voice husky and low. "Ask your questions, boy."

He looked over. "What is this place?"

"Valhalla," she answered. "'Tis the sanctuary for chosen heroes that have perished in battle. We train," there was a pause, and her head touched the elevator's ceiling as she listened to the quiet music, "till the day Heimdall's horn is heard and we are called to fight in Ragnarok, by Odin's honor."

His head spun. The elevator ticked down from the fifteenth floor, sending his head into a frenzy. The numbers on the panel kept changing. They flickered in and out, going from as low as two to as high as three thousand. It flicked to thirteen. Bad luck. He shuttered. Nevertheless, her words made no sense. The compartment hit level ten, and suddenly, he remembered. "Odin," he murmured. "*Right,* like from the kid's books, Norse mythology."

"*Myth?* The All-Father may be dead, but certainly not *myth.*" Her hands moved rapidly, like making the sign of the cross, but instead, she pressed her clenched fist to her forehead, mumbling something into her arm. A prayer.

As a child, he read picture books at the local library with stories about a Rainbow Bridge and a mystical hammer. *Stories.* Just stories. The elevator ticked again. He raised his head, staring up at the ceiling. His mother spent her entire life painting, and all around their house were watercolor pieces of a golden city, a brilliant castle within the center. Stars that shone during the day, and a chariot pulling the sun across the sky. Even a rainbow, trapped beneath a crystallized bridge made from diamonds and rubies, glistened in the inanimate painting. She said she recreated a dream, images haunting her during long nights. The paintings always replicated the old myths. Sometimes, his mother painted a man with a harsh jaw and a scar dragging through his left eye. But they were stories.

Milo wasn't sure why he remembered it. "Then all the stories -" he paused when she shot him a dangerous look. "*Sorry* - all the, I dunno, *stuff* that happened in those books," he said, "the rainbow bridge and Asgard, that's all real?"

"Real as the day Sol brings."

"So there's no God?" He frowned. "Like just one."

She eyed him silently.

"I didn't attend church often, but I liked it." He cracked his knuckles. "My aunts would make my mom and I go on Easter. It's like the whole 'Jesus is Risen' thing. I wasn't a big fan of -"

"By Ymir's beard, boy. Does ye ever stop?"

He held up his hands. "I ramble when I'm nervous," he mumbled. Nervousness happened to be an outrageous understatement. Every time he spoke, his voice quivered, and his bottom lip shook.

The woman laughed. "Not the first whelp I've had to deal with," she said, "it's not as bad as ye think, lad. 'Ere's a little secret to help." She leaned down towards him and whispered, "Everythin' ye've ever thought exists, exists. Everythin' ye've been told that don't does. Simple as that."

He inched away in the cramped elevator. Milo pressed his hand against his chest. There was no heartbeat. He ignored the emptiness.

"Listen here, boy." He looked up at her. She became kind in the moment, almost motherly. Her armored hand covered Milo's shoulder. "The best way to survive eternity: find yer clan. Bare is the back of a brotherless man."

"I'm an only child, actually."

"By Havi, boy! Take the advice with a silent tongue."

The elevator doors opened to a wide, glowing room, where the smell of mouth-watering freshly cooked food swept past Milo's nose. "But I -"

Her hand moved and pressed against his back, shoving Milo out. He turned around to see her hitting another button, immediately shutting the doors. He didn't bother to try to stop her; instead, he stared, watching as the only guidance he came across disappeared without another word.

Turning towards the mess hall, he searched frantically for an exit. He assumed he was, somehow, involved in the most drawn-out prank in man's existence. The cameras would come out, and Oba - looking normal and *human* - would extend his arms, lips spread into a wide smile. He'd let out his throaty laugh. It would go away.

Milo knew he was too optimistic as he stared at his new surroundings. Long tables filled with platters filled the space, crowded with armored people sporting weapons and shields. A few children caught his eye - three kids younger than ten sitting together at a table, looking minuscule beside the warriors surrounding them. One watched him silently with an odd stillness - the child did not have the gleam of innocence in his eyes, nothing even close to resembling youth. Milo pushed through the crowd, passing by a man dressed in traditional Union colors from the American Civil War and a woman in a bright red kimono, all giving him odd looks, whispering under their breath.

Milo ran to the closest door. His sweater suddenly became too tight, clinging dangerously around his neck. He couldn't breathe. All he needed was fresh air. Fresh air. His sweaty hands fumbled with the doorknob, carved like a wolf's head. Milo thrust the door open and let out a shout.

The outside world was like an ocean with clouds dragging across the vast blue. His eyes latched on to women in silver armor riding on flying horses speeding through Valhalla's echoing sky. Emerald vines grew across the walls. It was an island, the tower floating in a calm sea. A dark shadow shaped like a tree reflected off the sterling white clouds.

He wanted to go home. He wanted Earth. He wanted burgers and shelves stocked in supermarkets with canned goods and perishables. He wanted chlorinated pools lit an oddly green, porch lights with flies and moths and sickly sweet tea. He wanted national parks and Mother's Day and planes and trains. He yearned to hold a Bible, one with thin yellowing pages, maroon leather binding, and engravings done in gold. Milo blinked. He felt possessed.

And it wasn't like his world didn't exist anymore - someone out there was in line at a McDonald's, another filling their shopping cart in a busy Walmart - it was just far away, the same way he'd read about Napoleon in history books. Real, but only to an extent, for how real can something be if it is not displayed? Robbers and murderers and doctors and authors existed, living in a world where they thought they knew it all. Criminals knew their crimes, doctors knew their medicine, and authors knew their words. And yet, what was it they truly knew? Milo stood within a mystical tower, without either a top or bottom, growing and shrinking, sitting upon the line between life and death, and could only remember the last time he went to the movie theater. What movie was it? How much was the ticket? Where did he sit?

Milo frowned. He wanted to go home.

He hung his toes over the threshold and leaned forward, feeling the cool wind pull him into an endless sky. And he was practically out the door, halfway into the neverending blue with closed eyes and an open embrace. But he was grabbed, yanked back into the building, and with the door shut harshly, rough hands dragged Milo across the floor.

"Should've let him fall," jabbed a girl. "He would've come back anyways. That's how it works, right?"

"You really want to test that?" rebuked another voice.

Milo slowly lifted himself, turning to see two people watching him. "Thanks," he said, eyeing them cautiously.

Their clothes were identical to his, the woven triangle logo sitting over their hearts. The girl looked annoyed to be there, dark hair pulled into intricate braids down her back. Light from the surrounding candles lit her skin beautifully, like a raven's feather in the sunlight. At the girl's right was the most normal-looking man he had seen since his arrival, and he flashed Milo a pearly grin. He stood only an inch or two taller, sporting broad shoulders and a charismatic smile that shone across his dark skin. Wavy dark hair was pulled into a bun, the sides shaved. Handsome, Milo realized, would be an understatement.

The girl shrugged. She looked like she needed a hug. "We're all dead," she said, "so it doesn't matter much."

"I'm Silas Whitney," the boy said.

"Milo Bohr. I'd say it's nice to meet you, but -"

"Oh, it is." The girl grinned. "This is probably the best day of my life - er, death?" She chuckled. "I don't even know anymore! Name's Kali Caddel."

Silas shook Milo's hand. The moment they touched, the same burning pain he felt along his skin with the mystery girl surged back. Rather than a permanent pain, it sizzled to an irritated burn, numbing flames licking at their fingertips. Silas dropped Milo's hand within the second, looking around the room awkwardly. "Welcome to hell," he said sheepishly.

A shudder ran through the building when Silas said *hell.* The warriors close enough to overhear eyed him dangerously, glowering as the walls shook and groaned around them. Milo chose to ignore it.

Kali laughed. "This isn't Hell -" a rumble echoed from the tower, "it's great here." She turned on her heel and walked towards a table, dipping her finger in a bowl filled with whipped cream. "I doubt there is free food in Hell. At least, not according to *my* Church." Kali nodded her chin at Silas. "Feeling any better, pukey?"

He glanced at Milo with his lips pressed together. "I threw up for about an hour before you got here. Last time I got that sick -" he burped, " - *this sick* was when my uncle's best friend's little brother's friends drenched themselves in honey and rolled in hair clippings on their mom's salon floor. Looked like pre-pubescent oily Chewbacca's." He rubbed his stomach. "I got all the pictures."

Milo shrugged. "I got none of that."

"Babies *can* come out all hairy like that," Kali said, "just ask all the pregnant moms having heartburn."

"*Please,* by God," Silas started, holding his hands in a begging motion, "explain to our feeble ignorant ears what the *hell* you're talking about."

"I'm not kidding! Heartburn during pregnancy means the baby will be like a mini King Kong. My cousin had it bad during the second trimester, and her baby popped out with so much hair the doctor couldn't find his baby junk."

Silas laughed. "I don't think that's how it works."

"*Huh,* that's 'cause you've got a narrow-minded perspective," Kali snapped, "ain't you ever heard of families saying crazy stuff like that? Bet your grandma does something wacky, like those voodoo witches."

He blinked. "My grandmother hasn't remembered her name in five years."

Kali stared at him.

"If telling yourself that helps you sleep at night, then *sure,* my grandmother is a witch."

She grinned triumphantly.

Milo swallowed. "Sorry to break up whatever *this* is, but do you know what's happening?" He walked towards the table. "Like, seriously, what kind of hospital looks like this?"

Silas sat down, pushing a plate away. "I woke up feeling like shit," he grumbled. "I had the craziest dream of getting stabbed," he said, "and when I opened my eyes, I was here." A shadowy look crossed his eyes, a tremble rippling through his arms. He shook his head, blinked a few times, and smiled reassuringly at Milo. "But like I said, it was a dream."

Milo followed suit, sitting beside Silas. He wondered who the boy was trying to convince, but he didn't have the heart to say it might have not been a dream. "I met this girl," he began, "and my best friend, he became - is, I guess, a monster. I thought I died." Needles ran up his arm as he brushed by Silas, like swiping against flames. Milo ignored it again.

"You did," Kali said with a shrug.

He tried not to be surprised at her careless attitude - why would she be obligated to protect a stranger's mind? She busied herself with the endless supply of food scattered across the table. Maybe she happened to be a naturally calm person. Milo frowned. For some reason, he had a hard time believing that.

It took everything to bite his tongue and keep quiet. The last thing he wanted to do was put himself in an even worse situation. He took a deep breath and picked up a shining goblet. Filled with an amber-like liquid, it reminded him painfully of the whiskey he drank the night before. "Did you meet a girl last night?"

Before they could answer, men marked with war paint and women with hijabs approached, brandishing stained spears. One thing was the same about them: their eyes held hate, a raging darkness hidden beneath the color. Milo looked away, feeling awkward, like the first day in the high school cafeteria. The strangers weren't moving, though; a nervous chill ran down Milo's spine. He messed with his food and avoided eye contact.

"Look at the whelps," one said, speaking like she recited a song. Her hijab was a deep red, casting a frightening shadow over her skin. Milo watched in awe. She looked magnificent - something otherworldly. Stark paint lined her jaw and cheekbones, harshly lighting her skin. And her accent, thick and like an orchestra, carried brightly across the chaotic room. His chest filled with butterflies. "What warriors are you, little shrimps?"

Milo looked around the table. If they were meant to be warriors, someone would be disappointed. Kali scooped an outlandishly large spoonful of whipped cream in her mouth. Across sat Silas, who tried to shove bread in his trouser pocket, while Milo poked and prodded at meat with a miniature pitchfork.

"I didn't realize that bullies were considered warriors." Silas nonchalantly dropped the bread on the floor, smiling at the group.

The courage Silas carried brewed an envy within Milo. He wanted to rip off the boy's charismatic smile and slam it to the floor.

But he didn't want that. At least, that's what he thought. Ever since he was a kid, spikes of uncalled-for anger burrowed within his chest. Therapists didn't help much, no matter how many his mother found on stellar recommendations. There was a dormant anger somewhere deep within him. He ignored it, catching on to the warriors growing irritated with Silas's unwarranted confidence. People with pointed spears probably didn't do well with the nineteen-year-old attitudes.

"We don't want any trouble," Milo said, glancing at Silas.

One leaned dangerously close to Milo's face, his breath like steam from a lake on a cool morning. "You scum come into Valhalla," the warrior exclaimed, voice clouded with a German accent, "proclaiming you are heroes, but no Valkyrie chose you. You - *all of you* - have broken the rules."

The man slowly backed away, muttering something to his group in an unfamiliar language. He racked his brain for the fables he used to read but kept coming up blank.

"What the hell is a Valkyrie?" Milo asked no one in particular.

"Don't you know about Norse mythology?" Kali dropped the spoon, moving on to a shimmering goblet. "You're here 'cause you have some Nordic relation. That's normally how the stories went." She swirled the cup around, raising it to her lips. "Not just anybody gets welcomed into Valhalla."

"I'm Italian."

She rolled her eyes, downing her drink. "You're Norse. It's why you're here."

"I thought I died a hero!"

"Didn't you hear those assholes?" she snapped. "We broke the rules. It doesn't matter how we died," Kali paused, chewing on her lower lip, "no Valkyrie brought us."

"Once again," Milo said, "can someone please tell me what a Valkyrie is?"

Silas bumped his elbow into Milo's. "They're those ladies." He nodded towards the woman standing in the shadows, away from the warriors. They wore sterling silver armor, hair flowing behind them like capes. Long swords were strapped to their belts, glinting dangerously in the soft light of hanging torches. Something was painfully obvious about them - maybe the unnatural beauty they carried or the brightness from their armor. One snapped towards Milo, her eyes alight with a brightness like steel's edge. He jumped away.

Kali sighed. "The woman of Valhalla. They go to our world and bring dead heroes back here."

Milo searched their faces. None resembled the girl from the bar, though he hoped she would be here. He looked away somberly. Her absence stung him more than he thought it would.

"You said something about a girl?" Silas wasn't looking at him.

He nodded. "There was a girl last night I had never met before. It was odd," Milo looked back towards the Valkyrie. Odd was more like an understatement. He hadn't told them about the dreams; midnight thoughts sounded like too much information to share. "I just hoped you guys might've seen her too."

Silas shook his head. "Sorry, man. I don't remember what happened to me." He rubbed his hand across his neck, exhaustion filling his eyes. "I did overhear these two Viking-looking guys talking about a war, though. But I couldn't recognize the names they mentioned - something 'heim' and Odin or Thor."

Drums banged in time with each other. Doors at the hall's head swung open, an amber glow filling the room with warmth. A procession entered, marching with the drums, a short man at its center. Bald and dressed in fur, the man slammed his staff against the floor with each step, beard swaying. Milo could hear clicking from his intricate braids, adorned with beads. The warriors shouted and clapped with pride, arms raised above their heads in welcome.

A chant grew across the hall. Their table was silent compared to the others. Kali didn't pay much attention, focusing on the whipped cream. Milo glanced at Silas: the other boy stared at him peripherally, his gaze resembling a red laser point. Milo quickly looked away, feeling as though he saw something he wasn't supposed to.

Raising his short arms into the air, the hall grew silent in anticipation. The old man climbed onto an elevated stage, looking out at the warriors, a crooked smile pulled across his wrinkled face. Younger people, faces almost childlike, stood beside the old man, arms decorated with lavish clothes and drapes. Their skin, lit ominously by the firelight, grabbed Milo's attention. They were each different shades of green, one as earthly as freshly mowed grass, another housing a color so dull it melted into old leaves. None moved, standing like ornate decorations. The crowd settled in their seats, appearing calm for the first time since Milo's arrival. Only the Valkyrie remained stiff like steel, eyes scanning the room in a heavy silence.

"My children," he shouted, voice strong and echoing throughout the chamber, "welcome to the Feast of Feasts," his arms raised, "the Day of all Days - bringing the undead to our home, Valhalla, the heaven of the Almighty Odin, blessed with the hand of Frigg and kiss of Baldur!" The man clenched his hands into fists, punching the air before shouting, "Valhalla!"

A chant began: "*Valhalla! Valhalla! Valhalla!*"

The old man quieted the crowd. "Tonight, we celebrate our new warriors to serve the almighty Odin." He thrust his cane, a raven carved into the top, towards the table where Milo sat. "I am The Master of Valhalla. Come forth, warriors."

Milo guessed that the eerie silence floating through the hall meant they weren't wanted. Kali dropped the spoon and proudly marched towards the front where the Master stood. Silas, hands buried in his pockets, waited for Milo to get up. Milo sighed and followed behind, pulling and popping the bones in his fingers. The crowd parted as they approached the Master, moving away like they held a disease.

A murmur rippled across the hall.

"They're cheats!"

"Those ain't warriors!"

"Feed them to Heidrun!"

What the - an image appeared before his eyes: a goat silhouette against a tree's shadow. He wasn't sure how, but instantly, he became aware that *Heidrun* was a goat who sat upon Valhalla's top. The sudden knowledge shocked him, rolling through his brain like it was common, something anyone might know. Milo looked at the Valkyries standing in the corner. One grasped her sword, a sneer painted across her bony face. He looked away, feeling the walls close in around him. Milo stood beside Silas on the elevated stage. He reached into his pocket, hoping the painkillers would still be there, or even his inhaler. It was empty.

Up close, the Master stood under five feet, wispy reddish-gray strands making up his intricate beard, delicate braids tied in patterns. Tattoos marked him, runes scoring his old skin. Underneath the rough exterior were gentle eyes, a chocolate brown. Fear and comfort, a dull ache, and a sudden warmth mixed in his chest, pooling into Milo's soul with the same consistency as oil. He recoiled.

The Master looked over them, a wide smile on his thin lips, revealing a few golden teeth. "You three must have plenty of questions," he said, "that I am willing to answer. But first, I invite you to sit at my table and join the feast."

Silas cleared his throat. "And then you'll tell us how to go home?"

The room exploded with hearty laughter, men and women shouting to each other over the noise, while Silas glanced around, confused. It hit a mark in Kali's sharp exterior. She shrunk back, almost hiding behind Silas's beanstalk frame. Milo began to see the Master's answer before he spoke. A pang began in his heart as the crowd reacted chaotically, his gaze catching onto his company's dreary faces. He avoided looking toward the laughing audience, watching as the old man formulated his next words.

Don't say it, he thought. *Please.*

The Master slammed his cane against the ground, a wave coursing through the room. It grew painfully silent. He turned his head back to the trio. "I...you're not going home."

Milo's chest began to burn, and the headache reappeared behind his eyes. A heaviness burrowed within his back, traveling through his limbs and towards the heart. For a moment, he became stone, stuck in place and never moving again. And then he exhaled, and the world around him faded into a colorful blur. One thing mattered and rushed through his head.

You'll never see your mother again.

That phone call before Oba went crazy replayed through his mind. His Mom, back in their little yellow house, sat beside the front door, waiting for him to come home. He remembered what he said to her: 'I won't let you down.'

Milo swallowed his vomit.

Suddenly, his feet were moving, and he sprinted out of the great hall, not caring about the pressure squeezing his lungs together and trapping the air in his throat. The tears were hot against his cheeks, burning their way down to his chin. He clawed at the walls, tripping over his bare feet as the halls got narrower and colder. There were no windows. No air. The burning continued within his veins, pulsing and erupting in his blood.

He slid down. The walls covered him like a blanket, and he crouched against the hall's corner. Chills ran through him as his death replayed, moments upon moments erupting in his temples, burrowing in his throat. There was a conversation, something Oba said to him that he couldn't understand, too foggy the night before, but as he hunkered down in the halls of Valhalla, listening to the *fake* heartbeat in his chest, he shut his eyes, and remembered:

A hand grazed against his elbow as the rain pelted down around him. Milo turned to see Oba staring, his dark eyes narrowed. "When we first met, you had no friends," he began, his words quiet and melting within the raindrops. "Why?"

Milo couldn't find his voice. It was filled with the whiskey's leftover drops, strained from shouting over the bar's loud music. Milo had no answer, even if he had the will to speak. All his life, he never fit into any place. People weren't comfortable around him. His mother used to say the energy he held within his soul was too strong for regular people to handle. Milo liked to call it bullshit. He shrugged.

Oba looked away. "You were my friend, and for that, I thank you."

All Milo could think about was the mystery girl and what he planned on having for breakfast the next day.

"Your father would be proud."

That caught his attention. Milo looked over at Oba. His head was angled upwards, facing the sky, letting the rain fall and drench his face. It sounded like a friendly thing to say. Oba couldn't have known his father. Milo couldn't, however, shake the feeling Oba knew more than he was saying. He reached towards his friend, grasping at his wrist.

No words came out.

Oba turned, not bothering to wipe the rain from his eyes. "If you can tell me where the rest of them are, I can spare your life." Something changed on his face. His dark eyes held another meaning Milo couldn't place. Oba pulled his arm away, leaning towards his face. "Do you understand?"

Milo remembered that. Oba was strained, his voice suddenly losing its native accent. He felt himself shrug. "What?"

The rest was clear.

Super-sized Oba.

He opened his eyes, and one thing was for certain.

Milo Bohr was nineteen years old and was a dead warrior in the Norse heaven known as Valhalla. He did the only thing he could do in a situation like this.

He screamed.

IV. Yrsa the Wild

Grazing her fingertips against the circular pendant resting on her collarbones, Astrid looked up at the Drunken Dwarf Pub's ceiling. She could make out her scrawled handwriting, carved messily into the stone if she squinted. It read her name, and beside it, much neater and more visual, was her sister's name. The little girl's favorite rune was etched beneath, a long line with a shorter one striking through the middle at an upward angle. It meant a good harvest and bountiful blessings. Countless years have passed since Astrid last found herself in the pub. When she imagined her return, she hoped it would be on more pleasant tidings.

Before the war, it was common for Astrid and her little sister, Frey, to find themselves within the Drunken Dwarf, using it like a sanctuary, one close to home, always bustling with friends and family. If she concentrated, Astrid could almost see the little blonde head sprinting in front of her, knocking into legs and pulling down stools. Frey was the youngest in the farming family, and yet she was the one who found herself within its center, the absolute life of the village. Astrid knew from the moment Frey could speak she did not belong in their world of farming cattle and surviving off harvest. She was named after a wondrous god, after all. She dreamed of parading through the streets alongside her gods, dancing with flowers in her hair.

Used to be.

The day never came.

Frey's world ended before it got the chance to begin. Divinity never touched her. Love missed her heart. She wandered through Death's fields, only a child, a young soul ripped from Asgard, and returned to Yggdrasil. It was what the girl adored that killed her, what she prayed to that tore her limbs apart, dropped fragments of her dead self along doorways, along fields, along shadows. Astrid felt heavy with longing.

A hand touched Astrid's shoulder. She flinched, instinctively reaching for Hofond as it stung the skin upon her back. Her hand lowered. If any Asgardian knew a god's blade rested upon her person, hell would break loose within the already crumbling bar. She raised her head, eyeing the barman. His hand was raised, pointing towards the dimly lit back corner. She followed his point with her gaze. Half covered by shadows, half-lit by small torchlight, was a hooded figure, an ambiguous glow radiating around the short table. The barman's hand lowered as she quickly approached.

Astrid slid into the chair across from the silent figure, blowing out the stubby candle between them. She pushed the dripping wax towards the table's edge without a sound - the more darkness, the better. The figure gasped, sounding like a tired laugh mixed with a cry. With a steady hand, the figure pulled the hood from their face.

"Little warrior," the figure said, voice as cool as icy water, "what a surprise."

Fae.

Astrid sighed, leaning back against the chair. The Fae held pale, blue skin, casting an eerie glow in the darkness, shadows cast by the sharp angles. Her ears sharply pointed towards the ceiling, rings forged from gold and silver pierced into her. The tattered clothes she wore hung loosely from her thin limbs, but the dim light from her Vanir marks still shone - no matter how much light Astrid quenched, the godly blood the Fae held could never be diminished. Pure silver marks designating her as a Vanir were covered as much as possible - Vanaheim creatures were no longer accepted on Asgard's streets.

The Fae smiled, crystallized and pointed teeth glinting. "I was surprised to see your little calling on my doorstep," she said. "Plenty of years have passed since I gave it to you."

Astrid shrugged. "Favors don't expire."

Calling a Fae creature was simple: place the designated token upon their domain. The last time Astrid found herself face to face with the Vanir before her, it ended with a smooth stone being placed in her hand, colored a deep blue. Astrid placed the stone at a small garden pond on her way to the pub. At first, she hoped the Fae wouldn't show up - she could find another way to find information. But as she sat there, hope rushed through her veins. It was better than nothing.

"They do," the Fae replied with a grimace.

She watched the Fae with a weary eye. The deep purple orbs that stared back at her glistened with magic - Astrid flinched away. Before bed, her mother told her little folk tales about the Fae walking through Asgard at midnight, the flowers they'd pick and twirl into crowns, and the names they'd steal from passersby. And there was always one thing to remember: *never give the Fae your name.*

The Fae exhaled, wildflowers spreading between them. Astrid did her best not to breathe in the magic the Fae conjured. It was a protective air to keep the barman occupied while they spoke, averting prying eyes. Breathing it in could do many things to Astrid's mind. The

Fae stopped her magic-wielding, satisfied with her work, leaning back in her seat with a *creak*.

"Why here?" the Fae asked. She raised her hand, tracing the same Nordic rune the little Frey would scrawl into the wood. The Fae frowned. "So much of the child lives here. I can still smell her spirit."

Astrid flinched again. The creature nipped at healing wounds, picking at scabs along her soul with tainted fingertips. One little pull and she unraveled, everything buried inside split before the Fae, secrets, and treasures ripe for picking. She needed leverage. There was once a time when she knew the creature's name, whispered across the covers at midnight, a blue-eyed dawn watching her.

"Trying to remember, little warrior?"

Astrid smiled. "You're too smart for me."

The Fae leaned forward, nimble fingers tapping against the table. A vine slipped out from her sleeve. She tilted her head, scars lining her collar. "You carry something -" the Fae paused, eyes fluttering, "- *priceless*."

"It was a gift," Astrid said. Hofond burned against her.

"Yes," she muttered, "the all-seeing one." The Fae's eyes peeled open, the purple orbs as black as night. "You wish to leave Asgard."

Astrid cleared her throat. "Do you still answer questions?"

The Fae smiled, her eyes fading back to their purple hue. "For you," her smile grew, "I could."

"Could?"

"I'd hate to call you *little warrior* when we are so obviously friends," the Fae said. Her head tilted again. "Aren't we?" Her eyes glowed eagerly. "Friends know each other by *name*."

Astrid laughed. "The young Prince once called me Tora, but only when Sol carried the sun across the morning sky."

"And at night?" Her face was stern and cut like a diamond. "What did he call you then?"

"Yrsa."

The Fae abruptly laughed. "Yrsa the wild," she mocked. "The pretty Thor called his secret lover Yrsa?"

Astrid sunk into her chair.

The Fae leaned back in her seat, eyes never leaving Astrid. "I wonder what his betrothed would think." A softer laugh came between her thin lips, caressing the air between them. "One day, you'll find that funny."

Astrid rubbed her eyes. "What shall I call you?"

"Rundi," the Fae replied. "Give me your questions, Yrsa the wild."

"Where is he?" she whispered, glancing over her shoulder. "The son of Odin."

"Son?" she repeated.

"Thor."

"How boring," she drawled, resting her pointed chin against her palm. "When the Old Havi fell, Thor disappeared soon after," she replied with a tired shrug. "At the winding river edge, waiting." A shudder ran through her, a soft glow illuminating beneath her clothes. "*Waiting*." Her eyebrows furrowed as the color grew in her eyes. "I see," she said. "He waits for *the other*."

"The what?" Astrid jumped forward in her seat. She fought the urge to grab the Vanir. "I don't understand -"

"We never do." Her eyes faded, the Vanir marks dimming to a dull glow. "I have answered it with all I can. Another, Yrsa the wild?"

"How can I find him?"

Rundi lifted her head. Her fingers rapped against the table, flower petals shaking from her sleeves and scattering across the wood between them. "That depends, Yrsa."

"On what? A price?"

She shrugged. "It is not me you'd need to pay." Rundi snatched Astrid's hand before the warrior could pull away. Her claw-like fingers gripped her harshly. Rundi squeezed, leaning forward till her sharp nose touched Astrid's. "How far will you go, little Yrsa?"

Astrid tried not to move, feeling herself relax within the Fae's tight grasp. She steadied her breathing, paying attention to the amulet pulsing at her throat. "I'd travel through death." And as the words came out, she wondered who she was trying to convince: the creature or herself.

Rundi stared for a moment before dropping her hand. But within a movement as quick as a breath, her hand reached forward again, and the Fae's fingertips scraped against the amulet beneath Astrid's shirt. It spiked in energy at the Vanir's touch, growing so hot Astrid worried it would burn straight through her chest. The Fae laughed, pulling back and falling delicately into her seat.

"One day," the Fae whispered, "I think you will."

Astrid was silent but did not flinch. Fear should not be shown, even though the phrase *I think you will* hung darkly over her like a storm cloud. Nevertheless, Astrid looked upon the Fae, held her enthralling stare, and smiled. She breathed deeply, waiting for the Fae to continue.

Rundi looked pleased. "Did your mother ever tell you the Berserker tale?"

"Of course."

"The strength of a wolf, boar, and bear lies within their hearts," Rundi explained, voice low and almost musical in the still room, "bestowed upon them by consuming Odin's blood." She smiled, the pearly teeth glowing in the shadowy darkness. "It is said that their hearts beat in tune with Odin, a beacon towards their Master's life force."

Astrid nodded. "I know the stories."

"And when Odin fell," Rundi said, "so did they."

"What's your point?"

Rundi's smile grew. "One still beats. It pulses in fragments, magic far gone. But pulses still."

"You're saying that a Berserker still lives?"

"Whether she lives or not is rather a personal preference." Another laugh escaped. "The Berserker still *exists,* Yrsa the wild." The color in Rundi's eyes grew bright, flashing excitedly as she added, "The warrior's eyes grow the brightest towards their beloved."

"Where?"

Rundi smiled wildly. "Midgard."

It was an impossibility, a Berserker living. She yearned to run. Even the idea of traveling to Midgard forged an unwillingness within her. The Fae watched eagerly. The creature soaked up her response like light. Astrid feigned a smile, tried to imagine reuniting with her Prince, and showed teeth. This was what she wanted.

"Your help is -" she paused, catching herself as Rundi grinned. She smiled, holding her glistening gaze. "It's appreciated."

Rundi frowned. "Appreciation can be shown in other ways."

"What do you want?"

The Fae shrugged dramatically, playfulness in her eyes. "Times are hard for Vanir like me," she began, tracing her finger slowly around a carving in the old table, "the rebels are fighting Aesir and Vanir alike."

"If I could find Thor -"

"Don't be a child," Rundi interjected. "You scoff at godly help but place all your hopes and strengths upon Thor." She laughed spitefully, raising her eyebrows. "And what is he compared to you?"

"Flattery comes easy to you, doesn't it?"

"Heimdall bestowed the Hofond upon you. This is not flattery. How ignorant can you truly be?"

"Cut it out," she snapped, lowering her head as heat swarmed to her face. "I can't give you protection, Rundi."

"You misunderstand," she said. "I need you to *remember* me, Yrsa the wild. There will come a time when," her eyes grew cloudy, "you will be cast into darkness. And only I will be your hope."

"*That's* the payment?"

"Give me your word, little warrior," Rundi said, "that you will not forget me."

Astrid stared. The simpleness of it sent prickling sensations down her spine. The word *give* hung on Rundi's tongue like honey. Her mother used to pull Astrid and Frey close into her chest, whispering *never give a Fae-one anything.* The act itself felt harmless. Even the enigma of being cast into darkness didn't bring much fear. But it was different, then, with Rundi's eyes watching, this deep intensity burrowing in her throat. It was heavy, electric against the air, building to something she had long forgotten. She settled back in her seat, letting out a breath.

And then she smiled, proceeding to sign her life away carelessly.

"I won't forget you. You have my word."

Energy bounced between them. Rundi inhaled sharply, the marks lining her skin glowing with light. It took only a second: power and a dull quiet after. Rundi fell back, breathing heavily. Her bright eyes fell on Astrid.

"Find the Berserker, and your destiny will begin."

Astrid wasted no time. She flew out of the seat and shot across the bar before Rundi finished speaking. Her hand gripped onto the amulet. The invisible protection Rundi created faded as the warrior wafted through, the anticipating heat from Hofond, ready to be wielded, fueling her quickened pace.

She would be ready for anything.

V. Death is Only the Beginning

You'll never see her again.

Milo hung onto his curled legs, hot tears streaming down his cheeks. He didn't care how childish he looked, crying for his mother. There was no time for him to live without her, to know how to survive without his Momperpetually at his side. He yearned to beg and scream for her. His throat felt raw and scratchy, deep and guttural whenever he made a sound. His chest burnt from crying.

Eventually, he heard a light tapping. "Go away."

"C'mon, Milo." Silas pinched at his shirt.

Pushing himself up, Milo wiped his tears with his sleeve. "God," he breathed, cleaning his glasses, "I must look like an extreme wimp right now."

Kali snorted. "Wimp is an understatement."

"What happened to you?" asked Silas.

Milo shrugged. "I just lost it. I mean, doesn't the fact that you're dead freak you out?"

"Does more than freak me out," Silas muttered. He raised his eyes, throwing a comforting smile. "It'll be, well, everything will work out. Somehow."

Kali, on the other hand, leaned against the wall, chuckling.

"I don't think it's funny," Milo snapped.

She smiled. "It might not be funny, but it sure as hell ain't sad."

"Listen to my words. We are *dead*. There is no going back. No home, no more family. Nothing." Standing just a foot away, he noticed she was so short that she only reached his elbow.

"Take a step back, Milo. Just because you're bothered by it doesn't mean I have to be."

"It's like you don't have a heart."

She froze. Her face twisted into a grimace. "So what?"

He wanted to fall into a hole. It was the last thing he wanted to say. They watched him. He forgot who he was, how he spoke with razor edges and a forked tongue. His hand raised to his chest. He was hollow. Milo took a step back. "That wasn't what I meant, Kali. I shouldn't have said it."

Kali pushed past him. "Whatever. We were all gonna die anyway. Can we go back to the food now?"

"Stop for a second," Milo said, "and think. What's gonna happen now? We go back there, act like everything's okay, act like those people back there are normal and don't want to kill us - *again* - eat all the food we can, and then what?"

"At least we aren't alone," said Silas.

The space between them grew eerily silent. Milo's knock-off heart raced inside him, beating uncontrollably. His own words echoed in his mind. What would he do now? The small group didn't meet each other's gaze. It was sinking in, and Milo could only wish it was a dream.

"Maybe we could talk to that old guy back there," Silas said, "he could help us."

Kali scoffed. "He tried to talk to us, remember?" She threw her icy stare towards Milo. "But then quick feet over here had to run outta there like his behind was on fire. If you coulda just stayed calm, we might know something by now!"

"But I -"

"It doesn't matter now," Silas said, grabbing onto Milo's shoulder, "we stick together and figure it out. Fighting won't help the situation."

Milo pulled away, slinking back against the wall.

Sighing, Silas leaned on the wall beside him. "I wonder how long it'll take to hold funerals."

"Took a week for my Uncle." Kali stared at the ground. "Wake and funeral and reception."

"I hope mine's good," Milo said. "You know, awkward conversations with old people you never really knew, bad cheese plates, malt liquor." He smiled. "A whole life in 48 hours." He pushed himself off the wall. "You know what's weird? I grew up off paper plates - my mom and I moved around so much that there was never any point in real ones. But the first time I used real plates was at a funeral. They felt so heavy."

"Your childhood was depressing," Kali said. "Like seriously."

Silas snapped his fingers. "First funeral for me, I got a back massage from Underbite Laura in the bathroom."

"What?"

"A back massage."

Milo laughed. "Did you say underbite?"

"Yeah," he replied, "got four Lauras in the family. In my defense, I was about thirteen, and she referred to herself as Laura with an underbite." Silas grinned. "Felt like Beyonce taking a trip to Bora Bora in a yacht."

A shadow, elegant and lean, passed behind the trio and turned down the hall. Milo's eyes fixed on the movement. There was a click in its step, short heels tapping against the tiled floor. The voices around him faded. The shadow moved with a familiar twist, curling around the corner and gone in a blink. His interest grabbed, and Milo walked through the group, completely entranced.

"Milo," Silas called, "where're you going?"

He turned down the hall and saw the figure more clearly - a woman, her dark hair pulled into a braid, entered the feast, unaware of the group following close behind. With olive skin shining like gold underneath the firelight, she was an image Milo spent months adoring. His anger erupted, but beneath, electricity bumbled in his chest, sprouting into butterflies and sparking flowers to grow along his spine; nothing changed the blunt effect her presence had upon him, the blatant and never-ending urge to hold her. It was the woman from the bar. Everything, however confusing and blurry, is tied together.

"Don't do anything -" Silas began.

Milo shouted: "Hey!"

" - *Stupid.*"

Within the mess hall, boisterously loud laughter echoed against the walls, and the armored Valkyrie moved to an empty table, eating and chatting quietly as the party stormed around them. Sitting at a long table overlooking the feast, the old man remained near the front. His lips moved rapidly as he spoke to his companions. A plate soared and crashed against the opposite wall just as the woman from the bar stopped walking.

The woman spun around. She smiled. She bore no friendly recognition, instead a snarl before devouring her prey. Amber eyes glistened as her gaze landed on Milo. An ache grew in his chest, a tug at his stomach. Her gaze flickered to the others behind him.

Silas sucked in a quick breath. "*You?*"

The shock rolled through him. Silas did have an experience with the mystery girl. He rushed into jealousy, wondering why Silas's skin grew a bashful red. He shook his head - *you don't even know her.* But then the dreams returned to him, and every night, seeing her unnaturally beautiful face haunted him. She was his dream. Milo glanced towards Silas, trying to hide the growing resentment.

"Right," she said. Her head shook, a curl falling to the length of her face. She chewed on the skin around her fingertips. "Look, I'm sorry, but -"

"Who the hell are you?" Milo tried to ignore her nervous tick, but it stabbed him in the heart - *she was so normal.*

"What?" Her Scottish accent sounded deeper, more natural within the afterlife.

"You're the reason I'm here, right?" he spat. "Well, I think it's time for some answers."

"Not from me. If I were you, I'd keep the questions to a minimum." She gazed over the crowded feast hall. Her lip turned up in an amused smirk. "Dead men tell no tales."

Someone from a nearby table listening in boisterously laughed.

"*To agori tha einai to proto tha pesei kato!*" someone shouted.

Milo fidgeted in surprise. The language felt ancient and strong in his ears, almost vibrating. But as it passed into his head, the words unscrambled and melted into a recognizable paraphrase. The voice repeated in Milo's head: said something like *that kids' gonna get pummeled.* He would have to remind himself later to reminisce that *he somehow knows Greek.*

"Don't walk away. You did this to me," those burning eyes flickered over, "so it's damn well time to fix it."

And somehow, without Milo even realizing it, he offended her, which was the worst decision he ever made. Suddenly, she was there, moving faster than sound, and her fist tightened around his collar, lifting him off the ground. Heat shot across his skin. Milo gulped as he stared into her darkened eyes, and if it was any other time, he'd take some time to appreciate how much strength she had in her arms.

Silver grooves scored her skin, drawing out a bear's face along her own. Her head turned as she held him, her gaze falling upon the old man.

"Why can't your kind ever listen?" she hissed.

He shrugged. "We're quite friendly when you get to know us."

"Aye, sarcasm," she drawled, casting another look towards her audience, "that's original." She threw him, his back slamming against the tiled floor. The crowd bellowed with laughter as he struggled to push himself up, the pain suddenly zapping through his body like wildfire. A choke gurgled, blood pooling behind his teeth. He blinked as spots covered his vision.

You'd think, he thought, *death would stop the pain.*

"Do yourself a favor," she said, "and stay down."

Milo never considered himself a smart kid. His grades were all right in school - never good enough to fit in with upper-class intelligent kids who always wore polo shirts and dress pants. When it came to street knowledge, he proved to be even worse. If a beautiful girl he somehow fell undeniably infatuated with through misty dreams stood before him, he'd soon realize his inability to turn away. If he was told to walk away, any will to move his legs left his system. If he was told to quit the sarcasm, somehow, it was the only language he knew.

And if strong women who could destroy him in seconds told him to stay down, he found himself standing, fists clenched and full of rage, ready for the pain. With every fiber in his body, knowing she could beat him to a pulp, Milo was unable to stay away. And even then, when there was still so much to learn, Milo already knew he belonged to her. He just wanted to feel something.

The hall filled with shouts in every language possible, all calling for a fight. The different dialects blurred together, pooling into his mind as fractured English. Her hand shot out as he approached, smacking into his jaw. Falling to the ground and knocking his chin against the tile sent real, tangible pain through his head. He pushed himself back onto his feet, spitting on the floor.

He felt alive. Physical and true proof there was no way in hell he was dead. The dead couldn't possibly bleed. When the girl sent her fist flying into his stomach, knocking the wind from his lungs and sending him gasping on his knees, he told himself the dead didn't need to breathe. Dead people couldn't feel pain after their hearts stopped.

The only thing the dead could do after being washed away, gone, forgotten, and buried is remember the life left behind.

Milo drifted away as the world became blurry around him, not feeling pain or having the will to breathe. His head fell against the cool ground. Nostalgia ran through his heart. The floor reminded him of bed - a thought that almost conjured a laugh. He settled into the floor, limbs going numb beside him. Out of all the ways he might've imagined his death, the one he found himself in happened to be the worst. Once his eyes closed, his mother appeared blurry and bright against the rushing darkness. And the reality set in.

He was, indeed, dead.

VI. Goddamned Troublesome Elbow

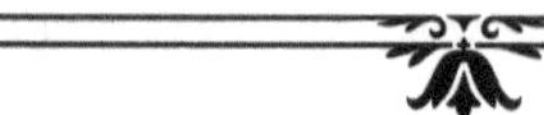

War had no effect on the rainbow bridge. At the Stone Quarters edge, where the protective trees and forest began, the worn-out trail towards the bridge was held. Centuries of movement through the path naturally created a narrow, rugged road lined with rocks and shrubbery. No one, Vanir or Aesir, dared touch the sacred pathway to the portal between worlds, especially not the bridge at its end. With Heimdall's magical blade, Hofond, the portal at the end could be activated, and the door to realms would be opened.

Closing it was an entirely different matter.

She passed through the trail quickly, not stopping to think about what the Fae, Rundi, told her. The Vanir's last words echoed in her ears like a manifestation of excellence: *find the berserker, and your destiny will begin.* Regret leaked into her heart. She hated herself for asking Rundi questions. If her mother was still around, she'd have no issue telling her how wrong she was. But now she was on her way to a realm she never wanted to end up, building hopes based on broken riddles and fragmented answers.

The trees thinned out, growing sparingly near the bridge. Astrid paused, looking upon her exit. The bridge began at the stark cliff's edge, stretching into a thick fog across the Chasm. Stories said that Odin, wanting to unify all the realms for a new era of peace, caught a rainbow from the Vanir Queen Freyja's cloak and trapped it beneath a cage forged in the Svartalfheim's labyrinths. Odin's wife, Frigg, conjured the fog, hiding the Bifrost from wrongful eyes. Together, the King and Queen of Asgard fashioned a way for all realms to meet and come together as a unified people under a singular Aesir King. Then the Vanir-Aesir War began, and prospects for peace vanished. Astrid's mouth grew dry as she approached the cliff, eyeing the never-ending drop into shadow known as the Chasm.

Astrid stood with her toes hanging over the edge. The rainbow bridge sat a few feet away, radiating a soft glow, shimmering iridescent colors trapped in jewels. Astrid knelt, balancing on the edge as Hofond beat rhythmically against her spine. She stared into the darkness and never felt more at peace. Something rustled in the trees behind her.

She unsheathed Hofond, wielding it high, the blade slicing across her face. The rustling grew louder as she inched from the cliff, twirling the sword defensively. She stopped before the trees, and a friendly face appeared from the shrubbery.

"Oi there, little one," the man said, "watch where you point that thing!"

Astrid breathed a sigh, lowering her sword. Tumbling out from the woods like a beggar on the streets, the god Ullr gave Astrid a wink and playful gesture as he stepped into the sun. The afternoon light snapped against his sculpted face, radiating marbled statuesque skin, a faint kaleidoscope reflecting beside his bare feet. Tattered clothing hung loosely around him. He raised a hand, pulled chestnut-colored hair behind his ears, and dropped ocean-filled eyes upon Astrid's surprised gaze.

He rolled his shoulders, and the clothes shifted, revealing runes lining his torso. Black paint smudged his fingers, like always. Ullr grinned. Astrid scowled. The archer god proved to be nothing but a pain in the past. Even though he was a part of Asgard's royal court, requiring his constant presence in the realm, Ullr spent his time being a pest rather than a royal. He picked up rune sorcery as a hobby, drawing little symbols upon the royal guard's golden armor.

Ullr reached down, flicking leaves and twigs from his trousers. "Mighty well to see you," the god said. He eyed Hofond. "If only under better circumstances."

"What the hell are you still doing here?" She felt breathless. *Two gods in one day,* she thought. At any other time, she'd feel honored, glowing with pride beneath the gods' gaze. Instead, she felt outlandishly mortal. Her skin was thin, translucent under the sun, and heavy with exhaustion and chronic pain. Ullr was in hiding, exiled from his home through war, but it looked as though the royal life never left him. She swallowed her anger. And with its dismissal, Astrid imagined him as her old friend, a fellow warrior who fought by her side, who would take a blade for her. A blade, however insignificant to his divinity.

He smiled. "Glad to see you're still a hag."

"Don't be witty," she snapped. "There's a war going on right behind you." Gripping onto Hofond, Astrid thrusted it forward, getting closer to Ullr. "If the rebellion knew you were here -"

Ullr laughed. "I'd like to see one of them toads try anything," he said, pearly cheeks growing red, "who the bloody hell do they even *think* they are? Troublesome, I tell you, they are just -"

Astrid sighed. "Ullr -"

"Maybe if they weren't such goddamned troublesome elbows, we Aesir could handle it!"

"Honestly, Ullr," Astrid said, "I don't have time for this."

Ullr faced the bridge. "Lucky to leave, ain't you," he said, poking her harshly in the shoulder. "I've been hiding out by the bridge. No one comes down
here, you know."

She nodded silently. If she wasn't already used to the 'always watching' concept of the gods, Astrid would be concerned Ullr knew her plans. He was merely looking out for her, she told herself. She felt like a child.

"A group of rebels went through the fog not a long while back," Ullr continued. He eyed her with a quiet voice, lips puckered with amusement. "Waiting for you, I suppose."

Surprise didn't even touch her. Astrid turned, staring at the flowing wall with a leveled head. Her purpose hadn't changed: she'd cross the bridge, pass through the wall, and open the portal. Rebel soldiers led by Sigyn didn't bother her anymore. Not when she was so close to the Bifrost. She bumped into Ullr's side with her elbow.

"Don't worry about me, old friend."

"Heimdall wanted me to tell you something."

"What is it?"

"You need to destroy it."

Astrid straightened. "Destroy what?"

"The Bifrost," he replied. "Keep none of them from traveling, you know? No one wants this disaster to spread."

Hofond became weightless in her hand, like holding a feather. She wasn't sure what gave her the most anxiety: the thought of *her*, a mortal Asgardian, destroying a creation forged by Dwarven steel and godly magic, or there not being a portal, trapping thousands within a war-torn land, trapping herself in ungodly territory. Ullr watched her, twirling a blade of grass around his slender finger. His lip twitched with tension.

Astrid met his gaze. "It was born from the gods," she said. "I am only a soldier, not like you. A mortal hand can't destroy something of such divine nature!"

"You put us on too high a pedestal." He frowned. "Always have."

"All I have is a blade -"

"The Hofond," he snapped, irritation burrowing deep within his eyes, "is the strongest weapon within Asgard, gifted to you - *just a soldier* - by its only owner." Ullr reached out, touching her cheek, his thumb grazing her nose. Immediately his divinity dripped onto her, like the sun's unfiltered gaze. She was gold beneath his eyes. "No god got you out of that prison, Astrid. It wasn't even Thor that saved us all those years ago in battle." He turned her around to face the fog. "Destroy the bridge."

She pushed him off. "And what of everyone trapped here? And coming back -"

"There's nothing left to return to. Asgard has fallen," Ullr said. "It is only the lost Prince that can save us."

Astrid pressed her lips together. "So I open the door and destroy the bridge behind me."

"Drop the whole lot of them in the bloody Chasm for all I care."

"Right," she whispered, "forgot about the rebels."

He patted her on the back. "You can handle it, soldier!" he called out, backing into the forest.

"Not without some help," she said, reaching around to grab him before he sneaked away. "How can I get past the rebels to open the door? All I've got is the key."

"I've been turned out of my home," Ullr said, "I got nothing!"

"You're a god of war. Turn your pockets out."

He grumbled, digging through the rags he wore till he found a pocket. He revealed a leather pouch, jingling with metal. Astrid's interest was piqued with silver coins, differing between carvings of Frankish Midgardian emperors or the gold used to trade in Asgard's markets. She snatched onto it, eyeing Ullr as she pocketed the coin. He groaned with an eye roll. "What's Viking Silver gonna do for you in Midgard, eh?"

"You owe me thousands from the pub, Ullr," she laughed. "Take this as a down payment."

Astrid waved for him to continue looking. From another pocket, he held a handful of *morke,* shadow bombs capable of casting a blanket of darkness over any terrain. *Finally.* She grabbed onto three, stashing them in her pocket. Anything else Ullr had was useless - paint vials and charcoal stubs.

She extended her hand towards him. "It was good to see you," she said. "You know, *before.*"

"You'll find your way back." Ullr grasped her hand.

"If I can't -"

"Asgard will not survive without you." He touched her face. The divinity moved between them again. "Achieve your destiny, and you will save us all."

They held each other for a moment before noise came from beyond the fog, an echo bouncing into the Chasm. Dark clouds crossed the sky dramatically, covering the sporadic sun burning bright above. Ullr backed away, reentering his forest, melting into nature. Astrid approached the rainbow bridge, watching as faded silhouettes danced across the gray wall. Hofond hummed in her palm, slightly inching forward on its own, eager to reach the Bifrost.

Astrid retrieved the *morke* from her pocket. A long time ago, riding her horse beside Thor during a rainy afternoon, Astrid made her first - and only - visit to the Bifrost. It was foggy in her memory - sharp colors, the rainbow brightest on the other side of the wall. A moment came back to her. Hofond protruding from a keyhole, the blade plunged within as the portal opened from above.

Astrid held Hofond close and inched through the gray wall. Voices grew sharper with every step. Astrid paused at the edge, where it faded into white and translucence. A golden room filled with carvings on every wall told the story of the Aesir building the Bifrost. The ceiling was open and built like a globe, showing the universe with twinkling galaxies and exploding stars. Twenty-four pillars framed the room, each decorated with statues and sanctuaries for every Aesir god and goddess.

The holy room looked untouched. Hofond's slot at the building's far end, behind the circular pedestal within the room, stood ready to be used. A wide, golden cone littered with jewels pointed its narrower end towards the pedestal, the opposite end facing the star-filled ceiling. All she had to do was place Hofond in its spot, and the cone would open. She'd stand at the pedestal, state where she wished to go, and hope it worked. All the while, somewhere in the middle, she'd destroy the bridge and remove as many enemies as possible.

You've had worse, she thought. *Even if you haven't, pretend.*

Six rebels stood between her and the exit. Another, taller and broader than the rest, stood upon the pedestal's top, poking her spear into the cone's center. Two more rebels were by Astrid in the fog. They spoke in hushed tones, Vanaheimian, a language she couldn't translate. She listened again - *that can't be right.* Asgardian rebels, fluent in the Vanir language, their natural and century-old enemies? Astrid blinked. It didn't matter.

She gripped onto the *morke,* raised it high above her head, and threw it with all her force. The small ball shot over the two rebels beside her, smashing into the crystalized ground beside the six. An explosion, followed by a plume of black fog, stretched through the room within seconds.

Shouts echoed into the emptiness.

She ran out of the fog towards the closest pair, sliding the sword through the left's chest. Hofond penetrated Royal Guard armor like nothing, sliding through the metal without a sound. She pulled the blade from the chest, turning it towards the other in a single motion. With a clash, her blade sliced against the armor, drawing blood. Astrid lept, keeping the rebel's arm down as the sword stole another life.

The *morke* grew fainter as the rebels reassembled themselves in the chaos. Astrid dragged the bodies into the fog, swiping at the blood but only managing to smudge it into the rainbow-colored floor. She dropped them, running along her cover, pulling another *morke* from her pocket. As the air settled once more, and the rebels breathed with relief at their ability to see, Astrid slid out, skidding the *morke* across the floor. She skated across the glass on her knees, gripping her sword as the bomb made its harsh contact with the ground, bursting into chaos.

Screams erupted through the fog. Astrid paid no attention. It sounded too much like a choir. She wielded Hofond through the darkness like another arm, dragging it wherever she saw fit. Shouts and echoes scattered around her, pulling the rebels in different directions. All she could do was fight and let the sword take control as the darkness clouded her eyesight.

That was when she smelt it.

A sweet scent of oranges and spices filled the room. It was intoxicating and lingering, clogging her throat with distaste. Her eyes searched for its source: *bla ild*. It grew pungent with fruits and citrus when activated. Years ago, during the Bifrost's creation, the Aesir Jord built spires with bonfires at the top, a brilliant deep blue flame always roasting, designating Asgard as the strongest realm. The fire was incredibly powerful and lethal if in the wrong hands. It was named *bla ild,* and after an illegal gathering, the power became weaponized.

Astrid knew the smell from anywhere. She dropped down within the fog, crawling across the floor towards it. If she could get her hands on those bombs, they'd be strong enough to destroy the bridge. The rebels were probably planning on using a small one, controllable enough that catastrophic damage could be averted. Astrid crawled faster. She needed it all, and fast. Four rebels remained, one being the superior officer, some armed with bows, all with sharp swords. They were beginning to adapt to the situation: finding the wall and hanging onto each other.

One rebel, young and scrawny, fumbled with the *bla ild* - trying to strike the match to light the leather casing. Blue flames lay inside the casing, and the explosion would be earth-rendering when it came upon heat. Astrid lunged, grabbing the rebel from behind with her blade pressed against a pale neck. She covered the rebel's mouth and dragged Hofond across their skin. The body flinched and fell limp, dead in Astrid's arms. She tossed the body, snatching onto the *bla ild* and matches.

Astrid placed the *bla ild* in a row, five leather spheres by the wall's base, where the rainbow bridge began. She struck the first match -

Thwip!

An arrow spiraled through the air, lodging into the wall beside Astrid's head. She glanced up, looking over her shoulder towards the dark behind her. It began to fade. She stumbled, the matches tumbling out of her grasp and clattering into the Chasm. She whispered a swear and raised her hands, cupping them against her lips.

Thor once taught her sorcery tricks during their time together. Things to whisper under your breath to borrow magic from the gods. Maybe there'd be a price to pay later, maybe not, but what mattered was that it was a way for mortals to get something extra on their side. Astrid breathed deeply, remembering his words.

"*Ved Odin's skaeg,*" she whispered, "*giv mig ild[1].*"

She breathed in from her palms, holding her breath as she lowered her hands. Astrid dropped to her knees as another arrow flew through the air, missing her nose by a hair. She kept her hands level with her lips, still holding a breath that began to burn her throat. Another flurry of arrows came from the fog. Astrid focused, staring at the *bla ild.*

And finally, she breathed out.

A column of fire rolled out from between her lips. It shot through the *bla ild,* lighting each leather ball on its way. As the last activated, Astrid shut her mouth, silently sending a prayer to whatever god happened to be listening, and sprinted into the dying fog. She pulled the last *morke* from her pocket, just moments from crashing it against the ground beside her feet, when a rebel stepped into the light, pulling the string of their bow back in a swift motion -

An eruption of unrelenting pain came from her side, prickling needles and pinches. An arrow lodged into her left side, the thin wood going all the way through, the arrowhead poking out from Astrid's stomach. She touched the wound sitting above her waistline, blood silently squeezing out at the slightest movement. Astrid slammed down the *morke,* falling into the stark darkness. She fell against the cool ground momentarily, nose pressed against the floor. Red painted her hands. Mortality, she realized, held onto her throat. She groaned, pushed herself up, and did not look down.

Gripping the Hofond in one hand and holding herself together with the other, Astrid moved like a ghost through the fog. Screams echoed around her, shouts sprouting up at every turn, calling

---

[1] By Odin's beard, give me fire

for reinforcements, begging for a description of the assailant. Astrid's skin crawled. She ran into something, bending her stomach on the pedestal. She exhaled sharply - *praise be!* Astrid raised Hofond.

Explosions came from the bridge.

"The *bla ild*!"

The bursts slammed into the sanctuary, shaking the golden walls and sending shudders against the rainbow floor. The screams grew louder and more violent. Astrid clung onto the keyhole, watching a rebel run out of the fog, staggering while the ground shook, to see through Frigg's protective wall. The rebel ran back within the second - the rainbow bridge collapsed, crumbling and falling into the Chasm. The rebel panicked to her comrades: "*There's no way back!*"

Astrid took her chance. Sweating and gasping for air, she plunged the Hofond into the keyhole, activating the portal, the Bifrost, Door of all Doors. Another shudder ran through the room. The cone above shifted, slowly moving towards the pedestal. Cracks spread into the gold as the rainbow bridge rumbled in its death. It didn't matter if the entire Bifrost fell into the Chasm - the portal opened, and the door unlocked. All realms lie inches away, vulnerable to anything. Astrid ripped the Hofond from the keyhole. The portal remained gaping wide.

Pulling herself towards the pedestal, Astrid dragged Hofond behind her, grasping onto the arrow to keep it from moving. The fog was disappearing. The rebels could see each other easier now, and their eyes were set on the intruder inching towards the keyhole. Astrid moved quickly, climbing the steps as another arrow slipped past her. A rebel began to come up to her left, brandishing a steel-tipped spear.

Astrid collapsed onto the pedestal. The universe lay above her, moving and stretching through the cone above her head. All time slowed. The rebel rushing at her became miles away. Astrid stared into space, and it watched back. She exhaled.

Midgard.

The spear dragged against her left ankle, spilling blood onto her shoes as the portal removed all of them from Asgard. Astrid gripped the sword, curling around the pedestal as the universe swallowed them whole, reading their thoughts and taking their knowledge. She let it happen and watched overhead as the world broke and remade itself, turning into something horrendous and murderous. And with the illusion of flying, the Bifrost took Astrid and the rebels from the collapsing room in Asgard, sending them soaring through time and towards another realm. Behind were the golden castles and mystical festivals in the streets where Fae danced.

Midgard was ahead.

VII. Thalia

Twenty-four hours after death, the body takes on a greenish-blue color.

Milo remembered his forensic science class quite well - rigor mortis set in at four hours, and the worst had yet to come. The bladder and bowel were already emptied - a lesson that received an audible response in the high school classroom - and blood pooled at the body's bottom as its temperature quickly dropped. As he slept, he wondered if his body was still there in the city streets. Maybe the police found it by then and made the doorstep house call to deliver the news to his sleep-deprived mother. Maybe there wouldn't ever be a body.

He wasn't too sure how the Norse dealt with death. He did know that sudden death meant eternal visions - a recurring theme for the Nords.

He stood upon Valhalla's roof. He couldn't even know if this was the top, he had no idea. Milo was at the edge, the wind rushing behind him, lifting the sweater off his hips. In the distance, near the middle of the horizon, a magnificent tree grew into the never-ending sky. Milo only saw its base, the rest covered by hanging fog and thin clouds. He approached the tree with quick steps, his subconscious taking control. It did not feel odd or misplaced, as though his eyes were always meant to look upon the winding tree.

Yggdrasil, a voice whispered.

Milo continued until he was only a few feet away from the tree. Brilliant colors splashed across its trunk, painted pastels along the leaves, and life itself carved within its auburn lumber. The sound echoed from above, where the intertwining branches could be seen in the clouds. He could've sworn he saw a goat's silhouette -

Here comes the boy.

The hairs stood up on his neck. The voice had the same texture as glass, translucent and empty, reflecting upon his self. Milo turned. Three figures wafted through the upended roots of Yggdrasil, pouring a steady stream of silvery liquid behind them. Their silver pathways melted into the tree moments after the figures made their way, sinking into the roots like medicine. Milo moved closer. *What the -* the dream delved into the weird. The figures were at least seven feet tall, with nimble human-like bodies. Hair the length of lakes trailed down and pooled onto the grassy floor beneath their taloned feet. Milo paused just beside their path and watched as they moved unbothered in their mission.

Milo's lips parted, trying to ask a question, but only air escaped, wisping out like bubbles in the ocean. He felt muffled, filled with water. The first figure turned their head to show a blank, crystallized face. Eyes twinkled back at him.

We are the Norn, spoke the figure. Their voices rang loud and clear even though they never opened their mouths. They continued to pour the liquid upon Yggdrasil's roots.

Milo stood and watched silently. A thought ran through him: *I want to know.* It surprised him. He wasn't sure what he would want to know.

The Norn turned in succession, their voices shrill, swaying as if it were a song:

Two siblings, light and dark -
Breed a war of worlds upon the mountaintop.
As one is slain by the moonlight,
We breathe the air of Ragnarok!

In seconds the vision changed: the tree decayed quickly, collapsing from its massive height and tumbling down in heaps. The Norn were gone, nowhere to be seen, but their voices still echoed in Milo's ears. He fell to the ground, pulling himself into a tight hug as everything died around him.

It dissipated.

For the second time in twenty-four hours, Milo woke up in an unknown bed with a very foggy recollection of how he got there.

He forced his eyes open. The ceiling above moved slowly, a tall blonde soaring through the painted blue sky on a golden chariot. Milo blinked as his vision focused. Waking up in an unknown room didn't bother him anymore. It was oddly comforting, the only routine since his end.

"Is he gonna die?" Kali's quiet and calm voice came from the bed's right side.

"He's already dead." It was her. Her voice was stern, heavy with an accent. His fists clenched as he ground his teeth together; the similar sensation of needles running up and down his arms began in her presence. She laughed. "I wouldn't worry. He's awake."

Milo groaned. "Didn't realize you cared, Kali."

She shot a glare at him. "Just because I asked doesn't mean I care."

His lips spread into a toothy smile. The aches and pains left almost as soon as they came. It was like he had no injury in the first place. He sat up abruptly. Standing at his left, Silas jumped back in surprise, sharing apprehensive looks. Milo raised his hands, rubbing his eyes as Valhalla's brightness settled in. And as he remembered who stood beside him, a lump clogged his throat and pulled his hands, he kept his eyes closed. There was anger and glee, forging this tightness in his muscles, an urge to slam his head till he fell back into a deep sleep.

His fake heartbeat sputtered. "Hey, where's that -"

"Look before you speak," Silas blurted, jerking his head over his shoulder to the looming figure at the bed's end.

With her hair still pulled back into a loose braid, with a few curling strands framing her face, the girl tilted her head and crossed her arms. She leaned towards him and sighed, moving around the bed to get closer.

She sat beside him silently. She snatched onto his hand, deep callouses rubbing against his skin. Holding his hand with her left, she dragged her thumb from his palm down to her wrist. As her thumb moved, sharp needles pricked against his skin, a faint shadow staying behind in its trail. She drew two more lines, diagonally aimed outwards towards his other fingers, near the original line. It was like an archaic tree.

Everything around him grew blurry, colors meshing together into one blurb. Comfort washed over him, calming the erratic surge in his heartbeat and soothing his quickening temper. He leaned forward, all the balance he might've ever carried evaporating. He fell into her, forehead smacking against her wide shoulders. Hushed laughter came from the left. He pulled himself back up, blinking rapidly as the world sharpened into reality.

"It means *Eolh*," she said. "A rune for protection and healing."

Warmth radiated from his palm, where the lines she drew still hovered above his skin like a shadow. Everything smoothed over within him, and the heavy comfort turned to safety. His senses sharpened and rattled him to the core. For a moment - just a sudden second - he forgot he was trapped in Valhalla. But it was all coming back to him, and as he raised his head, the girl pulled away, standing from the bed. She avoided the three silent onlookers in the wide room, moving towards the opened door.

Milo shouted: "*Hey!*"

"Not again," Silas muttered.

The girl paused, not turning around.

"Who are you?" he breathed.

She exhaled, and suddenly, the mood changed. The room became dimmer, though there were no windows or light sources. Milo raised his hand. The paintings along the ceiling shifted, melting into darker colors and deepened shades. Nighttime grew above them, storm clouds brewing as a man pulled his chariot across the sky. Milo lowered his chin, noticing the girl watching him. Her eyebrows furrowed, amber orbs swirling with an unrelenting interest. The burning against his skin dulled until nothing was left.

Then she blinked. "My name is Thalia."

Thalia.

Milo exhaled, the name clicking within his brain like a puzzle piece. He never realized a name could work so perfectly. Hesitancy crossed her eyes, a worried smile lingering on her lips. Thalia looked between them with a wildness, like there was a sudden need for everyone to approve. He watched as her hand raised to her lips nervously, chewing on her nails.

"You don't look like a Valkyrie," Kali drawled skeptically.

Thalia laughed uncomfortably, lips pressed together with narrowed eyes focused on the floor. "That's because I'm not one," she said, leaning her shoulder against the wall beside the door. "I do jobs for the Master - hushed ones. Off the record." She frowned, looking like a painting with hooded eyes and delicate hands. "We have a deal: he gives me a place to stay, and I run a few jobs for him. No questions asked." Her amber eyes stuck onto Milo. "The things I did were not personal," she said, "it was business."

"And the dreams? How the hell did you do that?" Milo interrogated.

"Dreams?"

"You -" he stopped, watching the shadows dance across her face. The white lines drawn in the shape of a bear's face glistened against her skin. "You have no idea what I'm talking about."

"That wasn't me," she said. Chewing on her lip, she quickly added, "What dreams?"

"How about we just get back to the important stuff?" he replied, shooting her a pointed look. He climbed off the bed, standing beside Silas. "You're not a Valkyrie, but I sure as hell doubt you're human."

She pressed her lips together. "You come from a place called Midgard - Earth," she began, looking between them, "in your realm, there was this skaldic poem about King Harald Fairhair, ever heard of it?" Silence came from the audience. Thalia's eye twitched momentarily in annoyance. "Of course. Bloody *damned* Midgardians -" she cleared her throat, "- in the poem, the warriors of Odin are sung about as legends. Beings built from the magic in his blood, *berserkers,* bear-skinned and red with blood, unrelenting war machines." Thalia extended her hands. "I am one."

Milo raised his hand, rubbing his fingertips along his eyes. *Of course,* he thought, *like the day couldn't get any weirder.* "If you got us here," he said, "take us back."

"What?"

He shrugged, turning to face his companions. "That sounds fair, right?"

Silas burst with that shimmering confidence. It brought needles up along Milo's arm, but he ignored it. "More than fair."

"I like it here," Kali added, her voice a faraway echo.

Thalia became a statue, her face solemn and grave. "There's nothing to go back to. Your bodies are gone, there is no way -"

"No, no, what about that hand thing, huh?" Milo raised his hand, tracing the lines she made on his palm. He moved across the room. "Look, starry eyes, this doesn't matter to me. All that crap Oba said," he paused, his heart aching for his best friend, "warriors and whatever and thunder. I don't *care*. And I mean, why the hell should I? All the dreams, the towers, those things, and the tree and you. You and *you*! I care about my mother," he breathed, "her name is Natalie. Natalie Bohr and she is all alone because of you people."

The darkness stilled, and the air grew stagnant.

Milo exhaled. "So take me home."

"I don't know what you expect me to tell you."

"Something!" he exclaimed. "Anything about why we're here!"

"Look around, Milo!" Thalia snapped. "*You're dead*. You can't go home because you're just a soul - there isn't a body anymore. This isn't some story about being the chosen ones. You died. All of you, and the sooner you get that, the sooner you'll start to move on." She held up her hands as if to calm herself. "For some reason, the Master wanted you all here in Valhalla rather than elsewhere. Take it as an honor. One day you will fight in Ragnarok and have everlasting glory."

Silas scoffed. "I lived a normal life! Getting stabbed in a football field was not the way for me to go."

A laugh blurted from Kali. "You're kidding, right?"

"There was writing on the ground, in the dirt," he said. "Like a rhyme or something. I just -"

"So what about Oba?" Milo interrupted.

Thalia frowned. "What about him?"

"He attacked me -"

"Killed, "Kali said. She shrugged. "Might as well get used to it."

"*That* happened," he snapped, "and then what? A blue giant just waltzed through Manhattan while leaving a squished guy on the pavement like an ant?"

Thalia shifted around uncomfortably. "He was a Jotunn." She glanced around. "Which you obviously know nothing about. A Jotunn comes from Jotunnheim, the realm of ice giants. Someone sent the giant after you."

"Where is he now?"

"Gone."

Milo's mouth went dry. "You -"

"I took care of him," she said. "Nothing to worry about."

He staggered backward. Oba's face grew clear in his eyes. "Gone," he whispered.

A hand tapped his shoulder. "Maybe he'll show up here," Kali said.

"What?"

"Your friend," she said.

Silas nodded. "We don't know how any of this works, man. Just be positive."

Milo wasn't hearing them anymore. Nothing positive lived within him. Thalia the berserker backed out of the room, her almond-shaped eyes never once leaving him. She paused at the threshold, eyebrows furrowing before scurrying out, leaving them in silence. Milo sighed.

"She's gone," Silas said as light began to peer back in.

Silence overtook the group. It wasn't an ordinary silence, but thick like ice, just thin enough to be translucent, a shattered mirrored image. Milo touched his stomach. There was an aching growing there, empty but full, pulsing painfully above his belly button. He looked at his companions: they were all stuck in the sickening dread. *Everlasting glory* resonated as *eternity* and *alone*, trapped remembering a previous life with an illusion displayed before them.

Silas spoke first. "It'll be okay." He smiled. "Even if it isn't, it'll all be okay."

For a moment, it was better, easier to swallow, calmer air spreading between them. They tried to remember childhood, only to realize with this everlasting death, in no time, those moments might fade, sounds grew dull, and all they remembered were the seconds before their worlds went dark. The ceiling above their heads changed again, melting into the sun and morning sky. Milo wondered whether Thalia's arrival or departure changed the ceiling's paintings. He lowered his head, smiling at his friends as he sat on the bed. "I don't think there was anything she could've done," he said.

Silas eyed him. "You said it yourself -"

"*She* couldn't have done anything."

"Let me guess," Kali drawled, lying lazily across the bed, resting her chin on cupped palms, "*you* know someone who can."

Milo shrugged. "What's stopping us from going to the Master himself?"

Silas nodded. "We can ask for help."

"No," Milo replied slowly, "I'm thinking more like breaking and entering."

VIII. Crackhead Nightlife Debris

"Get outta here," a voice called out, "she's in the damn window!"

Burning heat seared into Astrid's ankles, slowly spreading to her bare hands and wrists. Piercing glass spread all over the body, poking into her skin. The arrow, parts snapped off in the Bifrost-portalling process, became a dull pain, stagnant and durable as she came to her senses. She lay down, legs hanging over something that pricked into her calves and exposed her to sunlight. Her body from the knees up was cold, lying against a fallen bookcase and smashed glass. Astrid inhaled as she sat up, hearing wood creak beneath her weight. Her training came back in a rush.

The Midgardian is ignorant, her instructor had said, *and territorial. Do not take their instability as defenselessness but fear. It is only the unknown they have yet to conquer.*

"I can see that, sir, but I'm gonna have to ask you to -"

"Not till you get this crackhead nightlife debris outta *my convenience store!*"

"Sir -"

"These damn hipster meth-heads. I've been tellin' you people down at city hall!" The voice huffed. "Can you believe this?"

"Sir."

A crowd waited for her outside. She crashed through a vendor window during her journey in the Bifrost. Waking up then, she guessed it was early afternoon, in a raging city. Astrid squinted as she took it in sharp neon colors and bright lights shone chaotically towards her, paired with bellowing shouts and echoing demands wanting to know where she came from. Everything settled, and Astrid took it all in.

"Hey, lady," the voice shouted again. "Gonna pay for all this?" It came from a short man, with a pinched face and a boisterous belly, who reeked of horrid smoke and strange meat. A weirdly shaped leather pouch was in his hands and he waved it in her face. "English, right?" he drawled, screaming at her.

"She looks Middle Eastern, man," a passerby commented.

"Money for damage! *No checks!*"

Another man stood behind the shop owner, dressed in navy blue, glowing slightly in the sunlight with medals decorating his coat. Something buzzed with noise on his shoulder. He reached for it, muttered inaudible words while pressing a button, and walked up to her. His other hand held onto something attached to his belt holstered on a leather sheath.

"Ma'am, are you intoxicated?" he asked, sounding bored. "Ma'am?"

Astrid lifted herself from the ground, shaking the glass away from her skin. A sudden heat in her right hand scared her, rushing into a pulsing heat within her palm. She looked down - the shimmering Hofond was still there, dirtied a bit with dried blood, but still magnificent. She took a few steps, scanning the crowd: mechanical vehicles reeking of polluted gas rolled across their streets noisily, pedestrians moving along mindlessly. They held blank faces, looking like robots as they passed emotionlessly through the city.

Towering skyscrapers rose above her. Moving pictures glowing with painfully bright neon colors decorated the buildings, blaring electronic sounds. An earth-quaking boom rippled into the sky. Astrid looked towards the pale blue color above: a beast, stiff and long, shot through the sky, moving at a steady pace through the thin clouds, shaped like the English letter *t* with striking wings. She flinched, holding her arm up defensively. The growling Midgardian dragon disappeared past the towering buildings.

Fear plunged into her, and she held her chest as though she fell apart. Immediately she yearned for home, for familiarity as passersby watched her with muddled stares. A few mouths curled into gruesome scowls, muttering dark things to each other as they hurried away. It was suffocating, it was cruel, it was dark in a chaotically bright place, and it was heartbreaking. Astrid clung to her amulet, clung to Hofond, clung to her chest. The devils of Midgard approached, and her faith was all she had left.

It reminded her of war, the first battle she fought as a Royal Guard alongside Thor. It reminded her of the same fear, the same notion that crawled up her throat. There was an outrageous difference between her and the Prince: he flung himself into war, wielding a mighty hammer in one hand and a glittering sword in another.

The golden curls she once admired were lined with a leather strap, armor shined three times over brilliantly showed lightning bolts etched onto his chest. Even in battle, he wore his ebony crown, a purple cape draped across his shoulders. He moved like a snake, barely touching the ground, twirling and crossing through the enemies as though he were practicing an intricate dance. Astrid watched from a distance, noticing how he admired the blood staining his hands, how he struck a breast after the heart stopped beating, how he snatched the wealth from the ones he conquered.

Astrid watched and feared for her soul: *how do I love the angel of death*? But it was not hard at all. Her eyes barely remained on the blood, but instead remembered how he closed the dead's eyes, how he carried bodies back to their loved ones, how he committed the proper burials, how he prayed to his father to guide the Valkyrie towards the worthy. He was good, in a way.

But as she stood there, in Midgard, she knew her memories were obsolete, and the emptiness within her chest yearned to run from beneath the prying eyes of the clueless.

Her eyes caught onto something down the streets, twinkling between the rushing vehicles. Golden armor, three more followings close behind. Holding a spear high above her head, aimed to throw, it was the rebel group leader from the Bifrost, survivors glowering behind her. Astrid gripped Hofond and moved to run, but a sharp pain came from her side. *Blasted arrow,* she thought, grasping at her bleeding wound before spinning around on her heel.

"Where the hell do you think -" the voice started, a hand snagging onto Astrid's elbow.

She flung around, Hofond just hairs beneath the short man's chin. He gulped loudly and waved towards the stunned man in blue. Astrid inched towards him, keeping the sword inches away from his sweaty skin. Her lips parted, and she whispered, "Don't you *dare* touch me, dirty man." Astrid lowered the blade as she moved back, noticing the approaching rebels as the man in blue started to run towards her.

With a swift motion, gripping her sword in one hand and her wounded side in the other, Astrid sprinted down the street, shoving past the ignorant passerby. Shouts came from behind her, the man in blue echoing she was required to listen to him. She kept running as a familiar voice rang through the air, like the rebels from the rainbow bridge. Fear rippled down her spine: suddenly she was in a realm she never knew, with nobody to rely on besides the scattered riddles and gifts received from friendly faces. Truly, Astrid was alone in a crowd.

She reached up, clutching her pulsing amulet.

Give me the berserker.

IX. Warriors of Thunder

At his core, Milo was unsure of who he was.

People never preached about his qualities or complimented his laugh. Oba entered his life with such suddenness that it didn't feel real, like a blurry illusion spreading across his fragmented life. He was trapped in a maze. His murdering giant of a best friend was the first and last connection he experienced in years. And even then, in the end, Oba was gone.

But something changed, and Milo died and other dead kids were making him feel so painfully at home. He inhaled their presence with a feverish intensity, an aching fear latching onto his back as a whispering voice repeated in his ear: *the best things never last.* He shooed it away; it was easier to be dead with friends rather than alive and alone. And when it came to breaking and entering - he eyed his company, all of them barefoot - he found them to be a very capable team.

The halls, they came to realize, were as ambiguous as Valhalla itself. Unlike the feast hall, the tower's inner maze brewed an unsettling silence. Doors upon doors, identical in their woodwork of whittled wolves and ravens, lined the walls, none leading to the Master's chambers. Milo quickened his pace, sliding alongside Silas. The confidence wafted off him with every stride.

"Think we'll ever find it?" asked Milo.

Silas shrugged. "Doesn't matter, I guess. We'll come across the man himself eventually. Maybe he'll just talk, no questions asked."

"Maybe."

"And maybe we'll find the room and something that says we were transferred to a mental hospital -" he thrust his hands forward, "because that is the only goddamn logical reason for this. I'm talking, fully drugged, hallucinogens, strapped down to a hospital bed or something. Seriously, Milo - that or some other crazy conspiracy theory an internet junkie conjures up. Governmental probes, experimental medicinal products. Whatever it is, it's not death. I was not stabbed on a football field. *I was not.* And that girl -"

"What was she to you?" He heard the anger in his voice.

"Nothing, really," Silas muttered. "She introduced me to a college recruiter after a game. Weird thinking about it now, but on the night of the big game, it was *that* recruiter."

"What about the recruiter?"

Silas glanced at him. "The guy who stabbed me. Same dude she introduced me to."

Milo didn't know what to say. Speaking did not seem to be the best option, with this irreversible anger sitting behind his teeth. He pressed his lips together. The group continued through the halls, tossing looks at the passing doors.

"I'm not making accusations, though," Silas said. "Just saying maybe. You get it, right?"

Milo nodded, shrugged, and stuffed his hands into his pockets. He rubbed his skin against his trousers' rough material instead of popping the bones in his fingers. He shrugged again. "Maybe," he said.

They came to another turn. Wide double doors were at the end, and intricate artwork and symbols were engraved in the wood. The group stood there, silently staring. Sounds echoed from behind, slowly getting closer. The glow from the double wooden doors became incredibly inviting, like the only thing Milo could see.

"That'd be too good," Kali blurted. "I mean, seriously. Those can't be his doors!"

Silas laughed. "For the last twenty-four hours, nothing has made sense. That's his door." He snatched a torch from the wall, holding it close to his chest, and sprinted down the hallway, moving so nimbly that barely any sound came from him.

Milo hesitantly put space between him and Silas. Milo skipped over his feet, fumbling till Kali reached and pulled him upwards by the shoulder. She cackled. Milo stuck his tongue out.

"Hell of a lock on this thing." Silas prodded at the keyhole.

Voices echoed from down the hall. "Keep your voice down," Milo whispered.

"Just means we need to get in sooner," said Kali. "Get it open!"

Milo jiggled the wolf-carved door knob. He traced the keyhole, eyebrows furrowed together. Winding lines crisscross each other an inch down the metal. He said, "I can pick the lock to get outta detention early, but I've got no clue as to what this is."

"We could wait here for him to come," Silas said. "He'll sleep at some point, right?"

Kali snorted. "Wasn't the whole point of this for you big shots to try and placate your ego and break in?"

"Don't blame it on us," Silas snapped, "we all agreed to do this."

Shadows danced across the hallway.

Milo gripped the handle and shook it again as if a miracle would happen.

"Yeah," Kali griped, "wiggle it again, that'll work."

"How about *you* try to help?"

Making a face at him, Kali sarcastically grabbed the handle. Like clockwork, the pieces within the intricate lock shifted and clicked, falling into place. The grand doors shuttered and released, the door knob turning effortlessly when Kali pulled her hand away. The door creaked open.

"Did that just happen?" Kali whispered.

Silas prodded at the lock. "What're you, a master lockpicker?"

"I barely touched it." Her eyes grew wide as she stared at the door. "Barely."

More voices came from down the hall, growing louder.

"Now's not the time to question it," Milo said, rushing them to run inside.

They hurried into the room, doors slamming shut. Silas slid his torch into a placeholder hanging from the wall. Other torches roasted around the room, a giant fireplace with roaring flames on the far left. The warmth expanded around them, engulfing the three dead warriors in an embrace. It smelt like firewood and old books. Tall windows lined the back wall across from the doors, covered by decorative curtains and velvet tapestries. Paintings scattered across the walls, like the ones Milo's mother used to create, sent a pang of homesickness in his chest. Bookcases took up any free space, filled with leather-bound texts. At the center was a round table, littered with stray pages, opened books, and fraying maps. Colorful jewels could be seen beneath the papers, radiating across the painted ceiling.

Kali drove across the room, spreading her arms wide as she collapsed into a cushioned rocking chair layered. "Now, *this* is Heaven," she mumbled as though her mouth was stuffed with marbles, giving them a deadpan stare.

"Are you eating?" Milo asked.

Kali pulled herself from the cushions. "So what," she shouted through a mouthful of bread, "when you're hungry, you eat, right Mr. Smarty-pants?"

He laughed. "Where'd you get the food?"

"Right, I totally forgot." Kali yanked a wrinkled brown paper bag from her pocket, unfolding it to show the three overlapping triangles parallel to the ones on their sweaters. A small script was written beneath it: '*Valhalla warriors - remember to eat three meals a day!*' Another line: '*Deep down, we're still mortal. Deep, deep, deep down.*'

Kali opened the bag, dancing happily in her seat. "After your little moment in the grand hall," she started, chewing on more bread, "the feast started and I was starving but goody-two-shoes over here -" she jutted her thumb towards Silas," - insisted we went after *you* instead. Luckily for me, Valhalla has the same mindset as my elementary school and has to-go bags."

Milo found himself laughing, forgetting where he was as the noise spread quickly through the room. Silas scowled, shushing him quickly, and moving around the room.

"Here for a reason, remember?" Silas walked to the table. "I think we might've hit the jackpot, boys."

"*People*," Kali called out, "or did you forget about my existence?"

Silas groaned. "It was a moment, Kali, and you ruined it with technicalities."

"He was trying to be badass," Milo said as he walked by.

"I wonder what time it is," Silas mumbled. "Time feels universal here if that makes any sense. There's no sun, but it's always light. No moon and no darkness. I can see shadows change in the sky, the shape of something in the clouds, reflected off its position on the roof. Beyond that," he trailed off, eyes suddenly afraid, "beyond that we're ships passing at sea. Nothing to tie us to reality."

"Tomorrow can be different," Kali said with a shrug.

Milo ground his teeth. His eyes clung to the pages, but nothing resonated. The conversation irritated him. "Tomorrow doesn't exist anymore."

The others tiredly looked towards him.

"I mean, not to sound like a dick, but what exactly does time mean in death? *We* put names to hours and days and weeks and years. *We* decided to have daylight savings. *We* built those time zones. Why should any of that exist here?" He traced the pattern on the rug with his toes. "No tomorrow. Tomorrow is today, and today is tomorrow. Yesterday was the same as now and now is the same as yesterday." He shrugged. "What changes?"

"Cool it, Nietzsche. Anyone ever told you that you're outlandishly narrow-minded?" Silas poked through the papers on the table. Shadows crossed his eyes like sunglasses.

"That would be a first, actually," Milo muttered sardonically.

Silas kicked something across the room. "You believe in God?"

He raised his shoulders.

"How about faith? Or hope?"

He blinked.

"Maybe time isn't real," Silas said, "but the order of it is. What would we be without a successive calendar telling us where we stand? Wouldn't that be the same as faith? Believing in God? Believing in whatever supreme being you think is out there? Or whether there is nothing at all, but only our decisions? Time isn't tangible, but I'll ask for it like a glass of water. Time, order, and faith always mean something, even when it doesn't."

Something about his words sparked a heated jealousy in Milo's chest. Kali looked towards Silas with wide, curious eyes, admiration lodged in her throat so tightly she was breathless. How could anyone not look at him like he was the center of the universe? His face was bright and open, colored like an ancient copper statue, with pointed hazelnut eyes, wide and enveloping.

Milo stared, imagining himself tackling the boy to the floor, imagining starting a fight and blood staining his fingertips. He looked away and the image was gone, replaced with a dull emptiness in his stomach, a hunger he couldn't recognize.

Milo spoke harshly. "Do you think God hears when you scream? How about when you cry? Is there a God then, or an intangible voice echoing all the pain right back to you? What does your order and faith do then?"

Silas didn't look at him. The venom in Milo's voice was obvious enough for him to keep silent. After a long pause, the other boy raised his eyes and landed his direct stare upon him. "I do," he said. "And that release you feel after screaming, the euphoria that burns your throat, the hoarseness that's left behind, the emptiness in your chest now that all the anger's gone, caught by the wind - I think," he raised his hands as if to stop himself, "I *know* it comes from my God. Maybe it's a stupid thought, especially now being here, but it keeps me going. And you don't gotta believe in a God, man, to have faith. Try to have some faith sometimes, Milo. You wouldn't look like such a dick."

He blinked. His companions avoided looking at him, moving their attention towards the papers and books. Milo remained gobsmacked, staring at Silas's face as he looked through the Master's belongings. Light slid down the boy's cheek. A tear. Milo turned away.

He didn't know why he was like that. He longed to be good, for Kali to look at him the same way she watched Silas. He longed to see his hands and not be afraid of their capability. He longed for peace. He longed for everything for so long that it felt more like home than his own bed. He stood there, waiting for more, waiting for the light to hit him, waiting for his soul to change, waiting.

The silence settled like oil. Milo dug his hands across the papers. Countless languages were written in letters and forms, a different one for each. If he concentrated hard enough, he could decipher it in his brain, letters flipping around till it looked like English. A whacked-out steroid form of dyslexia. He tried not to stare at one for too long. The words *Aesir* and *Vanir* repeated, but nothing stuck. The words rang outrageously reminiscent of something Milo couldn't put his finger on.

He figured, eventually, there'd be a map resembling the United States. It would either be that, or they'd come across folders with their names on them, listing all the reasons why they were there. An easy route. Milo sighed as he began to reach the end of the pile. He knew better than to misplace hope.

All that was left was a book near the table's curve, buried beneath parchment. Milo uncovered it to see a golden title engraved into its leather cover. The words were gibberish in his brain. Even with the translation abilities, the title remained ubiquitous and unrecognizable. He reached for the spine, but with the brush of his finger, a discolored vision rippled before his eyes.

Brothers stood upon a mountain amid a violent battle; a silver ring, housing a raven emblem, was grabbed from the air, and clutched into a possessive fist; a woman wielding a magnificent sword crossed a bridge made from rainbows and into a fog.

He opened his eyes and realized the room was eerily silent, tense, and stiff. Silas's gaze locked onto something behind him. Milo flickered over to Kali, doing his best to not move a muscle, and saw her frozen in the same shock. Milo backed away from the book, turning towards the double doors, suddenly breathtakingly aware he was being watched.

"Just as I said," said a short figure illuminated by the torchlights, "they might not be the smartest -"

"Not the smartest?" interrupted a Scottish female that set a fire to Milo's chest. "No one was even keeping watch at the door!" She moved further into the room. "This lot makes up some lousy criminals."

Milo scowled. The Master moved in from the threshold, holding his cane tightly, stopping at the table, seemingly unbothered at the teenagers breaking into his room. The old man grabbed the book with golden engravings.

He frowned. *What were the odds?*

Something slapped against his cheek. Milo flinched, raising his head to see Silas staring pointedly at him. Milo grabbed what was thrown: bread. More specifically, half of a croissant. *Seriously?* Silas glared, making gestures towards the Master. Embarrassment rushed into his chest. *Silas wants me to talk?* He felt like a child, gesturing loudly towards the other boy to speak up first. For a moment they were snapping and pointing, jutting chins and mouthing obscenities. He turned. Thalia watched, eyebrows raised amusingly. Milo glared and faced the Master.

"I think we deserve some answers," Milo said.

The Master opened the book. "You do," he said, "and that is what I will give you." He set his cane down as the others approached the table. Thalia wandered around them, pacing the same way a wolf would in snow's cover. "What do you want to know?"

Milo exhaled and everything escaped his body. Questions bellowed inside his brain, each one yearning for attention. But then he was standing there and everyone stared and everything was on fire when *she* looked at him. A singular thought took over him like an explosion, lurching forward and resting on his tongue: *why does everything feel okay right now?* The idea of Norse gods and goddesses existing and him being a dead warrior eternally preparing for the end didn't sound too bad. And it frightened him into speechlessness. Milo stared at the Master and wondered if it would be too selfish to ask if he could stay and never leave.

The old man's stormy eyes met his own. His lips widened, flashing golden teeth. "You want to know why you're here."

Milo glanced around. The others eagerly nodded. He followed suit in a lag. The girl stared, a shadow drenched across her eyes. He glanced, and the world stopped. Quickly he snapped away. "Yes," he mumbled. "Thalia said we died -"

"That is what the berserker was told," the old man said, "but there is much more." The Master gripped his cane. "Centuries ago, the Norn told me of there being a day when the Warriors of Thunder would be reborn."

Thalia huffed. "*That's* what this is about?" her point became accusing. "Old man, you told me -"

He cut her off with a guttural sound, turning back towards the trio. "That might not make much sense. Norn are -"

"Three women at Yggdrasill," Milo whispered as he stared at his feet, "right? They can see the future," he sniffed loudly, rubbing his thumb against the sweater's cotton edge, "or fate, you know." He lifted his head, anger coming from his chest, spreading throughout his limbs like a low heat. He gestured at the Master. "And I dunno what kinda shit you dragged me into, wise guy, but I'm out. Do you hear me?" Milo got closer, heat swarming to his cheeks. "Judging by the whole warriors and thunder thing, I'm guessing you know my friend, Oba," he sneered. "But if that is what killed me, I'm done. I don't want anything to do with the thunder thing, the dreams, any of it."

The Master twitched. "The giant," he said, eyes flickering to Thalia, "he mentioned the Warriors of Thunder?"

Milo shrugged, disappointed in the man's reply. "Yeah. But I don't want it!"

"Are you a child, Milo Bohr?"

"Just about!"

The old man stared. "What you want matters not," he said, pointing to a page in the book. "Your life has been predisposed before it's beginning."

Silas tapped impatiently against the table. "And what did these Norn women say, huh?"

"Three beings of many natures were destined to die all at once," the Master said, "forged from different bloodlines, powerful in their own right. Together they'd be the Warriors of Thunder, destined to follow the heir of the Bleeding Throne into battle. I have searched before, but there have never been better prospects with you three," he said. His smile deepened to show curved dimples. "But now, by the *ord af de kvindelige skaebner*[2], now we have them, in the ripeness of a new age, in our darkest hours!"

Milo's thought process stammered at the language switch-up. He raised his hand, halfway leaning against the table for support. "You think that we're -" he pointed to his friends - where Kali ate potato fries from a hidden pocket in her sweater, and Silas tried to pocket something shiny by shoving it down his pants - then back to the Master, " - *us,* are the legendary heroes you've been waiting for?"

"Power is not visible to our eyes," the old man replied. "You all carry something that proves you worthy to be our warriors."

"Hold on now," Silas said. He pushed aside papers, sitting on the table with a velvety maturity as he crossed his legs. "You said these

---

[2] The word of the women fate's

are the 'darkest times' and last time I checked, the economy wasn't *that*
-"

"He means war," Thalia said. "We have been in an age of war
for centuries." Her piercing gaze shot towards the Master. "He thinks
you're the three destined to follow Thor into battle and reclaim Asgard
for the Aesir, right, old man? Still looking at those books, aren't you?"
Thalia looked at them. "You're putting the fate of worlds upon
children!"

Milo's head raced. Words he couldn't understand - Aesir,
Asgard, or even Thor - pooled into his brain. The illusion of having
sense over his life flew out the window. He shook his head. *They got the
wrong guy,* he thought. That made sense. The Master's calm exterior
began to fade, a vein popping out like a vine in his forehead. Before the
old man said anything to Thalia, Milo knocked his knuckles against the
table. "Back up," he said. "What war are you talking about?"

"This is bullshit," Silas laughed. "Honestly, Milo, you're gonna
believe all this?" He eyed Thalia, resentment behind his gaze. "War like
that isn't on Earth."

All his previous lamentations of faith and fate were gone. Milo
smirked. Everything had its limits.

"She said Asgard, idiot," Kali quipped.

"Oh, like Asgard is a real place."

Milo gestured towards the bickering, leaning towards the
Master. "This - *this* is what you've started," he said. "Could someone
just answer my questions before these two airheads destroy each
other?"

"It's been going on for centuries," Thalia replied. Her eyes
looked bronze in the fire, landing upon him with such a gentleness he
averted his gaze. "When Midgard - Earth - experiences a, let's say,
massive natural disaster, it's from this. Ever since all realms became

connected, what happens in one will be felt in another. Product of the Aesir-Vanir War."

There came those words again. Milo eyed her. They sounded like wind chimes against her tongue. "How's that even possible? For their war to affect us back home. It seems, I dunno, outlandish."

Thalia's face grew hard. "Gods are capable of anything."

"What do we have to do with a war of gods?" Milo asked, crossing his arms. "You said it yourself. We're just children, right?"

Her eyes flickered to the Master. He nodded, leaning heavily against his cane. Thalia moved her attention back towards them. "There is a goddess, Freyja, and she is the Queen of her clan, the Vanir. Before the war, all the realms existed peacefully, and as a sign of their alignment, Dwarves forged Freyja an offering of magic, jewels, and priceless pieces to build a necklace: the Brisingamen. It was the kind gods killed for." Thalia absentmindedly traced the decorative markings on the wooden table. "So when the Aesir gods invited her to dine with them, it wasn't surprising when Odin tried to -" The tower rocked as though hurricane winds slammed into its side. Thalia rolled her eyes. "You'd think after the god's death all *that* would stop."

The Master shrugged. "A name carries power," he commented. "Don't try to soil it."

"I wasn't trying -"

Milo knocked his fist against the table. "C'mon, you're just gonna leave a story like that?" He gestured for her to continue. "Honest. Finish the story."

Sweat trickled down her temples. She breathed heavily, like a weight sat upon her chest. "The All-Father Odin tried to kill her," she said, "for the Brisingamen."

"Thought Odin was the good guy," Milo said.

The tower rumbled again.

Thalia smirked - *pure,* his fake heart fluttered - and said, "Never said he was. There are no good guys when it comes to gods. You'd do well to remember that." She snagged two paintings from the wall. The first she set down expressed a forestry scenery, creatures and plants scattered around a creak. Eighteen figures flowed across the painting, graceful and dark. "The Vanir clan." Her fingertips recoiled.

A girl lurked in the painting's shadows, wielding a bow. The other Vanir moseyed across the landscape away from her. The clan shared twirling tattoos lining their skin, glowing mystically. "They rule Vanaheim. Lawful creatures, bound to magic." She set down the second painting. "The Aesir," she said, and the floor spoke back with thumps. Thalia stomped. "Beings of Asgard."

Milo inched closer. He counted twenty-five people walking amongst a field of flowers, a brilliant castle in the distance. He felt hypnotized. There he was, fighting the unbelievably strong urge to reach out and touch it, as though it could take him into their world. It seemed right, like a missing piece within his story. And the figure towards the front, a stark scar rippling across his eye, reminded him of home, even though Milo wasn't too sure he knew what that felt like. He put his hands under his armpits.

"Politically fueled by their yearning for power," Thalia continued. "Centuries of bickering and showing off has led to treachery and war," she paused, glancing over at the Master before she said, "an exiled Aesir formed a rebellion within Asgard. The outer villages fell in a few months, the cities in a year. There is nothing left."

"What does the rebellion have to do with a clan war?" Kali asked, entirely engrossed. Her food was placed aside as she leaned forward on her elbows, staring up at Thalia.

"It's just been a lazy rebellion," Thalia said. "They're a powerhouse of amateur soldiers with the will to plow through the great city," she raised her shoulders defensively, "but that's just what I believe, of course." She frowned. "The rebels conquered the city through the Royal Guard. A commander let their leader in and it led to the King's death. The only heir to the throne, missing within days of the invasion. I *know* these gods, and this rebellion," she waved her hand, "it's just a cover for clan domination. The Vanir are behind this. Controlling Asgard means power over all the realms." Thalia shoved a finger at the Master. "*He* believes the old stories and lullabies that the Warriors of Thunder will find Thor, restore him to the throne, and end the war."

"And you don't?" asked Milo.

"I don't believe in ghost stories. Old wives tales that give out meaningless hope." She sighed. "The Aesir could do better than Thor." The tower shook. She raised a middle finger to the ceiling.

Milo let the smile slip as he watched.

"Don't be childish," the Master grumbled, "take it seriously, Thalia."

Taps came from Silas. He swiveled till he faced everyone, legs twisted underneath him. He looked like he was trying his best to retain a laugh. "So," he cleared his throat, "you want us to find Thor? As in, *Thor*, the Norse mythology Prince. God of Thunder."

"It's your destiny," the Master said. "All of you! Can't you feel it?" He waved between them. "There's an intense bond between you - friendship, family, loyalty. It's because your souls have always been connected, tied by the Norn's words." He raised the book with gold engravings. "Everything you are and will be has already been written."

Milo's back straightened. He swallowed. "What does it say?"

The old man set the book on the table, flipping through the pages. The others inched closer, trying to get a good sight at the writing, only to realize it was all in the mystery language. Milo jumped onto the table, sitting a little ways away from the group. A prickling sensation started on his right; he turned to see Thalia passing, eyes fixated on him. Time slowed, and their gazes locked, an invisible force keeping them from looking away. Milo took the pain as she curved around him.

Milo turned back to the Master. Scars marked his cheeks. Up close he looked war-scorned, paper thin skin and wrinkled fingers riddled with rings and jewels dragging along the pages. When he stopped, the Master looked oddly afraid. A line drawing took up half the page. It showed a towering castle, three silhouettes standing at the base. Below the drawing were four lines. The page cut off there, obviously torn.

Silas sighed. "This is ridiculous."

"Quit it," Milo snapped.

"The Norn spoke this the day Freyja proclaimed war on the Aesir," the Master said. He sighed, licked his lips, and spoke:

> *At the time of summer's storm,*
> *The Warriors of Thunder will be reborn,*
> *Whom the walls of death cannot hold,*
> *To return the lost Prince to the Bleeding Throne."*

A stunned silence settled over them. Milo dropped his hands to his knees and felt the clammy skin through the cotton. His eyes closed, listening to the hum beneath his skin, listening to the echo across the room, listening to the soft steps as Thalia paced. He cracked his knuckles. The pops echoed within the quiet. *Summer's storm, walls of death, bleeding throne.* A shudder rolled through him.

Kali spoke first: "Does that mean we find Thor?" Eyes looked blankly back at her. "It's a prophecy, right? Those things tell the future. It says -"

"It says the Warriors of Thunder would die during the rain on a summer day," Thalia said, "but even though they're dead, they'll return to the living to *try* and find the Prince." She ground her teeth, nostrils flaring. "I hate prophecies." She stared dejectedly at the floor.

"'The Lord whose Oracle is in Delphi neither indicates clearly nor conceals, but gives a sign.'"

Kali blinked. "The Lord what?:

"It's Heraclitus," Milo said, glancing at Thalia, "she's saying prophecies never point to a direct answer, but more like give hints." He hopped down from the table, taking a step towards the old man. "But it means we can go back."

"Not in the way you think," he replied.

"Sorry," Milo drawled, "does 'land of the living' mean something other than 'being alive' to you?"

"You're dead, Milo," the Master said. "Returning to Midgard can only be done through the tower's magic." His frown widened. "*Living* something you are incapable of," he shut the book, "ever."

"Riddle me this, then," Milo started, crossing his arms, "why the hell do you think it's us?"

The Master smiled. "You know that as well as I," he replied. "There's something within you that believes this all makes sense. Can you truthfully tell me this is not your reality? How can you say your previous lives are the one, true reality?" He grasped his cane and left the table, approaching a glass case. "Valhalla should make you feel at home," he called over his shoulder, "and each other." The case popped open with a puff. "You must believe all things happen for a reason. Every one of you being here," he turned, "is not an accident."

Milo stood by his companions and had the feeling he'd have an asthma attack.

"You are the Warriors of Thunder, and your destiny awaits. It is rare," the old man said, "I come across the opportunity to send Valhallians on a quest." He waved for them to come towards him. "Today I do it with honor," the Master smiled, "you will go to Midgard, where upon your arrival, the key to finding Thor will show itself, and bring the lost Prince back to Asgard."

Milo looked around - their faces warped in shock. The walls caved in, and suddenly he was outrageously aware of what he had gotten himself into. He held his breath. Waited to see if any spots would cloud his vision. Waited for the need to gasp for air. There was nothing. He wasn't breathing, only stuck within the involuntary habit of inhaling and exhaling. And it was then Milo realized there would be no more turning back.

He made a mental note: one, they were not his companions, but something pointedly more; two, there was nothing within him designating him as alive; and three, he *really* needed to pee.

He nodded. "All right, old man," he said, "looks like you got me."

"Me too," Kali added. "I'll have to clear my schedule, though."

Silas huffed. "This is crazy!" he shouted. "I am *not* some reborn warrior. I'm nineteen," his confidence faltered as he cracked like glass, "and I've got a scholarship to the perfect college! A full ride! Do you know how rare that is for a guy like me? Five percent of its student body is black. *Five percent!* I'll never get a chance like this again." He moved to storm up to the Master. "So what you're gonna do, old man, is take me back!"

Milo shot out, stopping Silas from doing anything he'd regret. He met his friend's eyes, trying to give him the look of *Please don't do anything stupid.* He pushed Silas back, hissing to him as quietly as possible, "he's going to send us *home,* jackass!"

Silas grunted, shoving back against him. Recognition and knowing flashed across his eyes. Milo rolled his eyes and dramatically winked. They stared at each other, Silas not being able to stop his lip from quivering.

"I can't handle this," he whispered, "I'm just a kid, man."

Milo sighed. "I know. But I mean," his mouth turned up, "it's not like you've got anything else to do, right?"

"Fine," Silas said, "I'll try."

"Good," the old man said. He turned, grabbing things from the case. "I can give you three days to find the key." Chalk sat between his index finger and thumb, and as he waddled up to Thalia, she rolled her sleeve up, extending her arm forward. "The only reason why your souls can be present here in Valhalla is because they're attached to the tower," he explained, dragging the chalk along Thalia's olive skin. "Leaving would naturally result in immediate annihilation." He finished drawing: there were three black triangles, each overlapping the other, going up in a line from her wrist to her elbow. The Master raised the chalk and said, "This was a gift from the god, Ullr. Rune sorcery is a hobby of his."

Thalia pulled her sleeve down. "It's how I can leave," she said. "Valkyrie magic lets them leave whenever, for however long they want. Some of us," she looked over her shoulder at the old man, "don't have those luxuries."

The Master moved to Kali next. She gave him her arm. He began to draw the lines, and said, "There is much I can not tell you. The moment you leave Valhalla you'll be on your own." When he finished, he retrieved more items. He placed it in Kali's hands: a long staff twirled and decorated at the top with a dark jewel, and a leather-bound book, decorated with symbols and runes. "Laevateinn once belonged to the Aesir," he explained, "it can only be used by beings who hold the possibility of magic. This book will teach you how to control your ability."

"I don't -" Kali started bashfully.

"Stop questioning everything," the Master said. "Take Laevateinn. Three days from now, when Valhalla calls you back, this is how you come home. All of you."

She swallowed. "Three days?"

"The runes only last for so long, Valhallians," the Master explained. "You no longer have mortal bodies. Your souls are kept alive by the power of the tower, and without it, the runes are the only thing keeping you tethered to life. If you are not back by the time they fade, I do not know where you might end up."

After a few moments of struggle to get Silas to cooperate, the old man finished with Milo. He grasped his wrist, moving the smooth chalk along his skin in quick motions. "Once you find the key," he said, "Kali will use Laevateinn to open a portal back to Valhalla. Together we will find the path to Thor." He finished the rune, backing away from Milo.

"You keep mentioning the key," said Milo. "What is it?"

"That is unknown as much to me as it is to you," the Master replied. "I know it exists and comes from Asgard. Without it, the Prince will never be found." He reached into his pocket, and approached Thalia, placing a silver chain link in her palm. "Take this, warrior."

Thalia released a startled laugh. "Gleipnir," she whispered, "as I live and breathe! How did you get this?"

"Don't mind that," he chuckled. "It is a chain link from Gleipnir, the only restraint capable of holding the great wolf Fenrir captive. Something of great value can be the only thing between life and death," he advised, "remember that."

Milo stepped towards them, raising his hand. "Is *she* coming with us?" he winced. The venom dripped from between his lips like oil. He sputtered.

The Master laughed it off. "I already gave her the rune magic," he said. "You're only noticing it now?"

"I shouldn't go, Master," Thalia said. "Being out there, *now -*"

"Destiny written by the Norn applies for you as well, my friend," the Master said. "You, berserker, were born to be their guardian." He collected a sheathed sword from his bookcases, tossing it over his shoulder towards her.

Thalia grabbed it from the air, tossing it almost immediately back. She raised her eyebrows at him. The old man nodded, throwing a double-bladed Viking ax the length of Milo's torso toward her. She looked satisfied, sliding its wooden base through a loop at her belt. Her gaze turned slightly, sharply stabbing into Milo like a brick.

"I won't fail you, Master," Thalia said, hitting her fist against her chest. Her gaze fell over the warriors with a heavy resentment. "*Them,* however, can't promise anything."

The Master became solemn as he approached the group, eyes hanging pointedly onto Milo. "I can only assume word has spread of your existence," he said, "so you must move with haste and remain unseen. Creatures of the Vanir will hunt you, and I doubt the Aesir would help you. Death shall haunt you upon every corner - Midgard is the battleground for beings that will want nothing more than to have your souls for themselves." He got exceptionally close to Milo, grasping onto his wrist with a rough, wrinkled hand. There were mountains in his eyes.

The Master hissed: "*trust no one.*"

Milo, effortlessly and without hesitation, proceeded to say only one word.

"Motherfu -"

* * *

Valhalla's top floor had a magical portal in the wall.

Milo chuckled thinking about it - he never thought he'd be in such a position: realizing he stood in a wide room with the back wall missing, instead a golden door in the fog's midst, a few silver steps leading up to it. Milo stared, eyes lost in the swirling surrounding it, tendrils extending into the room like lanky fingers. He didn't want to look away - a raging fire burnt into his chest, spreading across limbs and swallowing him whole. Milo figured the less he moved, the quicker it'll pass, and the sooner it'll be over. He exhaled sharply.

"Raise your arms."

Thalia walked directly in front of him. She held a belt, the buckle unsnapped. Her amber eyes stared demandingly, motioning at his arms. The others got the same belts attached to their waists by the Master and a green-skinned boy with a friendly face. Twirling marks scored the boy's arms and flowers fell from his silver locks. Every time he opened his mouth to speak, the Master shushed him, tossing a glare. The boy frowned and lowered his head.

Milo swallowed as Thalia sighed impatiently and forcibly lifted his arms. She inched forward, moving her hands around his waist. She smelt like the woods across from his house during the winter, when everything froze over.

"What's with the green boy?"

She glanced over. "He's a *tjener*[3]."

"A what?"

"*Tjener*," she said. "Slaves devoted to serving the Valhallaians."

"You're kidding, right? The afterlife practices the most immoral system known to man?"

"This isn't heaven, Milo," Thalia said. "It's a power complex."

"What I see is a white man ordering a boy of color around."

The next time she looked at him, there was something unrecognizable in her eyes. "You're just," she said. "That's good."

Milo's gaze clung to the young boy. The *tjener* followed the old man, eyes colored like the Milky Way's strands, dejected and stuck to

---

[3] Servant

the floor. His gaze flicked to Silas, to Kali. They avoided the green boy, avoided speaking when the old man was near. Milo sighed. *I won't forget,* he thought. *I won't forget.* He turned away, back to Thalia and her cold stare.

Whatever pleasantries Thalia had were gone. She became angry again, face sculpted from ice and silver. He avoided looking down. It only angered her further. "You may hate me, warrior," she spoke with a steel tone, clicking the belt, "but I might be the only thing between you ending up with eternal damnation or a peaceful death." Thalia pulled back, reaching down to pick up something from the floor. "You'll have to deal with me," she met his eyes, "for your sake."

Quietly, he said, "I don't hate you." Everything within him became quiet. He held back from speaking more, afraid something stupid would find its way out. She reached again, sliding the sword into the belt's loops. Nothing about her body language looked angry anymore, just slow. She moved as something dragged her back. Guilt pegged him again. Milo ignored the will to hold himself back and whispered, "I liked you. Back at the bar."

She moved herself in the opposite direction, hands flinching till she held them tightly behind her. A glow burned deep within her amber eyes as she watched him. "We can't -" she stopped herself, clearing her throat before taking another step back. "That was before I knew you were on my list."

"List?"

"The souls the Master wanted me to collect," she replied.

"Yeah," Milo snapped, fidgeting with his new belt, "You seemed different."

Her eyes hardened. "You don't know me."

"I could," he said.

She stared and her eyes narrowed. "Have you ever wanted to be a god, Milo?"

He frowned, taken aback. It wasn't something he spent time pondering about before. It sounded ridiculous in his ears, like something he wasn't meant to consider. There weren't many questions where he couldn't forge an answer, however, fibbed or fudged it might be. He looked into her eyes and noticed how unnatural they were. Rims of the midnight sky, flecked with golden stars and amber strings, building galaxies within her iris. It hurt to stare for too long.

"Depends on what you'd define as god."

"Don't overthink it."

He stared at his feet. "I wouldn't think so," he admitted. "If I had the chance, I wouldn't take it."

She watched him like she knew something he didn't. A secret, barely visible, trapped between her lips. She twitched but did not speak.

"Would you?"

"Never," she said, too quickly, "I'd never."

Milo stared at the darkness swirling around the door portal. He could've sworn he could see his reflection, Thalia standing before him like an elongated shield, arms tanned with lumber and calves carved from stone. "Why'd you ask?"

"There are many ways to figure out a person," she said, "and the question of eternity is one."

He found himself lacking words when it came to her. Watching her was easy, admiring the sharp edges lining her throat or the wildness taking control within her hectic braids and curls. Imagining what it might feel like to hold her hand was torture. Yearning to lean down, to get as close as possible, to feel nothing between them, tasted like forbidden fruit. He smiled. His pulse ran like a drum in his throat. All he knew was that if she walked away, leaving him there staring into the upcoming portal, would be the worst pain.

"I had this friend, once. Before we lived in the city. Guess you wouldn't even call them a friend, really. More like oddly forced neighbors living in the same apartment complex." The portal was mesmerizing. "We took our bikes to this lake instead of going to school. It was weird, we barely even talked to each other the whole time, just staring into the water, waiting."

"Waiting for what?"

"The moment."

She watched him.

"That single second where time stopped, and all that mattered was the lake and the flies and the birds. The moment when all the noise turned off, and all that was left would be our souls, finding their way back home. The moment when you knew it was worth it." He peeled his gaze away from the portal, glancing towards Thalia. "Eventually we got tired of waiting, and he went into the lake."

"What happened?"

"He never came back out."

She didn't speak.

"I like to think that he's a god somewhere, with all the answers. Maybe one day he'd let me in heaven, you know? Maybe he'll see me and -" he stopped himself. She watched him intently, then, without the implication of looking away. He swallowed and licked his dry lips. "Maybe he'll see me."

"At the bar -"

"I shouldn't have let you walk away."

"What?"

He looked down at her. "You shouldn't have walked away."

Thalia's frown deepened as a blush burnt across her cheeks.

"Well," he said before she could, "I think I'm falling for you." Something barreled into his throat, surprise maybe. He never said something so truthful aloud. Either way, he couldn't take his eyes off her.

"Why would you do that?"

He reeled himself back, sudden unreasonable anger once again spiking in his fingertips. "Why does anybody?" he snapped. "Better yet: who asks something like that?" Her eyebrows raised. He swallowed. "Look, I like you, all right? I like you."

"I didn't ask you to."

"Nobody ever does."

Milo wasn't sure if she heard him. Before the air left his throat, she was gone, hurrying back to the Master. There was no response on her lips. Whatever she felt was under lock and key trapped somewhere he could not see. He watched her as he slunk back to his friends. For some reason, he felt empty.

"What happens when we get home?" Silas blurted.

Kali shrugged. "Find the key. Even though we have no idea what it looks like."

Silas waved her off, grabbing onto Milo's elbow. "That's not what I meant." He reached up, smacking Milo's cheek. "C'mon, buddy, peel away the eyes and tell me the plan."

Milo blinked. "Plan?"

"You winked at me earlier," Silas hissed. "How are *you* getting *me* home?"

"Honestly, I don't really know what to tell you," Milo said, backing away from his overbearing friend. He straightened out his sweater, rolling up the sleeves. "We don't even know where we'll be when we step through that thing and, you know, maybe if we *find* the key and bring it back, the Master and all these other crazy people can find that dude -"

"Thor," Kali interjected.

" - *whatever,* so we don't have to!" He leaned in to add in a whisper, "They can't stop us from going home then."

Silas settled down by that point. He fiddled with the dagger on his belt, looking uncomfortable with it beneath his elbow. But he wasn't fighting it anymore and stood at the steps, ready to step into the unknown. The Master watched as the warriors gathered.

"Innocents are suffering from this war," the Master said. "The Warriors of Thunder were born to stop it." He held onto Kali's hand. "Do not be afraid, young one: this is your birthright. Take it with outstretched hands and growing hearts - destiny stands just beyond that -"

"*Door*," Silas shouted, "we get it, old man. Quit it with the dramatic motivational speech, would you? Man's never been to the 'don't do drug' assemblies."

"Silas!" Milo exclaimed, stifling down his laughter. "Let's just get this thing going, all right?"

"Stupid," Thalia muttered, moving up the stairs towards the golden door. She ripped it open, wind shooting out at them. The Master backed away as she stepped partly in the shadows. "Think of Midgard," she called, her voice distant from within the portal, "remember each other. And try not to throw up." She submerged into the nothingness.

Milo smiled. "Click your heels three times, kids," he said, hitting his heels together as he moved up the stairs. He put his back to the beckoning darkness, ignoring the lull in his stomach urging him to collapse into it, and gazed over his new friends, calling out in a sing-song voice, "There's no place like home!"

And as they laughed, Milo fell backward into the cool emptiness, accepting it without hesitation. It brought him into peace, like a motherly hug - he closed his eyes.

Milo happened to enjoy parts of death.

"Herjan"

GODS
AND
DEVILS

X. Manhattan

Darkness yielded into colors and shapes. Sounds brightened and became sharper, forming coherent languages. A horrid smell entered Milo's nostrils, something scuttled by his left ear, and he heard a door open above, and footsteps along a fire escape. Car horns honked wildly in the distance, shouts and laughter echoing. The smells surged: bagels and hot dogs and coffee and wet pavement. Another noise, erupts across the air, piercing police sirens -

Police sirens!

Milo's eyes popped open.

The sickening aroma of old trash and rat colonies, buried in the deep allies of Manhattan, somehow comforted Milo. He flung his head back, inhaling deeply with a newfound sense of pride and homesickness - and *immediately* gagged. He burst into laughter as he rolled onto his feet, the afternoon sun falling upon him like a lighthouse. His smile widened; the city was just a little ways away, only dumpsters between them. Hordes moved along the streets, the industrial wonderland blurry in the background.

The rest of the Warriors of Thunder staggered to their feet, faces warped in disgust. Thalia stood as straight as a needle, eyes scanning the buzzing street, her hand holding a tight grip on her double-bladed ax. She pulled off her leather jacket, tossing it over in Kali's direction when she complained about being cold. Scars curved up and around her dark skin, sweat forming around her biceps. Thalia tied her hair up in a single motion, eyes never leaving the noise. Milo dragged his gaze away when she gripped onto her belt, taking slow steps down the alley. He reached down to help Silas off the ground.

"Let me guess," Silas groaned, swiping dirt and trash off him, "you're from this shit-hole."

Milo laughed, peeling an empty chip bag off his back. "It's not a shit-hole," he said. "Where're you from, huh? Someplace better than -" he extended his arms, " - *Manhattan*?" A few birds exclaimed loudly in their presence. Sounds from the road continued to echo through the alleyway. He shrugged. "It's not for everyone."

"Virginia," Silas replied. "Ever been?"

"Never had the time to travel," he chuckled, "or the expenses, for that matter."

"I've lived all around," Kali said. "My dad's a military guy, jumps between bases." She smiled, pride in her brown eyes. "My favorite was Germany. Only eighteen and I've seen the world."

"Obviously not all of it," Milo muttered.

Silas chuckled.

"You know," Milo began, leaning against a dumpster can, "when I was a kid, we -"

"*Hey!*"

They jumped around. Thalia paced around a few feet away, her ax fastened in her hand. She raised it, pointing the weapon at Milo. With glowing eyes, she gritted her teeth together and said, "What the hell do you think this is - social hour?"

"Give us a break," Milo huffed. He raised an eyebrow, all inhibitions flying out the window when he asked, "Wanna tell us where you're from?"

Milo felt a slight breeze below his chin, Thalia's ax sitting a hair's length away from his neck, glinting in the afternoon sunlight. She moved a fraction and the iron scraped him, clipping a few hairs. Thalia held the weapon with no hesitation, everything in her eyes saying she'd kill him in an instant.

He raised his hands defensively. "I'm sorry," he mumbled.

Thalia's face grew hard. "There are things more important," she said in a heated whisper, "than what *you* want." She stepped closer, the cool blade of the axe rubbing against his neck. "You aren't a child anymore, Milo Bohr. It's time to grow up."

He gulped as she lowered the axe, turning her attention towards the others. He wanted to be swallowed up and pulled away from the alleyway.

"We need a plan," Thalia said, moving around Milo as though he didn't exist, "the key must be found."

"The Master said it would be right here," Kali said, kicking an empty soda can across the alleyway. "Are we supposed to look through the trash?"

Milo blinked rapidly, trying to shake the buzzing from beneath his skin. Dirt sat on the bottom corner of his glasses. He yanked them off, cleaning with his sweater as he stared up at the building to his right. Something about it kept catching his attention. He focused on it: red bricks, three stories high, windows lining the fire escape. He snapped, sliding his glasses back. It was the Italian bakery his mom took him to on Sunday mornings. It was a ten-minute walk from the house.

Maybe there is such a thing as hope. Everything put him so close to his mother. A quick sprint could get him standing at his front door, ringing the doorbell, and leaving everything else behind. The others were wrapped around finding the key. He eyed Thalia - her ax was out, fixated on something in the distance. He looked around quickly, spotting a relatively clean t-shirt hanging on a low dryer line, and pulled off the Valhalla-issued sweater. Pulling the shirt over his head, Milo turned to see Thalia's head jerk in the opposite direction. He swiped an old jacket too big for him, covering the sword.

"Going somewhere?" Thalia called out, still facing the street.

"Just been thinking about the key plan, is all," he said, giving her his best team-player smile. "The key is bound to show up at some point, right? I mean, the Master said it'd appear when we arrived." Milo, satisfied with the coverage the jacket gave his sword, began to casually move down the alleyway. "How about this?" he called, "you guys stay here and I'll go see my mom, let her know I'm okay, and -"

"By Ymir's beard," Thalia breathed, rubbing her forehead, "how many times am I going to have to tell you?" Her eyes fell upon him with pity for the first time as she said, "You're dead. Let your mother grieve! We only have three days until we return, and the key must be found. Whether you care about this fight or not, I don't care - but you know what? *Lives* are at stake. Have some morality."

"We don't even know where it is," Silas said. "Give him a break and let him go."

"It's really not that simple. Do you have any idea the creatures that prowl Midgard for snacks just like you three?" She raised her gaze. "You danger-prone fools."

"It would take *nothing* to go see her," Milo pleaded. "I'd barely be gone!"

"If I have to go through this with you one more time -"

There was a scatter from behind. Kali choked on the air.

From the alleyway's entrance, guarding a city burst at the seams, came a menacing group. They were like the warriors of Valhalla, weapons extended and glistening with heavenly silhouettes. They wore sterling golden armor, blood, and dirt staining their hands and faces. Milo walked as if to meet them halfway, confidence lingering over him from being in a familiar place, but was stopped by Thalia's hand latching on his elbow. He met her poignant eyes, and saw an enveloping warmth, unlike the fiery pain prickling beneath his skin. He fell into line with the other warriors, eyes clinging onto her as she approached the newcomers.

Thalia stood in their way. "*Finn en annen rute[4]*, Asgardians."

"*Se, sma Valhalla-sjeler langt hjemmefra[5]*," the leader replied with a laugh. The others chuckled with her. Blood stained her neck. It was the same color as his. Somehow the thought calmed him. The Asgardian wielded a spear, leaning it on her shoulder as she towered over them. "Move out of our way," the woman said in English, her accent strange when compared to Thalia's, berth-like operatic singing. "Little mouse."

Thalia looked over her shoulder. "*Run,*" she whispered. And within the second, her arm flipped around, ax swiveling below the Asgardian chin. The woman boisterously laughed as her companions retrieved their weapons, lunging on Thalia.

Silas grabbed onto Milo's and Kali's arms. "C'mon!" he shouted. "She said run!"

Milo yanked himself free, unsheathing his silver blade. It was heavy in his palm, the handle soft with fur as he gripped it. "Can't leave her now," he said over the loud clashes, "not after that whole *have some morality* speech!"

There was another clash. Thalia's ax duplicated and became a pair, twirling around like an artist painting a blank canvas. Three Asgardians attacked her, jabbing with pointed swords and spears. He watched her move and it was like snowfall, sudden and constant, falling with a dangerous gracefulness. Silas armed himself next to Milo,

---

[4] Find another route
[5] Look, little Valhalla-souls far from home

holding his sword high. It looked like a needle in his hands. Silas looked down with a wild gaze. Milo remembered his childhood lightsaber, remembered the stick he'd snatch from the backyard to attack a tree trunk, and remembered watching kids turn pens around their fingertips like knives. He imagined how foolish he'd look.

Silas was grinning. "Cool, right?"

Milo feigned a smile. "Like gods."

The fourth Asgardian, the snarky leader, stormed up to the Warriors of Thunder. She swung her spear like a rope, shaking it forward to slice across Milo's cheek. He jumped back in pain, steadied back to his feet by Silas. Tears burnt his eyes as he slashed the sword flippantly at her. Inky blood slid between his lips. Hot iron and ash and honey. The woman slashed her spear against his wrist and the sword skidded across the alley.

Milo extended his arms, holding the others behind him as much as possible. He extended his neck as he backed away from the woman, searching for Thalia further down the alleyway. An Asgardian sprawled on the ground, an ax buried deep within his skull. Milo flinched away at the sight to see Thalia scrambling towards her other ax.

At his right, Kali slipped beneath him, thrusting Laevateinn forward. Energy shot from its scepter, slamming against the Asgardian's golden-covered chest, shoving her backward. Kali screamed, waving Laevateinn wildly over her head.

"*Kali*," Silas breathed, "what was that?"

She clutched Laevateinn close to her as it glowed and hummed. "I have no idea!" she exclaimed. "It was like, I dunno, second nature, and the next thing I know," Kali paused, mimicking the magic with her hands.

"The old man was right," Milo said.

The trio stared at each other in fear. Something undeniable just happened before them, something they could no longer ignore and call a bad dream. Together they sunk into their reality, unsure of how to carry their shared trauma.

Then the Asgardian's spear smacked into Silas's jaw, sending him doubling over. She raised her spear and aimed at Milo's chest, crazed accomplishment in her eyes. The Asgardian pulled the weapon back over her head, and -

"*For den Blødende Tronen*[6]!"

Soaring down from the fire escape, a woman taller than them all landed on the Asgardians' shoulders, plunging a wickedly gruesome great sword beneath the armor's collar, through the skin below. She screamed, hands clawing at her chest, collapsing when the mysterious woman pulled the sword free. Behind them, Thalia rose like a statue, scarlet blood staining her hands and chin, the bear marks on her face humming with a heavenly glow. Three bodies scattered at her feet, all frighteningly still.

Milo stared at them. Death, he knew, came often in everything - whether it be drooping flowers or collapsing stars. In a way, he considered it to be a beautiful process of renewal. But before him was only decay, blood seeping into the ground, a low-hanging stench slowly rising towards him. His chest felt like it was vibrating. One head was split, eyes staring directly at him. He was trapped in Death's gaze, and could only remember how bad the paint job was in his living room.

Thalia touched his elbow. His arms shot out, flailing, trying to shove her away. His lips parted like a fish, only seeing the dead man watching him. She held onto his wrists like manacles. "Stop," she said. "Look at me." She grabbed his chin. "Can you see me?"

And he saw her, death and all.

"I see *you*," she said. She pulled him away from the bodies. He was unsure of what she did, but the panic melted and when he looked back at the dead man, his eyes were closed. He was asleep.

---

[6] For the Bleeding Throne

Their savior remained still in the alleyway as Milo was guided back toward the group. The woman held her sword defensively across her chest. He slowly moved around, trying to get a good look. Wide, dark eyes took up most of her face, lighting up against the brown in her skin. Hair the same shade as chestnuts fell halfway over her head, the other half braided in intricate twirls and puzzles close to her scalp. Her clothes were taken right out of a museum - old trousers, dirtied white pirate-like shirt gaping down the middle, and puffy at the sleeves. A leather vest tightened over it, tied delicately at the stomach. Her eyes investigated the surroundings, knuckles bright against her sword's hilt till her gaze landed upon Thalia.

Falling to her knees, the warrior slid her blade into a sheath at her back. "*Velsigner deg*[7], Heimdall," she whispered. Raising her head, her eyes fell upon Thalia, and she called out in a heavy voice, "Hail, mighty berserker, warrior bred from Odin's blood!"

Thalia fidgeted beneath the staring eyes and reached down, pulling the warrior up. "Relax yourself, *kriger*[8]," she said, patting her awkwardly on the shoulder, "we are all the same here in Midgard. Show your truth: why have you come?"

"I come from the war-torn Asgard," she explained. "The rebels latched on to the Bifrost with me, and for that, I am sorry. I'm pleased you're all unscathed however," she raked her eyes over the Warriors of Thunder, confusion turning into recognition and eventually skepticism till she continued, "*Alive* you may be. I have come for the berserker." The warrior turned to Thalia again, eyes tired and pleading as she stated in an unwavering tone: "Asgard is dying and the key to restoration is relocating the missing Prince and returning him to the throne."

"What does that have to do with me?" Thalia asked.

---

[7] Blessing to you
[8] Warrior

"Berserkers are linked with the blood of Odin," the warrior replied, "it is your instinct to be as close as possible to anyone who holds his blood." She straightened, holding onto her sword. "You can lead me straight to his youngest son, Thor."

Thalia grimaced. "Your name?"

Her confident exterior stuttered. She recentered herself and retracted. "I am Astrid," she proclaimed, "daughter of merchants and loyal servant to the throne."

Thalia sighed. "You're one of the Royal Guard."

"Yes," Astrid said, "which means I will stop at *nothing* to restore my kingdom. I need the berserker -"

"I'll decide what it is you need," Thalia snapped, her cheeks growing an angry red.

Astrid cocked her head. "I don't back down that easily, berserker."

"*Hey,*" Milo interrupted, sensing the tension was about to reach a boiling point, "we're looking for the guy too, all right? People like us," he paused for dramatic effect, looking over his shoulder to see the other Warriors of Thunder watching him tiredly, "well we're pretty screwed, but got a knack for finding supernatural things without really wanting to."

Astrid blankly stared. "I don't - what does that mean?"

"It means we can help each other," he said. He looked over to his friends and shrugged. "Jeez, she acts like I'm speaking Klingon or something."

A hand reached, tapping Milo's shoulder before twisting around him like a shadow. Thalia stood in the distant city light, the sun standing above as the afternoon carried on. "Whatever happens next, first things first: we need to find someplace hidden and safe. I don't trust Midgard for a *second.*" She twirled around on her heel, moving down the alleyway and towards the city.

The Warriors of Thunder moved past Milo, Astrid eyeing them hesitantly as she followed, gripping her side as though she tried to keep herself together. Milo remained behind, watching them walk without a thought of turning around. His gaze moved to the brick building. There was a tug in his stomach, an urge pulling him towards his home, his mother. The thought of her being moments away killed him. He knew he shouldn't leave. All the ideas behind being heroes stopping a terrible war and recovering a lost Prince sounded wonderful in his ears, but he remembered the dead bodies and the way they ripped through him as though he were nothing but air.

Milo knew what he was going to do before it happened. And somehow, he only felt elation. There was no guilt. Maybe it designated him as heartless. He was not the hero. He waited till the company integrated themselves within the busy Manhattan streets, barely paying attention to who was around them, and took a sharp right, running in the opposite direction. As everything grew familiar, the trees and curves within the streets, Milo extended his arms and lifted his chin till his eyes burned from the sun's gaze. Everything that was real touched him - the wind, the smell of the streets, neighbors mingling, the quiet constant pattern life showed.

Milo smiled at the sky and screamed.

"Fuck you, Odin!"

XI. Helicopters and Promposals

Hofond hummed eagerly for more battle.

Heimdall's blade was already stained with death, but even as it sat sheathed, pressed against Astrid's back, a magical heat radiated from the steel. Its stagnant presence calmed her as she stood alongside strangers. Each held a brightened, dangerous quality that stood out like Sol's sun. Even the berserker, the one she had so desperately searched for, felt off.

"Well knock me down and steal my teeth, you donkey," the short Valhallian girl, Kali shouted, "*Gandalf* is the best wizard." A dark staff was in her possession, radiating a darkness all too familiar. Laevateinn was something Astrid had encountered before but under many different circumstances. At the time, it still lay in its creator's hands, the exiled Aesir, Loki. The girl's hands held onto it closely, its divinity echoing a deep glow against her obsidian skin.

Astrid glances over her shoulder at them. The first thing she noticed was the girl's natural beauty, and in another lifetime, Astrid saw herself fancying a girl like the Valhallian. There was a sharpness in her chin, a straight edge in her jaw. Her slender hands seemed to always be dancing along the wind, moving around gracefully. Astrid pressed her lips together as she looked away.

Astrid moved along a little ways ahead of the dead warriors, sticking close to the berserker's heels. The city was behind, a run-down neighborhood on abandoned land a yard ahead. They hadn't paused in the trek from the alleyway, moving quickly away from the bumbling Midgardian crowds. Astrid appreciated the speed - her vision grew blurry with exhaustion, her hand tired from clasping onto the arrow still lodged within her side. The arrow no longer stuck out, but the thin wood was buried painfully within. Turning slightly to see behind her, blurry figures moved around, talking boisterously.

"If you crap on *Dumbledore* one more time -" the charming Valhallian, Silas, began playfully. "*Merlin* is the inspiration behind practically all fictional wizard tropes," he said, "like you, Kali, with your stick and all."

"Did you just call me a fictional trope?"

Muffled laughter.

"Honestly," Silas replied, "if the shoe fits."

They fell into another bit of laughter. She never imagined the dead to be in such high spirits. In a way, their unwavering ability to find joy caused Astrid to experience extreme jealousy. She kept her gaze forward, ignoring their rising voices.

"Know your house?" Silas asked.

The girl chuckled. "Slytherin." She huffed. "I took the test once and lied on all the answers, but somehow *still* got Slytherin."

"That shit just knows."

"I had a snake, once. Burmese Python. We named him Marty and even though he wasn't mine, he loved *me* the most." She laughed confidently. "My step-brother bought him after getting high in a

Walmart parking lot. Once that high wore off - *god,* he was so scared he couldn't even go into the same room as Marty."

"Did you talk to it?"

"You know, sometimes. When I fed him."

"Yeah," Silas said, "Slytherin for sure."

She stuck her tongue out. "No comments from the peanut gallery, Hufflepuff." She laughed. "*Hey!*" Kali jogged to walk beside Astrid. "You're from Asgard, right?"

"Aye."

"What kinda animals do you have?"

Astrid blinked. "Mainly the same as Midgard's. We hunt game in our woods and fish in creeks." She shrugged. "Not much is different."

The berserker scoffed. "How about you tell them stories of your homeland, *kriger?* Tales of *dodsengler* and Fae. The truth behind Asgard's golden spires and great castles."

There was silence. Astrid stared at Thalia. *Dodsengler.* Old magic whistled through her ears. She used the ancient language, once spoken fluently in Vanaheim and rarely among some others. If an average Northern Asgardian warrior spoke in the ancient tongue, she'd be perplexed, but maybe it made more sense for a berserker to be well-educated in the languages. She wasn't too sure how to respond, though, since she had no idea what it meant.

"Tell us a story," Silas called out, "please."

She hesitated, searching her mind through all the old stories her mother used to spin. She said, "it has been foretold that the eldest son of the All-Father shall die by another god's hand." Astrid held onto her wound. "Baldur is the Aesir's pride. All of Asgard adores and cherishes him. As the King's sons came of age, the realm expected the eldest, Baldur, to be crowned next. When it came time for the naming of the crowned Prince, Havi the High One disappeared from the land.

He rode to consult a seeress about his firstborn's fate. It is said the seeress almost told Havi all of Baldur's end, but paused, never revealing the killer's face." She smiled, but it felt wrong. "We praise Yggdrasil he's lasted this long."

"Wait," Kali interjected, "this dude's still alive."

"Not *dude*. Baldur, High Prince of Asgard," Astrid said. "He remains under secret care with a watchful eye. Many years have passed since he walked the realm's fields, remembering the smell of his home during the spring. Whether the war has touched him or not, we might never know."

"If Thor's missing, why can't they just bring back Baldur to be King?" Silas asked.

"Neither Frigg nor Odin would risk putting Baldur on the most vulnerable seat in all the Nine Realms," Astrid replied. "The moment his fate was discovered, Odin rewrote the accords, naming Thor as Heir to the Bleeding Throne. The Aesir believe in what is written, the laws and traditions that have made Asgard the prosperous realm it's known for. It is why finding him will fortify Asgard. With a true King, one with the All-Father's blood and title, the Asgardians might be united once more."

"I mean," he said, "it's not like they're plastering his name on the center of a basketball game billboard for some stupid promposal. If everyone loves him so much, they'd protect him, and make sure he stays on the throne, right? At least, that's what I'd do. If one of you ended up King, and were good enough at it, taking a bullet or sword, ax or whatever, would seem worth it. For the future."

Astrid watched him and became pleasantly surprised. She didn't expect to get any formidable responses, but he delivered one without even realizing it. He hummed something beneath his breath, eyes raised to the dimming sky with snapping fingers and a bouncy step. The other dead ones did not acknowledge it either. They moved aimlessly alongside him, every once and awhile adding to his tune as if they knew it too. The berserker, who remained ahead and withdrawn, held her chin tilted towards her shoulder, quietly listening in. Pride laced her eyes.

Before Astrid responded appropriately, a dead one jumped in a puddle.

"This kid from my high school did one of those promposal videos," Kali said, "jumped out of a helicopter and everything."

Silas laughed. "Where was the proposal?"

"On the parachute, duh. It was badass. But then he landed badly and shattered his pelvis - ended up never going to prom after all. He did get arrested, though." She shrugged. "That was exciting."

"For jumping out the helicopter?"

"Nah, he stabbed some guy."

Astrid widened her strides to get away from the chattering. What they said made little to no sense - whether it was the *helicopter* or *promposal*, she was at a complete loss. They seemed happy, though, which gave her less to worry about. The last thing she needed was to bond with dead teenagers.

A collapsed house, the roof caved in and gone, surrounded by trash mounds and friendly pecking birds, came before them. Thalia did not hesitate to jog through the open door, ducking her head as she swung inside. Within a few moments, she ventured back out, waving her ax for them to follow. Astrid picked up the pace.

The sunlight struggled to enter the building, leaving the room dark and full of shadows. Pieces of the roof scattered across the floor, and a ruined fireplace collapsed in the back corner. Astrid fell into the old staircase, creaking and cracking beneath her as she tried to roll off her side. Pulling her hand away, Astrid looked down - her palm was drenched with blood, dried and thick against her skin. Muttering a curse to herself, she pressed her hand back down.

"Are you wounded, *kriger*?"

The berserker knelt to her right, cautiously holding her hands out. An auburn curtain cascaded down her shoulders, the strands lucky enough to catch the sun shining a deep honey. Buried in the curls was a singular braid near her neck. It was a Northern tradition Astrid knew well, from her brothers in the Royal Guard. Warriors from Asgard's snowy Northern terrain wore many braids for different reasons. One, she believed, symbolized being unbeaten in battle. Astrid eyed the berserker's hands carefully as she scooted away.

"Only tired," she said, "my journey has been hard."

"All this for Thor," the berserker said, rolling back on her heels. A faraway daze took over her eyes as she stared, tracing her finger along the intricate designs on her ax's blade. "How deserving is he really of the throne?"

Astrid stared, feeling as though she'd been struck. "It's his birthright," Astrid snapped. "How long has it been since you've been in Asgard, berserker?" she asked, "my loyalties lie with the throne, which is in Thor's care now. A war rages in my realm - whether he is worthy or not is outside my duty. Peace needs to be restored with familiarity. The people know the Aesir, the children of Odin. Only they can be trusted."

The berserker was silent, a smile widening upon her lips. "My name is Thalia," she said, reaching forward to grasp her, "let me look at your side."

"I've handled worse."

"I practice rune sorcery," Thalia's stare was unwavering. "You saved those three *jaevla dukker*[9] back in the alley when you could've let them get slaughtered," she spoke genuinely, a soft smile on her lips, "I

---

[9] Fucking dummies

would like to repay you by healing your wound. I'm not nice so please say yes before this ever happens again."

"Aye," Astrid said with a laugh. She removed her hand, the blood staining her white undershirt. The pain ricocheted through her as she leaned against the fallen staircase, the young Valhallians quickly approaching from outside the door. "Do what you must."

Thalia leaned down, looking over the arrow incision before pressing her hand against the exit wound. Astrid watched, skeptical of the berserker's sorcery. Rune sorcery was Ullr's trade, the only person she'd experienced it from. Light fell from the collapsed roof, sliding across Thalia's face till she lit up. At that moment, with her skin like bronze and eyes like fire, the berserker felt as though she tumbled out Astrid's memory. Something about her in the light rang familiar, coming from a time Astrid yearned to go back to. Clouds crawled in the way and the light faded. She pressed her finger into her palm. *I'm not dreaming.*

A strong heat came from the berserker's hand as her index finger traced little lines against Astrid's stomach. Footsteps came from the doorway when Thalia began to raise her hand, the thin cylinder of wood following. A sharp yell echoed between them.

"Sorry," Thalia said, "it'll be-"

The arrow flung across the room as the Valhallians entered the creaking shack. Relief washed over her as Thalia's runes began to stitch her skin together, restoring the blood loss and curing the fatigue.

"Better when you don't know it's about to happen." Thalia rubbed the blood away with a rag.

There was a grumble of throats clearing simultaneously from the doorway of the shack. Silas pushed the other and hissed, "Not at the same time! Jesus!"

The pair stood together awkwardly, bumping into each other with their elbows, giving *eyes* to who should talk first. Astrid watched, the agitation still finding its way to creep back up her throat. She eyed the berserker - the warrior was not too engrossed in her medicinal sorcery anymore, irritation beginning in her gaze.

"If one of you doesn't talk," Thalia muttered, "I swear on Mani's chariot -"

"He's gone," Kali blurted.

Thalia blinked with confusion, but her hands were frozen, and the mending process paused. "Who is?"

"Milo," Silas replied. "Obviously. Haven't heard his blabbermouth in a while, haven't you?" He buried his hands nonchalantly in his pockets, staring off to some random point in the sky.

The berserker's steely gaze shot towards the Valhallians. "How long have you known?"

Silas raised his hands defensively. "Look, we saw him take a different turn a ways back. The guy has a right to see his family, don't you think? I didn't say anything to give him some time. None of us had enough time."

Astrid remained silent as the berserker kept a stone-like expression. Something raged beneath her, but Thalia trapped it inside, staring at her fellow travelers with no recognizable emotion. She continued to draw little runes along Astrid's stomach, the healing moving with a sudden intensity. The dead ones watched, waiting for it all to be released. There was something within her silence, the need to remain calm and collected, that snatched up Astrid's interest. She concentrated, trying to remember what the missing Valhallian looked like - stood a hair shorter than her, raven curls lining his angular face, stormy eyes hidden behind the glare of Midgardian glasses. *Stormy eyes.*

Paranoia grew in her chest.

Secrets she couldn't imagine festered within the company she found herself in, and as she gripped Hofond, she muttered a quiet prayer to Heimdall.

Please, watch over me, All-Seeing One.

XII. City of Gold

Standing at his house's driveway, Milo wished to swallow his sadness, his guilt, his fear - not sugarcoat it, but rather swallow it raw, unfiltered, naked, let it curdle his insides and shrivel on his tongue. He was not, however much he wanted to be, satisfied. The yellow house reminded him of before, and it reminded him of how he lived in the after, of how he might forever teeter along the edge of living and dying. He wanted to sink into the ground, to melt against the sun and burn till the guilt swallowed him whole. The others were gone, hopefully someplace safe, and he was alone, surviving still in a state of longing for everything and having nothing.

The window at the far right was visible through vines, showing the kitchen counter and Natalie's home-grown herbs. A shadow passed. He exhaled, lowering himself to a crouch beside the tangled bushes. He paused a few feet from the window.

Light streamed in like puzzle pieces on the tile, plates from previous dinners unwashed in the sink - he promised his mother he'd wash them when he got back from the graduation party. A bad taste spread through his mouth, coating his throat with acid. Coffee cups are scattered across the table in the back. Lightheartedness rescued him for a moment: his mother liked to pour herself coffee, drink halfway, leave the cup somewhere, and get another cup with the thought the previous was finished, discarded someplace unbeknownst to her. It was calming to see a trait from his past life.

The shadow danced by the window again. Natalie Bohr leaned against the counter, an old flip phone pressed against her ear. The pale blue dress she wore glowed gently in the sunlight and her brown curls paused at her jaw, bangs twirled out from her gaze. Rounded glasses teetered against her nose, a breath away from falling into the sink.

Milo felt breathless at the sight of her. She hadn't slept in a while, and by the coffee cups scattered around, her energy came directly from the caffeine. Realizing he was close to her again shocked him so much he was glued to the spot. He watched her hang up the phone, and toss it harshly into the sink. She flinched at the sharp clatter and an irritated scream echoed against the window. He watched, stone cold and trapped, as she snapped towards the dirty dishes. Before taking another breath, Natalia flung herself, slamming her fists into the plates and pelting them across the kitchen floor. Crashing and wailing muffled against the window as her face grew red.

With the plates destroyed, Natalia laughed in disbelief, tip-toeing around the mess. She paused at the table, eyeing the newspapers, paint, and half-empty cups. Her tall figure collapsed into a chair. Milo backed away from the window as she sat there, the bad taste coming back to his mouth. He swallowed, touching his throat as the air grew heavy and hot.

Milo crossed the front lawn, peeling the old jacket off along the way. He dropped it on the grass, collapsing onto the driveway with a *thump.* All thoughts in his mind melted into soup, becoming nonsense and incoherent in his brain. The sun came heavy upon him as one thing dawned: *I can't see her.* No matter how much he wanted to run through the door, wrap his mother into a hug, and tell her he made mistakes but he'd be better. He wanted to be better for her. But in the end, Milo knew Thalia was right. He slowly raised his arm, covering the sun with his limb to see the marks the Master drew on his skin. The first triangle faded. There'd never be enough time to explain it all, to put an entire life into three days, to say everything they ever wanted to before he was gone.

Thus he lay there - sweating - reminiscing about being alive and wondering if the girl with amber eyes would beat him up again for leaving. His lip curled down. Maybe it was what he deserved.

A rumbling came from down the street. Instinct took over, and energy erupted into his veins, rushing like the primordial ocean within his blood. Milo unsheathed his sword, its unusual weight from before nonexistent. Rolling up to his feet, the sword slashed defensively as he tried to see what was coming.

A jet black Chevrolet Corvette, the engine giving off a predatory growl, drove creepily towards the house's mailbox. Tinted windows blocked Milo's view from seeing the driver, the sun's rays showing only a blurry silhouette. Milo, still gripping onto his sword's hilt, skidded across the driveway, toppling over the bushes and rolling on the grassy side. The next time he looked, the Corvette parked in the driveway. Milo paused.

The door behind the passenger seat flung open. Inside was darkness - no light reaching the car. A few birds flew overhead.

A figure stepped out. Reaching beyond six feet, the man wore a dark suit, hiding skin colored molten gold. A uniform mustache sat on his upper lip, and beneath a bushy beard trimmed along the jawline. Midnight hair rested at his shoulders, braids pulling strands from his face. Even from a distance, the man's coal eyes stood out like a black hole, forever echoing into darkness. Everything about him triggered an alarm in Milo's brain: the massive stature, the frighteningly perfect and symmetrical beauty of his face.

The scariest, though, was when he noticed the man looked directly at him.

The atmosphere changed. Milo staggered as he rose, the sword clattering from between his fingertips to the ground. His gaze locked with the darkness across the driveway, and everything else burnt away. With a quick thought, Milo tried to pick up his feet and run towards the house, to his mother. Nothing moved. A numbing sensation spread into his arms, all feeling gone.

Milo Bohr.

He flinched. The voice was low and methodical, like keys on a piano, playing an intricate melody. The coal-black eyes never left him, the voice coming from his closed lips. Milo lifted his leg to step backward, the old mismatched shoes he found in the alleyway weighing a ton. The mysterious man's head tilted, his arm extended towards the backseat. A smile widened across his lips.

Milo Bohr, the voice said, *take a seat.*

A noise came from the window. Milo, stuck in place again, peeled his eyes away from the strange man beckoning him into a car, and turned to the house. Natalie's shadow passed by the front window, flicking on the radio and cleaning up shattered plates and bowls. Milo looked back. "No," he said, almost under his breath. He forced a step closer to the house. "I can't leave her."

Get in the car, said the voice, *or she dies.*

Milo's knees went slack as he bent, stomach turning over. For a moment he was worried he'd have another panic attack, right there on his mother's front lawn. But something came over him, like a wave crashing against the shore, and the fear anxiety, and tension dissipated. Milo raised his chin, back straightening and feeling returning, and he stared down the man standing in the driveway. And as he reclaimed his sword, sliding it into the sheath at his belt, Milo became sharply aware of what was to come.

He moved through the hedges, crossing the driveway, and paused to stand before the man. Towering over him, the strange man did not move, coal-black eyes stuck directly on following Milo. Keeping a tight hold on his sword, Milo turned to the Corvette's backseat door and crouched down.

A few things happened at once: the leather seats inside the sleek car disappeared as soon as Milo got close enough, his foot already inside the door, a chasm of expanding darkness taking its place. Holding the same aura as Valhalla's portal, Milo fought the urge to collapse into the chasm, comfort and calm wrapping around them.

Rough hands grasped onto his shirt, bunching it into fists. He was pulled out of the chasm for a moment, given a quick glimpse of his neighborhood street and the man's shadow leaning over him, before the hands shoved him through the car door with an incredible force. Milo shot into the darkness without friction, free-falling through the nothingness. He blinked and face-planted into something hard and stony. He opened his mouth and inhaled grass.

Milo lifted his head.

A city of gold towered over him.

XIII. Ragnarok

"If you point at me one more time -"

"What're you gonna do about it, Kal?" the charming Valhallian, Silas, teased, wiggling his eyebrows as he waved a finger in the short girl's face. "Admit that you're wrong," he paused to wave his hand over her eyes, "and maybe I'll stop!"

The little Valhallian swatted his hand, pouting as she looked to the berserker for assistance. "We can't just leave Milo," she shouted, her shrill voice echoing through the abandoned shack, "you said it yourself: we can't be left alone in the city, but you're just gonna leave him out there? We don't even know if he's in trouble - and he probably is."

Astrid crouched at the collapsed staircase, watching silently as the argument raged. The wound at her side was practically nonexistent, only a fading scar, a memory to prove it even happened. When the undead trio waded into the shack and informed their guardian of Milo Bohr's disappearance, the berserker finished healing Astrid and reprimanded the warriors as if they were her children. The berserker's hands, obviously calloused and rough, slapped against the back of their heads, her words mixed with the language of her people and the one of the Midgardians. Once the berserker was satisfied, Thalia perched herself on the fallen roof, eyes raised towards the sun hanging high overhead.

Astrid hardly interjected; not much of what they said rang any clarity within her. The Midgardian tongue was one she never quite mastered. Not only was the realm of Midgard expansive enough to have countless languages of its own, but Midgardians spoke in a way she could never understand, no matter the actual language. It made it hard for her to keep up - the quick replies and sarcasm so effortlessly thrown in that the line between truth and illusion blurred. Many other Asdardians shared the same sentiment: even Odin himself, after his years of wandering the nine realms, returned with a hardness towards Midgard. Their speech reminded Astrid of a time when she overheard the King discussing the peculiar realm with his closest advisor, Tyr.

* * *

Hushed voices echoed in the hidden council room behind the Bleeding Throne into the golden great hall. During her late night shifts patrolling the castle in Asgard, Astrid never caught Aesir lurking about. The royal council went to their lands after the day, but the few without holdings resided in the castle. Astrid crept closer to the room, peering around the corner, curiosity getting better.

"We'd be better off closing its doors," a gruff voice explained, "no travel in or out."

The speaker was Havi, King and Wanderer, who returned from legendary adventures. Astrid froze, staring at the All-Father in awe at her crooked position. The candlelight sent embers across him, skin-colored bronze and eyes full of brewing midnight storms. Raven locks fell down his shoulders, braids twisting together at his scalp. Even amid night, Havi dressed battle-ready, a leather guard across his chest and a fur cloak around his shoulders. His mystical spear, Gungnir, leaned against the table beside him. Though dormant, Gungnir radiated an enveloping energy that swayed even Astrid. Her countless years of training to withstand such magic disintegrated to dust within its presence.

"Close Midgard?" Tyr repeated. "My Lord," he paused, laughing nervously, "you *must* hear the ignorance in your words. Countless creatures call Midgard their home, thanks to our mistakes as leaders. It would be immoral to trap the innocents of the realm with them. Just think of Jormungandr, my Lord, the world serpent."

Hearing the King's most trusted advisor speak directly made Astrid unsure whether she should laugh or frown. Only Tyr could speak to Havi with such familiarity. Tyr, who could only be found by the King's side, was the solitary god to address Havi as *my lord*. He hung close to his King without hesitancy; it was his duty as the Aesir to preside over law and justice. His words were adored, always cherished, no matter what they might truly mean. The young girls Astrid's sister used to play with admired Tyr as the most handsome Aesir. Astrid watched him: tufts of white curls pulled behind his ears, Fae-like violet eyes, short compared to the Aesir but tall to the average Asgardian. He wore a tunic wrapped with leather and animal hide draped over his shoulders. Across his temples sat a woven crown made from vines, thorns plucked and shaven down. She shrugged. His beauty was otherworldly, almost like it wasn't her right to look at him. She eyed him skeptically.

"I think of the beast every night Ymir lets me lay my head to rest," Havi steadily replied. "The Norn plague my dreams of coming tidings, Tyr. A darkness stronger than I've ever felt resides in the shadows." He turned, his shadow jagged and disfigured across the floor. "The end of all endings lies in the land of man."

Tyr frowned. "What have you seen, my Lord?"

"The beginning of our fall," Havi said. "I watched the cosmos collapse upon our golden towers, war raging across realms till even Yggdrasil could feel its scar. I felt the last exhale leave my brothers and sisters. I have heard the scream of a wolf, the call of Heimdall's horn. Yggdrasil cries out to me: the annihilation of all is bred in Midgard." His fists clenched around the table, the *crunch* of his strength echoing into the great hall. "I'll send every mortal soul to death if I must to prolong Agard's existence."

"You don't mean -"

"Yes, Tyr. I have seen Ragnarok."

The air left her throat. She pressed her palms against the wall, forcing herself to stay upright as her knees locked together. Her body shuddered. "Help me," she whispered. "Yggdrasil, help me." The prayer sounded empty. When she looked back around the corner, her heart dropped to the ground.

Why do you watch?

Odin the One-Eyed stared directly at her.

Astrid flipped around, scampering away from the council room. She moved across the great hall towards the side exit leading to the barracks. Her heart pounded. Whether it was from the King's gaze or his words, Astrid didn't know, but it haunted her endlessly. *Ragnarok* was a word rarely spoken aloud. Where she was from, it was considered bad luck, bringing bad tidings. She stopped at the door, turning over her shoulder to see a different shadow pass by the other entrance for the council room behind the throne. Its shape was unrecognizable, but put her on alert: *other eyes watched nearby.*

✳ ✳ ✳

The memory faded. Bickering rumbled through the shack like scurrying rats. She held onto her amulet instinctively. There never came a time for Astrid to try and figure out what the hushed meeting meant. The King was rarely seen afterward, and Tyr kept to himself with the Hooded One gone. Ragnarok was never mentioned again. Fear crawled up her throat. She wondered if it was possible for something as dark as Havi claimed to exist within Midgard.

"Milo made his choice," Thalia whispered, eyes glossy and distant.

Kali scoffed. "You can't just *say* that!" She crouched, holding her head in her hands. "The first day will be over soon," she muttered, raising her head to rest her bony chin on scuffed knees, "we haven't even found the key, and now Milo's gone." The Valhalla trousers she wore curled up to her knees, dark leather over the fading blue sweater.

It was the fourth mention of a key and numbered days. Astrid stared, considering letting herself question it. But the amulet hummed, and she remembered: *find the Prince, save Asgard.* She eyed the berserker.

Astrid lifted her head towards Midgard's solitary sun. Time progressed slower in the mortal realm, more than she anticipated. Asgard had already seen another dawn. The destruction Sigyn and her rebellion caused in the short time was unbeknownst to Astrid. It was the unknowing that proved to be the most panic-inducing. Knowing the condition of her home would be near impossible with the Bifrost destroyed. It was coming close to her having to make a decision: help the company she stumbled upon and, presumably, fix the damage she caused with her arrival, or abandon them to find Thor on her own, with no mystical guidance from a berserker to offer. Total solitude. No gods. Both parties' paths might have led to the same place, but the boy was gone, and she grasped at nothing. Astrid continued to watch the girl. It came down to a singular question: how much of her soul did she have left?

"It doesn't matter whether he comes back or not," Silas said with his hands crossed behind his head, "I'm not gonna be vaporized 'cause we didn't make it back to the tower in time. We're gonna find the key with or without him, simple as that." He approached the berserker, tapping his shoe against her foot. "Wouldn't you agree?"

She eyed him. "It's logical."

"Logical shouldn't apply to people like us," Kali said.

Astrid's eyebrows furrowed. "What are people like you?"

The Valhallian looked at Astrid tiredly, almost afraid to respond. Her gaze fell over her friends as if for approval, turning back towards Astrid with her lips pulled down in a frown. "Family," Kali finally said, "we're alone and dead and apparently in the middle of a war that's been going on for *centuries,* but none of that matters because we've got each other. I barely know the guy - and I'm still not even sure if I *like* him - but if I disappeared, he'd come for me. All we have left is each other," Kali paused, ethereal eyes holding onto Astrid's, "don't you get that? We died. We *died.* What else do we have, if not each other? I'm not losing anything else today."

The berserker sighed. "We're not losing anybody."

"There's no key without Milo," Kali snapped.

Thalia scoffed. "Not *everything* revolves around him," she said, frowning at her lap. An ax lay on her knees as she rubbed a rag against the bloodied blade, cleaning the sterling silver. After a tense silence, Thalia sighed again, turning her attention towards Kali, who stared unrelentingly. "Fine," she snapped, "tell us why you think we can't get the key without Milo."

"Everything progresses because of us three," she explained, "wouldn't it make sense for nothing to work out correctly if some prerequisites were missing?" she shrugged, "it's what the prophecy said in the -"

"Prophecy?" Astrid knocked to attention. The air grew frigid. Prophecies, in Astrid's time, were empty. The outlying villages in Asgard found nothing but stories within them, riddles formed to twist a mind to the god's will. Her later years were spent in godly company, where soothsayers and prophetic tellers were divinity in the flesh. For years, she avoided getting anywhere near one. Her father would grumble about an old superstition before the fireplace, barely speaking louder than the crackling flames when he said *words of the ol Norn hags land ye in the hands of death herself.* "Could you share it with me?"

The berserker shrugged. "Go ahead," she said, "couldn't do anything worse."

"It went like, 'the three Warriors of Thunder will be reborn, whom the walls of death cannot hold, to return the lost Prince to the throne'," she paused, "there are more lines, I think, but the page was ripped back in the Master's book."

"Warriors of Thunder," Astrid repeated. "That was a myth."

Thalia nodded. "In the past era, aye, the story of legendary reincarnated heroes has only been an old wives tale, but in time before, the Warriors existed to follow a different ruler. Every era holds a new ruler chosen by the Norn to be the bringer of peace, a unifier of all the realms, left to be protected by legendary soldiers." She jumped down from her perched position, sliding the ax into her belt. "They were never a myth," she said, "only forgotten."

"How can you be so sure it's *them*?" Astrid asked, getting a few insulted looks in response.

Turning her head, Thalia eyed her suspiciously, lip perking up in an amused smirk. "You don't really want to ask that question," she said, "there's a part of you that just knows it's them. At least, for a bunch of Midgardians, there's something unusual about them." She shrugged. "You can be skeptical about it all you want, but it's not like you can logically deny it. Not when it came straight from the Norn."

"I suppose you're right," Astrid replied. "It's an honor to be in the company of the Warriors of Thunder, then. If we all seek to restore the line of Odin to the throne, my journey aligns with yours." She raised her fist, placing it across her chest, lowering her head in a respectful gesture. The movement was so familiar it surprised her. Her arm dropped. "Tell me about the key."

"The Master said we'd find it right away," Silas explained, "but we've got no clue what it looks like or if it's even a legitimate key. All we know is that we can't find Thor without it."

"Then we should leave the boy."

"*What?*" Kali yelled.

Astrid raised her hands and said, "If the key leads to Thor, it's our priority."

"Did you hear anything I said? We can't be separated."

"The one you're fighting for doesn't seem to think so. That boy left for selfish reasons; it doesn't seem like he cares much for you lot."

"Right," Silas jabbed, "like you wouldn't do the same thing if you had the chance." He stood beside his fellow Valhallians with his chin jutted, defiance painted on his face. "He didn't betray us," he said, "if we were anywhere near my family, I'd be long gone! What matters is finding him and the key before we have to go back to Valhalla."

Astrid pulled the amulet off from around her neck, dark hair snagged in the rusted chain. The light caught onto the jewels' surface. "I know not where the crown Prince lies," she placed it in Thalia's palm, "but before his disappearance, a *heks* tied his life force to this amulet. It beats along with him."

"Old magic," Thalia whispered. Her eyes raised. "The jewel itself is quite priceless," she continued, "it's dangerous to cross realms with such valuables, it might catch the wrong eye."

"Knowing the Prince is alive usurps the possibility of thieves," was the only calm response the warrior could muster. The arguing and bickering sparked an ache in her back, an inferno enveloping her in the sudden anxiety of *failing*. Every moment they went against her was another second gone in Asgard. She sighed, reaching to take the amulet back, feeling eerily cold without it. "My oath demands I put the royal line above all else," Astrid dropped the chain around her neck, "I'd love nothing more than retrieving your friend, if that is what the majority wants, that is what we shall have."

"Great," Kali said, "then we should -"

"I wasn't done. Ignore my words, and we will reap the costs." They watched her, only the berserker unfazed. "If the Norn have proclaimed to you to find the Prince, you do just that. We need the key."

"But with -"

"All right," Silas drawled, snatching onto Kali's wrist before she did something reckless. He pulled her behind him and turned to Astrid, shooting her a smile before he said, "You said the majority wins, right? Let's have a vote, quit the back-and-forth arguing, and whatever."

The berserker waved for him to continue.

He smiled with feigned authority. "All for finding Milo?"

The Valhallian trio lifted their arms, nodding confidently to each other.

Astrid kept still, eyeing the berserker as she stood in the growing shadows like a statue. Neither moved. Hope sprung alive in her chest.

"All for not."

She raised her hand.

Thalia remained still. She crouched, arms wrapped around her legs as she stared above at the lowering Midgardian sun.

"The whole point is to vote," Silas snapped, "c'mon, play fair."

Thalia's gaze flickered to him, the glare terrifying enough to make him jump. She straightened, holding onto her ax as though it balanced her. "My destiny is to be the warriors' guardian," she said, turning till her honey-colored eyes landed heavily upon Astrid, "and it is for that reason alone I say we find Milo."

"That reason alone?"Astrid repeated, her voice rising.

"I didn't stutter," Thalia snapped. "These three are my responsibility, *including* Milo. A key can wait." She moved slowly, taking creeping steps till she was a foot away. Her bronze arms were littered with ivory scars. "Your prized Prince has been missing for a while now, *kriger*. He can wait a few days more."

Astrid looked away as the berserker brushed by, moving towards the shack's doorway. She lifted her chin, barely turning to see the other woman's silhouette over her shoulder. She paid no attention to the Valhallians watching with hesitant eyes, hands perpetually gripping their tiny swords.

"And how do you suppose we find him," Astrid called out, "with all of Midgard at our disposal?"

"Not something for you to worry about," Thalia replied. "I know where to go."

Astrid followed behind the company. Her new companions were the victims of a time limit - she noticed the marks along the berserker's arm, the dark lines drawn in the same manner as Ullr during his rune sorcery escapades. It was a separation spell, granting the Valhallians freedom from the tower that grants them existence after death, only for days. The realization smothered her irritation. They were children forced into the Norn's hands. She stepped into the dying light, heat bathing her face.

She watched the Valhallians and gripped the amulet.

"Odin," she whispered, "give me strength."

XIV. Ásgarður

It can't get any worse was a phrase Milo got used to telling himself while growing up. Eventually, after his mistakes and bad luck, the words lost meaning, and he spoke them out of habit.

So Milo straightened, placed a hand on either hip, and took in the sights. Below, dressed in lights and colors between striking mountains, stood a wide city surrounded by ivory and towers. At the city's center were five spires reaching into the sky, painted an oceanic blue. Flames danced at the spires' tops. Within the protective circle of towers was a golden castle. While the castle looked like heaven on earth, its surrounding kingdom wilted like a dying flower. Even from Milo's distance at the clifftop, he saw the scorched farmlands and burning villages. Buildings smoldered on the city's outskirts, and a low-hanging smog traveled through the streets. A clash of life and death living beside each other: an entire population crawling towards its death while a beautiful and heaven-like sanctuary sat at its heart, untouched.

He nodded. "Could be worse," he called into the wind.

A silence responded.

Milo wasn't too worried about his displacement - obviously, Manhattan was a long way away, but he died and *somehow* still made it home. His hand instinctively gripped his sword. No matter what came at him, he knew he'd make it back to his friends. The confidence spread into him like he'd taken a shot of something, a deep burn crawling beneath his skin till it enveloped him whole. And it was something else. The castle, however, from the Middle Ages it seemed, rang oddly familiar.

Awareness pricked at his neck as he recognized the way buildings stood, the way light reflected on the castle walls.

Milo stepped closer. *The paintings.* All his mother's artwork decorating their living room held the same vivid image of a golden castle. But his connection to it felt older, an ancient memory stowed away further back than Natalie Bohr's artistic hobby. He knew where the darkness took him from instinct, an ancestral memory suddenly shooting to the surface. Not needing someone to tell him where he was removed the fear. He was always meant to show up there. The Norn circling the tree of life in Valhalla crossed his mind - *fate.*

"*Ásgarður,*" Milo said, the old and foreign language sitting on his tongue as though iron weighed it down. The word translated itself as he spoke, dissolving and reshaping till it became something he recognized. He walked backward, the kingdom growing fainter in the valley's shadow. He bent down, clutching his knees as he struggled to catch his breath, shoving a singular word between clenched teeth: "Asgard."

"*Bingo,*" someone said from behind him, "as the mortals like to say. *Hmph,* the idiosyncratic qualities of the twenty-first century. I've always enjoyed the mortal dialect. Eloquent and foolish at the same time."

Milo didn't bother to fling around in surprise.

"Give -" he gulped down air, "me -" another sharp inhale, "a second!" Finally, he managed a deep breath. Every single asthma attack he ever had growing up came rushing back in that moment. He wanted to laugh and cry at the same time. He raised his head to the sky, and a shocked shout blurted out from his mouth. "What!" Milo exclaimed, pointing upwards. Three suns decorated the sky. The shock melted into awe, and joy from seeing something so naturally stunning. A chaotic light rippled across the painfully white sky, balls colored a burning yellow, and deep red fixed within his vision. He exhaled, lowering his gaze till he saw the unfamiliar speaker. "Sorry," he said, shrugging, "I dunno if you saw, but I had a legitimate moment back there and needed a second to, you know, take it in. And you know what? I've had my fair share of strange and mysterious interruptions from freaky aliens like you, and I don't think you *deserve* a good entrance."

Watching him from a few feet away like a nosy teenager, the mysterious figure slouched and inched closer. His hands were buried in his jacket pockets, dressed overly snug for the warm spring weather. Dark hair curled around his ears, mostly tied into a busy ponytail, trailing down the back. There was a boyish curve in his cheeks, a peachy color tinting his golden skin. Even though he looked as young as Milo, the boy held no aging splotches, blemishes, or scars. But then, he noticed the eyes.

Two dots of coal stared at him. And as the boy moved closer, the darkness overtook him again. Milo rushed backward, almost tripping over himself before regaining balance. The boy watched curiously, playfully tilting his head. His lip pulled into a smirk, flashing brilliantly white teeth, a few sharp.

The boy paused, hands buried in his pockets. "You're an odd one," he said after the drawn-out silence, "not what I expected."

"You're the guy," Milo said, gripping his sword.

"Been called many things," he replied, "never *the guy.*"

Milo blinked, confused about whether or not he should be concerned for his safety. As long as he didn't stare at the boy's eyes for too long, there wasn't much fear. He released the hold on his sword, wrapping his arms around his chest. Beyond the boy was a cliff that cut off sharply into darkness. If the need ever came to run, he'd have to remember to twist around towards the city. Even though he doubted it would offer him any solace.

"But it was you," Milo said, "you brought me here." He glared. "You're the one who threatened my mother."

The boy nodded and shrugged. "Really," he said, a mischievous twitch in his lips, "*truly* sorry about that. Figured this version of myself would be easier on the eyes for you. Had to get you here, and...*well,*" the boy paused to laugh, jumping in place as though he was cold, "Natalie knew what she was signing up for a long time ago."

Walking with a bounce, the boy passed Milo, stopping to look at the view. Milo quietly followed, his illusionary heart beating quickly. He popped the bones in his hands till it hurt, dread beginning to make its way to his mouth. The questions, the fear, the need to scream, all lodged within his throat. As a bad taste took over his tongue, he stood beside the boy, following his gaze towards the castle.

"How could you possibly say that? As if you know her?" Milo questioned, so quiet it fell unheard in the small proximity between them.

The boy continued to stare. "Let bygones be bygones, my friend. Did you enjoy Oba? He was a good actor, yes? Sad, though, the the berserker had to be rid of him so soon. I quite enjoyed the show," he continued with a loud voice, the smile returning. "But, we are practically family."

Milo staggered. *Oba.* The anger swarmed into his belly, an overpowering burning sensation rumbling within him. He clenched his fists, and the boy watching, a smirk growing across his lip at the sight. Milo refused to meet the boy's dark eyes. "Who the hell are you?"

"Can't guess yet?" he asked, the smile curling into a Cheshire grin as he turned towards him. Extending his right hand, the boy waved it through the air, deep smoke unfurling from his palm. The smoke became thick like fog, forming into a flat sphere and blocking the city entirely. The boy leaned closer to Milo and said, "Let's have a hint, shall we?"

An image formed within the fog, colors filling and spreading till Milo recognized it. Walking in the falling sunlight, passing by familiar streets and sidewalks, was Kali, lips puckered as if she was deep in thought. She still wore Thalia's leather jacket over her Valhalla sweater, the old trousers dirty and worn out, tied to stop at her knees. She tossed Laevateinn between each hand, absentmindedly catching it and throwing it over.

Milo shook his head, feeling a sudden emptiness in his chest at his friend - he never realized how much he missed them, how quiet everything was with none of them around. He turned to the boy. "I don't understand. That's Kali. What do you gotta do with Kali?"

"Wrong detail."

"Laevateinn? She got it as a gift, it's not really hers."

The boy frowned. "Wasn't the Master's to give."

"You say it like it's yours." Milo chuckled, nudging the boy with his elbow when he received silence in response. He laughed again and turned to see his companion staring at him with a blank expression. A pin dropped. Milo faltered, taking a step backward as he looked back into the boy's jet-black eyes. When the laugh came for a third time, it was a nervous sound mixed with little pops in his knuckles. Slowly, he repeated: "You say that like it's yours."

"Gods don't normally forge their own things, you know," he said, crossing his arms as he went on, "but Laevateinn came from my own hand. Imagine my surprise when something as prized as my creation falls into some *halvavlet dod kriger*[10]." He spit on the grass.

Halfbreed. Milo stared. *Why would he call Kali a halfbreed?*

"I don't mean to be rude," he continued without giving Milo a chance to understand, "you Warriors of Thunder are diverse in all matters, I get that, but these versions of you are outrageously unexpected." He touched his chin. "I'll have to have a word with the Norn, then. Skuld'll know what to do." The boy stopped, turning to see Milo watching him with gaping eyes. He chuckled. "You've got no clue what I'm talking about."

"No," Milo replied. "No idea."

"Can't help it. Easy to talk to people with our blood," he explained, leaning against a nearby tree, "we radiate to each other. Even though you don't know what I'm saying, you could sit and listen forever, and that's not just because my voice is too soothing for you to handle."

Milo blinked. "*Our* blood?" he repeated. "You still haven't even told me who you are."

The boy swiveled around. With a flourish, a magenta fog enveloped him from the feet up. As it cleared, the boy's clothes changed into something similar to what the warrior girl, Astrid, wore, with a richer flair. Purple decorated his uniform, a clock falling behind his shoulders. He lowered his arms, bowing dramatically till he faced Milo again.

"Loki, son of Fárbauti and Laufey, god of the Aesir," he bellowed, "at your service."

Oh, Milo thought, *it seems it's gotten worse.* There wasn't much he knew about gods, except for the one he'd remember on every other

---

[10] Halfbreed dead warrior

holiday, but as he stood there, two different things became shockingly clear: one, the god could easily be a kind friend; two, the god could much as well be the thing to end Milo for good. He grabbed his sword.

The god eyed him. "You need not fear me, Odinson. I bring you no harm."

Odinson.

Milo stood there, frozen, neck jutting forward a little way, staring at Loki with an expletive lodged in his throat. *Odinson.* Something about the word sparked every nerve within his body. It held something so eerily familiar it repeated in his mind like an echo. Images flashed repeatedly behind his eyelids, a striking pain coming along with it. He staggered. The images flashed again, sharper and clearer for him to digest: a tanned man stood before him, jagged and rugged face scared with age and battle; dark tufts of silvery and raven-colored curls pulled from his face, one eye crossed out with a pale scar. Two ravens sat upon the man's shoulders, a wolf's severed head below his feet. The man extended a hand, outstretched fingers reaching toward him with a dazed familiarity.

Min sonn[11], he breathed.

Milo steadied himself, blinking as the man's voice remained in his ears. He licked his lips, raising himself to face Loki. The god watched, showing a faint smile.

"Odinson," Milo repeated.

"You can hear."

He frowned. "Why would you call me that? That would mean *he's* my father. The All-Father, or whatever you people call him. Odin. It's not true. My dad is a deadbeat, some slouch that ran off the second he could, leaving my mother alone to survive with a child." Milo

---

[11] My son

chewed on his gums, kicking the grass. "A child, for god's sake. Would your king do something like that?"

Loki replied with an unfaltering stare: "yes, I believe he would."

"You think he's my -"

"I don't *think*, I *know* the old man is your father," Loki interrupted, "Milo Bohr, you are the youngest son of Odin, late King of Asgard, half-brother to Thor and Baldur. Your blood boils beside the Vanir, our fated opposites. Your skin *burns* with power."

Milo laughed. "That's impossible."

"How?"

"Aren't gods thousands of years old?" he asked, nerves riding up his throat like a tidal wave. The skepticism faded slowly - nothing seemed too impossible anymore, and after saying the word himself, Milo realized how much his brain didn't deny it. "My Mom was a waitress when they met, and he'd just gotten out of the army. He wanted to be a doctor or something, I dunno."

"A veterinarian."

"Right, he had a thing for animals. Mom went through this entire phase of painting wolves and birds 'cause of him. And he was around her age, you know? When they were together. Not some ancient grandpa Norse god."

Loki smiled. "I've been around long enough to fall into the *ancient* category," he paused, holding his hands beside his face, "and the aging process has been glorious, don't you agree?" he wiggled his eyebrows suggestively. "I've managed to retain my handsome youth."

"But aren't you a shapeshifter," Milo asked, "or is that just a myth?"

The god scoffed. "I hate that word. Myth," he mumbled under his breath, "nothing is a myth, and the sooner you realize that, the easier this will be."

Milo crouched, rolling back on his heels to fall on the grass. "Back to my dad," he said slowly, "how can you know it's me? That *I'm* his son?"

"Before the war, traveling between realms was ordinary, and the king spent many years making sure peace existed throughout all lands. He remained in Midgard longer than usual, returning to the castle a ...*changed* man. Suddenly, neither Thor nor Baldur was good enough to be named the Crown Heir to the *Blodende Trone*," he paused, "the Bleeding Throne, I mean. He even gathered for the Aesir clan to meet and arranged for the Vanir tribe's Queen to visit our realm. It was the talk of the town."

"I've heard this part."

"Yes, I'm sure the berserker knows her tales. Imagine our surprise when the King of Peace tries to kill Queen Freyja for some sparkling jewels around her pretty neck." He scowled. "The point is that Havi returned from his journey, and I acted upon speculation of something precious lying within Midgard, something he was willing to go great lengths to keep hidden." Loki's black stare burnt into Milo's soul. "And I found a child."

Milo swallowed. "How did I -" he stopped short, staring at his calloused hands, "*I* did this? My birth made him do all that?"

"The Norn did not write your story for it to be shameful," Loki snapped, his face warping into something older, a being built before time. His voice grew gruff, old, and scored with age. "Your birth brought along a new age, the turn from Odin's rule to another. He was *always* meant to summon Freyja on that day and perish. Do not let the gods write your life, Milo Bohr. Do not give them the power." The god pushed himself off the tree, a new urgency filling his words with a tremor. "Do you not see it yet, Odinson? Natalie Bohr kept you safe from prying eyes - moved you everywhere, never staying too long in one place, no one ever really knowing your name. Odin frantically rushed around Asgard, lobbying to separate Midgard from Yggdrasil's branches, not caring for his other sons. He was *afraid,* boy. He was afraid of what might be with his elder sons upon the throne. Your father rewrote the accords and named another the Crown Prince of Asgard, Heir to the Bleeding Throne."

"So Thor's not going to be King?" Milo stared off into the distance. As he became more familiar with the Aesir and Vanir politics, he became more confused than ever. He craved ignorance.

Loki sighed. "The thunder boy *could* be king if the Aesir wished it, but they are an old clan. They'll want to follow the accords, as tradition commands. And as of," he paused, raising his head towards the widest sun in the vast sky where a piercing light flashed across like a shooting star, *"now,* all Nine Worlds bound by Yggdrasil knows."

Milo blinked. "Wait, knows what?"

"Who the All-Father left the throne to," Loki hissed, "keep up, Odinson!"

"You still haven't even told me who he named as the heir."

Milo was whisked to his feet with a swift gust, the god's hand wrapped around his throat with an iron grip. "Why is it that Odin's offspring always have the same *outrageously stupid* quality?" Loki spat, his fingers pressing into Milo's neck. He rolled his eyes and dropped Milo to the ground.

"What quality -" Milo coughed, touching his neck, "- *quality* would you say that is?"

"You're naive." The god faced the city. "He named you the heir."

"No."

"Read the accords myself. Your father hid it well from the council, but my eyes are everywhere. Before the war ever started, you had already been named the next king of Asgard. Thor never would've known." He tilted his head. "I suppose he does now, on the assumption he still lives."

Milo stepped back, moving as far away from the castle in the valley as possible. The god watched him as though he were an experiment, not moving from the cliff's edge.

"Believe me," the god said, "took me by surprise as well."

All he could think about was his ninth-grade counselor meeting. The counselor told him it was time to find his niche and dive into something he'd want to practice for all his life. Milo sat there for the entire hour, listening to the man's rambles about possible careers as he zoned out. Nothing stuck then; for the following years, he remained aloof and carefree about his future. When graduation came, the possibility of doing something with his life felt so overpowering he could've suffocated. Finally, he was ready to do something, *anything,* to make him feel like being in the world had a purpose.

Then he died.

As he stared into thick darkness at the cliff's pit where the god stood, Milo Bohr realized his father was Odin, a one-eyed god spoken only about in books and poems.

Everything tumbled into place.

"What does this mean?" Milo asked, calling out to the god over his shoulder. "Me being his son, a Warrior of Thunder, a Prince. What does any of this mean?"

"It means you have a duty," Loki replied, miraculously appearing at Milo's left. "The Aesir blood of a god that runs through your veins makes you more than a mere mortal, dead and reborn again. Power rests dormant within you. Tremendous abilities, worthy to be shouted between warrior brethren on the cusp of battle!" He pressed his hands together, adding, "And now that your existence is known, every creature in *Niu Heimar*[12] will be hunting you. The only way you'll survive now is with your powers, not without."

"That's ridiculous. I don't have any powers."

Loki chuckled. "Course not, nothing's woken them up yet."

"Let's keep it that way, all right? The less anyone needs to know, the better. If I'm really his son, then keeping quiet's the smartest thing, right? That's what my Mom's been doin' all these years. Guess dear old dad was doin' the same." Milo's head suddenly shot to the god. "Hey, why the *hell* did you tell the world who I am? How's that gonna help me?"

"I'm an Aesir, Odinson," Loki said, "I don't work to help you."

"Fine. What's in it for you?"

Loki smiled. "I'm merely the messenger. Your destiny was delivered to me by the Norn themselves. I accept my part in pushing you down the right path - with my own twist on it, of course. Need to make a living for myself." He pulled his hands apart, and within his palm sat a ring. Forged from sterling gold, the ring radiated a strange energy. At its center was an intricate engraving showing a wolf's profile. "It's your heirloom, left to you as a sign of your birthright."

Milo laughed with a shudder. Scratching his neck, he took a few steps back. "Look," he started, "I can get on board with the reincarnated warrior thing, that's fine, and you know what? The dad-god thing I can deal with, too. But a throne? A crown and political position that leaves me in charge of an entire kingdom I know *nothing* about?" He laughed, "and you call *me* naive!"

"Don't be so dramatic," Loki muttered, "no one's asking you to retake Asgard right this instant." He dropped his hand, and the ring disappeared. "But *morally,* I need to know that once I bring you back to Midgard, you won't be slaughtered. The world can sense your rare

---

[12] Nine Realms

blood." He reached towards Milo, grabbing onto his shoulder in an almost friendly way. "Take the ring, Milo Odinson. Accept your destiny."

He frowned. "I don't even know what my destiny is."

The world became dimmer, as though a great cloud passed over the many suns decorating the afternoon sky. Cold air followed, and dread pooled within Milo's stomach. The god stared at him with an echoing otherworldliness, so obviously an alien, so obviously of another species, entire universes trapped beneath his skin.

Milo wished he didn't say anything.

A brilliant light overtook Loki's eyes, and magenta fog spread from his fingertips, dripping onto the ground beside their feet. And as Loki's lips parted, the words tumbling out permanently sealed Milo Bohr as a member of Norse myth.

"You must find the spear, reclaim the throne, and save Asgard."

Something heavy sat upon Milo's finger. The ring magically appeared on his right hand as though he'd put it on himself. He reached to take it off - *no, no, no. I am not a king,* he heard his voice repeat. *I am not a crowned Prince. I am not.* It wouldn't budge. The jewelry was stuck on there, unwilling to leave. He groaned, but before he tried to yank it off again, the god intervened violently.

With a sweeping motion, Loki grasped onto Milo's collar, lifting him off the ground and stepping to the side to dangle him over the cliff's edge. Below was the tragically deep chasm, forever plunging into a never-ending abyss. Milo reached up, clasping the god's wrists as a surprised shout echoed between his lips.

"*What are you doing?*" Milo screamed.

"Apologies, Odinson, but I need the god in you to awaken," Loki said, "it's about time for some fun, don't you think?" The god laughed, slowly shifting into the other form. He grew taller, hair falling out like a wave across his back. A kaleidoscope erupted from his skin as he changed, only his eyes remained. The god grew older, hair falling into curly locks down his back, a beard twisting into a series of braids along his chin. He held Milo away from him, hovering above the darkness. As he rolled his neck, cracks echoed from the divine bones. "That's better," he mumbled, giving Milo a cheeky grin. "How about it then, Odinson? *Loslat guden.*"

The god released him.

Milo swung at the air as he fell, grasping for anything to save himself. The darkness swallowed him whole, the wind hitting his back like bricks. Loki's figure looming over the cliff's edge, quickly grew blurry, eventually puffing away as though he was never there in the first place. And as he fell, wondering if this would be the time he would *truly* die, his mind translated the god's last phrase to be his final thought.

Release the god.

The boy's blurry figure disappeared into the Chasm within seconds. Loki stared, ignoring the pang in his chest. It was the one issue with time, he realized. Emotion, feelings, love, and regret remained prominent within him, no matter how long he lived. His divinity mattered little. God or not, there was pain, there was grief, there was guilt. Every death tore his heart away. Every cry tainted his soul. But it was the memories - *the memories* - that were stark enough to bleed into his reality, heavy behind his eyelids until he eventually forgot where he stood in the present, his thoughts blinking out like dying stars, only stopping when he couldn't remember his name.

Loki.

He opened his eyes. Odinson was gone. He was alone.

"My love."

Behind him, fuzzy and unfocused, stood Sigyn. Not Sigyn herself - she remained in Asgard's golden towers, invading villages as she took the Bleeding Throne - but a fragment, a piece of her soul, stretching across space till it reached him. Even in her weakest form, Sigyn looked like a piece from reality: midnight skin, golden armor fitted over a shimmering gown, and crystallized eyes. He smiled.

"Worry not, my Queen," he said. "It is done."

"The boy has the ring."

"Yes."

"And you're *sure* it's Andvaranaut?"

He winked. "I know my gold, Sigyn. It is Andvari's Ring."

"So it begins," she said. "It will ruin him."

Loki nodded, turning back to face the Chasm. He tried to ignore how much it hurt. "Indeed, my Queen," he whispered.

Sigyn had already gone, leaving him there again, staring into the darkness, wondering what would happen if...*if.* In another world, he truly believed Odinson would be his friend. He smiled. If only other worlds existed.

"The end has begun."

XV. Song of Yggdrasil

The moment the dead went silent, Astrid realized she had a real problem on her hands.

Wrapping themselves up in their thoughts, the pair became silent and quickly in their search for Milo. According to the berserker, she knew exactly where to go. They followed her without question, marching trustfully behind. None were alert to their surroundings, not even Thalia like she knew enough about her environment to not be worried. Astrid yearned to hold Hofond beside her in case, but the Midgardians scorned her for trying. It wasn't *normal* in their world. Instead, her hand continuously jerked towards Hofond's hilt at every sound and shadow. She kept to the back, staring at the Valhallians hanging their head low in somber silence.

She smiled, an idea entering her mind. Astrid picked up the pace, sliding between the two boys.

"*Bah*," Silas spouted, flinching in surprise, "aren't you supposed to be bringing up the rear or something?"

Kali laughed.

"Oh, *oh!*" exclaimed Silas. "Wasn't trying to flirt," he added, "if that's what you thought. Just thought you were -"

"You flatter yourself," Astrid interjected. "Didn't think that at all." She continued, jogging to catch up to the speedy berserker.

"No," Thalia said. She raised her hand to her lips, chewing scarred skin.

Astrid frowned. "I haven't said anything yet."

"Why else would you be running up to me?" She sighed. "He gets under my skin," she whispered, "under my skin, my mind. Somehow he figures out some way to irritate the hell out of me."

"Who?"

"*Milo,*" she hissed. Thalia gripped her ax, tracing the engravings with her thumb. "Sorry," she muttered, "it's been quiet, and silence makes me think, and all I can think about is how angry I am."

"Silence, exactly," Astrid repeated. "That's what I wanted to speak with you about."

Thalia eyed her hesitantly.

"Would you know any songs for the road, my lady?"

A loud laugh bellowed from behind them.

"*My lady,*" Kali mocked, "do we all have to call her that?"

Silas chuckled. "We're reincarnated warriors," he said, "can we have fancy titles?"

"*Hold kjeft[13]!*" Thalia shouted. The teens laughed quietly. She looked back towards Astrid. "What makes you think I know any songs?"

Astrid shrugged. "All Northern warriors I know sing before battle."

"Northern?"

---

[13] Shut up

"Your braid," she said, "correct me if I'm wrong, but Northern Asgardians wear braids to symbolize their rank in battle. When I saw yours, I just assumed." Astrid leaned towards the berserker, lowering her voice as she added, "The silence is deafening, my lady, we could use a little song."

Thalia stared at the ground, chewing on her lips. "Fine," she hastily groaned, "but only if you stop calling me that. I'm not your lady." She inhaled deeply, closing her eyes as the exhale came low and slow. Calmness waved over her. Birds whistled in the distance, a light breeze rustling the nearby shrubbery and tree branches. The company's steps became quiet as Thalia's eyes opened, and she parted her lips to sing:

> *"Ask veit ek standa,*
> *heitir Yggdrasill*
> *hár baðmr, ausinn*
> *hvíta auri;*
> *þaðan koma döggvar*
> *þærs í dala falla;*
> *stendr æ yfir grœnn*
> *Urðar brunni."*

As the verse came to an end, the listeners collectively held their breath. Astrid paused, waiting for the berserker to continue. When she noticed the embarrassed blush spreading across Thalia's nose, Astrid looked away, letting the smile form on her lips. It was a common chant, lyrics sung and spoken in all nine realms, known in Midgard as a Skaldic poem. It was a poem of good luck, a direct prayer to Yggdrasil and the life it holds within it. Even her sister, Frey, used to sing it while working the family farm. Hearing it again brought sparks to Astrid's stomach, the streets beneath her feet becoming unsteady. She raised her head, holding onto the slowly falling sun.

"Thank you," Astrid said.

"It was beautiful," Silas added, "can you do it again in English?"

Thalia threw him a pointed look.

"Hey," he said defensively, "all I'm saying is that I'd enjoy it a hell of a lot more if my brain wasn't trying to translate at the same time." Silas buried his hands in his pockets. "It's nice, though. Soothing. Better than the weird silence."

"I wouldn't mind hearing it again," Kali requested. "Make the time go by." She kicked a few stray rocks in her path. "I feel like we're all worried about what we're gonna find there."

"Worried to find your friend?" Astrid's interest was piqued.

She frowned. "More like worried we *won't* find Milo. It's not like we have the best track record. And I know we haven't known each other long, but something about being reincarnated thunder warriors or whatever makes me think it won't be as easy as we hope."

Silence overtook the company again. Astrid sighed, falling into step beside Thalia as the sun fell behind the trees and city towers. The neighborhood they walked through cast shadows along the road, holding dark alleys and suspicious figures lurking around every corner. Kali's words were foreboding, the tension she mentioned before coming back to swallow them whole.

Thalia exhaled, and the song came out as pure as before:
"*I know of an ash tree,*
It is named Yggdrasill,
A tall tree, sprinkled
With clear water;
It came from the dew
That falls on the valley;
It stands always green
Over Urd's well."

"What's Yggdrasil?" Silas asked.

"It is the center of being," Astrid replied, "all nine realms come from its branches, the heavens in its trunk, and hells under the roots. Upon Valhalla's top, Yggdrasil sits, tended to by the Norn, always living and forever dying. Without it, there is nothing, and with it, nothing is nonexistent."

"Either I've been drugged," Silas said, "or none of that made sense."

Astrid laughed. "It's not supposed to. Life is a paradox, just like the tree itself. Being always has been, meaning it never *was* or *will be,* existing constantly throughout time: immutable. Midgardians have been studying the concept for centuries - the philosopher Parmenides, for instance." Her hands raised to the sky. "Yggdrasil is our being. Its branches strike your sky the same way it does in Asgard. No matter where you call home, we all hail from the ash tree and will one day find ourselves back within it. If you concentrate hard enough," she lowered her voice to a whisper, "you can hear it calling you home."

The dead ones held their breath, listening. At the head, Thalia chuckled, looking disappointed. Silas stared at the sky, his curious, bright eyes narrowing inquisitively, while Kali stared at her staff, eyes locked in a trance, staring at its dark jewel.

"And Urd?" Silas asked. "Is that a god or something?"

"No," Thalia quickly said, eyeing Astrid, "it's short for something. Urðarbrunnr is from the Old Tongue, meaning 'The Well of Urðr,' sometimes called Mimisbrunnr. It sits at the ash tree's base, normally where you'd find the Norn. *Mótefni* was brewed by Mimir and poured into Urðarbrunnr. It's the elixir the Norn uses to care for Yggdrasil's branches."

"Isn't that just a story?" Astrid felt like something was in her throat. "Mimir doesn't *actually* exist."

Silas raised his hand. "Who's Mimir?"

"The Wise One," she replied, watching Thalia curiously. She heard of him last in her mother's old tall tales.

In the story, her mother recalled, Mimir was an old Asgardian who stumbled upon the Mimisbrunnr, a well of everlasting knowledge. Without thinking, he drank from the well and saw untold things unexplainable by the mortal tongue. As a price for taking such knowledge from Mimisbrunnr, the Asgardian was fated by the Norn never to leave the well's service, guiding anyone who came upon its path. Thus, travelers and heroes who sang about it in poetry would journey to Mimir with countless questions. Astrid didn't care too much for the story as she got older - her mother used it to teach them a life lesson, not to share history.

"It is said that Havi, who you know as Odin, sacrificed his eye for a chance to drink from Mimisbrunnr," Astrid told the dead ones, "the water gave him great knowledge and wisdom. Maybe the well holds unthinkable power, but the Asgardian man Mimir? It's doubtful."

Thalia smirked. "Do you have a faith issue, *kriger*?" She laughed to herself. "For someone who puts so much confidence in the gods, you take little care for their lesser companions."

"Mimir isn't a god-friend. He's a story told to children."

"Wouldn't most stories be based on some kind of truth?" Thalia boldly challenged. "If you were to ask any soul in Asgard, they'd swear to you Mimir was Odin's wisest counsel. Some might argue the wisest to be Tyr, but he's *merely* a god. Mimir holds something higher." She laughed again, clapping her hands together. Thunder echoed through the clear sky. "Enlighten me, *kriger*, but how different is believing in Yggdrasil versus Mimir? A tree that supposedly connects all worlds - living and dying *at the same time* - or an ignorant man too thirsty for his own good?"

"Yggdrasil has reached beyond its home to me." She paused, not wanting to speak further, but the Valhallians stared with unwavering concentration, waiting for her to continue. It made her unsettled. How long had it been since others yearned for her voice, and called for her stories? As a child, she was known as a silver tongue, proclaimer of fables and fiction, but as the years went by, the urge to speak faded, and she hid behind her blade, watching herself in her companion's armor. Astrid looked at the dead ones. "Haunting dreams used to plague my nights as a child. I was told they were visions from Yggdrasil trying to warn me about my future. This stubbornness I have was worse as a child, and I laughed in the Seer's face."

"Did she curse you?" Kali asked, her little voice like a child's.

"No. She didn't have to. The Seer knew what was coming next for me - that was revenge enough for her."

Thalia nodded. "Your dreams came true."

"Every last one of them." Astrid swung her arms as she walked. "From that time forth, I did not dare doubt Yggdrasil, or any wielders of fate for that matter. Gods receive my respect because their authority demands it, and peace asks for it. Yggdrasil *earned* it by showing me." She hopped over a crack in the road, looking towards the dead ones. "Mimir's tale was my mother's favorite to tell at the bedside. For me, it is only a story."

"You won't believe in him for her sake?"

Astrid laughed. "If you knew her, you'd never ask such a thing. My mother did not hold the respect I do for the gods. Her heart carried resentment and craved change. Those dreams died with her. Believing in Mimir does nothing for her, or me for that matter. His existence did not stop the rebels from invading Asgard. His drinking from the well did not save anyone. His story is but a story, as is the fate of most men."

Silence swept between them. Astrid sighed.

"Sing some more, Thalia," Kali called, "Aristotle over here is giving me a headache."

Laughter ensued. Even the berserker, eyes filled with an uneasy hardness, allowed herself to smile, a laugh similar to a robin's song echoing in the neighborhood. The Valhallians walked around Thalia, chattering and joking with each other. Astrid watched from a few feet behind - the music helped, indeed. Their mindless chatter calmed her heart and made the environment more comfortable. She fell into rhythm with the company.

Something about Thalia's laugh brought Astrid into her mind, memories dropping from her eyes like tears.

Six years before the invasion began, Thor's betrothed entered the realm. Astrid had been assigned to the Princess's arrival, ordered to walk with her caravan through the city and into the castle walls. Dressed in her shiny golden armor, a helmet guarding her face, she watched the Princess's silhouette from her position, wondering how much Thor might love her. And the intrusive thoughts came and went, scoring her entire day with deadly ideas and vicious stares.

The pair's engagement was merely political: she was Skadi, the Vanir Queen's daughter. Not once was the Princess seen during Aesir and Vanir's affairs, and she was never expected to attend. Instead, Skadi roamed Vanaheim's icy mountain peaks in solitude. It was more than surprising to see her in negotiations. A marriage between Aesir and Vanir was unheard of, never seen before in all nine worlds. The clans naturally fought, always arguing over useless things. But they could put the feud aside and come together. Astrid only prayed it wouldn't have to be Thor.

When the Princess exited her caravan for a moment's rest, taking in the heavy sunlight, Astrid burnt up with relentless jealousy. Skadi proved to be *more* than beautiful. Otherworldly and indescribable. Danger and cuts lined the goddess's fingertips, but gentleness curved her brow. Despite her luxurious aqua-blue dress that showed off her toned muscles and curves, her eyes were what held any soul captive. The marks of a Vanir trailed along her chestnut skin, colored a shade as dark as coal.

At the end of the day, Astrid took the Princess inside the castle walls and left her there, watching Thor come to meet her from a distance. Before then, she had last seen the Prince training, wielding spears, jabbing and coaxing the air in Asgard's countless fields. There was a difference in his eyes, though, something only his father held. Stricken fear overtook her at seeing him, bare-chested and barely panting. One day, he'd be King, marry his Queen, lead armies, and become a legend. She, however selfish, would remain obsolete, desolate, ripped in half. As she saw the godly maliciousness pool out within his training, Astrid pitied the goddess betrothed to him and wished she could escape the cage that Astrid would never be able to.

She fell back into step behind the company, quiet and deflated from the haunting moment. The company lowered their voices but still spoke, swept up in whatever conversation they delved into. Thalia was a little ways ahead, jogging away from the street. The berserker quickly disappeared into shadow with the setting sun, falling out of vision. Astrid reached, unsheathing Hofond and running towards the unaware Valhallians.

Silas was mid-speech: " - ever get McDonald's again. Unless Valhalla gets delivery."

"Mcdonald's isn't even that good," Kali replied, "haven't you had Windy's? I mean, Windy's is - no joke - the *best* fast food restaurant of all time, and I will fight you if you wanna argue otherwise. And some people like Five Guys, but it's not even -"

Silas blinked. "Why'd you say it like that?"

"What'd I say? Windy's."

"The fast food place, right?"

She punched him. "Yes, dummy, what other Windy's is there?"

"Okay, but Kali, you're saying it wrong," Silas said, trying to hold back laughter, "it's *Wendy's,* not *Windy's.*"

"That's what I said! Windy's!"

"No! Wendy's!" He leaned closer to her. "Wen-dy's. Wendy's."

"I'm tellin' you -"

Astrid slid between them. "Where has your guardian gone?" she hissed, ducking at the sight of a dormant vehicle.

Silas gave her a look. "Put the needle away, man! I'm telling you, that guy you said attacked you when you got here? Yeah, a *police officer?* One of them sees you with that, they'll come trotting over, and people like us gotta avoid those kinda situations, you know?"

"All cops are bad cops," Kali said in agreement, "just saying."

"You gotta get a license or something, I'm not getting arrested -"

"Can you *hear* yourself when you talk?" Astrid sneered, Hofond burning in her palm. "The berserker. Where is she?"

Before the Valhallians reacted, a figure leaped from the shadows, knocking into Silas with a loud grunt. Thalia looked wild, her amber eyes alight like a burning blaze. "Follow me," she ordered, "here's the house."

Astrid clutched onto Hofond as she crouched, running along the path Thalia created. The dead ones scuttled behind her, their footsteps meshed together to sound like a large animal. Thalia paused behind rounded bushes, her ax tight in hand.

A cozy home was painted a dim yellow and covered with overgrown vines at Astrid's right. Flowers and weeds grew anywhere available, creating a suburban jungle within the front lawn. Her eyes caught onto a window on the house's side wall: a brief glimpse revealed a bed layered with blankets and fluffed pillows. Grief tinged her heart. She couldn't remember the last time she slept in a bed. The war destroyed her home, the land she grew up in, and scattered any belongings she might've ever had. It left no more parents or siblings, no extended family. Even at the castle barracks, she possessed no bed. Not even Thor's chambers were her own. And in chains, her bed was wherever she found sleep.

At the front windows, Astrid watched a shadow walk by. She could see little from the low lighting: long legs, a worn-out dress, bandages wrapped around fingertips. *The boy's mother,* she thought. She hid behind the bushes beside Thalia, watching as the other Valhallians lined up at her left.

Silas whistled. "Boy, look at that car!"

"Keep it down," Thalia whispered.

"Milo never said anything about a Corvette, did he?"

Silas shrugged. "Not to me. Don't think they're the rich type, though."

"It's not Milo's," Kali interjected.

Astrid watched the machine. "How can you tell?"

"By the people in the car that are obviously *not* Milo."

As she spoke, a noise came from the Corvette. Both front doors snapped open, the right backdoor following afterward in a slight lag. Two looming figures, oddly tall to fit in such a machine, stepped out. They wore matching suits, sunglasses shielding their eyes. Something about the way they stood, arms slightly hanging lower than normal, shoulders slouched forward and down, put her on edge. Nothing about the encounter seemed Midgardian.

The final passenger exited the Corvette. Standing at least six feet tall, the man appeared like a statue, firm and solid in the hazy evening air. Traditional Southern Asgardian braids lined bushy curls above his ears, falling back into the midnight hair stretching down his shoulders. Astrid reached, touching the messy braids in her hair - she wore it the same way as most Royal Guards did. His eyes colored pitch black, he gazed calmly around the house, and he spoke to his companions, popping a button on his suit absentmindedly.

"You know," Astrid whispered, "he looks sort of like -"

A twig snapped behind her. Astrid flipped around. Darkness looked back at her, trees standing luminously within it. She could've sworn she heard footsteps, something crawling inconspicuously closer to their hiding place. There were a few broken branches scattered around, leaves broken and dying, and a divet within the soft soil, as though something pressed down upon it. Astrid raised her eyes. A singular curl of smoke floated above her, dark and shadowy till passing through falling light: purple. All too familiar. She raised her hand, running it through the smoke. It dissolved.

It can't be.

Astrid turned back towards the hedges.

The man moved towards the front door. As he walked, his companions followed close behind. The man lifted his hand, and purple fog swallowed them, revealing their true appearance. Within the same second, they exited the fog, appearances altered into their true selves. Robes colored purple and black replaced the man's suit. The dark eyes remained constant, still staring menacingly toward the quiet house. Behind him, the man's companions exited the fog.

"Jotunn!" Thalia choked in surprise.

Astrid staggered backward, almost falling as the earth swung beneath her. Fear ricocheted within her chest. *By the grace of Odin,* she thought, *do not let this be who I believe.* She stuck Hofond into the ground, yanking herself back up to see the trio march towards the house.

The two figures behind the man held oceanic blue skin, antlers extending from their foreheads, and veins protruding at any visible place. They were alarmingly grotesque, with jutted teeth and bloodshot eyes, dried blood and dirt staining their arms. Their suits fell into rags, tattered and ripped, axes and swords gripped in their hands. Thalia's first guess proved correct: Jotunn were icy creatures from Jotunheim, tangling deeply with the Vanir clan.

"*Vær med meg*[14]," Astrid breathed. She turned to the berserker. "They've broken the treaty. Jotunn could never step foot in Midgard."

Thalia scoffed. "The treaties died the moment your King tried to kill Freyja."

She snapped over, ready to argue, when grumbling whispers came from her left. Astrid and Thalia whipped around to see Kali trying to bury the Laevateinn underneath her clothes. A bright light came from its jewel, causing the staff to shake and rumble with energy. Kali yelped, dropping to her stomach with a *thud*. Her small frame covered the staff, almost snuffing out the jewel's light.

"Turn it off, Kal!" Silas hissed.

"*What do you think I'm doing?*" she screeched. "Please, please, *please,* turn off! Go to sleep!"

Laevetinn was wide awake.

Only at the arrival of its true master could the staff act in such a way. The energy it used was its own, Kali's goals didn't matter. She looked towards the man. The trio paused at the door.

Pitch-black eyes met hers for a split second, and she remembered.

All she wanted to do was run. With a quick turn, she could sprint off into the wooded areas of the neighborhood, leaving the dead ones and the berserker behind. The amulet hummed at her collar. Once, she believed there was nothing left to fear. But there stood the bringer of death, an old friend, a new enemy, a god that could rip worlds apart with a snap.

Astrid grabbed the Valhallian. The light from Laevateinn burst in the darkness. "It doesn't matter," she whispered, "he knew we'd be

---

[14] Be with me

here before we ever arrived." She pointed to the staff. "Do not be afraid to hide it, dead one. Naturally, it calls its master, and he has already heard."

"Master?" Kali repeated. "But that - isn't that -"

Thalia shot up, eyes wide as she stared at the house. "Loki," she said, "the Deathbringer."

"Valhallians," Astrid commanded, standing from behind the bushes, "remain out of sight, take up arms only when you believe death is required. Take no life unless your own is at stake." She jumped over the bushes. "Protect each other." She extended her hand towards the berserker. "Care to fight a god, berserker?"

"Bless you, *kriger*," Thalia said, her ax duplicating to be a pair, "you know my heart."

Running beside each other, the pair kicked down the front door.

And the silence was deafening.

XVI. Loki the Deathbringer

Loki watched himself exit the Midgardian machine, waiting for his Jotunn companions to catch up. Their arrival was unexpected - a last-minute gift from Sigyn. They'd be his fighters, little placeholders to keep the warriors busy while he got his work done. While lately, he'd seen himself taking a more pacifistic approach, the Norse were not specifically known to be peaceful. He looked down. The company knelt a few feet away from him, cowering behind the greenery. He scowled.

Four outstandingly peculiar beings, hooded by shadow and shrubbery, stared at his other form with perplexed expressions. The two young ones were obviously prized pickings for Valhalla, even if they weren't snagged by the Valkyrie. The tower existed off the power it received from its inhabitants, warriors forced to remain in the realm till Ragnarok's horn blew. The stronger the soul, the higher Valhalla grows, and the longer Yggdrasil survives. Midgardians were Valhalla's majority, adequate in their own right but useless.

He crouched behind the smallest Valhallian as her hands curled tightly around Laevateinn's darkness. With a deep breath, Loki coughed, laughing in surprise. The girl held a distinctive air about her: purity, a golden heart beneath the heightened physique, scarlet blood tinged with bronze. *Odd.* He had never come across a child both of Midgard and Alfheim. Elven magic lay within her veins, giving her mortal body a godly favor. Loki stood up, smiling down at her. *If only.* Centuries had passed since he had an apprentice, the last being the *idiot* Ullr, and all he did with his teachings was play tricks on the Aesir royal court.

Valhalla earned a good soul with the girl. He'd leave Laevateinn with her for the time being. It watched over her, keeping her safe till the moment came for her role to surface. Eventually, she'd have her day, and the front seat of the show would be his.

He idled through the trees as the company squabbled about his appearance. They fumbled with Laevateinn as it burst with light - a simple trick with a flick of his fingers. His eyes were glued to the tallest in the group, dark waves pulled into braids along her scalp. They were in the Southern style, he noticed. She pulled the little one to her feet, mumbling about Laevateinn's power.

She looked devastatingly like a dream in the dying light. Loki softened. Astrid reminded him too much of the days before. He locked her up in the cells beneath Asgard's castle halls for good reason. Keeping her away from battle worked best for him and Sigyn. Not only was she the safest there, but the fool commander Esther remained compliant, and the restless Sigyn operated in the city without the warrior's interference.

It used to be during late nights when Loki led Astrid through Asgard's golden halls, glowing in the firelight. As a mortal, the godly halls of the castle instinctively filled her with fear, so she'd hold his cloak, sticking to his side. Those moments made him feel as normal and young as her, not a being that had been living since time's beginning. It was the way divinity worked: being in the divine's gaze let the divinity seep into the mortal; being in the mortal's presence let mortality trickle into the divine. When they parted, her mortality rubbed onto his skin, creaks echoing through his bones. She'd slip into the Prince's chambers, and he'd drag a knife's edge across his hand. For a second, his blood shone red, a thick scarlet reeking of iron sliding down bronze skin. *A split second.* Then immortality returned, and the blood turned a thick gold. He was mortal on those nights.

Their last interaction ended on a sour note despite the good times before. Being exiled from the Aesir royal court was the final strike between them: Astrid's love for the gods blinded her and made her ignorant of the real world. In that way, she was infuriating, belligerent, and hell-bent on protecting the clan that ruined her family. And for what, a mindless Prince with an outlandishly pretty face? *No,* he thought. He knew her better.

Without a moment's to lose, Astrid grasped the woman to her right, inviting her into battle as she unsheathed the glistening Hofond. The blade hummed erratically at Loki's presence. He stuck his tongue out at it. *Mind your own business, Heimdall.* The god spied on the warrior through the weapon without her even knowing. Tactless but effortlessly efficient. The pair made their way toward the house.

The Valhallians restlessly waited for their guardian's return. One of them, average height, handsome with smooth, dark skin, unsheathed his blade, watching the house with fearful eyes. The girl held Laevateinn protectively close.

Pity, he thought, *there's so much potential.* Guilt strung him up, hesitation crawling up his throat. *I still have time.* If he retreated, Sigyn would hate him, but his soul wouldn't be tainted. Hope grew. If he stepped back, the Aesir might offer him another chance on the royal court. Resentment towered over his emotions. Justice stood taller than any other false hope he might give himself. The bigger picture was more important than saving his soul.

Loki shrugged.

The emotion was gone.

He continued to his task. The handsome Valhallian stuck his sword deep in the grass beside the hedges, hands on hips defiantly as he looked up at the sky. Stars and constellations held his attention. Another Valhallian continued their conversation, voice low and incoherent in Loki's current state. Everything was a bit fuzzy, and his hearing was a little off. It didn't matter much - there wasn't anything they said he needed to know.

Loki approached the stargazing one. The boy flinched, a chill running through his body. He turned, looking in Loki's direction, but finding nothing. The god got closer, leaning down to get close to the boy's ear.

"*Hor pa meg,*" Loki whispered. His breath came out like smoke, colored a faint magenta. He inhaled, the spell coursing through his veins, and said, "*Listen to me.*"

The boy's skin grew cold, littered with goosebumps. His lip quivered, falling into a frown as he stared into space.

"*Have no mercy,*" he muttered.

Smoke trailed into the boy's ears. As it spread, color dripped into his dark eyes like ink, the brown fading into a magnificent purple.

Loki tilted his head, gazing toward the other Valhallian amid their discourse. The girl's head snapped back in laughter.

"*Kill them.*"

The god backed away, wiping his lips of the remaining magic as he left the young ones. A muffled yell came from behind him. Loki barely turned, catching a glimpse of fists flying towards the girl. She screamed. Laevateinn grew dark, falling back into its slumber. The girl's power called out pleadingly to him, screaming for help. Loki raised his arms, blocking it out.

Loki smiled.

Everything was right on schedule.

XVII. Long Live the King

The quiet spread through the house like slick oil on water, spilling and spreading, devouring everything in its path. Astrid yearned for her berserker companion to sing. She didn't care what, whether a shanty or prayer before the inevitable end, the air needed to be filled with something other than emptiness. The stillness came within like a sickness. She reached, barely touching the pounding pulse at her neck. She breathed a relieved sigh. The silence almost stopped her heart. And, from the impulsive habit, she pressed her finger harshly against her palm.

Am I dreaming?

She focused: a dark house, belongings scattered across the floor, shadows dancing around luminously against the back wall. Astrid lowered her hands.

No, I am awake.

Thalia bumped her elbow into Astrid's side. The berserker brandished her axes, crossing them defensively across her chest. The gesture twinged in Astrid - Asgardian warriors did not make those exclamations before the battle. They shouted, expelled a warcry like a final thought, their last words to the universe. Vanaheim's inhabitants were known for the motion - a technique to brandish power and stature. It was a silent moment, a show of strength, unification between warriors binding them as brethren. The notion was of comrades and companionship. If it didn't frighten her, Astrid might've found herself replicating it. She watched the berserker cross into the house's kitchen, pushing cracked glass from her path.

Astrid brought her palms to her lips. "*Giv mig ild*[15]," she whispered, sucking in hot air. Needles pricked her arms as the energy washed into her veins, growing strong and hard until the sensation reached her fingertips. She exhaled, and fire shot from parted lips, rolling into a sphere at her hands. The flames illuminated her face, barely spreading light around the house. The flames' warmth brought comfort, a soft light illuminating the path forward.

Thalia scoffed. "Even in war," she said, "your gods still answer your prayers."

"My gods," Astrid rotated to hold the fire close to Thalia, "are the same as yours."

The berserker grimaced. "They never belonged to me. And I'd never want them."

"What Asgardian warrior fails to pray to her gods? You're foolish for saying such cursed words aloud."

Thalia laughed. "And you're blind."

"How *dare* you -"

The lights flicked on within the house.

---

[15] Give me fire

"You know," an eerily familiar voice said from behind, "the Midgardians *are* good for something."

They turned, and Astrid's magical fire puffed out.

There stood Loki, the Deathbringer, the god of tricks and cursed fate. He was in the form Astrid could picture with her eyes closed. Hope pooled into her chest: *maybe he wasn't the monster anymore.* But he had a glimmer in his pitch-black eyes, an angry arch in his eyebrows. His skin was lit by the moon and his hair freckled with stars. No weapons in his belt. Within his clenched fist was hair, a middle-aged Midgardian woman slumped against the ground. Scarlet blood stained her porcelain skin, turning her dress into a shade of nightmares. The bright color seeped onto the carpet, spreading till it reached their feet.

"Midgardians harvest light the same way we collect blue fire," Loki continued, looking up towards the chandelier above them, "who knew such short, narrow-minded brains contained knowledge?" He shrugged. "Knowledge is not worth keeping a species alive." Loki's gaze hung onto Astrid. Hatred lurked beneath his skin. "Wouldn't you know something about that, Astrid? You and your beloved?"

She did not need to hear his thoughts to know what he truly wanted to say. She forced it to stay in the past. Astrid was not ready for it. She brandished Hofond.

The berserker's presence suddenly appeared beside her. "You're out of bounds, Loki."

He sneered. "I'd watch my next words carefully if I were you, berserker," he tilted his head, "or have you forgotten what it is I know?" His companion trolls appeared from the shadows.

"Let the Midgardian go," Thalia said, "and we can move past this."

"You're not in the position to make demands!" he shouted. "You have walked in on *my* plan. You've intruded upon a matter that *does not concern you.*"

"The *moment* you entered it became my problem." Thalia pointed her ax at him. "Be the good man you once were, Loki. Let her go."

Astrid watched. History lies between the god and Thalia. The berserker's story grew more clouded with secrets. The darkness faltered in his tense face, the strain easing. His lips parted, and he grew younger, frowning. His fingers loosened around the woman's hair. She groaned in response.

Loki looked at Astrid. "*No.*" The resentment returned. He yanked the woman, throwing her over his shoulder. She grunted, going limp. "My journey is only beginning," he said, "and I have gone too far to turn back now."

Astrid gripped the sword. The blade burnt her palm, screeching and screaming to be thrust into battle. She raised it toward her old friend. "And Thor? Taking him was part of your plan too?"

Loki frowned. "What would I want with that idiot?"

She hesitated, glancing towards Thalia. "Where is he?"

"How would I know?" he sneered. "The baboon went missing *after* my exile - or did you forget about that?"

"If this is about revenge -"

"Do not patronize me, Astrid." Loki clenched his fists, the darkness in his eyes enveloping the room. "You act as if you know my mind, but what is it you *truly* know? Enlighten me, warrior," he paused, walking closer, unafraid of the blade pointed at his chest, "how well do you know the gods you cherish? How well do you know the man you've so graciously given your heart? How well do you know about the war you fight?"

Her hands wavered. "I don't understand."

"Astrid -" Thalia interjected.

The god's hand snapped, and the berserker flung backward, her back slamming against the kitchen wall. Axes skidded across the floor. Hofond shook in Astrid's hands. She inhaled to steady herself, only succeeding to heave.

"All those late nights in Asgard's halls," he continued, "all those hushed conversations, whispering things like Ragnarok and a darkness growing within Midgard."

"It was you," she breathed. Something concaved in her chest.

Loki stood only a foot away. "Secrets passed between the Aesir council, the one you have spent your entire life serving. Astrid," he reached, touching the sword's tip, "what do you know about the beings who took your family away?"

Am I dreaming?

"I remember the little Frey," Loki said. "Eyes as wide as the moon, hair strung from gold. Wasn't it the All-Father who ravaged through your village?"

Am I dreaming?

"Not even nightfall could render him unrecognizable. A brilliant King wielding Gungnir, burning your home to the ground. And for what?" Loki was upon her. He touched her chin, raising her eyes. "Rumors of the rebellion festering? More secrets?" His stone-cold fingertips gripped her harshly by the jaw. "How well do you know your King, old friend?"

It wasn't a dream.

Before Loki could continue, the berserker retrieved her axes, snapping them across the god's wrists. He retracted, slinking back towards the trolls. "Lovely, Thalia," he said with a harsh laugh, "finally making it fun!"

"You stay away from her."

"Oh, come on! I'm *helping*! Astrid here is blind, you said it yourself! She looks at the Aesir with clouds over her gaze, not *once* seeing them for what they are." He glared. "Monsters." His grip tightened on the Midgardian woman. "I'm playing my part in a much bigger game, ladies. It's not my fault if you're too late to realize it."

"Riddle me this, Loki," Astrid shouted, Hofond burning in her hand, "what does all this have to do with a few Valhallians?"

Loki blinked. "Right," he said, "you haven't heard!" He snapped, glancing over his shoulder at the trolls. "Silly me, I always forget about the whole timing thing."

Before his exile, Loki studied astral projection, failing to successfully perform it. Astrid nodded. "There's another version of you out there."

"*Bingo,*" he said. "Should be arriving any moment now." He glanced out the window. "Won't be news for our little berserker, though," Loki smirked. "Another taste of those lovely lies."

Not even a second passed before light erupted in the living room. It grew and crackled till forming into an orb, levitating in the air as it cast a shadow across them. It was old magic, one only the All-Father summoned. Odin used it once before: to announce Thor's engagement across the realms, for peace. The Aesir council released messages to reach all nine realms. That is if they are aware of the tree's existence. Not just anyone could see a message from Yggdrasil.

Thalia choked. "That's impossible -"

"No," Astrid muttered, "the message was already created, any Aesir on the throne can send it." Her eyes snapped to Loki's smug smirk. "And Sigyn sits on the throne."

The god shrugged.

Light burst from the orb before a booming voice too familiar echoed through the house. Odin the All-Father spoke beyond death:

"Children of Yggdrasil, I, All-Father of Peace, Lord of the Aesir and King of Asgard, hereby declare Milo Odinson, my last born, as your Crown Prince, heir to the Bleeding Throne. All Hail Asgard, and long may he reign."

The orb swallowed itself, disappearing as though it never existed.

Loki laughed in stunned silence. "But you already knew that," he paused, turning, "didn't you, Thalia?"

The berserker glanced at Astrid. "There was no way -"

Astrid raised Hofond. A burning surged into her throat, crawling down her cheeks. Tears slid down her face. Like arrows, they struck her skin and flung onto the sword. The rage and hate took over, swarming through her.

She raised her eyes.

Loki smiled. "And now you know."

"Now I know."

Still holding the Midgardian, Loki stepped backward, his companions moving around him as tall shields. "I hate to cut this reunion short," he called out, "but I've got loads of things to do, with such little time." He touched the wall. "Take this as my final gift to you, old friend."

"Loki -"

The wall melted behind him, swirling and morphing till it took on Asgard's golden spires. He was already stepping into the portal, halfway gone when he delivered his final warning.

"Get in my way again, and it'll be your death."

The god disappeared.

Brandishing grandswords, the Jotunn growled, stalking forward.

"Think it's about time we killed something," Thalia said.

Astrid nodded. "It's about time."

The warrior ran, dropping to her knees and sliding underneath the troll's sword. She raised Hofond, and the blade eagerly sliced across the Jotunn's back *leg*, earning a pained shriek. It swiveled around, whipping its sword through the air. Astrid ducked, crossing Hofond over her chest and slashing down upon the Jotunn's chest. It shouted, clasping at its wound before collapsing. The blade came down upon its neck.

Thalia slammed her ax into the other Jotunn's skull, dragging the weapon's pair across its gut. The creatures fell to the floor beside each other, magenta blood dripping onto the carpet.

Astrid ran to the wall, where the god had escaped. She pressed her palm against it and felt the hard surface push back. The portal disappeared the moment it was conjured. Loki and the Midgardian with it. She turned, looking back towards the berserker.

"You knew."

"I had a hunch."

"What kind of *hunch* tells you Odin had another son?"

"It was only a hunch," she repeated. "We need to get ahead of this before it gets out of hand."

Astrid scoffed. "Aye, maybe try being honest from now on."

"I did what I had to, *kriger,*" Thalia said, "it's my responsibility to keep those dead ones safe, and that means not saying things like that aloud." She reconnected her axes, sliding them into the belt loop. "I'd say Milo knows, and Loki has just dangled him in front of every power-hungry creature in the nine realms. It's only a matter of time before something comes for him."

"But the throne -"

"*Doesn't matter*! We need the Prince. We need the key." She pointed to the marks on her arm. "All before time runs out. Do you still want your Thor? *Fine.* Looks like we've got his brother. It's just become a family affair." She stepped over the trolls, reaching her arm out towards Astrid. "Help me finish this, and I will personally get *your* idiot back on the throne."

Astrid stared. There was no trust left to spare. And the knot growing in her stomach told her to do one thing: *get out of there. Find Thor. Leave the bastard to die.* She closed her eyes and breathed in.

She took Thalia's hand. "For Thor."

Or so help me, I'll rip your heart out.

XVIII. Danger and Fists

Milo lost track of how long he drowned.

At one point, he's thrown off a cliff, and the next, he drifts through a murky sea - none of it made sense. There was the fall, a figure fading in the darkness, an everlasting chasm, then...*water*? Somewhere, the sea began, and eventually, there'd be the bottom, but all he could feel was lost. No sea life lingered by, leaving him alone in the cold ocean. His arms waved around him, but it didn't seem like he was moving. Milo swung upwards, thrusting with his legs, swimming but never reaching the surface. It made him feel like a child again, ignorantly stuck in the shallow end. He clawed, grasped, opened his mouth, and screamed for *Loki*.

Water surged into his mouth. Everything was cool and warm simultaneously, darkness spotting across his vision. His arms stopped flailing, and his feet ceased to kick. He melted into the ocean and faded into nothingness. It was like falling asleep; one moment, he'd lie awake, and the next, waking up from a deep slumber, never realizing he fell in the first place. And it was pleasant and calming in a weird way. He stopped worrying and realized there was only him and water and no foreseeable way out. Somehow, it brought peace, and he was ready.

Milo closed his eyes.

Remember.

The vision flashed: ocean waters snapped away, replaced with snow-peaked mountains and a frosty tundra. Shrouded with falling snow, a jet-black and shadowy castle stood in the distance. Below Milo's feet was an icy lake, creatures he could not recognize passing beneath. *Holy shit.* Hit foot twitched. Cracks sliced through the ice. Everything became still, the line between life and death thin as the cracks that moved around his feet. Someone screamed his name.

Find the spear.

The frozen floor caved in.

Milo collapsed into the lake, winter quietly chomping him down. Down he went, the waves wrapping around his ankles and wrists like shackles. It twisted him till he faced the rocky bottom. A long and dark spear sat on the sandy floor, intricate engravings of ravens and wolves at the top. Jewels marked its spine. Nordic runes like those Thalia drew in the bar lined the spear's body. Loki's demands crossed his mind. Milo snatched it.

Reclaim the throne.

The water and ice disappeared. A figure, taller than him by at least three feet, stormed forward, sprinting at full speed. A prism-like mesh of colors rising to a terrifying height. Around them were some greenery, burnt grass, and scattered ash, the sky a rising orange, about a handful of sun-like orbs hovering over the horizon. He could smell salt water and fire. The spear from the lake was in his right hand, a brilliantly golden shield in his left. The blurry figure got closer, just a foot away. Milo held the shield, lifted the spear over his head, and vaulted it.

The spear sunk into the figure's chest, and the world became painfully bright.

Save Asgard.

He stood before a tower on fire. Rubble and debris fell from the clouds, the never-ending tower crumbling. Screams erupted as men and women burst out windows, jumping to safety. Glass trickled on him like rain. It reeked with death. Blood stained the grass. Swords and shields clashed. Friends and enemies died. It didn't matter what side he was on: he could feel the end at hand. Milo raised his head. He saw a tree's shadow against the clouds, where the tower's top sat.

There was a crash.

Clouds and sky parted: branches the size of a football field fell towards him.

He closed his eyes.

Milo.

The ocean returned. *How long have I been dreaming?* He pulled his arm through the water, trying to see the runes the Master drew. The first triangle faded, but somehow, he still lived. He raised his head and opened his mouth. The water pooled in again.

Stop doing that!

He flinched, thrashing around in the water. The voice came again, unfamiliar and strange. Out from the darkness was an ethereal figure, glowing at the center with fiery embers. Crystallized eyes looked back at him, shapes and rays of light forming the creature's skeleton-like body. Water fell from its skull-like hair, foamy waves shaping into robes. It swam up to Milo, curiously inspecting him.

You keep making me bring you back, the voice spoke without a mouth. It tilted its head. *Don't speak. Nod. Shake your head. Every time you swallow water, you die, and I have to bring you back. It's annoying and rude.* The creature turned away, staring into the distance, the diamond-shaped eyes distorted and sparkling.

Milo parted his lips. The creature's diamond arm shot out threateningly. He nodded.

I am the fylgja, It continued, *fate's servant and watcher. Do you understand?*

He shook his head. *No, how could that make any sense?* He fought the urge to yell, waving his hand through the creature as though it was holographic. Instead, he rubbed his eyes, everything numb and wrinkly from the water.

The Norn created me, built me from the soil beneath Yggdrasil as a guide for the living, It explained. *I have seen the string that bounds your life to the everlasting ash tree - your story is far from over.*

Milo stared at the creature. There came a thirsty urge to strangle it. He shoved the thought away. He yearned for answers, for a light within the shadowy words presented to him. There was Loki and the Norn, dreams of brothers and war. Milo nodded at the fylgja. He wanted to know.

They need you.

He shook his head. *Who?*

Without its head, the creature said, *the Warriors of Thunder will fall. And now, their lives are in danger. Only you may be their second chance.*

If the water around him could've gotten colder, it did then. *Danger?* He nodded, teeth rattling. The last time he saw his friends, they were in the safety of Nordic warriors. The constant worry of a dangerous creature roaming was there, but something about how the creature spoke made it much worse. He nodded again, fiercely this time, and a passion sparked within him. *Anything to get me back to them.*

The fylgja got closer. *It's time to wake the god.*

Before he could shake his head, and scream that it was what Loki wanted, the creature already moved. He thrashed, trying to shove it away. The creature swam into him, fading into a light as it crashed through his chest. Milo's limbs flung as the burst ricocheted into him like a bomb exploding. Light spread across the sea. A switch flipped, and it raced back into him, a brilliant energy surging into his hands. The jewelry he wore hummed against his skin. He yelled, clawing at his hand. The pain spread, a burning heat filling up his throat and spreading across his stomach. He grabbed his neck. He screamed as tears united with the water.

Do not fight it, Odinson, the voice came. *You are what you are.*

His head flew back.

A man with silver-streaked raven curls and a scarred eye sat upon a scarlet throne, a crown around his head. A great black wolf lay beside his feet, ravens perched upon the seat.

Within your blood is the universal power of the Aesir, a bond to unite you as a godly clan.

The painting from the Master's room came back to him. Twenty-five outlandish beings stared at him as though they knew his life before it happened. A new figure appeared in the middle, stepping out from the golden light and standing alongside the others. It was himself, dressed in a fur cloak and armored suit.

Take the power given to you at birth; accept the destiny prewritten for centuries.

Another scream rippled from his throat. Acid ate him from the inside, swimming through his veins and consuming every part within him. He was aflame with the power, alighted like the sun's core. Euphoria tied in with pain. It was raw and powerful and forever. He was nothing and everything, built from the divine and sculpted by the mortal. He no longer knew who he was. Like a wave, it crashed into him and pulled back, taking something away. Bits and pieces of the ocean remained, life scattered from different origins to recreate something new. He was the same but different, calling himself Milo but meaning Odinson.

Find the spear, reclaim the throne, and save Asgard.

He was new, golden, and bright. Spring blended into summer when the days became long and the earth grew again. Mountains could shake at his footsteps and air whistle into a hurricane with his exhale. From his fingertips could grow a light as glorious as the sun, undying and immutable.

Milo Odinson.

The pain stopped. His heirloom ring did not burn any longer and sat upon him like a feather. His skin tingled like it did when he woke in Valhalla for the first time. There wasn't fear as there was then. It was instead the way a knife sliced through paper - without friction. He reached up, arms like rubber tubes, and grabbed his glasses. They snapped without much effort, floating as little pieces through the gray water. There was no longer a need for them. His eyes were no longer his own.

They need you.

At once, he remembered them, the people he left behind. Their faces rippled behind his eyelids like photographs. And they were strong, each of them. Without him, they'd live on and become their own. No matter what the creature said, they did not need him. It was the other way around. *Always* the other way around.

Then, he understood what the old man meant. In other centuries, he knew them. In different winds, he breathed their air. He heard their hearts beat in separate lands and ran to catch them. Whether there were hundreds of suns or none, a moon or two, they would be there, an unsolved puzzle, moments trapped in a body, souls imprisoned and yearning for release, gasping to unite as one. He knew, then, in death, they found each other. In life, they would search; beyond that, their chests would pool onto the land like the sea. He would know them in any face, taste their being with a single breath, and recognize their souls like an old friend. That was when he knew.

Milo.

He raised his head. He could see the rippling surface.

Find them.

Milo swam, surprised at the strength within him. He pushed till he crashed through the top, gulping down air. It was sandpaper against his throat. He choked on reality's appearance. Clawing at the muddy shore, he snatched onto the grass, dragging himself onto land. He collapsed against dirt, legs still submerged.

The lake was only a few yards away from his home. There wasn't any time to be surprised: somehow, the deep chasm within Asgard carried him back home. An old bicycle stuck out of the water. For a moment, he felt lost, unable to search through his memories to find the way. He felt empty.

Milo lay there, discerning the line between reality and illusion. It was night, the moon slowly rose, and the house across the street was where he broke his leg for the first time. He once borrowed paint from the blue house. His mother sold paintings at a yard sale a few blocks down. He met a dog at the street corner, begging to keep it only to find the owner. Nine houses down were his own, and his mother would be inside. *His mother would be inside,* which was reason enough for life to return to his limbs.

Ignoring the yearning to collapse, he pushed on and wobbled to his feet. Milo grasped at his belt to find it empty; his sword left on the grassy cliffs of Asgard. "Danger and fists, then," he muttered.

And he was running, sliding a moment as the mud rubbed off his shoes. Everything whipped around like a dream, melting together like water and paint. His life passed by in scattered colors and wisps of air. He kept running, leaving it all behind. None of it mattered. The gods, the war, the death, and the life. He only yearned for home, for the feeling of fullness, of never going hungry, of comfort within a gaze. Thalia and her amber eyes, mysterious thoughts trapped within them, never looking at him as he hoped. Kali and Silas and they're forever bickering. Even Astrid, the Asgardian warrior he knew little about, saved their lives without a second thought. He remembered the woman from Valhalla: *find your clan.* He ran faster.

Shouts echoed. Sudden cries followed a pained scream.

Kali.

He pushed himself further.

The light caught his eye. His father's ring shone unnaturally in the moonlight like a fallen star striking the sky. It grew painful, shocking a nerve within his hand that shuddered throughout his body till it stopped at his feet. The surge became euphoric.

" - let me go!" Kali screamed. "*Please,* god, Silas!" She sobbed.

Milo sprinted, skidding as he got closer.

The windows were alit with color - shadows danced chaotically behind the shades, thundering noises beyond the thin walls. The Corvette was gone. There was nothing to prove it existed. Along the hedges beside the driveway were the Warriors of Thunder.

Kali laid on her back, propped against her elbows. Crimson trailed down her lip, sliding down her chin and staining the Valhallian sweater. Across from her was Laevateinn, half buried in the bushes. Silas walked towards her, breathing heavily, his hands bunched tightly into fists. He lunged, and she helplessly rolled out of the way, but not fast enough. Silas's fist slammed into the nape of her neck.

Flying backward, Kali shrieked in fear. She clawed at her throat, coughing like an animal as she lurched, vomiting on Milo's front lawn. Her wails propelled him and flung his legs towards the driveway. He leaped over her, not stopping as she shouted in surprise. He lunged, tackling Silas to the ground.

Everything went dark.

He was unsure how long he punched his friend's face. The pain dulled after a while, and eventually, the bones became rubber and the skin butter. The image of someone he knew disappeared. Someone he cared for wasn't below him. Within it all, amidst the movements and strikes, he got lost. Somewhere, he got dropped off, running at high speed while he remained behind, watching from a distance. The new version grasped the reins, narrow-minded in the fact someone he cared for was in trouble - who cares the one inflicting harm would also be a friend. But *he,* Milo, sat in darkness, realizing it was happening, unable to do anything.

He screamed.

Sometimes, he wished death was quiet.

XIX. Together

Bones cracked beneath Milo's knuckles. Legitimate bones.

He wasn't sure how many bones made up the skull. Biology class was years behind him, assuming he paid attention in the first place. How hard could they be to break? Maybe a baseball bat slammed into the nose. A strong enough fist hits the jaw at the right spot. Once, as a baby, Milo fell from his crib, knocking his left temple against the tile floor. His mother rushed to the emergency room, screaming and crying for somebody to save her baby boy. It turns out babies have oddly flexible skulls. There was a little scar to prove the accident happened, but no broken bones. At his school fights, blood was drawn, hands bruised, cheeks swollen, and teeth knocked out, but never the crunch of bones.

This time, though, he felt it.

A cracking like popping bubble wrap or a fortune cookie snapping. The grooves on his knuckles pressed hard enough to result in a rumble, the vibration running up his arm. Each time, the adrenaline spiked higher and higher. His veins rushed with energy, lifting his arms and lowering them, lifting and lowering.

It didn't matter. Silas wasn't awake anymore.

It didn't matter that someone screamed from behind, begging and pleading for Milo to stop.

It didn't matter when rough arms wrapped around his neck, trying to yank him away.

It didn't matter that he pulled back just to slam the intruder to the ground.

It didn't matter.

It didn't matter because he no longer knew who he was. Because deep down, there was a scary part that didn't want to stop. Something lay within his arms, trickling to his fists. Whatever it was, it was hungry and asleep for too long. It regained control. Milo never held the reins.

His eyes closed.

The blood became too much.

Milo raised his fist.

Crack!

He punched.

Crack!

He punched.

Crack!

He punched.

Crack!

He didn't even feel tired.

Milo wasn't sure how long he was there. He couldn't remember if the sunset was before or after it started. When it was over, Milo couldn't put his finger on the events leading to it. He remembered his mother at the kitchen window, watching the Corvette slide up the driveway, standing on a hill above Asgard alongside Loki. He stared at his hands. Beneath the blood sat his father's ring. Beneath the blood.

He stumbled, toppling over and collapsing in the street. Thalia followed - her shadow lurked in his vision, tall and grand like an empty suit of armor. He blinked. A memory: Thalia pulled him off Silas, wrapping her arms tightly around his torso. He fought at first, thrashing and shouting as his fists slammed into her sides. She didn't move. Her arms tightened as she moved backward. His eyes squeezed shut - *there was too much blood* - and his arms moved, still smacking against something. Eventually, he stopped, and she let go.

Stars twinkled above them. He watched Orion, barely visible beyond the faint clouds. As his eyes lowered, the red on his hands caught his gaze again. He swallowed. *How can there be so much?* He dragged his hands along his trousers, leaving behind damp blood. *Why is there so much?* He kept rubbing.

"Stop."

Thalia crouched down. She reached, gently grabbing his hands. Without thinking, he flinched, yanking them away, watching as she refused to let go. Pulling out a plastic water bottle, she dumped it into his palms, drenching his skin. She retrieved a towel from underneath her elbow, cleaning the blood off.

He watched. As she positioned herself to sit on the road, her shirt rode up, and he caught a glimpse of a purple bruise growing along her abdomen. It swelled, bronze skin the shade of roses and violets. She looked frail, then, wounded like a human.

"I did that."

She pulled her shirt down. "I've handled worse." Thalia raised her eyes. "It's fine, Milo." Her voice lowered to a mutter. "We've all had those days."

"Days? I almost killed him."

"No," she chuckled, "Silas is already dead."

He glared. "You know what I mean. I did something awful."

"Sometimes being awful is the only way to survive."

"But it's not living."

"Well, Milo, spoiler alert: *you're dead.*" She shrugged. "Awful comes with the job."

He closed his eyes.

"According to Kali, you saved her life," she said. "Something happened to Silas."

Milo nodded. "He attacked her -" he paused, realization waving over him, "*Kali.* She must hate me."

"She was scared. First, her friend attacks her, and then her *other* friend joins in the fight. Give her time," Thalia said. "Whatever happened back there wasn't you or Silas's fault. It all comes back to that damn Aesir." She shook her head. "Always the Aesir."

"Loki."

"Guess you had a run-in with him." Her hand touched the ring. "How much did he tell you?"

"Enough," he replied. "Does the Master know?"

She shrugged. "Probably. He's not quite the poster child for straightforward. I had my suspicions."

"About me?"

"Couldn't help it," Thalia smirked, "you were never the average Midgardian."

Milo smiled. He looked towards his house. The living room windows glowed dimly, casting shadows upon the front lawn. They moved through the house, on the grass, almost pacing. The front door creaked open, and Astrid carried garbage bags over her shoulders, shaped oddly like gigantic limbs. He shuddered. He peered into the house, and even in the distance, he saw Kali sitting on the couch, arms wound tightly around her chest. Silas was nowhere to be seen.

The door quickly shut as Astrid reentered the house.

"Where is he?"

"He's fine," Thalia said. "Stop worrying."

"I beat the ever-living crap outta him. How can I not worry?"

"If we're lucky," she finished cleaning his hands, "you hit him hard enough."

"What?"

"I've got a hunch that whatever happened to him came from Loki's spell. There's no way to counter it with rune sorcery when I have no idea what the original spell was. Sometimes, and I mean *rare,* a good pounding can knock it right out of him." Thalia shrugged. "Just a hope, I guess."

"But I didn't kill him," Milo asked, "right?"

She smiled. "No, you didn't kill him. He'll have scars and bruises tomorrow, thanks to the runes I applied. He'll be fine."

Milo fell backward till he lay flat against the cool pavement. Stars stared back at him. Sounds from the neighboring city echoed through the trees. And for the first time since he died, Milo felt at peace. In the same spot years ago, his mother assembled her handed-down telescope. Late Saturday nights consisted of peering into the sky, listening as his mother regurgitated everything she knew about the moon. When winter approached, they bundled up and snuggled close with steaming cups of hot chocolate. Milo instinctively raised his hands, holding them above his right eye like he held the telescope. Orion still looked so far away. He dropped his hands.

Mom.

A lightbulb flicked in his mind. *How could I forget?* He turned towards the house. Shadows moved by the window. The warriors must be getting acquainted with his Mom. He knew what she'd say - eyes crinkled with age, framing her gentle face - *you've found them, Milo, your people.* She'd be raging mad, smacking him on the neck while simultaneously hugging him and grounding him till the ripe age of *never.* He smiled. That's all she ever wanted. Because, one day, as she liked to warn parentally, she wouldn't be around, and he'd need somebody. Thalia crouched beside him.

He cracked his knuckles, and a sharp pain darted to his elbow. Bruises line his hands, scabs, and skin scrubbed away. Milo pushed himself up, shoving his hands into his pockets. It was the last thing his mother needed to see.

"You met my Mom yet?" he asked Thalia, walking towards the driveway. "Because she'll love you." He turned, walking backward. "Something about you looks like a painting, you know? Or a sculpture. Don't get freaked out if she grabs your face, okay? It's just what she does."

Thalia stood. "Milo."

"And some people think she's a basket case," he continued, "but she's just never been a people person. Like you. And she's the prettiest Mom on the planet - no doubt. No offense to your mom, but I'm guessing she doesn't live on Earth - never thought I'd say *that* aloud -"

"*Milo.*"

"What'd you guys say to her anyways?" He laughed. "Guess 'hey, Mom, I died, and I know you screwed a Norse god' doesn't come in a greeting card. But you never know with Hallmark. She's probably got questions. I mean, *I've* got questions. Do you think she'll tell me? About him?" Milo paused, standing in the driveway. He looked down. Crimson decorated the pavement beside his feet. He blinked. "She'll wanna paint this over. Blood doesn't come out of driveways, huh? Wonder what the Humphrey's will think. They were always -"

"Milo, *please*," Thalia shouted. "You can't go in there. Not yet."

"Why not?"

"Because what you're expecting to find isn't there."

Milo looked at her. Those amber eyes dimmed in the darkness, taking on a chocolate shade as she watched him. Like hot chocolate. He flinched. The ring on his finger grew heavier.

"I don't understand," he replied.

She frowned but remained quiet.

"Is she dead?"

Her shoulders raised. "I don't know."

"Loki -"

"He took her," Thalia interrupted, "she was alive when he escaped. I'd take that as hope. It might be the last for a while."

"*Hope*?" he repeated. As though the monster from before never left, Milo stormed up to her, forcing his hands to remain in his pockets for fear of hurting her more than he already had. "Some crazy homicidal maniac has my mother, and you categorize that as *hopeful*?"

Thalia barely flinched. "Loki wouldn't take her if she wasn't important."

"What?"

"I doubt he's killed her," she said. "Natalie Bohr is alive, somewhere, trapped under Loki's thumb. That is hope, Milo. And the moment you start forgetting hope exists everywhere is when things like this -" she lurched forward, snatching his hand and touching the warm bruises, "happen all over again."

He whispered: "You - you did this."

Thalia dropped his hand. "I -" Her lip quivered before a wave of stillness fell over her face. She swallowed, lifting her head. "Natalie Bohr will survive."

"She'll survive?" he repeated. Aghast, he clenched and unclenched his fists. "*Survive?* What kinda condescending bullshit is that?"

Thalia stared at the sky, muttering foreign words with a scrunched up nose. "Look, I should've noticed you left," she said, "or know someone like Loki would be trailing us. I left the Valhallians out here, and look what happened." Thalia moved backward, trying to hide the twitching in her mouth. "And I *see* the way the *kriger* looks at me. She stares like she knows what's coming, but I don't. Aye, like it began with me."

The bubbling anger within him battled with the image of her on the brink of tears. His naive self never imagined her crying, never pictured such disappointment pooling out of her. He reached for her. The familiar anger bubbled in his stomach. His hand dropped. She saw the movement, eyes as wide as the sun. He tried not to look at her anymore. He didn't want her to see his rage brewing, he didn't want to see her watch him with such sadness. In the end, it couldn't be anyone else's fault but his own. He left to go home. Not the other way around.

She nodded. "It'll be fine."

"What's that even supposed to mean?"

"What?"

"It'll be fine," he repeated, "everyone says that like it changes things. Sure, I just found out my father was not only a god and a king but also died. He's dead. I never got to know him, to have those stupid, meaningless fights about him leaving me. But it'll all be fine, right?"

She grew red in the face. "It's what people say."

"It's gonna be fine," he sneered, "*I'll* be fine. Is there a fairy godmother or a magic wand? Maybe some pixie dust since all that bullshit seems to be real now."

"Don't be ridiculous," Thalia joked, "*Pixies* aren't real. Obviously."

He glared. "Seriously?"

"C'mon," she groaned, "people joke when they're scared or sad, okay? Get over it, and joke a little. You'll feel better."

"No, Thalia, I can't joke 'cause, unlike you, I have a life left behind that's worth saving."

She shot him an icy stare. "I'll ignore that because of the circumstances. Just this once."

He watched her with a heavy silence that sat on the back of his throat, growing like a sickness.

"Sorry, Milo, but honestly, what the hell do you expect me to say?" she raised her arms exasperatedly. "When you care about someone, you lie, okay? You say it'll be fine, the worst is over, and everything will improve. And you know what? I've got *no clue* whether or not any of it gets better. I haven't gotten there yet."

Milo's heart was a dried-up lake filling rapidly with an ocean. Warmth and coolness washed over him. He stared at her. She didn't look at him anymore; instead, she stared into the trees.

Everything stood still and raced at the same time. She held his gaze suddenly, with a blank stare. He would never be able to tell if she felt the same way, the same rushing emotion. He frowned. *She doesn't know. She can't tell.* Fear rushed through him like a nightmare. It was like those dreams where you fall, soaring down from the sky till the ground immediately rushed forward. She couldn't tell how he felt. She couldn't see his soul lit beside her, the fire pulsing beneath his skin.

He watched her and could feel nothing other than everything. Everything and nothing. And he wanted it to stop. He yearned to rip out his hair and scream and remove his skin and feel nothing but air on his bones. Days felt like centuries, minutes into moments. An entire life happening all at once. He wasn't sure what hurt most: the echoing in his heart or the dejection in her eyes.

Thalia kept her eyes down. He raised his hands to touch her or stop himself from falling; he did not know. He turned to the house and stepped forward. "Be honest with me, Thalia," he whispered, "how does it look?"

"Not good."

There was nothing left for him to say. Behind him stood his house, empty without his mother. Before him was *her,* watching him with a silent, perplexed expression. Both options left him feeling like there was a massive cave within his heart, a sudden chasm filled with nothing but air. Neither knew how to handle the situation - who would lean on whom? He looked away, embarrassed beneath her stare. And even though he yearned to run into his home and lock himself in his bedroom with the promise of never leaving, he had no urge to enter the house. To walk through the halls without seeing his mom. To see Silas there, unlike himself.

"It won't be fine," Thalia said. "It never has been, and it probably never will be." She walked towards him, extending her hand. She beckoned. "But we'll get through it. Together."

Milo stared at her hand. A part of him yearned to deny her, to refuse her hand and the notion that everything would be fine. But he looked into her eyes and couldn't imagine disappointing her. He smiled.

"Together."

XX. Daddy Issues

The dead don't sleep.

If Valhalla had a handout or orientation, Milo wouldn't have struggled to fall asleep in his old bed for hours. It wasn't until light dawned upon the house, fire streaming through the windows, that he realized.

Milo sat up. Nothing in his room had changed. Which sounded odd but made total sense. Time was scattered and cracked since Valhalla like he was dead for months instead of days. Barely any dust settled upon his wooden dresser. Still piled in his hamper, his clothes sat folded like he had just done laundry. He left the bed, snagged a shirt, and smelt the fabric. *Lavender.* Same detergent his mother used. He pulled the shirt on, the warmth wrapping around him like a hug.

From the shirt, slowly drifting down to the floor, was a dried-up flower. He frowned, picking it up as the petals snapped off lightly. It crumbled in his hand.

A knock. The door swung open before he moved.

"Do you people *not* drink coffee?"

Kali stood in the doorway, hands juggling boxes of *Twinings* tea and coffee cups. She marched inside without waiting, dropping her collection upon his bed with a hefty sigh. The old Valhallian uniform was gone, replaced with Natalie's old clothes. Dark, worn-out denim jeans hung long on Kali's legs, tightened around the waist with a peeling belt. Tucked in was a button-down, mainly light blue, except for the random paint splotches their washer machine never got out.

He smiled. "Those fit you nicely."

"Sorry," she said, "they were in boxes, so I just figured -"

"It's fine, really." Milo sat at the bed's corner, tossing a cup. "She was probably gonna donate them anyway. Better for them to be worn than sitting around collecting dust, you know?"

Kali nodded.

"About Silas -"

"I don't wanna talk about him," she said, "for now, it's better if we avoid that."

"Sure."

Kali moved around his room, eyes hungry and curious. Her fingertips dragged across framed photos and school books stacked neatly on his desk. She paused, snatching one up and holding it close to her nose. He pressed his lips together. He'd give anything to hear her thoughts, to know whether or not she'd hate him for eternity.

"Did you want coffee?" he asked after the drawn-out silence.

She shrugged. "Just didn't want tea."

"There's probably some hidden in the fridge. My Mom could brew an entire container of coffee grounds without realizing it.

Sometimes, I'd slip a few in random spots." He looked at his hands. "She probably found it, though. Drinks when she's nervous."

Kali dropped the framed photograph on his lap. "Who's that?"

He looked to be about thirteen in it. Raven curls wild, running amok around his chubby face. Beside him was another boy, roughly the same age, arm wrapped around Milo's shoulders. The pair were caught laughing, both wildly looking at the other. He smiled. The other boy had skin like lumber before roasting in a fire. Wide eyes hooded by bushy eyebrows creased with laughter. Braces shimmered in his mouth. He couldn't remember where he was in the picture, maybe a summer camp. Milo looked away from the picture, handing it back to Kali. It was unsettling to think about how much the boy and Silas looked alike.

"Old boyfriend."

She stared skeptically at him. "You're gay."

"I'm not anything," he replied, "I'm just me, I guess. I didn't like Andrew because he's a boy. I liked his laugh," he paused, pointing to the picture, "and his eyes. We were also kids, and he had every G.I. Joe action figure known to man."

"What happened?"

He shrugged. "What always happens. Parents paying for a Catholic school education don't like to see boys holding hands at their doorstep."

Kali placed the picture back on his bookshelf. "And Thalia?"

"What about Thalia?"

"Well, I'm guessing you don't like Thalia 'cause she's a girl."

"That obvious, huh?"

Kali remained silent, collapsing onto his desk chair before swiveling to face him. She eagerly waved for him to continue.

"I don't think I can describe it."

"Why not?"

Milo leaned back, staring at the ceiling. "When you have it, you just know." He shrugged. "That's what it's like with her. I just know."

When he met her eyes, tears streamed down her cheeks like airplanes.

"Are you okay?" he asked.

Kali flinched and blinked a few times. "Oh," she breathed, "*god*." She laughed, wiping her tears. "I didn't even realize -"

"It's okay."

"I don't think I'll ever get that," she whispered, "not again. Not after -" her words cut off.

"After what?"

"How'd you die, Milo?" she asked, avoiding his gaze.

At first, he froze, confused by the question. *Did I die?* And the moment was gone, and it all came rushing back. *Oba.* He closed his eyes. He never realized how easy it'd be to melt back into reality and shift into his old life as if nothing had ever changed. His father's ring stared back at him as he opened his eyes.

"My best friend turned into a blue-skinned giant and killed me," he said, "like any reality television show."

"Didn't think you had any friends."

"I didn't." Milo leaned forward, resting his elbows upon his knees. "And you? How'd you go?"

Kali looked at him. "I was shot. Right outside my car. And she..." her lip quivered, "...she was in the passenger seat, *watching*. He shot me. He shot me beside my car, and she saw. She saw."

"I don't understand," Milo said, "who saw?"

"Lana," she replied, "my girlfriend."

Milo frowned. "I'm so-"

Her hand shot up. "Don't say that," she snapped, "because you don't mean it. No one does, not when someone like me gets killed.

Not when someone like him pulls the trigger. 'Sorry' doesn't do anything. Prayers don't stop racism. It won't stop cops from firing their guns like they're on a battlefield. It won't get that murderer arrested. It won't give my father his daughter back. It won't make my life matter, and it won't make Black lives matter. It won't." Her eyebrows furrowed. "Obviously the man wasn't even a real cop. I should've noticed. He looked...different."

He swallowed, unsure of what to say. "I won't act like I understand," Milo said, "'cause I don't. And I doubt I ever will. But I'd like to think that, if I was there, or if it was Oba in that situation, I'd take it."

"Take what?"

"The bullet." He nodded. "I'd take the bullet."

Kali watched him. Nothing in her face changed, remaining incredibly still, staring with a slight twitch on her lips. "That's brave."

"My Mom said bravery doesn't mean not being afraid," he said, "but being aware and having the ability to push through."

She smiled. "Your mom's kinda cold. Like a stone cold."

"Sometimes, yeah, I think she can be." He laughed.

"Milo," she said, her eyes serious. She reached and grabbed his hand. Her cold fingertips ran over the dark bruises. "I don't hate you."

"But Silas -"

"Will be fine," she said. "You chose at the moment, and in the end, it saved him." She raised his hand, pressing her lips against the bruises. "I don't hate you," she repeated.

And something clicked within him. Kali became sharp in his vision, as though she was previously shrouded in darkness, and for the first time, he saw her. He forgot they were all thrown into a chaotic soup of destiny and war. They never had a choice. Silas didn't ask to be brainwashed by some vengeful-crazy god. Kali didn't ask to die in a way she feared all her life. She didn't ask to traumatize the love of her life.

He reached and enveloped her with his arms, filled with a feverish need to hold her together.

Kali chuckled against his shoulder. "Never thought I'd be hugging you."

"I've been told," he said, "I give some pretty darn good hugs."

She pulled back, smiling a wide, toothy grin before punching him in the stomach. "You should tell her, you know. If you're not a chicken."

"Huh?"

"Thalia," she whispered. Quiet rumbles came from the kitchen. "Have you told her how you feel?"

He exhaled. "Nope."

"What the hell are you waiting for?" she sighed, shaking her head. "Take my advice, Milo, and do something. Tell her how you feel, 'cause if there's anything I know, everything can be taken away in seconds." Kali stood, twirling around before snagging a coffee cup. She shook it beside her head. "I'll look in the fridge," she said, "thanks." She moved towards the door, a slight skip in her step.

Halvavlet.

Milo flinched. Loki's cool voice spread into his mind like a sickness. "Kali."

She turned around at the threshold.

"When I was with Loki in Asgard," he began, "he called you *halvavlet*. It means -"

"Halfbreed," she interjected. Her eyes were clouded. "Weird, right?" she joked nervously. "Guess being reincarnated warriors means infinite knowledge of languages."

Milo frowned. "Got any idea why he called you that?"

"I dunno," she replied. "Probably has to do with the fact the Master said I have the *capability* for magic. Probably also has to do with the fact I've never met my mom." She laughed again, leaning against the door frame. "We've been dealt some crazy cards, huh?"

He stood from the bed, walking towards her. "Like you wouldn't believe."

"Makes me wonder."

"About?"

She smiled. "I don't have a family, do I?"

Milo looked down the hall. Thalia sat at the kitchen table, using the natural light to draw runes along her forearm. An ominous glow radiated from them. Astrid paced and changed into regular-looking clothes - though it didn't fit her. The pants became capris; her legs were too long for Natalie's jeans.

"DNA doesn't make a family," he said. "None of us are the same, yet we are in every imaginable way." Milo leaned against the door, facing her. "You're my sister, and I don't need a blood test or shared last names to tell me that." He smirked. "You know, when I woke up in Valhalla, there was this Viking. Terrifying as hell. She told me the only way to survive was to find my clan. 'Bare is the back of a brotherless man.'"

Kali pushed herself off the wall. "That's probably the cheesiest thing I've ever heard," she joked. Halfway down the hall, she said, "But thank you, Milo. Really."

The pair walked towards the living room. Natalie's bedroom door was cracked open. As they passed, Milo turned, glancing to see Silas passed out on the king-sized bed. He looked tiny, buried beneath comforters and blankets, pillows displayed beneath his head. Half his face swelled into a tomato, the other side decorated with countless runes, an eerie glow radiating.

An audiobook played within the room.

" - *I was mad that I might be whole, and dying that I might have life, knowing what evil thing I was, but not knowing what good thing I was shortly to become. Into the garden, then, I retired, Alypius following my steps. For his presence was no bar to my solitude[16] -"*

The door slammed shut.

Astrid stood a foot away, her arm stretched across the door. "This way, Odinson," she commanded. Darkness clouded her almond-shaped eyes. The gaunt lines along her face made her seem pointed, sharp to the edge. "It's time we had a proper talk."

Kali shut the refrigerator door, pulling out the last container of coffee grounds. A doughnut stuck out her mouth as she began to fill the coffee machine.

"How much do you know?" Astrid shouted. Even in her Midgardian get-up, the Asgardian warrior held tightly to her long blade. It was the same length as her long legs, Nordic runes decorating the shinned silver. "How much did *he* tell you?"

"My father is Odin," Milo replied, the words sour against his lips. "Or, *was*, I guess. Odin was my father."

"How can we even be sure he's telling the truth?" Kali asked. "I mean, Milo, the son of a god? Sounds crazy to me. No offense."

Milo shrugged. "None taken."

"Not the Jesus type," Kali added.

"A madman often tells the truth," Thalia said.

"Loki is no madman," Astrid argued. "Irrational and vengeful, but never crazed. He is far too smart for that."

"Talk about daddy issues," Kali blurted.

Laughter erupted through the living room. Kali slammed her hand against the kitchen counter as she choked on giggles. Milo shook his head, chuckling under his breath as Astrid blankly stared. Thalia held her breath, staring at the ground with deep concentration.

Kali cleared her throat. "Sorry, that was inappropriate." She left the kitchen as the smell of dark roast wafted through the house. "If

---

[16] *The Confessions of St. Augustine*, "Chapter VIII, 19"

he's so smart, how do we know he's telling the truth? Just trust his word?"

Thalia scoffed. "*Never* trust the word of a god."

"Thalia -" Astrid tried to interject.

"And lucky for you, I've had my fair share of lying gods." Thalia eyed Astrid before standing from the couch and crossing the living room to Milo. She didn't hesitate to snatch his hand, gripping tightly to his index finger before quickly pricking him.

"*Hey*!"

She yanked him towards the kitchen, turning his finger so blood dropped on the counter. It fell silently, spreading into a minuscule pool. The company crowded around, watching as though they expected something spectacular to happen. Instead, it sat there, a scarlet red circle. Normal.

Milo frowned. He was *disappointed.* He swallowed, avoiding looking at his friends. *Disappointed?* He cracked his knuckles. He should've been glad and relieved. But if he was normal, what would he be? A dead boy who never amounted to anything. He watched the counter.

"Huh," Kali said first, "maybe he was lying."

Thalia tapped the table. "Wait."

Light streamed in from the window, striking the blood. Under the morning sunlight, it shone gold.

"*Shit,*" Milo breathed.

"Sorry, man," Kali said, "all families are a little messed up, right? No biggie."

"*No* biggie?" he repeated. "Loki told the entire universe I exist and that my friggin' name is on those stupid accords or whatever as the heir to some throne!"

Astrid left the counter. "The Bleeding Throne is not just *some* throne. It unifies all worlds. Whoever sits upon the Bleeding Throne rules the nine realms. They are the Guardian of Peace, guided by their Warriors of Thunder."

"Do I *look* like the Guardian of Peace to you?" He stormed out of the kitchen. "I'm a bullseye now. Loki said that everything is gonna wanna kill me - Aesir or not. And you know what? I'm pretty sure I didn't understand a *word* of what I just said." Milo raised his arms. "That's where I'm at by this point."

"Let's take it slow then, all right?" Thalia called out. "Tell me what he said. Exactly word for word, as much as you can remember."

Milo sighed, closing his eyes. "I am the son of Odin," he said. "The King went to Midgard for a long time, and..." Milo turned, looking at the photograph of his mother hanging from the wall, "and he met Natalie Bohr. They fell in love and had a baby. And for whatever reason, having that baby scared him. It scared him enough to wanna -" he stopped, touching his nose, " - cut something off from a tree, I dunno, I'm tryin' my best."

Thalia nodded. "Take your time."

"Odin went back to Asgard after I was born and was different. At least, according to Loki, he was. Both my mother and father did all these things to try and make it seem like I never really existed - it's why we were always moving." Milo crouched, rolling back to sit on the living room floor. There was an odd stain a few feet away from him that he had no urge to ask about. He looked back towards the others. "Makes sense, actually. That's why it all feels like a punch in the face. It's been *so* obvious. Everythin' right under my nose." He scratched his chin. "Odin changed the accords or laws or whatever, making *me* the heir to the throne instead of Thor. I still can't wrap my mind around why he'd do that. Why go through so much to make sure no one could find me, just to put me on a massive pedestal years later? What was the point?"

Silence responded.

"Anyways," Milo muttered, "he gave me this ring. Said it was my heirloom." He pulled it off and tossed it to Thalia. "And with it came my destiny."

Astrid inspected the ring over Thalia's shoulder. "Well, Loki wasn't lying on that part. This ring was definitely within Asgard's treasury. Thor and Baldur have similar ones." She eyed Milo. "Loki is a god, not a declarer of fate. How could he know your destiny?"

Milo shrugged. "Said it came from the Norn. He's just the messenger."

Thalia threw the the ring back. "You remember it?"

He nodded. "Find the spear, reclaim the throne, and save Asgard."

"Spear?" Kali repeated, steaming coffee in her hands.

"The Gungnir," Astrid whispered. "By Ymir."

"What is it?"

She looked at Milo. "It must be why they want you," she said. Why Sigyn sent Loki."

"Who the hell is Sigyn?"

"An exiled Aesir," she replied, "a powerful sorceress, once the Queen of her settlement. She led the invasion of Asgard and sits on the Bleeding Throne." She paced through the kitchen. "The Gungnir is a spear, arguably the most powerful weapon in all the nine realms. It was forged *specifically* for Odin after he took the throne, and his death led to its disappearance. No one knows its location."

"But I'm supposed to find it."

"Hate to bump in," Kali grumbled from the kitchen, "but what will we do about Loki? It sounds like he's the bad guy, and we're just gonna do what he wants."

"I say we kill him." Thalia shrugged.

Heated stares pointed back at her.

"What?" she snapped. "Oh, don't look at me like that. It solves the problem."

"We draw the line there," Milo said.

"What do you mean?"

"Taking a life isn't something I signed up for or any of us," he said while standing up, "we have to keep ourselves, you know? What'll we be if it's *that* easy to kill? What does that make us? I'm not a Viking or a god. You and Astrid have lived your lives killing, and that's fine, but we never have. And I'm not about to start."

Thalia silently watched. As though she didn't mean to, a smile twitched to life across her lips.

"Death is necessary," Astrid said. "All things eventually perish, and by the aging of the ash tree, the beyond might one day take us all. Do not be afraid of it."

"I'm not afraid. Hell, I'm *already* dead. But you know what's still intact? My soul. There is no argument you can give me that'll change my mind," he argued. "Killing a stranger is no different than killing your best friend. Why? Because that stranger was somebody else's friend. Somebody else's brother or sister, mother or father. What gives me the right to inflict so much grief when the same can happen to me at the drop of a dime?"

"And if the death of one saved many?"

He frowned. "This isn't the *Enterprise,* Spock."

Astrid kept her mouth shut.

"Justice means to be good without restrictions," Milo said, "your enemies become your friends. It's -"

"Plato," Thalia interjected.

Milo spoke at the same time: "Socrates."

She scoffed. "Plato wrote *The Republic.*"

"But Socrates is the mouthpiece."

"How about we agree to disagree, all right?" Kali called out. "I'm with Milo. No killing. It's not who we are."

Astrid sighed. "You can't save everyone." Her midnight eyes dropped on Milo. "Those who deserve the end shall receive it," she turned, looking towards the sword resting against the couch, "by the grace of my blade."

"Doesn't mean I can't try," Milo replied. "Why's Loki so pissed, anyways? Earlier, you called him vengeful."

"That's beside the point." She turned towards Kali. "Valhallian, you and your companions mentioned the importance of finding the key. Has that become any more clear for you?"

"No," Kali replied, "as far as we know, it's still back in that alleyway."

"And you're *sure* you need it to find Thor?"

Kali hesitated, glancing at Milo. Then she nodded. "I'm positive."

"Once the dead one is fully recovered," Astrid explained, "we return there and search for it. We don't leave till it's found."

Milo chuckled. "Who died and made you King?" he paused, tilting his head. "I guess *we* did..." he shook his head, "never mind. How about we take a step back, and you go back to telling us why Loki is doin' all this in the first place?"

"What makes you think I know?"

He shrugged. "Let's call it intuition."

"He's right," Thalia said, "you have a history with him."

Astrid flipped towards her. "And you, berserker? Your lies, cover-ups, and masks are growing *thin*. You think me blind, but you are ignorant. Dead ones you can easily fool. I am a different story." She shook her head before storming towards the front door. As she ripped it open, she turned, calling over her shoulder, "I can see through you like glass, Thalia. The next time you wish to pin your own discrepancies on someone, I'd look into a mirror."

And with that, the warrior left the Bohr house.

"Well," Kali said, "that went well."

Milo sighed.

Like she wouldn't believe.

XXI. The Land of Memories

Out of all things in Asgard, Astrid missed her sister the most. Standing there, lit by the morning Midgard sun, her mind only conjured the little Frey. She wore hoods colored a deep ambrosia like a religious symbol. And Frey's amulet, the Vanir god their mother so carelessly named after her, always hanging low at her neck, twisting with messy curls. Even as the other children teased and joked about an Asgardian named after a Vanir, Frey held onto her name like it guaranteed her life. After so long of pushing the young spirit out of Astrid's mind, forcing herself to move on within days, everything came rushing back like it never left. She stepped forward like a drunk, grasping mindlessly at the porch rails. She bent over at the stomach.

Loki.

It always led back to the god. If he hadn't brought those memories out from the shadows like he did, she wouldn't be where she was now: trying to claw her way out of the cage her mind built.

She pictured it as clear as day: a shimmering lake flowing at the valley's base, connected to a river that streamed between mountains and coaxed life through the kingdom. Riding upon their horses, the sisters regularly traveled across the lake, resting them at a wooden port near the eastern bank. They ran along the stream, the water carrying laughter and wisps of hair. Astrid chased her sister, watching as the girl extended her arms like a canary and flew. And even though their blood rendered them mundane, with no magic or purity trailing through their veins, they were goddesses.

Astrid gripped the porch rail.

Frey's voice echoed in her ears: *help me!*

Something cracked beneath her hands.

The Bohr household door creaked open from behind her. Astrid's hands clenched into fists, digging into the wooden railing and ripping it off. She flailed around, pointing the yellow wood towards her onlooker.

"I built that railing," the boy said, "I was real proud of it."

The wood dropped as she looked away. Facing Milo hurt more than she thought it would. His eyes, the color of storm clouds and lightning, were like his brother's, filled with an outrageous intensity. Even the curls lining the sharp lines in his statue-like face looked too much like his father. *How had she not recognized it?* She slowly exhaled, calming her beating heart. And with a new cautiousness, she swiveled around to see Milo Odinson. He still looked like a boy in many ways. It shook her to imagine him young: nineteen years in Midgard was a blink in Asgard. She lived through her traumas before he even spoke his first word.

"I apologize," she said. "Sometimes...there are days where the anger is stronger than my ability for composure." Astrid touched the broken railing. "It's a lovely porch."

He nodded, approaching slowly. "Wanna talk about it?"

"My rage or composure?"

"Both are *slightly* concerning."

Astrid kept her eyes lowered. "Is there something you need, Odinson?"

"No," he replied. "Thought you could use someone to talk to."

She swallowed. "There is nothing I need, Odinson."

The Prince remained silent for a few moments. He moved slowly, inching closer to her. Something about how he walked, leaning down in a hunched posture, chin jutted forward and right eyebrow permanently arched reminded her of a forgotten dream, a being lost to her reality. She held her breath and lifted her head by a hair to see him watching like an attentive creature, a ghost of someone she knew.

Her breath caught.

Thor.

As quickly as she looked, Astrid yanked away, crossing her arms behind her back.

"Can I ask you something?"

She nodded.

"Why can't you look at me?"

Astrid hesitated. "I don't know what you mean."

"Sure," he said, "then look at me."

She licked her lips and tilted her head. Fear sent chills down her back. She raised her chin into the air, shaking her head. "I spent years as a Royal Guard, Odinson. Aesir royalty is not to be looked upon by me," she explained, "we are not on the same, as you say, level."

"You're kidding, right?"

Astrid remained silent.

"I'm not Aesir royalty, Astrid. Doesn't being an actual bastard make me like, dirt or somethin'?"

She raised her eyes and looked at him. She sighed. *He is not Thor.* "You are the Prince of Asgard," she whispered. "Having your mother's blood makes you better than the other Aesir." She looked over her shoulder. "But if you *ever* tell anyone I said that, I'll slit your throat."

Odinson laughed.

"I'm serious."

"Oh," he said, eyes narrowing, "right, sure. You'll slit my throat." He shrugged. "I've had worse." The Prince chuckled, leaning against the wall beside the front door. His eyes hung onto Astrid. "Thalia wasn't trying to start anything with you."

"She lies as easily as the sun rises," Astrid sneered. Rundi had claimed Thalia to be her solution to recovering the lost Prince, and yet Astrid felt more behind and confused in her journey than before.

"Maybe," Odinson said, "but we all have secrets. You told her to look in the mirror, but you've got your fair share of lies, don't you? And I don't care, honestly. I've seen you with a sword, and I'd much rather have you on my side, even with all your secrets."

"Your point?"

Odinson's eyes grew serious. "Stop attacking my people. I think a part of me is beginning to put you in that category, but I swear, if you keep pulling that shit, I'll throw you out here."

She raised her eyebrows. "You'll," she paused, "*throw* me out of here?"

He frowned. "I-I mean," he laughed nervously, "well, you know-"

Astrid laughed. "I can't believe I never noticed."

"Noticed what?"

"How much you look like him," she whispered, "Havi."

The Prince nodded, suddenly more glum than before. He rested his head against the wall. "Can you tell me about them?"

"Your family?"

"I don't think that's what I'd call them."

She frowned. "The Aesir are your brethren, Odinson. In times of need, your soul will call out to them, praying for help. And if you shout loud enough, they might just answer."

"I never really believed in praying," he said. "I mean, I *have* prayed, but to God. Like, *the* God." He chewed on his lips. "My Mom never really talked about him. But she painted him and things he liked. It was the only way I got to know him."

Astrid nodded, crouching down till she sat cross-legged on the porch. "I am not the one to tell you of Havi," she began, "he was my King, nothing more, nothing less. What I know is the same as any Asgardian."

"How about Thor? You liked him, right?"

Heat rushed across her cheeks. "The lost Prince held the attention of many."

"And?"

"He is betrothed. The engagement was arranged to forge peace between the rival clans, a first step towards ending the war." Her throat grew eerily dry. "He disappeared before the wedding took place."

Odinson sat down across from her. "Hold up," he said with a growing grin, "were you dating my brother?"

"*Dating?*"

"Yeah, like, you know," he paused, "dating. Like holding hands, constant PDA type of deal." He smirked. "He was a stud, right?" He laughed.

Astrid blinked. "None of that made sense."

"Yeah," he drawled, "Midgard's kinda lousy compared to Asgard, huh?"

"I wouldn't say that. All realms have beauties, treasures," she smiled, "and faults. From my perspective, Asgard is heavenly, but it is my home. You might never feel that comfort unless you are here." She crossed her legs beneath her, straightening her spine as she took a deep breath. "Enlighten me, Odinson: what is 'PDA'?"

He laughed again. "It means 'public display of affection.'"

"Then, no," she replied, "whatever I did with Thor could never be in public. It would've tainted his name if the realm knew of our relationship."

"How'd you guys meet?"

She closed her eyes. "My father was a merchant, so he traveled across the realm often," she said. Her eyes reopened. The boy watched intensely. She conjured a lie. "Behind, he left a farm, where my mother and sister tended. I could not join them. My soul called out for something more. But when I approached my father about it, he expelled me from the farm and forced me onto the streets." It seemed likely, and judging by his face, the boy believed. How could she admit that his father destroyed her village and forced her upon Asgard's streets till she eventually joined his militant ranks? She found no harm in lying, for Milo's sake. "I roamed the kingdom, starving, till he found me."

"Thor."

"The Prince was the first person who saw me as me and not someone vulnerable enough to be walked on," she said. "He knew my past but chose to ignore it. Through him, I began to train in the Royal Guard, and eventually, I went home with my head held high." Astrid paused, staring down at her hands. "But he was never easy. Thor was something solid to lean against, violent and fierce and unmoving. Nothing more."

Odinson nodded. "And you love him."

She hesitated, glancing at the sky. "I feel the closest thing to love with him," she said, "that is all I am capable of."

"He's powerful," he muttered, "a god."

"Yes, the lost Prince is stronger than most may believe."

Milo clutched his legs closer as though he'd swallow himself whole. His eyes raised, and darkness was cast upon them. "But killable."

"Everything is killable."

"My father included?"

She sighed. "Odin was almighty."

"But he's dead," Odinson interjected, "wouldn't take something as almighty as Odin to be vulnerable, you know?"

"All things eventually end, Odinson, god or not. One day, it'll all just stop."

He shook his head. "Is it bad I find that strangely appealing right about now?"

"No," she said, "it means you're human. Having golden blood doesn't change anything about you, Odinson. Gods die the same as I will - as you already have. Worlds collapse. Beginnings become ends. Be glad you are of two worlds: living a life where you know it'll one day end is more humane than never knowing when the needle stops."

"I don't understand."

"Gods do not live according to the Norn's string. Their souls are tied to the cosmos, life forces united with the ash tree, Yggdrasil. When a god perishes, so much life dies with them. A god's death means the death of a world. You are lucky to never have to face such responsibility."

"So what died with Odin?"

"Asgard. The realm I once loved no longer has its soul. But I believe a child of Odin could bring it back."

Odinson scoffed. "Sounds like impossible hope to me."

"Maybe," she said, "I'd call it faith."

He fell onto his back without another word.

Pain struck her heart. A boy, practically still a child, torn between separate worlds without any true knowledge about his homeland. He based it on myths, paintings strung upon his walls, and books stacked in the bedroom. He knew nothing of the true Asgard. She grinned, reaching forward to grab onto his foot. He flinched.

"Wanna let go of my foot, Astrid?"

"Sit up, Odinson."

"Excuse me?"

Astrid's grin widened. "Sit tall like the Prince you are, and let me show you your home."

He narrowed his eyes, but sat up, twisting long legs beneath him. "I doubt now's the time to take a field trip to Asgard."

"We are not leaving the porch." She placed her hands on her knees, palms up. Slowly and methodically she breathed, relaxing the nerves within her muscles. "Long ago," she started, closing her eyes, "the gods spread the possibility of basic magic throughout all nine realms. All it took was a prayer, a quiet homage to your god, to receive a gift of your choosing."

Odinson watched skeptically.

"When I was in the Royal Guard, an old friend taught me how to share memories with another."

"Who's the friend?"

"Just an old friend," she repeated. *It would be unwise to say it was Loki,* she thought. She smiled. "What matters is that I can show you Asgard if it is what you wish."

He hesitated. Something held him back, information he had failed to share with the company. She didn't blame him. Lies to her were so common they were feathers against her chest. Whatever it was, he pushed it aside and met Astrid with cloudy gray eyes. "All right," he said, "I'm in."

Astrid grinned. "Replicate my stance, Odinson."

Slowly he moved his legs, and dramatically slapped his hands on his knees.

"Clear your mind."

"Wait a hot second," he interjected, "is this like those eight-hour 'dream reality' slash 'lucid dreaming' slash binaural beat videos? 'Cause I gotta say, I did those reality checks and listened to those videos but not *once* was I able to lucid dream." He tilted his head. "Well, one time I *did* make myself fly, but -"

Astrid slapped him.

"*Hey!*"

"By the ash tree, if you don't clear your mind, I swear I'll clear it for you."

Odinson rubbed his cheek but grew serious. Slowly he closed his eyes, one remaining open as Astrid closed her own. Eventually, his breathing grew heavy and long, deep within his chest.

Astrid opened her eyes.

Another Prince.

Curls-colored twilight hung around his face: sharp lines down his cheeks, pointed jaw, and jutted chin. As the morning light displayed itself around him like a halo, Odinson appeared more real than his siblings. Real and fragmented. While the eldest, Baldur, was known for his charismatic tongue, and Thor for his undeniably chaotic and rageful power, the last-born son before her held something different. Something no other Aesir contained. A scar, barely longer than her pinky, sat above his right eye, cutting into the brow. A front tooth was chipped. There was a permanent line across his nose, probably from where his glasses used to sit. Freckles decorated his chin and nose like chocolate chips, forming beautiful constellations along his tanned skin. Midgardian flaws scattered across him as though he was splashed with rain water, the leftovers leaving behind humanity.

That's it. Humanity. He holds humanity.

Astrid raised her hand, fingertips a hair away from his cheek.

He fidgeted, and she recoiled just as quickly.

No, she thought. *It's about Thor.* She closed her eyes and assumed the meditative position, but it felt almost impossible to clear her jumbled mind. *I swore an oath to the Aesir. Not to a group of Valhallians.* Astrid steadied herself.

"Hold onto my voice, Odinson," she whispered.

Behind her eyelids, images and colors splashed within the darkness. Patterns grew, splotched and sporadic, forming into memories and dreams. They filtered away as she searched, flipping through every detail till they stopped at her home. Slowly the pictures formed into worlds, spreading till dew and firewood entered her nostrils. Water splashed against her face. Grass, sharp and pungent, tickled her fingertips, dancing peacefully through the wind.

The Prince gasped. The images flickered.

"Remain steady," she muttered.

His breathing picked up.

"Odinson," Astrid called, "calm yourself." The memory sharpened. "Leave your body here, in Midgard, and let your mind travel. Follow me."

He evened himself, stretching across the place till his soul reached her mind. Together, they evaporated and exited their current time until they reached years before, stepping into Astrid's solitary mind.

She opened her eyes.

I'm home.

A wide village sat at a valley's base, a flowing river slicing through, beneath mossy bridges and cottages. Trees as tall as Asgard's castle walls marked the town's edges, their leaves falling like afternoon snow during the crawling fall. Townspeople marched past with bashful smiles and determined stares - harvest time approached. Farms were scattered across the village, each decorated with a wooden shed and a small house. Children rushed by, playing in the bright grass and picking violet flowers. Even Fae, Vanir folk discredited enough to be shunned from the realm, walked freely through the village, hoods down to show their peculiarly beautiful pinched faces, colored different blues and purples, Vanir marks drawn precisely along their muscles.

To define *perfect* would be to just look upon the village of Herjan. A land of peace, housing their own scars and war, reborn into harmony and gentleness. And there the pair stood, Astrid and Odinson, basking in the dozen suns above them without a care.

Astrid's arms extended. "*Home.*"

"This is crazy," the Prince drawled. He bent down, digging his hands through the earth and raising the soil to his nose. After taking in a deep breath, he laughed gleefully. His terrifyingly sharp gray eyes looked upon Astrid with an innocence she never expected. "Is this real?"

"It was," she replied. "This is only a memory. We stand within what I can remember."

He stood back up. "You're from here?"

"My family has lived in Herjan long before me," she said. Taking a few steps to the left, she raised her hand, pointing towards a gap within the trees. As the mountains rose, creating a deep valley in the middle, Asgard's golden castle spire reached into the sky, slicing through the air. Just between the trees could it be seen from Herjan. "There stands Asgard."

Odinson moved to see it. "Seeing it from a distance makes it feel not real, you know?"

She nodded. "I only traveled after..." her words trailed off. *After.* Something scuttled through the shadows behind bushes and ferns in her vision. She glanced over and saw nothing but children playing. "Herjan was all I knew."

"Does that mean something?" he asked. "Herjan."

"The Aesir named it Herjan, for you, it may mean 'warrior' or 'Leader of Hosts.' There was an ancient battle that took place on these lands. Centuries ago, the Jotunn threatened to invade the castle, but because of the mountains, the only way to it was through here. At the valley's base where the mountains meet. The Jotunn would follow the river," she paused, pointing to the water passing quietly into the town, "and eventually reach the castle. The people who inhabited this land were only farmers and merchants, maybe a few mercenaries passing through. Yet it was those untrained peasants who defeated the invading Jotunn, protecting their homeland."

Odinson nodded. "Badass."

She smiled. The shadow passed by her vision again.

"Is your family still here?" he asked.

She no longer heard him. Astrid stared at the silhouette. Bushes rustled as the wind rushed. A soft laugh, barely audible, carried along the breeze. It sounded oddly familiar. Astrid stepped closer.

"Are you guys, like, medieval or whatever?" the Prince continued on, oblivious to her attention being pulled elsewhere, "this looks straight outta *Lord of the Rings* if I'm being honest. No Hobbits, though. Do you guys have Tolkien? Bet it'd be cool as hell to read a book from here. Do you guys have books? Or is that a dumb question? Am I being stupid?"

Astrid stopped listening. Something hid behind a bush, laughing and giggling with a familiarity that chilled her to the bone. Quietly she approached, hand gravitating over her belt even though no weapon lay there. She reached, grabbed the bush, and lunged.

"Did I miss something?" Odinson called out.

Nothing. Astrid sighed. "Just my imagination," she said. "It's -"

A girl, no taller than five feet, ran behind a nearby cottage. Golden hair flew behind her, stretching into the air as she disappeared. Astrid choked, stepping quickly towards the passing blur.

Frey.

And she was running.

"*Astrid!*" the Prince shouted, his footsteps echoing behind her.

Quickly she ran to the cottage, sliding around the corner, expecting to see her sister waiting.

The memory changed.

Herjan was lit aflame by raging aqua-colored fire, swallowing the village in a single sweep. The fire spread silently, crackling on roofs and trees, jumping roof to roof, catching on the dry grass, and falling upon the villagers like rain. A young boy, not much older than Odinson, sprinted toward the stream, his back ablaze with Asgard's fire. Farmers ran from their land, sprinting towards the sacred water. Beyond the chaos, towards the opening in the trees where Asgard lay silently in the distance, clobbering horses approached, a menacing leader at their helm.

"*No,*" Astrid whispered.

A clammy hand grabbed her.

"Take us back," Odinson pleaded, "please, Astrid, take us -"

But she remembered. Like the back of her hand, she knew how it played out. There the steadfast enemy approached, the one man she cherished more than her own father. One who she believed provided Sol's light, who fueled their boats and strengthened their crops. A King in power for centuries, a King who had always been King. The Wayfinder, overthrower and Raven God, Evenhigh and Long Beard, protector, and hawk, God of riders and Mover of Constellations, Mankind's Father.

Come to destroy.

The memory was clear. She'd get on her horse, ride towards the King, and hold her sword high, screaming a battle cry with burning tears striking her cheeks like arrows. But the rest was an old story. She was defeated within a second.

Something heavy fell into her hand. A steel blade, glowing dangerously in the blue firelight, sat delicately within her clenched fist. Everything focused. Astrid raised her eyes, staring at the swarming horses quickly approaching. It could be different.

"I can change it," she breathed, "this time, I can save her. I can -"

Odinson blocked her vision. "Astrid," he shouted over the roaring chaos, "it's a memory! It's just a memory!"

She slammed the sword's hilt into his side with enough force to send him skidding into the lake. He landed in the water with a splash. In the distance, lit up by the blue flames, was the King, jumping from his eight-legged steed, Sleipnir, brandishing the ebony spear, Gungnir. From his empty hand, he dropped a frail, short body, obviously lifeless. Astrid stepped closer.

"*No!*" she screamed.

The young Frey, golden braids inked scarlet with fresh blood, laid slumped against the ground, eyes rolled back to show milky whites, blood stretched across her thin neck. Her translucent skin looked empty from afar, the blood drained to paint the grass a shade of war and death. The little girl's lips parted as though a final word escaped her in death's embrace, a final plea towards her assailant. The word echoed in her ears: *Astrid.*

She gripped onto her sword. "Frey!"

Odinson shouted from the lake: "Astrid, don't!"

But she was already running towards her King with the sword extended beside her. Euphoria and adrenaline elated her, springing her toward the battle. The King watched silently, taking long strides forward. Odin lunged with the spear, stabbing it through the air. Astrid dropped to her knees, sliding across the ground before slashing the sword's edge across his legs.

She jumped to her feet from behind him, dipping her blade beneath his midnight-colored armor, striking his back. A guttural shout came from the King as he slipped away, snapping the Gungnir back to slash her across the face. Astrid fell as a searing pain ripped through her body, originating from the sharp cut along her cheek and vibrating down till she rumbled with tortuous agony.

Gungnir.

The ebony spear's power was unimaginable - a single prick could take over a body with soaring pain. It was forged in lava pits, studded with spells and enchantments, twisted together by the divine. No mortal being survived its strike. Suddenly she was paralyzed, limbs snapping against the ground, neck pressed against her collar. No matter how much she willed herself to move, nothing happened.

Odin leaned over her, dropping close enough so she could see the stabbing gray and blue lightning in his narrow eyes, raven curls streaked with silver. Heat sprayed across her face. The fabled scar dragged through his eye, leaving behind a blind emptiness. His lip curled into a sneer as he watched her struggle.

All she wanted was to look away.

Please.

Reunite me with her.

The King raised his spear, aiming its sharp end at her neck. He spoke: "Long live -"

Golden blood trickled from his lips. It dripped onto her face, sliding down her temple like a tear. The paralysis wore off as her breathing spiked, a shaking hand raising to swipe the blood away. It reeked with honey, a heavy smell pungent with magic. It ripped the air from her throat. She looked down. A blade pierced through the King's chest from behind. Before the King collapsed upon her, he was shoved away, slamming against the ground beside her with a loud thud. Even in death, the god stared through Astrid as though she was translucent.

Strong hands grasped onto her biceps, yanking her upright.

"Are you crazy?" he shouted.

Her eyes were glued to Frey's body.

"Astrid," he snapped, "look at me."

She turned.

Odinson, tall and lean, held onto her. His glare softened, growing sympathetic. "It's not real," he whispered. "It's *not* real."

Astrid's shaking finger pressed hard into her palm. Her finger shot right through her hand. She breathed a sigh. "We're dreaming."

He nodded.

"She's already dead."

The Prince turned, looking towards the little girl. "Your sister."

The world around them grew dim. Astrid closed her eyes. The Land of Memories faded, slipping back into the darkest shadows, never to be touched again. She lost track of the Prince's hands as their souls journeyed back to their bodies, back to the warm morning in Midgard.

Astrid opened her eyes.

Bright light stabbed into her immediately. The birds' pleasant song overhead grew cold and empty in her ears. Odinson's silhouette stood stark and bold across from her, eyes wide and piercing as he stared. The anger was obvious before he even spoke.

"Was that a memory?"

"Yes," she replied, "at first, it was just a recollection, but somewhere...illusion blended with reality, and it became -"

"A nightmare. I thought you said Herjan was peaceful."

"Everything is once peaceful, as well as horrific. What you saw was Herjan's end and Valfodr's beginning. Now it stands as a cemetery. And for that, I am sorry." Astrid held her hands together, avoiding his gaze. "My mind was pulled away, and I lacked the restraint to hold onto it."

"My father...he did that? Destroyed your home? Killed *all* those people?"

"Havi the Wise One enacted his assault based on the Norn's warning. Rumors of rebellion gathering in my village brought the Aesir down upon it with a deadly hand. It is the hard choices of the Aesir that hurt the most, but are the ones we need."

Odinson's eyes grew wide. "You still love them."

"I don't *love* the Aesir." She felt the same as when she lied. "I respect them, I am beneath them. My duty is to serve the throne -"

"Oh, stop spoon-feeding me the regurgitation of what those assholes told you!" he shouted. A bright red spot, like a strawberry, formed above his nose, between his eyebrows as he became angry.

"Odinson -"

"My name is Milo. Milo Bohr. Not Prince, not Odinson - *Milo.* I am not your boss, I am not your royalty. I don't want your respect just 'cause my blood looks the same as theirs. That's somethin' you earn, and from what I've seen, none of them have!"

She remained silent.

"Odin killed your family."

"He had right to believe -"

"Your sister." He was calm despite it all. If it was Thor, she would've already been dead.

"Stop."

"Your mother, father. Every single person you ever knew in your life was slaughtered, and yet you still defend them."

"*Stop it.*"

"Because of some supposed rumors?" he asked. "That's not justice. That's not a King I'd want! And all those other Aesir just followed blindly behind him, and for what? 'Cause he happened to be 'bigger' than them? Stronger? More dangerous? You love them. Even now, after all of it, you'd give your life for him. For Thor -"

"By the ash tree," Astrid snapped, eyes stinging, "if you say another word, I'll -"

"You won't do anything. You won't." He shrugged. "Not because you like me, or because I wouldn't deserve it, but because I'm *his* son; I'm *his* brother."

Astrid looked away.

"Honestly, Astrid," he sounded tired, "I'm just sorry for you. I can't imagine loving and hating someone at the same time. Tearing yourself in half to appease everyone but yourself." Quickly his hand shot out to grab onto her own. "But I'm not my father. You're not my shield, and I don't expect you to take a bullet for me - er, sword, or whatever. I'd like to think you're my friend, and friends don't use each other."

And then, Astrid did the only thing that seemed correct for the situation.

She hugged Milo Bohr.

Without hesitation the Valhallian extended his arms around her, enveloping her within a warm furnace at his chest. *Odd,* she wondered, *nothing beats within him.* Indeed there was an emptiness as her ear pressed against him, almost instinctively searching for the heartbeat matching her own. Even as the illogical and naive mind might expect him to be cold and dead, Milo remained the opposite. His heart was too big. His empathy is too strong. And somehow, divinity lay within him. Eternity's staleness, space's darkness, lay somewhere deep within him that she could not find. The warmth he held was overwhelming, selfless, and immutable. She closed her eyes, and scattered images of Yggdrasil played like flashing photographs.

Even in death, the boy was alive.

"Aye," a cold voice said from the doorway, "this is cozy."

Milo retracted, looking over his shoulder to see the berserker. "What're you -" he started.

The berserker barely waited for him to finish. She stepped by, marching down the driveway with her hand firmly grasped on her wielding axes. "I'm walking the perimeter," she said.

Astrid watched silently as Milo's intense stare followed the berserker. His lip quivered when he turned back to her.

"Friends?" he asked.

She smiled. "Follow her."

"What?"

"People like us," she said, hearing the young Kali's words replay in her mind, "cannot sit on the sidelines when life carries on before us. Follow her, and stop holding back."

He grinned. "How do you know about sidelines?"

"Asgard isn't as *medieval* as you think."

Milo chuckled, looking at her one more time before leaping to his feet, and jogging down the driveway. She remained sitting, folding her hands as her heartbeat settled. The Land of Memories drifted back to where it belonged, leaving her soul back within her to heal. She breathed in deeply and exhaled slowly.

Footsteps clobbered back up the stairs.

Milo pressed a quick kiss to her forehead. "Thank you."

And the Son of Humanity was gone.

Astrid smiled and felt like the sun.

XXII. The Valkyrie

Milo wasn't sure whether or not his hands would stop shaking.

A heavy burden lingered upon his chest. Something latched onto him while he was in the memory of Asgard, attaching itself to his very being till he returned to reality. And whatever it was remained, hanging over him like a storm cloud, threatening to dump an eternity of rain on him. But his hands, thin and agile, shook with an earth-rendering force. The tremors spread till his teeth chattered.

A few feet ahead marched Thalia. Her steps were harsh against the pavement. Still, her grip fastened on her ax like danger would always be around the corner. Every once in a while, her head turned, her chin barely leaning across her shoulder. The glint in her eyes, though, could be seen from even Milo's perspective: a burning bronze.

Follow her.

He scoffed. *Why did I listen to her?* The embarrassment rode up his throat like acid. And yet, she was right there, radiating this electrifying sunlit energy. It hurt to look at her. He shook his hands. The tremors moved to his legs.

"You like the *kriger*," Thalia spoke smoothly.

Milo swallowed. "'Course," he said, "she's nice."

"Nice?"

"Somethin' wrong with nice?"

Thalia shot him a look, remaining quiet.

He jogged to catch up, spinning till he walked backward to face her. "Astrid did this thing to show me her village," he explained. "I dunno, some prayer or somethin'. It didn't turn out like I thought, but I *saw* him." He faltered, tripping over his feet. "Technically, I stabbed him."

"What?"

"She showed me my father," he said. "But it became a nightmare, and I had to stop him. But it wasn't real." He shrugged, turning back around. "It wasn't real."

Thalia sighed. "If it was an illusion, why are you still discussing it?"

"I was just talking."

"There are bigger things to worry about."

Milo stopped. She bumped into him, burns spreading down his back. His hands clenched into tight fists. He worked his jaw, turning his head away.

"What's the matter with you?"

Rage. That's what it was. The panting in his chest, the adrenaline pumping through him, it was all enough to put him on edge. He stepped away. She barely spoke, barely threw the attitude towards him, but he was ready to rip his hair out, rad un till the end, which eventually always came, and his feet bled. He kept moving backward, putting as much space between them as possible. The further he got, the stronger the tremors became, the more he wanted to scream and cry and *explode*.

Thalia sighed again. "*Fine,* Valhallian, don't tell me." She walked past him, those bronze eyes looking everywhere but him.

I ache for you, he wanted to yell. He wanted to grab, hold, and tell her everything he thought about the moment she stepped into his life. *You saved me.* With his bruised, bloody knuckles, she held him. He no longer recognized himself, but she was there. The night at the bar, the end to an uneventful and practically disastrous day, spun around to become a night he'd relive for the rest of time. And he knew, just by looking at her then and there, he'd die all over again to replay it. To immediately tell her: *I think you are the most perfect person to have ever existed.* He'd die every time to do it all over.

"I get it, Thalia," he said, surprising himself.

She paused.

"I really do," Milo continued, stepping cautiously towards her, "you don't care. I'm used to it. Well, I'm quite the negotiator, so here's your 'get out of jail free' card. You wanna take a backseat and not get involved? This is the chance." He licked his lips. "But you know what? I'm selfish. I'm selfish, and all I can think about is *you.* I don't want a crown, a throne, any piece of that kingdom. I want, *damn it,* I want -" If he could breathe, he would've stopped at that moment. He looked away sharply.

"Milo."

It came swiftly and all at once, the unmistakable fear swelling in his throat, jolting him into sudden awareness. Something between a scream and a cry lodged in his heart, trapping his words and thoughts into a little box. But it softened, and his skin was like honey dripping to the earth. Nothing was familiar about it, but it took over him as though it had always been around. It was everything and nothing.

Milo looked at her. "I want *you.*"

She exhaled. Her face burnt a deep red, and lips pressed together so hard they went white.

"And you," he said, "what do you want?"

It angered her. He saw it painted on her skin. A feverish stare, wildness trapped in her hair. She bit her nails, and when her eyes landed upon him, there was nothing but ice. "I want you to tell me a lie," she said.

He laughed. "What?"

"Aren't you tired of being tired? I want to be loved in the dark and my name forgotten in the morning." Thalia was not close to him, yet he thought he could feel her breath along his neck, her hands trailing down his arms. "I'm not good. I'm not a doll. I'm not made of glass - I am of jade, I am of stone, I am of diamonds. Break my heart or let me break yours."

He watched her.

"I am sick to death of nearly almost. Just-about. Hands away from each other." She held her face as though she wanted to scream, arms like lumber and eyes suddenly beads of coal. "I am greedy and hungry for real." Her gaze landed upon him, and the world fell away. "Give me everything. Give me your soul, and I am yours. Give me your heart, and I am yours. A thousand times over, and I am yours."

Only the way she looked up at him as her fingers intertwined with his was loud enough to speak the words he couldn't.

Thalia took another step. Her forehead rested against his collar. He didn't have to look at her. Milo already knew how she moved or how the wind pushed the curls out from her gaze. Her figure stood beside him like a key, and he realized she was always meant to stand there. Whether in death or life, their souls intertwined as they entered a new beginning throughout their days of everlasting eternity.

He squeezed her hand. *Together.*

"Milo," she said, her voice muffled by his shirt.

He smiled and felt like the sun.

Suddenly, with an unimaginable force, Thalia shoved Milo away, brandishing her double axes. She stared into the trees, where the sunlight did not reach. A rustling came from the branches, twigs snapping and leaves crunching as something approached.

"Behind me," Thalia commanded.

Quickly he moved, reaching for his belt but finding nothing. He pressed his lips together, about to implore Thalia for an ax when he was immediately interrupted.

"Lovely moment, berserker," a female voice said.

Another laughed. "Didn't take *you* for a *kjaereste*[17]."

Lover. He bit back his grin. It was not the time for that.

"Then again," another voice added, "you've always surprised us."

Thalia grunted angrily. "Come out of the shadows!"

The voices melted together in a cohesive laugh.

Out from the woods came three brilliantly shimmering figures. Three women, all dressed in sterling silver armor, their legs drenched in scarlet blood. Each held a spear, the end sharpened to a triangular point. The sun sparkled dangerously against them, the glare striking across the pavement. Mio heard Kali's voice: *Valkyrie,* she once said, *the women of Valhalla.*

Relief washed over him. "They're just Valkyrie."

"Stay behind me," she hissed, barely audible.

The woman in the middle, Nordic braids twisted within her red locks, left the pair behind her, approaching Thalia with a wide grin. She reached at least seven feet, towering over them with her weapon close to her side. Raven tattoos decorated her neck. She tilted her head. "Thought the Master was lying when he said you had become a

---

[17] Lover

guardian," she said. "The lads and I made pretty hefty bets against you."

Thalia did not lower her guard. "Why're you here, Sigrdrífa? There are no battlefields for you to purge."

"But there will be."

"Leave now," Thalia said, "and I won't be forced to remove you."

Sigrdrífa laughed bitterly. She looked over her shoulder at her companions, snickering. "Kill *me*, berserker?" she laughed again, more boisterous as she raised her spear, pointing its end towards Thalia's exposed neck. "*Dum bjorn*[18]," she spat, "I am Victory, Wisdom, and Power. I forge heroes of legends, berserker! And what are you, but a...how is it that the Midgardians put it?" She glared at Milo. "*Babysitter*." Her accent changed the word to '*bibesattir.*'

And without hesitation, Milo laughed. Quickly, he covered his mouth, but the laughing continued. "I'm - *god*," the giggles interrupted, "that's hilarious."

Thalia stared at him, her olive cheeks an unusual pink.

He looked at Sigrdrífa. "Who talks like that?" he shouted, doubling over. "'I am Victory', talk about a villain speech, am I right?" he bumped his elbow into Thalia's stomach.

Thalia launched her fist into his side. "Sigrdrífa," she said, "you don't scare me. Not anymore. Not with your empty threats. Your victories are in the past."

Sigrdrífa smiled. "So you know, then."

"Of Sigurd? Everyone does. You wouldn't shut up about him and Fafnir and your...what was it?" she tilted her head. "Poweress." She laughed maliciously. "I won't tell you again, Sigrdrífa. Take your posse, and go."

---

[18] Stupid bear

"Not till we get what we came for," the woman to the left said.

"Olrun's right," the last woman called out, "give us the Gungnir, and no one will be harmed."

Milo's eyes widened. "Gungnir?" he repeated. "Isn't that-"

"It's missing, Svava," Thalia interjected. "Everyone knows that. So how about you tell me why you're really here."

Svava, bronze-skinned and sneering, landed her pointed stare upon Milo. "The boy must know," she said, turning to the other Valkyrie, "it calls to him."

"Then we make him speak," Olrun replied. "But how?"

Milo had the sudden urge to scream.

Sigrdrífa smiled. "Simple," she said, "we bargain."

Like lightning crashing, Sigrdrífa zipped around them, snatching up Thalia like a rag doll and wrapping her in a tight chokehold. Axes clattered against the ground as the berserker thrashed, her feet off the ground.

No.

Milo lunged, but something snagged onto his wrist, yanking him back with such force a searing pain erupted through his shoulder. He shouted, falling to his knees. His arm fell limp beside him. A Valkyrie held him down.

Thalia was screaming: "If you *touch* him -"

"What," Sigrdrífa interrupted, "you will kill me?" Out from her clenched fist, beside Thalia's neck, came a thin needle, its sharp end laced with an emerald liquid. Slowly, the needle's prick approached Thalia's skin till Sigrdrífa paused, turning her gaze where Milo knelt. "This is *helvete kysser,*" she said, "Hel's Kiss. Deadly poison that delivers a slow, agonizing demise. I have been saving it for a rainy day," Sigrdrífa paused, tightening her hold on the thrashing berserker, "I'd say it's pouring."

Svava grasped Milo from behind, popping his arm back into place at his shoulder. He screamed, but the pain dulled and relaxed into a muscle sore.

"Now, tell me, boy," Sigrdrífa demanded, "where is your father's spear?"

"I don't know!" he shouted, "I swear! Just -"

"Every lie you utter brings me closer to giving lovely Thalia this poison. Try again."

Thalia slammed her head against her captor. "Tell them nothing, Bohr!"

"Please, I swear," he pleaded, "I have no idea where that *stupid* spear is!"

Sigrdrífa leaned the needle a hair closer.

No.

The rage pooled in like tears, streaming down his cheeks and dripping onto his clothes. His vision dimmed, darkened like he had slipped into a deep sleep. It was the same blackout he experienced with Silas - the existential feeling of exiting one's body, looking at the world from a bird's eye perspective. He recoiled, grabbing onto himself before his soul escaped. Heat radiated at his palms, paired with a burning bright light that shot like the reborn sun climbing over the horizon. And as quickly as it came, it left. He was just Milo, a dead boy trapped within someone he didn't recognize.

He looked upon the Valkyrie. "*Let her go.*"

Svava laughed. "My, look at the little Odinson go!"

"How angry can we make him?" Olrun called out, circling like a lioness.

Sigrdrífa grinned. "Come along, little Odinson, show us your god."

Milo raised his eyes to Thalia. Everything faded. She held onto Sigrdrífa's arm, her grip loosening as a soft smile spread across her lips.

Even there, standing with one foot in both life and death, she was the most beautiful person he had ever seen. Milo inched forward as the Valkyrie continued to mock and taunt him. She shook her head. He froze.

Her lips parted: "Survive."

Swiftly, Thalia jumped, leaning into the needle so the poison plunged into her bloodstream.

"*No!*"

Sigrdrífa dropped the berserker with a thud. "Well, *that* was an unexpected turn of events."

Milo skidded across the pavement towards Thalia. She twitched and moaned in pain, weakly grabbing onto her neck where inky blood stained her fingertips. Milo grabbed her, pulling her shaking body into his chest, ignoring the pain erupting across his entire body at her closeness.

Thalia raised her hand, dragging bloody fingers down upon his left cheek like a sharp scar. "Pray to them," she whispered, "pray to the Aesir."

"I can't -"

She gripped his neck, pulling him so close their noses touched. "You are a god, Milo," she hissed, metallic bronze eyes stabbing into him, "*pray*." Thalia released a staggering sigh and coughed, eyes fluttering close as she thrashed painfully within his arms.

Pray.

Sigrdrífa's stomping feet slammed against the ground as she stormed up to Milo, swooping to snatch him around the waist. He clutched onto Thalia, gritting his teeth together as her fingertips slipped away.

"I've still got questions, Odinson," she snapped, dropping him on the ground. "Maybe you'll listen to *him* more." Sigrdrífa twirled her spear, spinning around as she slammed its butt end against the road.

The pavement cracked beneath them, stretching till a gaping hole ripped through the neighborhood street. A roar exploded, releasing a piercing scream that could crack glass. Milo clasped at his ears. Rumbling echoed across the road like an earthquake, shaking till he toppled over. The Valkyrie remained as tall as statues, each watching the monstrous hole grow and grow with proud expressions. Milo wobbled to his feet, staring with wide eyes as something roared from below once more, climbing up from earth's fiery core.

"What the -"

A claw, scaly and long, larger than his house, shot out from the hole, slamming against the road. Another claw followed, and ebony talons and bony nails created deep grooves within the pavement. A beast surrounded with running magma, thick scarlet lined its body, carved from space, extended itself out from the radiating core, and fell upon the street. Its head was bulbous and enlarged like a crocodile's, and it pointed downwards, its lips unfurling to expose sterling silver canines. A forked tongue snapped out as the monster's body pulled itself from the earth's cage, bat-like wings snapping out at its back.

Milo, as any person would, *slightly* pissed himself. "That-that-that's -"

"A dragon," Sigrdrífa said, "Fafnir."

Trees snapped and collapsed like gunshots as the dragon's wings unfurled, slicing through everything as though it were paper. The beast's claw raised and slapped down upon a two-story house, destroying it without flinching. Milo reached, watching as a home he had passed for years collapsed into nothing. Two cars were in the driveway. He stared, wondered who was inside, and remembered the days he saw a little girl run through the bushes, chased giddily by his parents. He felt as though the beast ripped through him rather than the house, creating this gaping hole within. When the beast raised its paw, there was nothing left. He turned back towards the Valkyrie. They ignored the destruction.

"Once," Svava said, "the magician, Andvari, tricked the son of the Svartalfheim Dwarven King Hreidmar into harboring a cursed ring."

Olrun continued: "It's gold and jewels tainted the dwarven Prince's mind."

"To protect his prized possession," Sigrdrífa said, "he transformed into Fafnir, an ill-natured and greedy dragon." She turned to face Milo, with the dragon poised as a dangerous silhouette behind her. With a roll of her shoulders, brilliant wings unfurled from her back, colored a piercing white with sharp, pointed feathers.

"I am *so* overwhelmed right now," Milo squawked.

Sigrdrífa surged forward, the wings snapping to shoot her across the road.

Milo didn't bother to run. "Son of a bi -"

The Valkyrie slammed into him, grabbing him around the torso. The wind rushed as he squeezed his eyes shut, scared of what he might see when everything stopped. Sigrdrífa swooped down, her arm moving till she held onto his elbow, dangling him mid-air. Milo shouted as his eyes opened, seeing the Valkyrie flying above him, blocking out the sun. Slowly, his head turned, and he looked down below to see the dragon, Fafnir, widening his jaws to reveal fangs.

Milo thrashed around, grabbing at Sigrdrífa's arm. "Please -"

"Last chance, Odinson," she shouted over the rushing wind, "where is the Gungnir?"

He turned to look down once more, seeing Thalia's small, faraway figure against the street. He reached for her. *If she's dead,* he thought, *I can't do it. There isn't anything without her.* Milo stared up at Sigrdrífa. "Go to hell."

Sigrdrífa smiled. "*You* will."

She released him.

The air rushed around like a wave, slicing at his exposed arms and shoving his curls from his face. The Valkyrie grew faint in the distance as he fell, but he could just make out her smile, soft and genuine, pleased at the sight before her. He closed his eyes.

Milo.

A voice, faded and quiet, called out to him.

Min sonn.

He reached.

My son.

And a cry rippled through his lips.

Father.

Milo's eyes opened. "Help me!"

The surging air shoved and tossed Milo around, flipping him till he faced Fafnir, its wide jaws just feet away from swallowing him whole. And as a scream rippled at his throat, he closed his eyes and imagined *her.*

Thalia -

Milo's chest slammed into something hard and leathery, knocking the fake breath out of him. The beast roared from behind, echoing angrily through the city. He gripped his arms around the thing beneath him, slowly lifting himself to see a horse.

"What -"

My lord, a deep voice rang in his ears, *I am Sleipnir, stead of the Aesir, traveler of Odin.*

Milo held onto the horse's mane, looking over the side to see the streets running quickly beneath the animal's eight legs. *Eight legs?* He recoiled, counting the legs quickly. Eight legs. He nodded and shrugged. "Of course," he muttered, "my father *would* have an eight-legged horse."

It is time for battle, Sleipnir said.

"Battle?" Milo repeated. "I can't kill a *dragon*!"

Sleipnir raced down, clobbering against the air as it approached the pavement. Something sat in the road, casting a long shadow against the earth. Sleipnir swooped down, getting closer and closer to it till Milo could make out its shape. Quickly, he reached, snatching it up as Sleipnir passed, zooming back up to the sky. Milo raised his arm.

A hammer.

The leather-bound handle was boxed and heavy at the top, decorated with Norse runes. Milo raised it, the light jumping off its ebony body like a sunset's approach. Sleipnir neighed, turning his head as he curved through the air, facing the growling dragon, Fafnir.

"Mjolnir," he said.

Sleipnir faced the dragon.

Fafnir's wings extended. "Son of Odin," his scratching voice the same as a pounding bass drum, "you carry something...*priceless.*"

Milo opened his mouth, prepared to shout 'your mom', but feeling his mortality decided against it.

"*Forhekse deg*[19]," Fafnir growled, "return what you have stolen!"

"Stolen?"

"Fine, Odinson, it has been centuries since I've had a good meal." Fafnir lowered himself like a cat readying itself to pounce. "Time to join your father in hell!"

The dragon lifted off the ground. Milo raised Mjolnir, pressing his heel into Sleipnir's legs. The eight-legged horse darted through the air, zooming towards Fafnir with the speed of a bullet. Sleipnir dipped beneath the beast's snapping jaws, revealing Fafnir's reptilian neck, thick and protruding like a turkey. Milo slammed Mjolnir into the

---

[19] Curse you

dragon's jugular. Fafnir shot upwards as if he had a giant's strength until he fell on his back.

"*Yeah!*" Milo shouted, almost sliding off the horse. "Holy mother of god -"

Hold on tight, my Lord, Sleipnir said, *it would be unwise to fall where we go next.*

"What? Wait, I don't -"

Sleipnir shot to Fafnir's open mouth as the beast roared.

"Oh," Milo screamed, "that'll be a *no* from me!"

Hold on!

Milo gripped onto Sleipnir, lowering Mjolnir to his side as the horse got closer and closer to the beast's mouth. The dragon's breath, the same as sulfur, rotten food, and musty woods, like pavement after rain, overtook Milo immediately. He gasped, eyes watering. And before he could turn back, Sleipnir plunged himself and Milo into the *literal* pit of Fafnir's stomach.

With his eyes squeezed shut, Milo raised Mjolnir and launched it overhand with as much strength as he could muster into the beast's belly. The hammer shot into the dragon without hesitation, slamming against his insides. Quickly, Sleipnir retracted, all eight legs clobbering against Fafnir's shut jaws till they pried open, releasing the pair into the fresh air. They clattered against the ground, Milo launching off Sleipnir and skidding across the street. Mjolnir was nowhere to be seen, and even unscathed, Sleipnir left Milo there, clobbering along the air till he disappeared within the clouds.

Milo rolled over. Fafnir struggled, screaming and clawing at his underbelly with massive talons. With each strike, the dragon whimpered, gasping for air as the hole from whence he came called back to him, widening to swallow him whole. The burning red from the earth's core grabbed the beast as he screamed and thrashed, calling out in his native language for help from the missing Valkyrie. Milo staggered, watching as the dragon fell back into Hell, a final cry wailing between its jaws.

Fafnir was gone.

Thalia.

Milo ran towards the berserker's slumped figure, thrashing and convulsing even in unconsciousness. He knelt beside her, reaching down to touch her sweating cheek. He retracted immediately, shaking his hand. *She's boiling!* He never felt such an intense fever, burning so much it hurt with barely any contact. Sucking in a deep breath, Milo quickly swooped his arms beneath her, gritting his teeth to hold back the pained scream forming within his chest. After grabbing her fallen ax, Milo held her close and ran home.

He whispered, "gods be with me."

XXIII. In Which Everything Goes Wonderfully Wrong

There were three things Milo missed:

One: Natalie Bohr's smile.

Two: Oba.

Three: being ten years old, running into a nearby park at midnight - Natalie close behind - as winter's first snowfall scattered across the city, casting a heavenly glow upon the horizon; tiny footsteps littered the snow, and ten-year-old Milo preened with pride: he, within a silent, tranquil moment in a hurricane's eye, made the first marks upon a newborn season.

Maybe not in that order.

As Milo ran back towards his house, careful not to trip with Thalia mumbling and twitching in his arms, all he could remember were those three things. If there was any place Milo wished to be, it was the past: buried within his mother's warm embrace, laughing alongside the one person he loved as a teen, filled with naive innocence as he ran through fresh snow. His childhood flashed behind his eyelids like photographs.

Sigrdrífa's destruction was barely visible behind him. Whatever crater the Valkyrie created washed away, stitched up together as the Earth tried to heal itself. The house, though, was still destroyed. Trees snapped and decorated the pavement like Lincoln Logs. Sleipnir's footprints scattered everywhere like breadcrumbs. Milo left it behind, swallowing the guilt. He was dead, and there was an eternity to remember the destruction, the death he caused. Milo blinked back tears.

He clobbered up the driveway, slamming into the front door. It rattled beneath him, resulting in a few scattered and surprised shouts from inside. He reached with his left hand, juggling Thalia as she groaned against his neck. The door slapped open, smacking against the wall with a *thud*. Milo sprinted inside. He pelted to the kitchen table beside the back windows, flicking on the light before setting Thalia down on the cold wood. All the half-filled coffee cups were gone, and the dishwasher's low rumble echoed through the quiet kitchen behind him.

"By Ymir's beard."

Milo turned, breathless. Astrid stood transfixed in the entryway, staring down at Thalia's body with an unusually calm face. She moved into the kitchen quickly, remaining quiet as she pushed him aside, investigating Thalia with soft movements. Her gaze, harsh and stone-like, was stuck on the puncture mark on Thalia's neck, a little prick where blood trickled onto the table. Astrid swiped it away, grabbed a dish towel, and pressed it against her skin.

"Milo," she called, "tell me what happened."

He looked at her again. His lips parted; all that came out were short, quick exhales. Behind him, Kali's face warped with an uncharacteristic worry. He didn't need to look at her to know what she was thinking: *did he do that to her?* Milo figured he'd have the same response if he stood where she did. Silas lay in another room as proof. He blinked. The actual events that conspired moments before seemed fake, a foggy illusion created by his mind. He rubbed his eyes. *What happened?* Fear snagged onto him. All those moments, the dragon, the earth ripping open, the eight-legged horse, the hammer - how accurate were they? He looked at his hands. Afternoon light shot through the window and displayed across his palms like blood.

Thalia's eyes were open, just slightly, looking right at him.

Was it me?

"Odinson!"

He nodded.

It was my fault.

"Damn it," Astrid was saying, "somebody snap him out of it!"

His fists clenched.

I did this to her.

Hands touched his elbow.

"Milo," Kali said. She sounded afraid.

He looked at Astrid. "It was me."

"Sure about that?" she shouted. "*You* had poison?"

Kali sighed. "Maybe it was! He did *that* to Silas -"

"That was different," Astrid said. "Milo, look at me."

He raised his eyes.

"You didn't do this. I know that. But I *need* you to pull yourself together. You have to tell me what happened, or she *will* die."

Milo stared at Thalia. "There were these women," he said. "Sigrdrífa." It came down upon him like nightfall. A voice: *it wasn't you.* He looked back to Astrid. "Sigrdrífa!" He wanted to cry with relief. It wasn't him.

Astrid nodded. "The Valkyrie."

"She showed up with two others," he explained, "and she gave Thalia this poison, and had wings, and *literally* pulled an actual dragon from the earth's buttcrack. Like I'm talking Smaug, I'm talking Jabberwacky, I'm talking Serafina - all those, put together to create this weird nasty smellin' dragon from the *earth's buttcrack.* Now," Milo paused, holding out his arms, "picture me, riding this eight-legged horse with friggin' Mjolnir, busting through this dude's *throat,* I'm not even kidding, like -"

"Stop," Astrid snapped. "The poison. What was it?"

"*That's* what you got from all that?" Kali asked. "I wanna hear more about the earth's buttcrack."

"*Helvete Kysser.* Hel's kiss," he replied.

Astrid's demeanor faded. She looked back at Thalia, stepping backward. She raised her right hand to her lips and whispered something so quiet it looked like a breath before pressing her fingertips against Thalia's lips. "I'm sorry."

"What do you mean?"

"I am not a healer. There is nothing I can do to counteract *Helvete Kysser.* It is of the divine."

He blinked. "I don't -"

The table creaked and moaned as Thalia thrashed, eyes painfully wide and staring at the ceiling. A guttural scream clawed through her throat. Astrid reached to hold her, but the berserker's fist snapped out, slamming into the Asgardians neck with an unnatural force. Astrid slipped backward, choking and coughing as she struggled to regain her breath.

"*Hold...her...down!*" Astrid screeched.

Milo ran towards Thalia, snatching at her wrists even as the searing heat from her feverish skin spread onto his own. She cried persistently, screams, wails, and pained groans melting together to become the worst sound Milo had heard. Tears formed in his eyes as he held her, begging and pleading for whatever higher force out there to give her another chance, to keep her alive, to stop the agony, to give them more time.

"*Please*," he cried, "don't take her." He cradled her. She thrashed, slamming her legs and fists into his sides, her elbow lunging into his jaw, ripping his shirt and snagging onto his hair. All he could do was hold her. Press his lips against her forehead. Deal with the pain. Do it all over again. "Thalia," he breathed, "it's me. Come back to me."

Give me one more chance.

And in her place, he imagined his mother. He imagined Oba. He imagined Silas and Kali. He imagined his father from Astrid's memories, blood-colored gold drenching his skin. He imagined Astrid. He imagined even Frey, the young, innocent girl he would never know but whose soul somehow clung to his own. He carried the sins of his father. He imagined every Asgardian buried in Herjan. He imagined the boy he once was, the soul who loved reading, snow, and his mother and the world.

He held innocence and purity, something more precious than the finest jewels. Against his chest, the berserker settled, groaned with pain, and suddenly silent. Silent but alive.

Footsteps clobbered up beside him.

"He's awake."

Milo lifted his head. "What?"

"Silas," Kali said, "he's awake."

Shouting came from the guest room and down the hallway. Astrid bundled Thalia in her arms, pulling her from Milo's arms.

"Help your friend," she said, "I will tend to the berserker."

He stared at Thalia.

"Go."

"Put her in an ice bath," he said.

"A what?"

"In the bathroom, fill the tub with ice and cold water, the coldest you can get. Do you understand?"

She nodded. "To calm the fever." She sprinted towards the bathroom.

Kali touched Milo's arm. "He was calling for you."

"Me?"

"All he's said is your name."

His heart sank. Dread pooled within him, chills running down his back. He had no urge to go to him, to see his friend lying there, still wounded and suffering. But Kali was watching, eyes urging, already backing towards the room. She reached, beckoning with her fingers outstretched.

"He won't hate you."

Milo wasn't even sure if that's what he was afraid of. How would anyone feel when facing their loudest guilt, their most obvious mistake? How could he look upon his friend, knowing what he did? His fists clenched. That other thing, that monstrous being that took over the moment he tackled Silas, was not him. *It's not me.*

He stormed down the hall. "He should."

When Milo opened the bedroom door, Silas sat upright in the full-sized bed, the comforter tucked around him, pastel blue pillows stacked beneath him. Half-faded and half-prominent runes scaled his face, an eerie silver glow radiating from his swollen bruises. Dried blood stained his lip. His right eye was swollen shut. Bandages twisted like braids along his bare chest. A tattoo, cursive done so neatly across his stomach, Milo barely made it out, scored his lumber-colored skin. Silas, silent and still, stared directly into them as though they weren't truly there.

His lips parted: "*Milo.*"

"It's me."

Silas repeated. "Milo."

Suddenly, he left the room's threshold, shoved in by Kali. Milo inched closer to the bedside. "How do you feel?"

"Can you remember?"

Milo paused. His voice sounded different. "Remember," Milo said.

Silas tilted his head. Light shot through the blinds, slicing against his eyes like sunglasses. And there, in a split second before clouds passed, Silas's normally chocolate eyes became violet, a deepening purple, swirling and meshing together like a whirlpool. "I can," he whispered.

"His eyes," Milo muttered over his shoulder, "did you see that?"

She looked stricken with fear. "Just like -"

"Loki," Silas called out. "He remembers."

Milo turned back towards his friend. "What do you remember?"

"The end," he began, his head moving at a snail's pace till he stared directly at the two within the room, "the end and the beginning, the rotation of it all. I have seen," his eyes locked onto Milo, "everything you have done. Everything you will do." He closed his eyes and spoke words that did not belong to him: "'For in the great day there shall be a judgment, with which they shall be judged until they are consumed; and their wives also shall be judged, who led astray the angels of heaven that they might salute them[20].'"

Milo inched away. "Holy hell."

"What is it?" Kali whispered.

"The book of Enoch. He's quoting Enoch."

Silas watched them. "The death," he said. "The death. The death. The -"

---

[20] 1 Enoch 19:2

"I don't understand."

Silas's arm shot out with incredible speed, snatching onto Milo's throat with a claw-like grip. He squeezed, utterly ice-cold fingers pressing into his skin as he yanked, holding MIlo centimeters away from his nose, a hair away from each other's souls. And with a soft smile, lines wrinkling around his nose and eyes, Silas parted his lips and spoke words that would haunt Milo till his last breath. "You will kill us all."

Milo blinked. "Like...*again*? 'Cause, I mean, we're kinda already dead."

"That was supposed to be eerie, man," Kali said. "You ruined his moment."

"What do you know about his moment?"

"The hell you mean 'whadda I know,'" she mocked, "look at him! You stepped on his thunder!"

"All right, peanut gallery, just take a -"

Silas lunged, tacking Milo to the carpet. They rolled till Silas was above him, squeezing his hands around his throat before lifting him and slamming him back against the ground. It was a fruitless struggle, where Milo had no urge to try and get the boy off him. Words pooled into him, so loud and harsh he couldn't even deny them: *you deserve this.* He held onto Silas's wrists, choking on nothing as he wondered how long it'd last.

"Si -" Milo spat, reaching up to touch his face. A tear caught on his hand.

And as soon as it happened, a thundering sound hurdled in from behind them. Kali's hands were outstretched, shoved before her as though she pushed something away. The booming sound came from her palms, an invisible force erupting beneath her skin and throwing Silas onto the bed. There was no time to grapple with the power growing within her. She held Silas down over the comforter; teeth gritted together as the boy mindlessly fought, thrashing and screeching like a madman.

"Help Astrid," she shouted, "I'll handle him!"

"I can't -"

"We're *all* Warriors of Thunder, Milo. Maybe not as cool as Odinson, but we can handle each other." Her eyes grew worried. "Save Thalia, okay? We need her. Whatever it takes."

Milo sprinted down the hall, sliding as he twisted into the bathroom. Astrid filled the tub with water and dumped buckets of ice into it. Thalia lay dangerously still against the tile, eyes wide and unfocused, staring at the cracked ceiling. A twitch riddled through her. And the prick on her neck, no longer bleeding, took on an unusual color, a mix between a healing scratch and a growing bruise. It spread down her throat, down her collarbone, and beyond her shirt. But it was her hands that caught his attention. Milo knelt. Her fingertips were an ashy gray, bronze skin faded and sickly, the color spreading up her wrists.

"There," Astrid muttered.

Without a word, Milo swooped Thalia up, the fever still raging outrageously beneath her skin. He kicked his shoes off, cradling her close before stepping into the tub. Together, they lay in the ice bath, Milo shivering and chattering as the chill grabbed him. Thalia's fever sat upon his chest like a furnace, warm as everything else became swallowed within the cold. He held her close as they sank deeper into the frozen water, splashing it against her burning body. She barely shook. He figured his warmth could help, but it didn't seem to do much. He closed his eyes and tried to pray.

"Odinson," Astrid snapped, "you'll freeze, get out!"

"Wu-wu-wu-where s-s-she goes, I-I-I go!"

Astrid paused, staring at him before reaching into the bath, grabbing ice by the handful to press against Thalia's skin. The ice melted upon contact, sizzling as it dripped back into the still water. Their efforts were worthless, a circle of shivering and melting. As Milo grew incredibly stiff, the ice chilling him to the bone, he touched his nose against her head, the messy curls soft and comforting against his skin. Thalia's hand drifted through the water, sliding into his own with a shuttering twitch. And even though it still burnt like the sun, he intertwined his fingers with hers, not once feeling afraid.

Astrid stood, mumbled, "More ice," and vanished.

Whispers came from Thalia, which were too incoherent for him to understand. Her eyes fluttered shut. His frozen lips grazed her clammy forehead; static radiated through him, a moment of warmth. Milo swallowed, parted his lips, and spoke against her, "I sh-sh-should've kissed you when I had the chance."

And as it all seemed close to the end, her body sinking into him, a sharp ringing ran through the Bohr houses. Silence. It echoed again. Milo struggled to keep his eyes open. Another ring. He turned his head towards the opened door. Fourth ring.

Kali stood in the doorway. "Please, by god, tell me you have twenty dollars."

"Wha -"

"Don't be mad," she said, "but I need twenty dollars."

He licked his lips. "Kali, I-I have no idea wh-wha-wha-what you're sayin'."

"Twenty dollars, man. Two pizzas. You like pepperoni?"

"You buh-buh-buh bought a pizza?"

"No," she said. "Two. I bought two."

And while the urge to be angry was there, Milo swallowed it, trying to keep Thalia's warmth against his chest. He looked at her. "Wallet," he muttered, "in the bedroom."

"Thank god," she breathed.

"Wait," he called out. "You ordered *pizza*? N-n-now?"

"Look, death does not stop the hungry, okay? I'm starving, but I chugged a water bottle and never had to pee - explain that, copycat Jesus! How does that even work? Just wait: one of y'all is gonna wonder why you haven't taken a shit, and you'll come runnin' to me 'cause I'm woke, and -"

"*Kali!*"

"Right, doorbell." She ran, and after loud bangs from down the hall, she passed by the doorway again, and Milo heard steps snap across the kitchen tile. The door creaked open. Silence.

Milo closed his eyes.

He had always wished death was silent.

"Odinson."

No, he thought, *it is silent.*

"Open your eyes, Odinson."

No.

"Your journey is far from over."

He peeled his eyes open.

A young man dressed in a local pizza restaurant's uniform, colored violet and black, stood in the doorway. The boy reached up, pulling the crooked baseball cap off as he wandered into the small bathroom. Behind him was Kali, the wide pizza boxes stacked in her hands as she stared. Milo gazed up at the boy's face.

Ebony eyes stared back.

Loki knelt beside the tub, pushing the dark curls from his face as he inspected Thalia's wound. He frowned, tilting his head. He reached for her cheek. Rage fueled Milo's system, sparking throughout him like an electrical fire. Even though he only wanted to lunge, to tackle the god to the ground and never let go, he was frozen, unsure if he'd move again.

The god cupped her face, lifting her ever so slightly. He whispered: "C'mon, old friend."

Emerald green trickled between Thalia's ashy gray lips. It slipped into the air like a crawling snake, twisting around Loki's nimble fingers till he made a fist, and Hel's Kiss vanquished into nothing. Thalia's chest rose, the darkness fading from her fingertips and returning to delicate bronze. Milo raised a shaking hand, touched her cheek, and received the same spiking electricity he got whenever he was near her. The fever was gone. He touched her neck. The puncture wound was merely a needle prick, the bruising disappearing.

Milo raised his eyes. "Thank you," he whispered.

"I'm over here," Loki said, "not up there."

With his diminished strength, his head rolled towards the god, a permanent glare stitched into his eyes. "*You*," he groaned.

And before Loki breathed, Astrid loomed over him, hands shaking as her glittering blade shone in the artificial bathroom light. She pressed its edge against Loki's tanned neck.

"Remove yourself, Deathbringer," she said, "before I end you."

He raised his arms, a smirk lingering on his dark lips as he backed away, eyes never leaving Milo's. Astrid lowered her sword, practically leaping into the tub and removing Thalia gently before yanking him from the melting ice. His teeth chattered against her neck as the warrior gripped onto him. She moved quickly, too fast for him to see where, till she laid him down against a familiar couch, forcibly removing his drenched clothes. Her face shone beat red, eyes a deadly shade as she ran, layering blankets on him. And as he settled into the sofa, she returned with a damp towel from the kitchen, laying it across his forehead.

He murmured into the blankets. The towel was a delicate warmth against his face. He opened his eyes.

Astrid breathed heavily, wetness pooling in her eyes. "*You* are stupid."

"Thank you," he replied. "Thank you."

Darkness clouded his vision, and another figure stood in her place when they reopened.

Loki knelt before him. Jet black eyes crinkled like crystal, the midnight sky trapped within his gaze. If he had looked close enough, Milo could have sworn there were stars, cosmos, galaxies, and worlds upon worlds born and destroyed within his irises, pupils, and his stare. The most beautiful and precious darkness, right in there. Milo wished to look away.

"There is no greater terror than watching someone you love fall before your eyes," Loki said. The god smiled. "You endure so much pain for beings like us. Why is that?"

"Honor," Milo said. "I have a sense of honor."

"Humans. So careless and brave for being such minuscule things."

"You'd think," he drawled, incredibly tired, "if someone like you had all the time in the world, you'd know what that would mean. To have honor."

He turned his head. "What are you saying, Odinson?"

"How long does a god take to become the devil?"

Loki frowned.

"How many lives need to be taken till they don't matter anymore? How many brothers? Sisters? How about fathers or children?" Milo lifted himself from the sofa, the towel sliding onto the floor. "Or mothers? How many mothers do you need to victimize before enough is enough? What does death mean to you, Loki, or is it nothing because you've escaped it for so long?"

"Death is a woman I once knew," Loki replied, "and I fear her the most."

Milo collapsed onto the couch. "You can go."

"Is my soul too dark for you?"

"You'd have to actually have a soul for me to be afraid of it."

"Odinson," Loki chuckled, "the longer you avoid your destiny, avoid *me,* the more danger you put your foolish little clan in. *I'm trying to help you,* Odinson. The sooner you find the spear, the sooner you claim your throne -"

"Unless you're about to tell me where my mother is," he pointed, "there's the door."

The god watched him. He looked surprised, but it disappeared quickly, as though Milo imagined it. Loki's lips curled into a smile, harsh and deadly. The god stood, shrugging and placing the pizza delivery hat back over his wild curls. He snapped his fingers, and crumbled paper appeared in his palm.

"A piece of your prophecy, Odinson," Loki said, placing it on a dusty bookshelf beside the door. He did not turn around as he called out: "Remember me in your time of need, boy. I might one day be your only hope."

And in a furl of violet smoke, the god was gone.

Milo closed his eyes.

He wished death was quiet.

XXIV. Prophecies and Demon Dogs

Astrid found herself at the dinner table surrounded by family, her last memory of such an event too fuzzy to remember. Her father rarely stayed in the family's cottage. His days as a merchant forced him to travel the realm. The days he came back, though, were her most incredible memories. He'd return with stories of the Royal Guard, godly festivals that kept the streets lively and jubilant. The tales captivated Astrid and Frey, eyes wide with wonder as the firelight slowly dwindled through the late night.

In the Bohr household, the company ate at the cleared dining table and scrubbed clean from coffee stains and blood. The table was round and wooden beneath the late afternoon light streaming in from squared windows. The boxes Kali acquired, filled with food she called *pizza,* released steam and a pleasant aroma as they passed it around. Astrid stared at the triangular bread on her plate. She mimicked the others, picking up the slice and taking a full bite. Her face pinched up:

it dripped with grease, slices of meat burning her throat and filling her stomach. Unlike the kind she made from their cattle, the cheese stretched between her lips. Astrid held in her laugh at the Midgardian food. Her stomach impatiently gurgled for more.

Only one, however, stared at their plate with a sullen expression. Silas, the swelling gone from his face, picked up his pizza and proceeded to drop it, lips drooping. The purple hue was drained from his eyes. Wounds scored his cheeks and neck, his right arm twisted into a bandage. He lifted his head. Everyone at the table silently watched.

Astrid spoke first: "What was it like?"

"Huh?" Silas fidgeted in his seat.

"Being under the deathbringer's spell," she said. "How did it feel?"

Silas gazed around the table, pressing his lips together as all the companions waited curiously. "It was like dreaming," he explained, "perpetual dreaming while god knows what happened on the surface. My soul...my *being* was someplace else."

"Where?"

"The ocean. And not like I was swimming or driving a boat. It was like I was the ocean. I was the waves. Even though there was this lingering feeling something was going on, something was happening on the outside, I never wanted to leave. Even now, being here is one of the most depressing things I've ever had to do." He avoided looking at anyone. "How sad is that?"

Milo, who sat at his right, nudged Silas with his elbow. "Eat something, man."

Astrid watched as the dead one obediently ate. The Valhallians never stopped surprising her. Their devout loyalty, despite being pitted against one another, despite constant disaster. Their shared pain and trauma. With it all, with all the suffering and darkness, somehow, they threw smiles and cracked jokes. Even the berserker was as much a Valhallian as they were.

"Dead people digest food," Milo blurted. "That's a *Cosmo* cover."

"God, I missed pizza." Kali shoved another triangle in her mouth, letting out a mix of a laugh and wail. From her left, the berserker slid a napkin over. Kali sheepishly snatched it up.

"I missed air conditioning," Milo added. "Valhalla doesn't have vents."

Silas grabbed more food. "There's no sunset. No sunset, no sunrise, no moon. That's what I miss. The regularity of it all." He took a massive bite. "And Kuriegs. Definitely Kuriegs."

Thalia grumbled. "Forget it."

"What?"

She lifted her head. Her recovery from the poison was swift after the god removed its ailment; soon, she was back on her feet, her harsh stare even more angry than before. "The more you remember, the more you know you've lost," Thalia said. "Forget your past life: it's practically nonexistent now. It's the only way you'll survive."

Astrid held back her annoyance. The berserker had little restraint or tact when it came to guiding the dead ones. And as the warriors became deflated, the only one with no issues proclaiming what he believed spoke his mind boisterously.

"How long have you been," Milo paused and shrugged, "you know."

Thalia blinked. "Been what?"

"Dead. How long have you been dead?"

"What makes you think -" she stopped abruptly, blinking rapidly before shooting him a placid smile. "It's-it's more complicated than defining being alive or dead."

"It's really not. We died. Astrid's alive. And you're..."

"Drop it, Milo."

"But -"

"I'm serious."

Astrid swallowed. It was something she never stopped to think about. Rundi said the berserkers would've died with their Master, alongside Odin, but somehow one survived. Her eyes narrowed. Lies and deceit hung around Thalia like a storm cloud. She realized, though, that the unease it brought lightened with time.

"You mean to tell me you're something other than dead?" Milo snapped. "Don't piss on my leg and call it rain, Thalia. What are you?"

The berserker remained silent.

Astrid looked around. The would-be silence was filled by the chewing of his friends, careless of the tension. Milo, obviously pouting, stared at Thalia's head with an intensely gray glare. A towel still draped over his shoulders, his clothes replaced with a dry t-shirt and pants. The berserker moved her attention to the ripped paper left by Loki. The few lines written on it in black ink were in a lost language, one none recognized. Thalia had been fixated on it since she recovered, swearing she could translate it quickly.

"What's it like to die?" Astrid asked.

Kali huffed. "You guys sure have some good pizza talk."

"My sister," she continued, "I spent too many nights wondering if she was in pain that night. Where her soul wanders. What spirits she has seen."

Milo rested his forehead on the table. "It's everything and nothing all at once. A moment of fear, a moment of relief. A darkness. Empty space. But peaceful. A quiet so loud it hurts. Voices. Memories. All at once, you experience everything and nothing, till a second later, when your eyes are open." He looked at her. "Then you do it all over again."

Silas pushed his plate away. "Well, I was stabbed, so, you know, got a lot of pain."

"You whiny punks got nothing on me," Kali shouted, flexing her arms, "I was shot *twice*. Yeah, how 'bout them apples!"

"It's not a competition, Kal," Milo said.

"That's 'cause you're too much of a shrimp to make it one. You know I'd win."

"Are you playing the pity card or something?" Silas asked. "'Cause as a fellow black man, dying is dying. We all ended up in the same boat."

"I'm not shallow," she replied. "I'm just saying. How much you wanna bet my face is plastered all over Instagram? Turn on the TV and see how many are talkin' about *another* black girl shot and killed by some dumb police officer. Random white people sharing my graduation pictures with the 'long live' hashtag, you know? It'd be sweet if it actually changed things. Now it's just patronizing."

Astrid smiled. "I'll have to agree with you, dead one."

"*Me?* You wanna agree with *me* on something?"

"You could take them," she said. "You wield Laevateinn."

"I mean, do I? The only time I used it was outta pure luck. And honestly, after knowing who it really belongs to..."

"What about the book? I saw you reading it."

Kali sheepishly shrugged. "I'm still learning."

Thalia slammed her fist against the old table. Her lips curled into an ecstatic smile. "I got it," she shouted, "the prophecy - I've got it!"

Astrid dreaded her excitement. The Valhallians mimicked their guardian, looking at each other with a newfound hope. Astrid never took a prophecy as a good sign, and based on the shaded worry behind Milo's eyes, she suspected he felt the same. "Read it," she said.

The berserker stared at the fragmented paper. She swallowed. And spoke:

"One to rule and one to destroy.
Nothing can survive while one is alive.
Brothers march for the throne,
Bringing us closer to damnation forevermore."

They were silent. Thalia reread the words aloud once, twice, and three times. The fourth was barely audible, lips moving frantically with scattering eyes. Her eyes raised, touching upon Milo. She reread it. If the boy could get any paler, he did then, becoming the same shade as Mani's moon when streaking across the night sky. He didn't move a muscle. Something lay within him, a hidden and unspoken fear.

Thalia began to read it again.

"Stop," Milo said. "Just - please, stop."

"The brothers are the Odinsons." Astrid shrugged. "That much is obvious."

Milo shook his head. "Then that would mean I'd have to kill him." He frowned. "Or he'd have to kill me."

Astrid avoided looking at him. She felt ripped in half, everything within her spilling onto the table. If it were true, which the Norn always were, then he was right. One would be fated to kill the other. A god and half-god. One from thunder and the other - she glanced at Milo's face, seeing his cheek curve, the sharpness in his chin, the frail skin alongside his temples, his ears, his eyelids - the other. What would he become? She dragged her eyes away. And what being with human blood could defeat an Aesir who saw eons?

Nothing fought Thor and won. The world serpent tried, Loki set his own traps, and his cousins upon cousins vied for his name and fought for his ebony crown. Even the Vanir sent assassins, their highly skilled warriors, to try and bring his head home to their queen on a platter. And Astrid saw them perish at his hands, watched their blood stain his steel blade, watched him mercilessly rip through armies and worlds and empires and skies. He caught lightning, bent it to his will, built storms from his bare hands, and captured thunder with an inhale. She lived her life believing there was nothing he couldn't do.

She gazed upon Milo and wished Thor could not do this one thing.

"Loki keeps trying to get me to find the spear," Milo said.

"The Gungnir," Astrid said. "The mightiest weapon in all the Nine Realms. It would be useless in his hands. Why would he want it?"

Thalia shook her head. "Loki doesn't want it. He wants Milo to have it."

"But why?"

"Your guess is as good as mine," she replied. "Locating it could turn the tides of the war."

Silas rapped his knuckles against the table. "Shouldn't our priority be getting back to Valhalla?" He looked down at his plate. "It's not like we've got all that much time left either. Besides, doing what Loki says isn't the right move," he paused, glancing between Thalia and Astrid, "right?"

"I'm not leaving my mother," Milo said.

"Look, I get it. If I were you, I'd want the same, but what about us?"

"What about you?"

"What happens when our time runs out?" Silas raised his arm, poking the fading triangles. "What happens if we're here, and these tattoos disappear instead of being back in Valhalla? What happens then?"

Milo swallowed, pressing his lips together. He spoke as though a hand clutched his throat. "I-I don't -"

"This isn't me trying to be selfish, okay? I'm just saying there's much more at stake with us than with your mother. We can go back to Valhalla and get help to find her."

Odinson rapidly blinked. He looked younger, the falling light cascading across him. He clenched his teeth, worked his jaw, and stared blankly at a painting on the wall: a gray wolf staring back at him.

Thalia pushed her seat back. "We do not abandon family," she said. "All of us together have shared a wound through this war that passes into all realms. We're family now, meaning Milo's mother doesn't get left behind."

He didn't seem to have heard her.

"Finding the Gungnir can be the one thing to stop Loki," Astrid added, trying to catch the boy's attention. "No being can withstand its power."

"But what about that hammer?" Kali called out. She had the pizza box, sliding slices onto Silas's plate. "You know, when the dragon came outta the earth's buttcrack, you said there was a hammer."

Milo blinked, his eyes focusing on her. "Mjolnir. But it's gone."

"You lost it?"

"It'll come back to me, right? 'Cause it's mine."

Thalia huffed. "It's not your hammer. It came because your blood is golden, like the Aesir, its creators. It came because you called out to it, and Mjolnir is a servant of your clan. But it will not remain with you. Mjolnir waits for its purpose in Ragnarok," she spoke these words as though she had been taught to speak them all her life, "like us all."

Milo chuckled. "You know, everyone keeps bringing up this Ragnarok thing, and I've really got no clue what it means."

Astrid blinked. Her stomach dropped. She turned. Thalia experienced the same: eyes as wide as a cat's. She stared into Milo's skull as if to crush it. He looked between them.

Astrid repeated: "everyone."

"Huh?"

"You said everyone," she said, "who else mentioned Ragnarok to you?"

"It's really not that big of a deal -"

"Milo, Ragnarok is the end of all ends. It is the coming of destruction, the time Yggdrasil finally dies, taking all life with it. It has been foretold since everything's beginning. Now, Odinson," she leaned forward, "tell me who has delivered the warning of Ragnarok."

He remained quiet, almost afraid to speak. "I don't understand."

Thalia sighed. "Who mentioned it to you?"

"You guys," he said, "and in a dream."

"What dream?"

"Just a dream!" He grew defensive, that strawberry mark popping out between his eyes. "Big deal!"

Astrid pressed her hands together, trying to dilute her agitation. "Foretellings are often delivered through dreams. What were you shown?"

Milo frowned. The wall he held deteriorated, and tiredness overtook him, wrapping his arms around himself as though the ice bath still chilled him. "There was a tree," he said. "Like a weeping willow. Branches, vines, and leaves, with roots so large they came outta the ground. But it was sad."

"The tree," Silas repeated, "was sad."

"Like it knew it was dying."

Astrid barely looked at him. She already knew where his words led. During sleep, his soul traveled alongside Yggdrasil's tunnel branches till he landed before it, watching as the ghostly Norn figures healed the tree's roots. She had the same vision once, when her family name was predicted to collapse. At the time, it was fruitless, a dream she had whisked away as a product of her mother's vivid bedtime stories, but she understood its truth at Herjan's fall. For his sake, she hoped it was only a dream.

"These women walked around the tree, pouring medicine on its roots. And they were talking to me without ever opening their mouths."

Astrid closed her eyes.

"It-it was kinda like they were...laughing at me, you know? They knew my entire life before it ever happened. And then they said it." He paused as if collecting himself before he recited:

"Two siblings, light and dark -
Breed a war of worlds upon the mountaintop.
As one is slain by the moonlight,
We breathe the air of Ragnarok!"

And Astrid willed herself to meet his eyes. The Prince held her stare, fear lodged in his throat, in his eyes. And there, sitting around the table, Milo Odinson looked truly dead.

"But it was just a dream," he said, "right?"

She opened her mouth but couldn't speak.

"*Right?*" he repeated. "I'm not gonna kill my brother. Ragnarok isn't gonna happen. Because it was a dream." He looked around, saw the deflated expressions, and realized they avoided him. He stopped on Thalia, noticing how the one person whose eyes were permanently stuck on him stared at the paper, lips moving silently. "This is crazy."

Silas huffed. "That's *literally* what I've been saying this entire time."

Kali left the table, gathering plates and empty pizza boxes as she headed to the trash can. Astrid saw the shake in her hands, the plates rattling. Their fear interlaced with each other - what one felt spread across them like tremors after an earthquake. The Vahallian disappeared around the corner.

"The Norn have delivered worse fates," Astrid said.

Milo was silent. Staring at the painting.

"Whatever happens," she continued, "you won't be alone."

"That's impossible."

"How?"

He finally looked at her. "Gods are always alone."

Before she could laugh, reach towards him and squeeze his hands, exclaim *you are not a god,* and she would never let him become one, a thud echoed from the hall. Thalia leaped to her feet, clutching an ax. Astrid lunged for Hofond, lifting off the chair as she lost herself, giving a coarse shout: "Kali!" She pushed her chair back, moving to the hallway. She shouted again: "Kali!"

Silence responded. Her heart dropped.

A door slammed. Something snapped against the wall, back and forth. Footsteps were tapping. Astrid stood at the hall's threshold, a cool afternoon breeze gusting by. The berserker appeared at her right. Milo, the Prince armed with nothing but a pointed stare, was on the left. There was anger in how he stood, the tendons popping from his arms, sharp gray eyes taking in everything. It was familiar. A godly stance.

Astrid tried to steady her breathing. Fear lurched up her throat, gripping her heart and squeezing till she almost collapsed. The dead one was probably fine. Merely tripped or dropped the trash or slammed the door shut behind her. And even though she'd repeat the speculations, a voice lurked, whispering *you cannot save everyone.*

She opened her lips to shout again when the Valhallian slid around the corner.

Breathless and sweaty, she spun into the hallway, braids flailing around. Even in the hall's shadows, the dead one's obsidian skin had this otherworldly sheen, reminding Astrid of the Fae and their magic-tinged fingertips. More wind surged behind her, bringing along perfume or some natural scent. Astrid couldn't tell. But it was light, like spearmint and grass. Astrid felt euphoric as though she might sprint towards the dead one.

Kali gulped down air. "There's-there's-there's-there's -"

The berserker snapped her fingers. "Stop. Try again."

A clatter from down the hall.

Milo frowned. "What was that?"

"I opened the back door to take the trash out," Kali said.

"All right," he drawled, "did you leave it open or somethin'?"

"Whether I left it open or not doesn't matter."

He raised his eyebrows. "Why?"

"Because it's already inside."

A growl echoed from the back. Behind Kali grew a shadow, spreading along the hallway walls.

Astrid tightened her hold on Hofond till its handle cut into her palm. "What is inside, dead one?"

"It-it looks like a big dog," she replied, "like a wolf. But a-a demon wolf." She nodded. "Definitely a demon wolf."

Milo groaned. "You let a monster into my house?"

"I'm sorry! It was a puppy, man, I swear. I looked outside, and there was this cute little puppy, and she did this funny little roll -"

"You let a demon dog in for *fun*?" Milo screeched. "Why couldn't you just *laugh*?"

And before anything could be done, an intensified growl erupted from the hall, sounding like a bird screaming across the clouds.

It billowed, echoing and snapping till it whirled with a tornado's strength. Whatever the beast was, it approached, the shadow growing monstrous against the pastel-colored walls. Within the second, they crowded at the hall's edge and watched as a wolf, the same size as a kneeling bear, fur a stark gray and eyes a dripping blood red, stepped around the corner. It breathed deeply, each paw striking the ground like an earthquake. The wolf's massive head swiveled towards them, lips curling up in a snarl, growling and exposing unexpectedly pearly white teeth.

Astrid turned. That painting the Prince was entranced with held an eerie similarity to the demonic wolf, both having an odd serenity in their eyes. She looked back, grabbed Kali with her free hand, and inched backward.

"It is a beast from Hel," Thalia whispered.

Milo scoffed. "Lots of things come from Hell."

"Not your Hell," she said, "I mean the goddess, Hel. It is a child of hers."

He rolled his eyes. "Of course."

And with as much force as possible, Astrid shoved her companions behind her, brandishing Hofond's shine. In the wolf's eyes, she saw the goddess's ethereal reflection, the hair stretching to her ankles, midnight's sea trapped within it, tall like her Jotunn ancestors, broad with muscles, curved wondrously as an admiring sculptor forged her from clay. Her beauty was stark, blatant, and evident to the eye. Her dress was carved from snakes, her crown from a rose's thorn, death and dying, and the end staining her fingertips like mortal blood.

Astrid pointed Hofond towards the fragmented image within the beast's eye.

"I wonder how it feels," she shouted, "for a goddess to perish at my hand."

The wolf snapped its jaw, released a blood-curdling screech, and pounded down the hallway; Hel distorted as though she stood in a cracked mirror, scarlet lips as dark as a flesh wound, a gash across a stomach, blood spilling viciously against an obsidian floor.

The goddess screamed.

XXV. Hraesvelgr the Eagle

When the wolf came barreling down the hall, Milo remembered the first time he played hide and seek with his mother. There were still flowers laced in his hair from their first visit to Central Park. A giddy high lived within him as he ran, old enough not to be considered a child but young enough to avoid adulthood's trenches, leaping over cardboard boxes filled with wrapped dinner plates and mismatched silverware.

He avoided stacked furniture, skidded by the furnished television, and jumped around the telephone cord. His Mom quickly leaped after him, holding slender hands towards him as he was a foot away, forever grasping but never catching. Eventually, she swaddled him, pressing a mountain of kisses in his hair before whispering you're it and skidding down the hall.

Like a dream, he remembered: chasing after his mother, hands grazing the freshly painted walls, the divots in the tiles pressing against his bare feet, flower petals drifting down from his hair, scattering the floor behind him like breadcrumbs. He spun around a corner, expecting to see his Mom, but found another empty room. He went through the rooms twice. Did it all again a third time. The panic settled at the fourth, and his shouts for her to stop playing became desperate. Eventually, the tears pooled and slid down his cheeks like a waterfall. He erupted through the backdoor, almost ripping the screen off its hinges.

His Mom stood in the backyard, staring at the sky underneath a tree's shade. Her skin looked like paint in the golden light, slick and smooth, blemish-free beneath the sun's gaze. As if the sky were watching, the clouds parted, and through the tree's gaps came light, illuminating her cheeks and arms and the curve of her dress as though she were made of nothing other than diamonds. He ran to her, colliding with her chest as he wrapped himself in her embrace.

"Never let me go," he had said. "Not again."

And she held him, still staring at the sky. "Never."

The hallway was no longer bare. There were no boxes, no furniture needing to be built, no fragile objects wrapped in plastic. Instead, the wolf moved without care, maliciousness in its claws and in between its teeth. It slammed into the walls, the small space barely able to contain its strength. Framed photographs clattered. Paintings, ones Milo had never seen anywhere but their home on the walls, clashed and cracked. He fumbled with them as he ran, grabbing them as the wolf's jaws snapped at his heels, the howls sounding like a pained scream.

They found themselves trapped in Milo's bedroom. He set the paintings and frames down on his bed, careful not to ruin them more. He touched his mother's signature, ordaining the corners. Voices surrounded him, but he found himself unable to respond. They were angry, irritated with Kali's ignorance, scared at the beast slamming itself against the frail bedroom door, and laced with concern about whether or not Silas was Silas. A hand latched onto him.

"Milo," Thalia said, sounding far away even though her nose was inches from his jaw, "you need to leave the paintings."

Astrid was at his window, trying to shove the old pane up - it had been stuck for as long as he could remember. They considered smashing it. He could see the fear in their eyes.

"I'm sorry, but I can't kill a beast of Hel." She was afraid. "We have to make a run for it. Maybe trap the wolf in the house."

"It'll destroy everything."

Thalia sighed. "There's nothing left here."

"You're wrong," he whispered. "Everything's here." He pushed the paintings around, grabbing onto the framed wolf. He couldn't explain the magnetic pull, his eyes drifting towards the same painting repeatedly. Even as a child, he recalled the moments he'd stand before it, watching his mother drag her paintbrush across a pale canvas.

But there, in his bedroom's enclosure, a wardrobe pushed to barricade the door, howling banging on the walls, a calloused hand tugging on his shoulder, Milo reached and touched the wolf's painted fur.

What happened next was too sudden for him to understand.

There was a voice, someone he couldn't recall, whispering repeatedly in his ears, words overlapping and tripping over each other. And even as the words built a dull pain in his skull, Milo could not release the painting or drag his eyes away. The whispers became clear: *you have the blood of gods,* it began, *do not make yourself limited.* Images flashed like a slideshow: an icy terrain, caves the only sanctuary from the perpetually falling snow, and a little wolf, just larger than a puppy, tumbling out from the shadows. Bare feet melted the snow as they strutted towards the animal, dipping down and sweeping the wolf into their hands, carrying it on their shoulder towards a towering castle in the east.

He closed his eyes. There, within the mind's darkness, was the wolf. Half the size it was in the hall, panting lightly, fur coarse and long across its back, eyes still a sharp red, it whimpered slightly, trotting towards him. He knelt, felt the hot breath against his cheek, and dragged his hand through the gray coat. The wolf rested its head against his shoulder, its heart hammering against Milo's chest. He didn't need to speak. The wolf's voice entered his mind, not as heavy as he thought it would be, but more like a flute, neither male nor female.

I am Kára.

There was no reason for him to say his name. The wolf already knew.

She controls me.

Bare feet against the ice came back to him.

Spill your blood, and I may be freed.

He held onto the wolf's fur.

Present the offering, and none will die.

Milo opened his eyes. "Remove the barricade."

"Huh?" Kali shouted over the noise.

Everything sharpened. Everything in the room materialized around him once more, feeling the hand upon his shoulder, turning to see a bronze gaze upon him. He released his hold on the painting. "Move the barricade."

Silas made a sound of choking. "You're kidding, right?"

"Do I look like I'm kidding?"

"I dunno, man," he said, "I'm hoping you are."

Thalia held onto him. "Listen to yourself, Milo. You open that door, and you'll kill us."

"Do you trust me?"

She swallowed.

"Please, Thalia," he muttered. "Do you trust me?"

"Always," she said. "Always."

"Then let me go."

And contrary to what he expected, she released him.

He stood before the door. Silas and Kali pushed aside his wardrobe, photos, books, and knick-knacks, clattering to the floor. They eyed him impatiently as he passed, disdain clouding Silas's eyes. Milo forced himself to ignore it. He touched the doorknob. The thumping from outside paused. He swung it open.

The lights were out. Everything was darker, tinted with shadows from the falling sun and broken lamps. Milo heard panting from the living room, low and heavy. He exited the bedroom, hearing the door snap shut behind him. Creeping from the hallway, he peered around the corner.

Kára paced the room, her shoulders arched like a cat ready to pounce upon a field mouse. There were Nordic runes painted into her fur, lining her spine and underbelly, something he hadn't noticed before. It laced around her limbs like chains. Slowly, he crossed to the kitchen, his eyes never leaving the wolf. Kára acted as though she hadn't seen him, her hind legs stepping over his couch as though it were a worm beneath her paws. He stepped around the kitchen counter, snatching a knife from the set his mother cherished the most.

The wolf growled, low like a trombone.

"It's okay," he said, "I heard you."

Kára reared back as he approached, her teeth exposed.

"I'll free you."

Her eyes were the same color as a neck wound.

"Watch," he said. Milo raised the knife, extending his left hand. Kára growled again. He slid the blade against his palm, dragging its sharp edge across his skin till he ripped like paper. His blood was as normal as he expected it to be: a scarlet ribbon sliding down him and falling across the floor. It was only in the light it gleamed gold.

Kára stared. Slowly, she inched closer, her paws as large as his skull smacking against the ground like boulders. He resisted the urge to scream. Kára was only a foot away, sniffing the air as the runes lit up along her fur. Milo could smell the metal iron in his human blood and the golden heaviness within it, like maraschino cherries or chocolate. Together they took over the room, sucking out the air and leaving behind a sticky syrup. And when the beast stood only feet away, her body taking up half the living room, the wolf's tongue rolled out, swiping across his hand.

Slowly, his hand raised, digging his fingertips through the fur. A low sound like a cat's purr came from Kára. Her eyes closed.

"Milo," Thalia said.

Kára was no longer gigantic, like a Midgardian wolf, head tilted toward the ones she would have devoured. He turned to face them. The four lined up behind him, glancing between the dripping blood, the wolf, and the ransacked room. Thalia walked to him, wrapping his hand to stop the bleeding. Kali lowered Laevateinn.

"She won't hurt us," Milo said to Silas, who watched with a pinched expression.

The boy frowned. "That's hard to believe."

"Have some faith, would you?"

"Look at you," Silas drawled, "tryin' to school me about faith." He laughed, approaching cautiously. "So we've got a pet now, or what?"

Milo laughed, crouching down to touch Kára's coarse fur. She stretched her neck out. "Kára is not a pet," he said. "Hel enslaved her as a baby, forced her into captivity. She's free now." He dropped his hand. The wolf rubbed her nose against his face, letting out a high-pitched whine. He smiled and scratched her again. "But I think she's gonna stay."

Thalia finished with his hand. "It's odd, isn't it?" She eyed Astrid.

"This is a trait he did not acquire from Odin," the warrior replied.

Thunder shook the house. The sky was clear.

"Acquire what?" Milo asked.

Astrid smiled, patting Kára's head. "Odin was once the Enemy of the Wolf," she said. "His greatest adversary was Fenrir, a beast of Hel, much like Kára. He made a point to kill all wolves within Asgard. Like I said," she paused, shrugging, "you don't get that from your father."

And somehow, hearing it sparked something within him. *You don't get that from your father.* His mind drifted to the painting. He knew where it came from. Milo swallowed the emotion crawling up his throat. "What now?"

"It's time we ask for help," Thalia replied. "We have questions that need answers. As much as I regret saying it, we need the gods."

Astrid frowned. "You believe that to be wise? Amid war?"

"Wisdom isn't the question," she said. "It's knowing when mortality isn't enough. Which happens to be now. Have any coins, *kriger*?"

Out from Astrid's pocket came a pouch, jingling with sound. She pulled it open, retrieving a silver coin decorated with a long-faced man. "What god still accepts Viking money?"

"Calling him a god is a matter of preference," Thalia said. She moved to the front door, exiting the house without another word.

The group followed, Kára trailing behind.

Milo jogged up to the berserker as she positioned herself at the driveway's edge, raising the coin above her head to catch the falling light. "Is he an Aesir?"

"Not exactly."

"Vanir?"

"I...uh," she paused, "I wouldn't put him in that category either."

He sighed. "Then who the hell is he?"

"Immutable," she said. "Like any immortal. Just don't stare, okay? Or speak to him. Or move."

Silas laughed, crouching down. "So what're we supposed to do?"

"By the gods, nothing. Please, do nothing." Thalia took a few deep breaths, her figure increasingly relaxing until her eyes fluttered close. "Hraesvelgr," she shouted. The word sounded garish on her lips like a church bell clanging. It extended into the air, and immediately, the breeze picked up around her, tossing her hair. "I call upon you with a question, o' wise one. Accept my selfless payment, and grant my ignorance with your divine eye."

Everything became still.

And in a blink, he was there before them. The creature towers over the group, his back hunched. His face was pulled down as though his chin were a beak, a sharp nose stabbing out, with pinched lips pressed together like he held something behind his teeth. Feathers, colored auburn and brown coated his cheeks, scored his hands, and poked out from his tight collar. Everything he wore resembled rags, only the cloak dragging behind his bare talon feet radiated divinity. It looked forged from feathers trapped within velvet.

Thalia bowed. "Lord Hraesvelgr."

The god still looked over them. Slowly, his bright eyes waved over the companions, flickering momentarily with perplexity or amusement. Not until he stopped on Milo, his lip curled, revealing unusually perfect teeth. "What a...*precarious* clan," he spoke, and it sounded like feet upon gravel. "And greetings, Aesir Prince." He did not bow, however reverent his words. "I hope your days are not as tainted as your brethren."

Thalia's warnings to be normal disappeared within him.

"What's that supposed to mean?" he snapped.

"It means that my eyes have seen the ends of your people, and their own greed breeds it. What say you, boy, newcomer to the Aesir?"

"I don't care about money if that's what you're asking."

Hraesvelgr frowned. "Ah, your plight is with your human mother, the mistress."

"*Mistress?*" Milo shouted, rage boiling in his chest. "You wanna talk about my Mom like that again, bird brain?"

"*Milo!*" Thalia hissed.

"I merely speak the truth, not to offend," Hraesvelgr replied, unbothered.

Right. Why should gods care about how I feel? Creatures born with the burden of living forever but never truly living. Eventually, there'd come a time when toying with hearts packed with expiration dates would be their only escape. He saw it right there: Hraesvelgr watched him as though he were a science experiment, displayed to be graded and checked. The god's head tilted to the side. It was a game. Gods could whistle and start wars. They could touch the earth and summon a flood. They could cup the ocean in their hands and drop a tidal wave upon cities.

"Tell me this," the god continued, "how is your journey not one of greed if it is a selfish prize you seek?"

Milo kept his mouth shut. He had the unfamiliar urge never to speak again.

"You do not know how to survive without her, so you search for her hand as though her path is the sun in your days. Natalie Bohr of Midgard is but a string in your life, another temporal being subject to mortality."

"What's your point, birdman?"

"Son of Odin," the god's voice boomed, "I implore you not to be like the ones who carry your blood. The Aesir are bountiful, plenty, and ripe in the tree of life. As are the Vanir. They do not need another god to weigh down their yearning for power."

"I don't want power."

"But you wear the ring."

Milo glanced down, prodding at the metal. It looked like any old ring. He shrugged. "It's just a ring."

"Nothing is ever just anything, boy."

He rolled his eyes. "Can-can we quit it with the psycho-babble, please? My friend needs to ask you a question."

Hraesvelgr grinned. "How about this, son of Odin: pass my test, and your wish shall be my command." The god's hands, decorated with feathers, trembled. From excitement or fear, Milo couldn't tell. The god spoke: "Are you a coward?"

Milo was taken aback. "No."

"Are you a liar?"

"*No.*"

The god's pinched bird-like face grew dark with irritation. "You cannot trick me, Prince." The air around them grew stiff and stale, burning at their throats and scratching within them. "I am Hraesvelgr, blessed with the eyes of prophecy and tongue of gold." His cloak snapped out behind him. "My wings breathe air into your lungs. I am the master of wind, the father of eagles, the one foretold to drink from Baldur's blood in the coming of Ragnarok, to feast from the bones of the dead after the Valkyrie have claimed their precious souls. Fool me, you may try, but my eyes can truly see, and I have seen you: cowardice and lies." He closed his eyes and shuddered. "You are as tainted as the Odinsons come. I will pray for your soul."

Milo blankly stared.

Thalia no longer treated the god with respect. She stared him down like she did to the warriors, impatience lacing the shadows. "I have not called upon you for prophecies, Hraesvelgr, games or tests, but _"

Hraesvelgr shouted. The noise was like a crow's shriek, echoing between. "Do not talk as if I have not already heard your plea." His sharp, sun-colored eyes narrowed as he watched, stepping closer. She did not flinch. "You speak beyond a mask, child. A beauty, a pulse within you I have heard before, a distinct face from long ago. I respect your shadows, but do not take that as naivety. I know what you want, Thalia of the North, and I refuse to give it."

She looked unperturbed. "Is it a coin?" she asked. "Do you want more offerings?"

"I am not a negotiator."

Astrid sighed heavily to catch his attention. She didn't look him in the eyes. "Are you not a victim of the Aesir-Vanir War? Do you not wish to see it end?"

"It is sad that you think your actions might call a ceasefire."

"So," Silas said from the ground, "you're just gonna ignore us."

Hraesvelgr looked down upon him, eyebrows raising. "Your kind are the easiest to forget."

"That doesn't give you the right to decide if we live or die," Milo said. He inhaled, the air pricking at his throat. He breathed in once more and ignored the pain, accepting the sharpness to roll throughout his body. By the third breath, the resistance was gone, and he felt stronger than the god.

Hraesvelgr stared silently.

"Don't you know what it means to feel pain?" Milo continued. "How about love? Happiness? Depression? Can gods stand in our shoes long enough to feel the length of mortality, the burden of being alive? I have seen the first snowfall and never experienced a greater beauty. I have watched lakes freeze over and wondered how long I could run till my legs feel like rubber, my knees like water, and my heart like a hummingbird. Just because you've never been in my shoes doesn't mean they don't exist. Gods talk about us like we're a ripple in the water after you toss in a pebble, but damn it, *we are so much more*. And you think you have a right to let all those lives disappear? How *dare* you call me a coward? *How dare you*? *You* fear *us*. You fear our ability to keep living after our hearts are broken. You fear my strength. You fear the power I have for just a *human*. Try to say my people are easy to forget one more time, and I'll make sure my face is forever imprinted on the back of your eyelids."

Hraesvelgr stared. The god looked like an eagle: auburn hair pulled back like straight feathers, eyes a pitch black with a yellow flare spiking in the middle. As though a breeze chilled him, the feathers ruffled, standing up before cascading down like a waterfall. The god took in the frightened stares watching him, waiting for their reaction, seeing Milo's glare, the twitch in Thalia's hands as she gripped her ax, the curve in Astrid's elbow as she prepared to grab Hofond.

Milo swallowed and forced the fear back down his throat. Bit his tongue. Pinched himself. *What did I just do?* The remorse tripped his confidence over and toppled it down the street. Eyes pierced him till everything whittled down, leaving only his bare soul exposed before them. He wanted to take it back. To fall to his knees in shame, to beg for forgiveness. The wind grew sharp around them. *What did I just do?*

Hraesvelgr knelt, bowing his head till his lips touched the driveway. "Warriors of Thunder," he said, "sons and daughters of the First Age, I give my allegiance."

Silas was suddenly standing. The three of them, dead and alive simultaneously, stood together like a wall, Astrid and Thalia poised at either end like the spires guarding Asgard's golden castle.

"Say *what*?" Kali spouted.

Milo bent down, grabbing the god's swinney arms and guiding him back up to his feet before he could speak. Through the thin cloth, Hraesvelgr's limbs shuttered, feathers poking unpleasantly into Milo's skin. It was like holding a bird. The god kept his head bent.

"Please," Milo said, "don't treat us like we're better than you. Believe me, there's no way in hell -" the ground below their feet rumbled "- we are."

Hraesvelgr raised himself. "I pledge my allegiance to you," he spoke, voice forged from gravel and raven's caw, "as ally and friend, defender and brother. At times end, when Heimdall sounds his horn and the world's final battle has begun, I will be at your side, Warriors of Thunder, till death may part us." The god picked a silver feather from his feathered cloak, his eyes barely wrinkling at the rip. He turned, extending his hand and presenting it to Milo. "Take this as a token of my honor. Only whisper my name into the wind, and I will fight by your side, High Prince of the Aesir."

"You'll help us," Thalia said.

The god bowed his head. "My prophetic nature has its boundaries, but there is one thing I can proclaim for sure: the Gungnir sits upon Nifelheim, in the possession of my mother, Hel."

The air grew stale. Whatever it was, it did not come from Hraesvelgr. Mentioning the goddess pulled clouds across the sky, settled the wind till none existed, and brought a silence unlike anything Milo had ever experienced. He expected to feel cold, to become chilled to the bone when walking into death's domain, but it was quite the opposite. A painful heat riddled his spine, streaked beneath his hair, trickled down his arms like sweat. He scratched himself, swearing the heat was like ants crawling under his clothes. Kára trotted closer to him, rubbing her nose against his fingertips. He looked down at her. Her head tilted.

Astrid fidgeted. "Are you sure?"

"Would I be telling it if I was unsure?" he asked. "The spear is in her possession."

"Nifelheim is Vanir territory," Thalia said. "It would be suicide to travel there."

"What else are we to do, then? We risk crossing the goddess's path, but it is the only way to find the Gungnir. Without it, we are helpless." Astrid frowned.

"Then we go to Nifelheim," Milo blurted. "Everything is a death wish for us. I see no point in trying to fight it now."

Hraesvelgr stepped away. "Be swift, Warriors, for your coming days will be long, harsh, and buried in winter's cold. Be brave, and never forget who you are." He nodded to Thalia. She smiled, flipping the coin over the gap between them. Quickly, he snatched it, a twinkle in his eyes as he inspected the silver. Hope lingered in his pinched bird-like face when he looked upon them again. "And may the gods be with you." Extending his arms beside him, Hraesvelgr's cloak snapped out with the wind, breaking in half till there were wings, thrusting him off the ground and shooting him into the air.

"Hate to be the killjoy," Silas said as the god retreated, "but how do you guys plan on getting us there? Last time we went to another realm, there was a portal."

Astrid grinned. "Simple. We call on the gods."

Thalia was laughing. "Look at you, *kriger*. Following in my steps."

"Never said it was smart," she said. "But what else are we to do?"

Milo rolled his eyes. "What kinda god are you thinking about?"

"One that owes me a favor!"

And as the Asgardian made her way down the driveway, elated with her newfound idea, the same hope from Hraesvelgr warping her naturally stern face into something resembling a cloud, Milo became aware of a heartbreaking thought. He turned, taking in his house for what felt like the last time. *Nothing will ever be the same.* He wanted to run back inside, lock the doors, and search every nook and cranny for his mother because *she had to be there still.* He touched his eyelids. Maybe it was all a dream. Maybe if he pinched himself hard enough, he'd wake up. Maybe he should let something kill him for real this time, see what would happen.

Maybe.

Milo watched his friends follow Astrid away from the house, only Thalia hanging back slightly, waiting for him to start moving. He could see the mistrust in her stance, the thought lingering on her lips: *will he try to run again?* And for her, he wouldn't. He still meant those words he struggled to push out in the ice bath, whispered over the heavy air towards Astrid. Down to that last second, he knew he'd say them over and over again till his throat was raw with agony, scratched and hoarse.

Where she goes, I go.

Thalia raised her hand towards him. "Are you coming?"

He ran towards her, his wolf following at his ankles.

Milo took her hand, wishing he could turn back time.

XXVI. The Road to Hell has Daisies.

The company walked along the roads toward a lake Milo had mentioned, which was surrounded by thinning trees, mud, and dead grass. Astrid watched a rabbit scurry into a bush's cover. Crows circled above their heads. There were wilting daisies along the roadside. A gray discoloration hung over the company, a fear of the future. She ignored it, tuning back into the world around her, the young ones feeling like needles against her brain. For the fifth time, they begged her to tell a story. Eventually, their pleas turned specific, begging for firsthand experiences with the God of Thunder himself.

In the gloom of Midgardian neighborhoods, her mind only recalled their first fight. The moment Astrid understood, she willingly gave her heart to a beast who never planned to return it.

Astrid could not remember how it began. One moment, they were bare under the covers, intertwined and dizzy with the rising dawn; the next, he crouched before the fire, skin glowing the same color as the embers, her back pressed against the wooden bed frame, sturdy and cold on her bare skin. She wanted to fold into herself, to be covered with iron and gold. The room spun. She wasn't sure whether she would throw up or not. Her stomach was empty.

Thor held his knees against his chest, fine golden hairs twirling around his fingertips. His nakedness was stark but not bold within the concealed chambers. He was not trying to impress. Gods did not need to. "My creation," he said, "cannot be taken from me."

What had she said? There was talk of death, her yearning to run across hills and move mountains. Soft whispers of a future not involving the Prince. She knew when he said *my creation*, he referred to her. Her eyes narrowed. "Do you not wish for me to be free?"

"You speak as if chains hold your wrists," he looked at her with sun-lit eyes, "down to my floors. But if, Astrid, there were to be chains, who is to say they do not extend across realms? And if I, by my mercy, rid them for you, is that not creating you into something else?" Drunken lips dripping heavy words turned back towards the fire. He was the god she hated, the side that praised divinity over her beating heart.

"Is that what you call love? You act as though I should be thankful for your presence, for the mark your divinity has left upon my skin, but I feel empty. I feel like a shell, a discarded being used for comfort and smiles and shields. What am I to you? If I am your creation, and you are my god, I'd rather be like your fallen angels, discarded and independent, breaking into a new world with only your face in the distance."

He was still in the fire's light. "You are mine," he said, simply, a matter of factually, as though she should have already known. With a blink, he was gone, leaving her there, frozen, staring down an immeasurable cliff and begging for her body to jump.

It was the grief - the *shame* - that crawled up her throat, pushed against her teeth, and threatened to spill like an unwavering ocean. Her gaze landed on Milo. He wasn't paying attention to his fellow warriors' badgering but stared ahead, a storm gathering in his eyes. The one thing she refused to do was ruin him. She would not tell stories of his brother's faults, of the things he did, the crimes he carelessly committed, the lives he took without a blink. She would build something to describe his honor, something Asgard's poets sang during festivals, prayers devoted before his altars. She would remember an inscription on the countless statues, repeat the words a thousand times till she could convince him *Thor was good*.

Astrid touched her amulet.

Rain trickled down from gathering clouds. She glanced at the young Prince again. He seemed oblivious to it, his jaw tight and harsh like glass. The rain streaked down his cheeks. Drops fell from Astrid's nose, slipped between her lips, and caught in her hair. She breathed in. The rain was heavy with ghosts that day. She closed her eyes as they walked on.

"There is nothing to tell," she said once more.

The dead ones groaned in response.

They wanted tales of adventures, stories built from daring escapes and scraping by death, love, and happy endings. There were none. There were more Jotunheim invasions than she could truly recall. There were wars resulting in villages pillaged, children slaughtered, limbs left on doorsteps, and decorated pikes lining battlefields. There were fields still stained with the blood of gods and mortals alike. There were thousands dead. Thousands more were left wounded. Thousands more are still fighting for their lives. Thousands are trying to forget and live without the ghosts haunting them forever.

That was all Astrid had. Memories of blood spilled. Moments between feigned peace, her hand trailing Thor's back carelessly, searching for scars from their past battles but only finding skin as smooth as marble. She held onto Hofond. The rain continued to fall.

"Tell us of Thor," Milo said.

She imagined he spoke in her head.

"Astrid," he continued. "I want to hear."

And whether it was her fear of disappointing him or the strength laced behind his voice sounding so eerily like him, she nodded. "What would you like to know?"

He shrugged. "The truth."

She knew what he meant. The boy did not wish to hear fables or poetry; he did not want to know the praises sung in his brother's honor. He stared and wanted to know how his enemy thought, how they moved and swung their blade.

"He was born during the rain," she said. "Fresh spring. Asgard smelt of dew and blossoms and trees. Frigg's screams were so loud that she created thunder, the birthing pain felt across all realms. But Odin carved the Prince from his wife, using the Gungnir to tear apart her immortal skin before it repaired itself. Thor was fully grown hours later."

"Huh?" Silas blurted. "He was what?"

"Gods are not like you or I, Silas," she replied. "They experience centuries in a day, are born one minute and aged the next. The Prince quickly matured, but that does not mean he knew what being alive meant. He loved how Asgard's golden floors felt beneath his feet but had not yet experienced snow or the crunch of leaves. He believed the most angelic color was bronze, for it was his armor's color, sword, and statues that lined the throne room, but he had yet to see the brilliance of newborn flowers." She stared at Milo. "Thor spent years being trained by his fellow Aesir to wield a sword. The Norn blessed him at birth with great speed, enhanced endurance, and the gift of battle. There is nothing he could not do."

Milo tossed a rock and caught it in the same motion. "And when he lost?"

"I have never seen him lose."

Something like fear and surprise crossed his face. "Never?"

"Not once."

He raised his face to the sky, tossed the rock, and angrily caught it. The thunder slammed into them in response.

Astrid wanted to shake him. His questions were careless, strung from ignorance. The wind tossed them around, rain striking down, thunder echoing, and lightning screaming. No matter how far away Thor might be, he felt his brother's power and would leave nothing to chance. She had seen him do such things before Baldur was sent away: the first High Prince showed his power through leadership and charm, captivating all Asgardians. In response, the young Thor - who was no more than a decade old - tricked his brother into climbing the highest mountain with him and forced lightning to strike at their feet. The young Thor was unscathed, and being centuries older, Baldur was left to look like a frightened chicken for days before his matured godly healing took over.

She used to ask herself what she'd do for the missing Prince. In the past, she killed for him, plundered empires, and smashed skulls. But somehow, her answers would be thin, leaving her more empty than filled with love. Astrid looked upon the young Milo, and the question was answered without being asked.

Anything.

Milo was not finished. "When did you meet him?"

Astrid sighed. She could not remember her first encounter with the missing Prince. The days after Herjan's destruction were a blur. Thor told her it was a good thing not to remember. "You were a starving street rat," he said one night, their limbs tangled from a previous embrace, "the things you did are better forgotten." She curled a blonde strand around her pinky and nodded. In those days, his words were final for her. There was no convincing. It was a whole fragmented year, months of grieving before Thor eventually came across her in the castle. Her first memory with him was the clearest in her mind, sharp with vivid emotions and crisp colors.

It was her first war. With whom she could not recall, the gods were not as transparent with their knowledge as one may believe. She stood upon a hill, looking down upon the falling enemies. The limbs flew across the field, and death's smog hovered above their heads. Hel was so close she could smell her: iron and cedar. Valkyrie watched overhead. Vultures circled. But it was Thor, alive for a century by then, who caught her eye. He struck down the enemy King's sons like lightning. Ullr stood at Astrid's side. He placed a steady hand-colored clay on her shoulder. "Children cannot be permitted to live," he said. "Not when they may avenge their people."

Thor slaughtered a family name that day. Or was it night? She could not remember.

Astrid left the hill afterward. War's view from above was not meant for a mortal like her. What she saw was not for her eyes. Somehow, past the carcasses and severed heads, her feet led her to Thor. He raised his blade over the King. She touched his wrist.

"That is enough death for one day, my Lord."

He looked at her like one of the beautiful goddesses in Asgard's halls. And for her, he lowered his blade. The King lived till his heart shattered with loneliness, burying his children and wife in copper tombs beside the field where their blood birthed blossoms and tulips. Later, Thor told her he fell in love with her that day. When she asked why, his answer chilled her. "You were as dark as me," he whispered, "I wanted him to suffer, and so did you." Her confusion must have been evident on her face. He touched her cheek. "That King had to live with it. All the pain." She expected to feel horrified, slap him and run, fight for her honor, and exclaim her intentions were pure, unlike his own. Somehow, the words never came out.

But as she looked upon her companions, their stares drilling into her as they awaited an answer, Astrid vowed never to speak such memories aloud. They did not need to know Thor was a cruel Prince or she was as dark as him. "After my village's collapse," she lied, "he brought me under his wing within the Royal Guard." She smiled the best she could. She was surprised at how much it hurt. "He saved me."

As they neared the artificial lake, Astrid spoke no more. She quieted her confidence and tried to bring hope back to her lips, for dealing with a god meant wearing one's best face.

The lake hid behind trees, a broken wired fence half buried in grass, half exposed to the cloudy afternoon light. Bushes reaching her hips surrounded the lake, mud swirling and catching on the dried grass, dead from the previous summer's gaze. It was incredibly still like the lake knew what was to come. The animals kept their distance, and residents locked themselves indoors, trapping the company in an air-tight bubble. A few weak daisies sprouted by the lake's edge. She reached down, touched the petals, and watched them wilt. A butterfly skidded across the surface, its reflection cracked like stained glass. Astrid avoided trying to see herself in the lake's mirror.

"All right, *kriger*," Thalia said. "What next?"

She pulled the amulet over her head. "I call upon an old friend."

Kneeling, Astrid placed the jewel upon the water's surface, watching as it sank, the color melting into darkness. She rested her palms on her knees, slowing her breathing, picturing the god in her mind. His skin was a rustic brown, riddled with Vanir markings - shaped to resemble ocean waves, with the tides pushing and pulling beneath his jaw. His hair draped down to his knees, white with age and smelling like salt, water, and seaweed. Barnacles grew on his skin. And his eyes were like shells, colored pale blue, wide and intelligent. His face grew sharp in her mind.

Thalia's foot tapped against the dirt. "How could a Vanir owe you anything?"

"Not all Vanir are soulless," she paused, turning to look at the berserker, "like Freyja."

Thalia glared.

"Once," Astrid continued, "there was a Vanir god trapped within Asgard's walls. He was captured during conquests and forced to live in a bronze casket below Odin's statue in the castle's square courtyard." The lake's surface rippled. "Fortunate circumstances led me to find him, and weakness made me believe he did not deserve to be trapped in something so cruel." The rain fell harder. Wherever the lost Prince was, he could hear her, and the betrayal rattled with thunder.

"So you freed him," Milo said.

"He swore to one day repay me." The water pulled back. "Today, the tides turn towards us."

A man rose from the inky black lake. The water line stopped at his stomach, revealing a bare chest adorned with the intricate twists and turns of the Vanir ribbons. As she remembered, the god's beard rested at his collarbone, white with eternal life. His hair was pulled back in braids, like sailboat knots. Nothing had changed with his face. He was still handsome, like waves shaped his face. Only his bright eyes, outlandishly large, marked him as something other than mortal. Astrid's amulet was minuscule in his hands.

"Golden warrior," he said. There was something harsh about his speech, like water smashing against rocks. But it was not harsh with reproach, rather heavy with divinity. His lips were blue. "You look well."

She bent till her nose dipped into the lake. "Lord Aegir, King of the Seas."

"Rise, mortal."

Astrid stood, noticing how the berserker avoided looking the god directly in the eyes and how transfixed Silas was, awe trapped behind his skin. "I hope you've been well during the wars."

"Vanir are never well during an Aesir war," he replied. He rolled the amulet between his fingers. "My blessings have protected you, I hope."

She smiled. "I did not know you did such a thing." She touched her heart. "The moment I can, I will provide more offerings."

"Do not give me your gratitude. It is not a Vanir's place to guide an Asgardian through their journey. My people were...aghast, to say the least, at my actions."

"Then why did you?"

Aegir cracked a smile. "Your exiled gods find solace with us. One is known for his persuasion." His shrug washed the lake over their feet. "I did not think you would ever call upon me."

Exiled gods. She turned slightly and saw Milo's pointed stare fixated on her. They both knew who he referred to. *Loki.* Most days, she forgot they were once friends. Astrid spent her early days in the guard beside Ullr and Loki, and eventually, Thor and Sigyn joined the company. The five were a powerhouse on the battlefield, knowing each other's moves before they ever happened. When the war had escalated past peace's embrace, tensions grew till Loki and Sigyn were exiled; Thor suddenly turned a blind eye towards his previous friends, Ullr escaping through the woods into solitude, and her, left to be a mortal within the gods' halls. She forced herself not to be softened at Loki's gesture, even after what she did to him. It was not something she deserved.

"I would not have," she said. "But Asgard has fallen, and we need safe passage to a place only a Vanir can access."

Aegir's gaze flickered over them. "A Vanir."

"We are only mortals, lacking the ability to travel between realms."

His lip twitched. "Quite a company you find yourself with, golden warrior."

"They are Valhallians, sent on a mission -"

Something rippled through the water. Aegir's face warped, the lake swirling around him like a whirlpool. "Divine eyes can penetrate your masks," he snapped, the words resembling a crab's snapping claw. "Do you think your true identities go unnoticed?"

"I did not lie."

"Neither did you tell the truth."

"Depends on what you consider the truth," she said. "You understand why I cannot say such words aloud." *Warriors of Thunder. Odinson. Berserker.* All titles would be heard from miles away, the words holding power enough to be carried to the wrong ears.

Aegir softened. "Tell me, *Valhallians*, what is it you seek?"

"We need passage to Nifelheim."

"No."

Her eyebrows raised. "I beg your pardon?"

"A portal to Hel's land of the undead is impossible," he said. "You should know this. Your arrival would not go unnoticed. Hel's Dragur would be on you within moments."

Milo inched forward. "I'm sorry," he choked, "did you say *Dragur*?"

The god nodded. "Souls captured by Hel and transformed into her undead army. They are unbeatable. Eternal creatures connected to her divine life force." He smiled politely. "All of you would perish."

"That doesn't matter," said Milo, the glint in his eyes saying something different.

Kali meekly raised her hand. "Personally, I think it matters."

"If a god says we shouldn't," Silas said, "then I think we should figure something else out."

"No," Milo said. His voice ricocheted. Thunder rumbled. Clouds parted above, and the sun extended downwards. Astrid noticed he sounded unlike himself; his voice tinged with something unreal, a power bringing fear to mortal ears. "You're gonna take us there."

"Your blood is not fully golden, boy," the god growled. "Do not speak to me like your Aesir brethren."

"Look, I'm not trying to be an asshole, all right?" He looked around at their company, tired eyes staring back at him. "Last thing I wanna do is disrespect you. But what you've gotta understand is that I'm *not the Aesir*. Everybody keeps saying they're my brethren or my family, but they've got it all wrong. My family is *here*. You're lookin' at them. And I'm missing one person." He frowned. "You've got a mother?"

"Once," Aegir said, "I believe I did."

"Well, I've still got one," Milo replied. "Her name is Natalie, and I've gotta find her. You understand that, don't you?"

"She is not on Nifelheim."

"No, but there's something there that'll help me get her."

Aegir did not move. For the longest time, he stared, the lake growing eerily silent around his figure. Slowly, the god waded through the water, its inky darkness wrapping around him like a cloak. He dropped the amulet into Astrid's hand. "It is impossible."

"*Why?*" Astrid groaned.

"That amulet," he said, "it is useless to me."

"But the jewel -"

Aegir chuckled. "Is but a jewel, hexed with simple magic to be paired with a lost infant god. Indestructible magic surrounds Hel's realm, a wall that keeps most out. For me to open a portal long enough for all of you to get through would require power. *Real* power. That is merely a talisman." He shrugged. "A weak one at most."

"Lord Aegir," Astrid said, "all I have is this and the honor I risked for you many years ago. Is that not offering enough?"

"You know how this works, golden warrior. There is no way around it. My power to build portals comes from mortal's gifts, and I tell you again: what you give is not enough for what you ask."

Astrid neared her end. She was tempted to throw herself at his feet, bow till she was flat against the muddy ground, plead and scream till he changed his mind. But she knew he did not lie. They asked him to commit an act the Vanir considered treason. The convincing he'd need would be something divine. She lowered her head.

The berserker walked towards the lake. She stepped close to the god, her shadow stretching over Astrid. And then she was on one knee, holding out her palms to show a glimmering chain link. "Would this suffice?"

Aegir's face lit up. He reached. "Gleipnir!"

Astrid stared at the chain. It was a piece from the prison entrapping the great beast Fenrir, built by the greatest blacksmiths and blessed by the most bountiful gods. She watched the stillness in Thalia's jaw as she waited for the god to take the offering.

The god grabbed the chain, energy rumbling through him. "I can take you to Nifelheim," he said. "But it will take time."

"We can offer you hours," Astrid said, "but no more."

"I see," he replied, twisting his beard around a finger. "Hours I can manage. I will need to be as close to the sea as possible."

"And what might that take, Lord Aegir?" She preened a smile and pulled back her lips to show teeth. Time had taught her all gods were the same, no matter which clan they came from. They sought respect; without it, there would be no telling what they might do. At a different time, she may have expected Aegir to treat her as an equal, but with his chains gone, he returned to the status of *Lord* and *Sir*. Even the ones she once called friends expected the same titles.

He waved his arm through the lake, the water swirling like a tornado, the inky color fading into something lighter. "Only a detour," he said. The god's eyes grew dark. "I take sanctuary in Hjerte, a quiet Vanir village that pools my seas. There, you may find solace for a few moments. No beasts or gods are there to harm you on your journey. In an hour's time, I will have forged your passage to Nifelheim."

"Hjerte?" Astrid repeated. She squinted. *Hjerte*.

The berserker grasped at her elbow. "*Kriger*," she whispered, lips almost pressed to her ear, "we cannot."

Astrid pulled away. "That is gracious of you, great god of the sea. We will accept -"

"*Astrid*!" Thalia hissed.

She turned, just for a moment. She couldn't remember another time in the last three days when the berserker addressed her by name. The notion should have frightened her, but it merely brought distaste to her lips. She turned away and stretched her smile out again.

"Lord Aegir," she continued, "we accept your bargain."

The god nodded, and the whirling water glowed a faint silver. It smelt like snow and mountains and deer. "Enter, mortals, and you will be safe."

There was a long pause. She grazed Kali's hand and bumped her elbow into Silas. "Go ahead, dead ones," she whispered, "I will be right behind."

Silas first entered the portal with small steps. He sunk into the water, face warped by surprise as he delved, gone within an instant. Kali clicked her heels together three times. Milo chuckled. And without another sound, she entered the portal. Thalia, still afraid, stepped into the water, her sharp gaze glancing toward the god before disappearing.

Astrid gripped Hofond in one hand and tightened her fingers around the amulet in the other.

And as she entered the portal, hope filled the cavity in her chest.

* * *

"I offer you something else, young one," the god said into the quiet.

Milo paused before the portal. It rained again. His eyes had been caught on a patch of nearby daisies for some time, the previous conversation nothing but whispers in his mind. What caught his attention was only Thalia's anger, her rage, and fear. The sudden emotion made him suspicious and lit up this heat along his body as though someone was watching. Feeling that way about her hurt him as though a deep hatred for her lay dormant in him. He raised his eyes towards the god. Aegir was oddly beautiful in his own right. The same beauty which you'd find when looking upon the horizon.

"What?"

Aegir waded towards him. "I know what you are, and the company you wander with is...unlike you." The god struggled. He muttered something in a different language. "It is not here where you belong. With this power," the chain link reappeared in his hand, "I might change your course."

"I don't understand," he said. "Where else would I be?"

"Your father's halls."

"He's dead."

"The rest of your clan is not," he said. "There is Frigg. The eldest brother, Baldur. Cousins and such, gods with little name but wide lands." Aegir's eyes softened. "Even with Midgardian blood,

329

young one, your divinity remains the strongest. I might take you where you belong."

Milo laughed. The disbelief stopped in his throat. "They're my family."

"Mortals are no friends of the gods."

"I'm not a god!"

Aegir smiled. It was not pleasant, but it was like jumping into freezing water for the first time in summer. "I could make you one."

He scoffed. "Why'd you even want that? You're a Vanir, for crying out loud. You don't like me."

"There is little you know of our tribes, young one," he said. "We fight for land and power but are together, surviving through eternity. Aligning yourself with mortals is an insult to your power."

"God," Milo breathed, "you sound like a xenophobe."

The god ignored him. "If you cherish them, do you not wonder what your golden blood might do to them? How might it ruin them rather than protect them?"

"What's that supposed to mean?"

"You hold the masked one close to your heart, do you not?"

Milo froze. *Masked one.* He swallowed. "How do you -"

"Do you know what would happen if you were to love her? Truly, I mean."

He didn't speak.

"You have yet to feel your power, young one. But I know you have felt anger beneath your chest, rage and grief trapped within your fists." The god leaned forward, his skin like moss. "How about love? What would happen when you realize something in your palms could kill a warrior like her?"

Milo stared at the god and remembered Loki's rantings. He swallowed, pressing his lips together. "There's no way of knowing that would happen."

"But it could."

He shook his head. "I'd never hurt her."

"You will."

"*No!*"

"Young one," he said, "I can ensure it doesn't. I might take you away, keep you from seeing her face again. You would be safe and on the way to becoming an Aesir like your brothers."

Milo felt rage crawl up his throat. "Say that one more time, and I'll -"

"What," Aegir said, "you'll kill me with your mortal hands? Look at yourself. Without divinity, you are as little as they, ants crawling through the dirt, barely leaving a mark upon the world that you ever existed, your only chance of immortality being the name you leave behind. You are nothing, boy. Nothing without the golden streaks in your veins, nothing without your father's name, nothing without the quest you have been placed on. *Nothing.*"

He looked away. Without another word, he entered the lake, stepping into the shimmering portal and wishing everything would be silent. He took one last look at Aegir.

"Then I shall be nothing."

"Beyond Asgard's golden castles...
...Stood Sjel, a small and peaceful settlement."

SOULLESS

XXVII. Prometheus

They appeared in a land of snow and mountains, dusted grey at their peaks, stabbing the sky miles away. But, after a few seconds, Milo noticed that there was *no sky* but rather a curved rock, only a circular opening at the center to show a glimpse at the sky. He raised his hand, tracing the faraway ceiling with his fingertips.

Drawings done in scarlet red paint decorated the obsidian rocks, like prehistoric cave paintings. Down at the horizon, where the rock met the trapped snowy mountains, was a woman painted upon the stone. He frowned. It was a *bowl*. An entire village, filled with plains, mountains, snow, and houses, all kept inside a jagged bowl resembling a volcano's insides.

Beyond were buildings shaped like pyramids, charcoal-colored smoke trailing up from rooftops. A tall fire pit sat at the village's center, surrounded by rock and twigs. The inhabitants were cloaked, layered with furs and leather. When hit with moonlight, their faces showed twirling red paint, and tattoos lined their jaws and chins. They all had similar attributes: olive-tinted skin, jet-black hair that hung full and long down their backs, belts strapped with swords and bows.

But directly before the company, where the portal delivered them, was a lamppost. It was ordinary, and the top opened to carry an oceanic blue flame. The heavy snowflakes dropping into the fire did not disappear even as the snow trickled down.

Milo realized then, staring into the fire, what he said. *Then I shall be nothing.* His hands shook. Who was he, merely a boy, to speak to a god in such a way? Even more, why did he feel regret? Why was there guilt lacing his heart? Brought together, his hands rested over his heart, and for the first time, he did not flinch at the lack of a heartbeat. He didn't want to be a god. He sucked in a breath. He didn't want to be a god. His voice rang unfamiliar in his mind. Not that it mattered. Aegir was gone, and the company was once again in another land.

The Valhallians shivered in tangent.

"God," Silas muttered, "could've taken us to the Bahamas, you know?" He wrapped his long arms around himself, huddling down next to Kali. "Just wish the portals came with accessories. Like coats."

"This isn't Narnia." Kali laughed to herself when no one else did.

The Warriors of Thunder huddled close together for warmth. Milo pressed his feet into the snow, hearing that satisfying crunch. He raised his head to look for Thalia but only saw Astrid. She held the greatsword close to her chest and nodded her chin to the right. Thalia stood beside the lamppost, her hand tracing an engravement at its center. Above, the blue flame rippled and danced.

In the post's center was a carving of a woman, her arms crossed at her stomach, axes crossed over her chest. Pinched curls enveloped her face, almond-shaped eyes staring forward. Runes were inscribed beneath her image. Milo inched closer to Thalia, watching as her fingers intricately traced it.

"I remember this place," Astrid whispered. She grabbed a handful of snow and watched it course through her fingertips before looking back. "Hjerte is the land of Skadi, the winter goddess. It's," she paused, eyes glazing over the settlement, "still around. I thought it would've been destroyed by now."

"War taints many lands," Thalia whispered. "Just because you cannot see its scars does not mean they don't exist." Her eyes narrowed. "Aegir said his power was funneled here. His land must be destroyed."

Milo frowned. "So that can happen? Like realms can die?"

"As I've told you before," Astrid said, "all things rise and fall." She pointed to the west. "There's a stream. It must connect to Yggdrasil. Otherwise, he'd be powerless here."

"Is she here?"

Astrid raised her eyebrows. "Who?"

"The goddess," he replied. "Skadi."

Thalia froze. Her hand dropped. "Doesn't matter," she snapped. "The best thing for us is to lay low and wait till Aegir opens the passageway to Hel. Understood?"

She was on edge. Milo watched her face, the tense lines around her eyes, hands clenched at her sides. Aegir's words lingered, whispers warning him of becoming too close. His hand reached, and almost like she could hear his thoughts, she jerked back, wrapping her arms behind her.

"Why a lamppost?" he asked.

Thalia's eyes narrowed. "It is a piece of Asgard's eternal flame." Her angular face lifted towards the cracking fire. A soft aqua light cast long shadows along her face, her bronze eyes taking on a different shade. "Legend says the goddess brought it to her homeland as a mark of the alliance with the Aesir. The same fire protected Asgard's castle in its spires."

"So what's the truth?"

"Ever heard of Prometheus?"

"Yeah," he said, "he stole fire from Zeus. Brought it back to the humans, right?"

Silas came up behind him, shoes crunching against the ground. "His liver gets eaten every day in punishment. Tough luck for a god."

Thalia nodded but said no more. She looked away from the lamppost, keeping her eyes down, everything different about her face. "Come," she said, "we should get inside." Swiftly, she left the lamppost, approaching the town filled with low chatter and muffled music. No townspeople paid attention to them but followed each other one by one towards a longhouse at the settlement's most northern point.

The building must've been fashioned from wood, for the deep smell of lumber and leaves wafted toward them as they approached. There was something else: a sweetness, sickly like honey, mixed with a roasting pit, like meat on a stick. His stomach rumbled. Kali was right, he thought. The dead can hunger. Echoing laughter and music came from the building's wide doors, a reddish light radiating out like heat waves. Immediately, warmth spread towards them, beckoning for the company to come closer to its comforting hearth. Milo practically ran to the longhouse when he slammed into a chest, his nose smacking against a sternum.

"Watch where you're -"

"You Midgardians always surprise me," Aegir said, his voice oddly different from the lake - it was gentler, easier on their ears, not the godly resonating voice pounding down upon them. He was shorter, there, in the snow, barely a head taller than Milo. Cloaks resembling bear fur draped over his shoulders, a hood covering coily white hair. His skin surprised Milo: it was shaded obsidian like the rocks, deep and mesmerizing, blemish, and scar-free. And gone were his Vanir marks. "So careless with your words."

Milo gaped. "How-how...you're -"

"I have come to you in a familiar body," the god said. "It is best when lingering in mortal's midst for my true appearance to remain secret. For all our safety, do not call me by my name." He lifted his chin. "Call me Asbjørn, young ones."

Thalia grabbed onto his hand, gently pulling Milo back till she faced the god. "Why have you come, Asbjørn? Is it done?"

"I did not lie when I asked for hours," he said. "If you want solace in Hjerte's longhouse, you must look the part. Follow me."

Behind the longhouse, where the sounds became a distant reminder of warmth awaiting them, were wool cloaks, fur boots, and gloves made from black leather. Beside those was a wooden bucket filled with an inky red paint. The god motioned towards the clothes. "Take one each," he commanded.

The Warriors dressed in the cloaks, pulling the gloves on. Thalia moved to the bucket, dipping her right hand and grasping Milo with her left.

"What're you doin'?"

She grabbed his chin. "Don't move." She dragged paint across his face in graceful motions, following the grooves in his nose, the protrusion in his jaw, and the jut on his chin. Down her hands went through his eyebrows and eyes, pausing as her thumb grazed his lip. To their right, Asbjørn dressed the others, decorating their faces and necks with the paint.

Kali squirmed beneath the god's working hands. "I know this isn't cultural appropriation," she said, "but I *really* feel like this is culture appropriation."

"Promise me something," Thalia whispered.

He looked down. Quickly, his eyes darted towards Asbjørn, where the god watched with a pointed gaze. He turned back to Thalia. "Anything."

"Don't turn away from me."

"What do you mean?"

She frowned. "Just...no matter what happens," her voice lowered, "I am not your enemy."

And yet, her request sounded like a warning in his ears. He wanted to grab her, force her to explain what she meant and tell her *he* feared being the enemy in *her* eyes. In the moment they were close, where heat spiked his insides, he had no clue what might happen. How strong would the power be within his hands? His hand reached, fingertips grazing her neck. Goosebumps formed. As quick as he reached, Milo jumped back, extending her at arm's length.

"Let's get going," he muttered, pulling the hood over his head.

Asbjørn left them to enter the longhouse, disappearing into the snow. The longhouse was filled with townspeople laughing and shouting in unfamiliar languages. Fires roasted at every corner, drinking games happening sporadically at the wooden log tables. The walls were decorated with rusting weapons, shields, and furs. A small throne sat at the building's head; a man heavy with age and wool layers lounged with a tall cup resting against his lips. He did not notice their entry.

"Is that a pig?" Kali stared with a gaping mouth at meat twirling over a roasting pit. She inched closer.

Astrid touched her shoulder. "Come along, dead one." She grinned. "How about some food?"

Without another word, Astrid marched towards the feast, followed by Silas and Kali, the duo barely containing their excitement. Milo watched with amusement but didn't dare follow. Nausea swirled in his throat, Thalia still beside him. He yearned to push her away, shake her, and shout *why do you trust me?* All he could think about were Aegir's warnings. What lay beneath his skin? What could he do to hurt the people he loved? How could any of them trust him? His fists clenched. He did not even trust himself. Milo fell into an empty seat, staying away from the town's inhabitants. He grabbed a fork, twirling it around absentmindedly. It was like the night in the bar. It all led back to the bar.

"Aren't you hungry?" Thalia slid into the seat across from him.

He shrugged, avoiding looking at her.

"Reminds me of home," she whispered, looking over her shoulder. A smile draped across her lips. "All of it."

"When are you going to realize I don't care?"

Thalia's head shot towards him. Amusement twinkled in her eyes, lips poking up in a smirk. "What's with the attitude, Valhallian?"

"Just being honest," he snapped. His throat ached. "Sit someplace else if it bothers you." *Don't go.*

"I thought we were friends."

"You were wrong."

Her playful nature faded. "Well, you're lying."

"Thalia -" *I'm lying.*

"You're *lying*," she repeated.

He dropped the fork. "Stop yelling and just listen to me."

"No. No! You're trying to push me aside, aye?" Thalia pressed her lips together, leaning forward, knocking a jug filled with a honey-colored liquid over with her elbow. "I'm not. Not now. You're being a coward, and for what?" She pulled back, head lolling to the side. A snarky sarcasm shined through her paint-covered face. "What's scared you?"

"Do I look afraid?" He knew he was afraid.

"Yes, Milo Bohr," she exclaimed. "You look afraid. So how about you try the truth this time."

The air stilled. He gritted his teeth together, looking away from her pleading eyes. And there, with her attention fully drawn upon him, all he could do was be what she wanted. If she wanted his hands, he'd cut them off. "I'm afraid," he started, licking his lips, "I'm afraid that if I told you about the darkness inside me, you'd still look at me like the sun."

"Humans are as dark as they come, and there's nothing left to do but survive." She shrugged. "Why is that bad?"

"Because you have no idea how many times I've wanted to hurt you. *You*." The words fell out before he could stop himself.

His head dropped. His voice scorched his own throat, tore at his tongue, and stabbed his teeth. He covered his mouth, pressing his nails against the drying paint against his cheeks. And when he looked at her, she was not afraid. Even then, when heat swarmed within him once more, when he could've sworn a monstrous rage danced within his eyes, she watched him with a painful steadiness.

"There's this rage in me," he said, "something that isn't human, that looks at you and sees the worst." And nothing could stop something else from forcing itself out from within, all those fears dripping from his lips like blood. "I hate you, and I love you. *Do you understand?* I hate it when you look at me as though you can see what's in my head, and I love it when you look at me and see something I wish I were. I want to tell you I love you till my throat bleeds. Do you understand me?"

A newfound lightness overtook her features, that angelic smile dragging across her face. "I have my own mind, Milo. Decisions are my own, not yours."

He shook his head. "What -"

"I don't scare easily."

Milo's fists slammed against the table. The sound barely carried in the already rambunctious room. He wanted to scare her, to make her think twice about giving him her time. "You know what?" he spat, the same old venom filling his mouth as he prepared the forked words to stab her, "you act all high and mighty, afraid of nothing -

berserker Thalia, warrior of legends, but what are you really? As much as you can see me, *I* can see *you*. Deep down, you're just like me."

"And what would that be?"

"Dead."

Thalia's smile faded. An ashy color took over her face. The world around them faded. It was just them, her eyes staring at him with betrayal. She looked away, towards the snow drifting into the longhouse, towards the other Valhallians shouting with laughter, towards the man upon the throne. She did not look at him again. "Screw you, Milo," she whispered, her voice so quiet it barely carried along the breeze, "just...screw you." Thalia lifted herself from the bench as if caught in a trance, entering the snowstorm outside without another word.

Then I shall be nothing.

That same heat erupted in his chest. He didn't care anymore. His legs moved without him wanting to. The space between them was like the sea, forever growing and destroying, swallowing up lands and drowning sailors. The farther she moved, the more his heart ached, and the more he wished to collapse in sorrow, rip out his hair, and melt into the snow. Without remembering how he got there, Milo stood in the snow, eyes scanning the dark terrain till he saw her, once again by the lamppost, her hand tracing the engraving. He told himself to go back into the longhouse. Leave the space between them forever growing. It would be better this way.

He ran to her.

Thalia saw him when he was a few feet away. She lost her cloak and dropped it in the snow. Her gloves flung into the wind, the peeling red paint half gone. Not one part of her shivered with the cold. The darkness in her skin was most prominent against the pearly snow, resembling a tall bronze statue within a foamy sea. She didn't look at him.

"Go back," she said.

Milo shook his head. "I-I can't. I'm sorry, *god*, you have no idea how sorry I am."

"I don't care." She finally raised her eyes. They were glossy like glass. "What is this, Milo? One day, I'm like gold to you, and the next, dirt beneath your feet? Is this what divinity does to the Midgardian mind?" She stormed up to him, the wind tossing her hair around. "How about you do us both a favor and make up your mind! *Stop* trying to push me away, and tell me what you want!"

The burn erupted in his hands. He wasn't sure what it meant: he wanted to hold her, grab onto her, and never let go, but there was this other part screaming for him to run, to escape into those mountains watching in the distance. He shook his head for the second time. "I don't - I *can't* -"

"No," she snapped. "You don't get to play confused and question your feelings. You said it all loud and clear back there! So what is it?" Her eyes grew hard. "Love me or hate me?"

He couldn't stop the smile from slipping onto his lips. And everything was released with an exhale; the barriers fell, the warnings falling into faded whispers. He wanted nothing between them. "You're like gravity."

"What?"

"*Gravity*," he repeated. He inched forward, wrapping a chestnut curl around his finger. "You've got this *pull*. Like there is a rope tied to my wrists, and no matter how hard I pull away, you yank. You yank, and you yank till I'm wrapped in your orbit. And I can jump, but what's that gonna do? Eventually, I will land back on solid ground - *your ground* - and it'll happen all over again. And I'm not even mad! Because in the end, I *chose* to hold onto the rope. I *chose* to come back to you. And if you'll have me, I never want to leave your side. Never again."

She stared at him.

"Just say the word," he said, "and I'll turn away. Say the word, and I'll be whatever you need me to be. But know this: tell me you feel the same, and I swear it'll be me and you till eternity stops."

Thalia's eyes grew wide. Her silence was so long Milo feared she didn't hear him. "It's not fair," she whispered.

"What is?"

"I've been alive for all these years," she said, "and I've just now found you."

He smiled, everything within him filled with light. "You found me."

Nothing else mattered. He suddenly dropped down, lips crashing against hers, fervently needing to diminish the sea between them. Whatever storm raged within Hjerte was gone instantly, slipping into the breeze and disappearing. All that made sense was her face in his hands, her coarse fingertips grabbing onto his shirt, lavender and wood radiating from her hair. His arms wrapped around her, pulling her closer until he thought she might puff out of existence. They enveloped each other, souls meeting at the ocean's center, lighting up the desolation that had clouded him for so long.

He knew then there would be nothing more important than her in his arms, kissing him, loving him, looking at him like he was the sun.

And then everything went wrong.

XXVIII. Vengeance is Mine, Saith the Lord

Five years ago, centuries for the average Midgardian, was when Sjel's genocide occurred in Asgard's outskirts.

It was a time Astrid seldom forgot, always plaguing her memories like a parasite, always on her tongue, always waiting for her around the corner. Before Sjel, Astrid had her fair share of death, following her Commander into wars, aligning with her lover on the battlefield, and fighting alongside the ones she considered friends. Her regrets stopped piling on her heart during those days. When you believe it to be a just cause, the lives stolen at your hand become collateral damage, actions necessary to take. And for years, since those fatal hours at Sjel, that was what Astrid told herself.

She had to do it.

Astrid had to slaughter mothers, fathers, and children. She had to kill people who held no name, people who held wealth or nothing, people who were born seconds before, and people who lived to see the birth of gods.

It was the quiet moments when the dead ones were transfixed in the local magician's tricks that Astrid found herself remembering, sipping an ale so sweet her mind was sluggish with comfort and ease. Kára, the wolf, lay sleepily at her feet, her quiet breathing sounding like a heavy purr. As foggy as they felt, her eyes focused on the settlement's leader. He sat luxuriously on a wooden throne, elevated a few steps above the rest. A goblet decorated with rubies and emeralds sat loosely in his right hand, chocolate-colored eyes dragging lazily across the building. There was no crown upon his head, only fur decorating his shoulders regally. The man's head turned, and his eyes landed on Astrid.

Five years ago, Odin looked at her with the same heaviness. The Aesir royal council filled the throne room, surrounding the Bleeding Throne. Guards armored in gold lined the room's perimeter, standing at attention as the gods argued and bickered over the same problems they'd handled for centuries. Astrid stood the closest to the throne, feeling the divine energy wafting through her as though she were only an empty shell. She avoided looking upon the gods, for the Aesir, children of the sun, held the brightest halos and loudest voices. Astrid's eyes could only handle Thor, the young god, who flicked stones at Ullr from across the throne room.

"We cannot let it stand, my Lord," Tyr shouted. His voice, cool like an ocean breeze, was barely heard over his brethren.

Thor looked at Astrid then.

"You wish to enact crimes," a woman to the King's right said, "upon someone with no evidence other than suspicion. You, being of justice, speak nothing of the sort."

Tyr smiled. "And what would you know, Frigg, of justice? Of the Aesir Law?"

A hand snapped towards him like a lightning bolt. "Watch your tongue," another woman said, "that is the Queen you address, Tyr. Treat her with *respect.*"

Queen Frigg rested a tanned hand upon the woman's wrist. "No need for hostility, Gefjun. I take no offense to Tyr's familiarity." She eyed her husband upon the throne. "It is not *me* who should be concerned with his recklessness."

"I only wish to protect our authority," Tyr stated. He knelt to the King's left, touching the Bleeding Throne gingerly. "What would happen, my Lord, if the trickster were to turn on us? Who could say what he might be willing to do? Is it not our duty," he stood, gesturing buoyantly towards the council, "as Aesir to protect our realm from rogue gods?"

That caught Astrid's attention. She peeled her eyes away from Thor, who traced sorcery runes along his hands to conjure flowers between the cracks in the floor, and faced Havi, watching his stone face contort with concern. For a moment, she could've sworn it was fear. Not once had she considered the possibility of an usurper, an Aesir containing enough power to overthrow the great All-Father himself.

Immediately, she knew who they referred to: Loki was only a trickster before Deathbringer, an Aesir who sparked flames beneath his clan and found joy in their scrambling. And yet, that was never how she saw him. In those days, the god was only her friend, a shadow hiding behind the Aesir that guided her towards Thor during the long nights, forged a hidden entrance for them to meet, and protected them from prying divine eyes. She looked away.

Astrid assumed there had to have been a time when Odin the Hidden One was not upon the throne, a time when Asgard's halls were filled with different divinities, dangerous beings with coarse skin and angry eyes. It was unsettling to imagine. Different gods. Different wars. Her eyes caught on Thor. He watched her, eyes narrowed, head tilted with thought. He mouthed to her: *what is it?* She swallowed and moved her head an inch. *Nothing.*

When she turned back to Havi, the King stared straight through her.

"You are right, Tyr," the god said.

Frigg clasped onto the King's shoulder. "Think about this, Odin," she hissed. Wildness raged in her ruby-shaped eyes, platinum hair short around her jaw, her brown skin glowing like gold beneath the god's mighty light. "You might start a war."

"We have been in war for centuries," he said. "This is not a declaration, my Queen." Slowly, he stood, grasping the Gungnir and pressing it against the marble floor. "But tell me, how can we not speculate the worst if the boy is not even here? Where might the trickster be if not before his people, defending his honor?" He laughed, the sound more heinous than he probably meant for it to be. "If he were here, I'd have no suspicion."

"So, in his absence, you might consider the worst?"

Odin watched her. "I consider the safety of my realm, of my Aesir."

"Then," the Queen began, eyes as hot as lava, "*my Lord -*" she eyed Tyr " - what will you have us do?"

"An envoy must travel to Sjel," he said, booming across the throne room, "summon Loki, the trickster, and Sigyn, the sorceress, and demand them to speak before the King's oath."

The hall became silent. The gods eyed each other, lifting their shoulders and turning away, some even acting as though they never heard him in the first place. Tyr's steely gaze sliced over them, an eagerness lingering behind his lips as he waited for someone to speak up. Astrid held back her disdain for him. The god would never offer himself to be an envoy; he would never leave his King's side. She couldn't hold it against him. To be in Odin's sunshine was like being at the universe's center, with all eyes, all heat, and all attention focused on you. Astrid wished it for herself some nights but found it within her companion's eyes.

Thor approached the throne, dropping to one knee. His tunic, an ashy gray cloth touching his knees, tied around his waist with a leather band, glowed beneath his father's light. The young Prince bowed his head. "Raven God, I offer you my spear and sword. Allow me to be your envoy, my King, with my warriors at my side. I will return with answers or the trickster himself. If it is what you wish."

His mother, the divine Queen, walked forward like she was on ice, gliding down to him. "You would be a worthy envoy, my son." Her hand touched his chin, raising him till he stood. She was still an entire head taller than him with her powerful immortality. "But be cautious. Loki is older than you, and he knows the ways of our kind more than you ever will." Her hand touched his heart. "Use your compassion, not your sword. He is innocent," she glared at Tyr, "till he proves otherwise."

Odin gave his son a curt nod.

And so it was done.

* * *

Beyond Asgard's golden castles, past the green plains and forests colored by moss and bark, in the eastern point of Odin's vast realm, stood a peaceful settlement inhabited by quiet Nords. Mercenaries and Vikings, done with their nomadic travels, found solace and stillness with Sjel. Astrid never ventured too far from the castle but found the journey the most pleasurable moment during that fateful year. The company traveled on horseback to Sjel, Thor leading with

Ullr at his side. Astrid trailed behind, two other Royal Guards chatting mindlessly behind her.

When they arrived in Sjel, the sky was clear, Asgard's suns nearing the horizon, where the castle was a distant memory, unrecognizable between the mountains. The townspeople did not run to greet them. They were suspicious, eyeing the golden armor, the spear glinting upon the Prince's back, and a sword dropping from Astrid's belt. Where smiles and warmth should have greeted their company, stern eyes stared at them. Ullr grinned as they arrived, eyes wide with wonder as he took in the beautiful village.

"Oy," he shouted to Astrid, "see the plains, love?"

She smiled and nodded.

And there, in divinity's midst, Astrid felt herself growing older but not growing up, stuck in an impenetrable cycle caught within Thor's orbit. She was Tora and Yrsa, never Astrid of Herjan. She was a lover and a hidden woman of shadows and whispers. Wrinkles swam beneath her skin like worms, unseen by the gentle eye but glaringly obvious by her lover. *There*, he'd say, dragging a hand along her temple, *your mortality lies*. The smile he carried was pitiful, sympathetic. When she'd grow embarrassed beneath his stare, pulling at her hair to cover the age, he laughed, forgetting her mortality. His eternal essence drew a wall thicker than blood between them. She stared at him from her horse, ignoring the captivating beauty Ullr drawled on about, unable to appreciate life when everything echoed around the Prince.

She realized her heart was riddled with dark spots, like the fruit hanging from vines outside Thor's castle window. She wasn't sure whether it was soft from rotting or too many squeezing hands. It was fruit snatched up, pawed, and felt till realized it was no longer good enough, dropped back to the earth and forgotten. Maybe they were not ready for the fruit - or rather, she was not ready for their consumption, too sickly sweet, too pungent, too ripe. Her heart ached with what was to come.

Ullr was the happiest he had ever been at that moment. He would never be the same again.

* * *

When they came across Sjel's longhouse, Loki was already waiting. He wore rustic clothes, trousers, farming boots, and a shirt stained with dirt and grass. There was no crown upon his head. No throne within the longhouse. It was simply made with wooden tables lined with plates and goblets. Empty platters awaiting their next feast. A few townspeople wandered in and out, men brushing old brooms across the floor, women carrying hay for the horses. Sigyn entered after them, her midnight skin shimmering with the outside heat, eyes bright and alert at the visitors. There was a blade at her belt.

Thor laughed at it, an ebony crown settled between his wild blonde curls. "Afraid of something, Lady Sigyn?"

She stood beside her husband, hand resting on the hilt. "Your arrival is unannounced," she said. Her head tilted to see the entourage behind him. "And you bring a fighting company. Tell me, Prince of Asgard, should I be afraid?"

Loki grasped her shoulder and whispered something in her ear. "We are all friends here, are we not?" he flashed a brilliant smile, the one that could win over instantly. "Come, join us at the table, would you not?"

"We are not here for a polite gathering, Loki," Thor said.

Astrid removed her helmet. The other guardsmen behind her muttered in disapproval. She took steps to stand beside Thor and Ullr. Maybe she was disrespectful, stepping into an authority that was not hers. But her mind was drunk with memories, moments of happiness and friendship. "We come from the King," she said, "there is no need for hostility."

"Always the naive one," Sigyn spat. "Do you forget your mortality, little warrior?"

She frowned. "Never."

"Enough," Thor shouted. Thunder echoed in the cloudless sky. "You were summoned to the council, Loki. You were missed."

"I did not feel my presence was necessary," Loki said. "You are here now, aren't you?" He sat at a table, still smiling. "Tell me, Prince, what did I miss?"

Thor sighed. "It is said the people of Sjel have been gathering. Scattered talks of an usurper within your quiet little town. Does that sound familiar to you?"

"Sounds like rumors to me."

"What are rumors, if not whispers, based on truth?"

Loki frowned. He no longer jested. Quickly, he glanced at his wife, back towards the townspeople curiously glancing over. He sat as still as a statue. "What is this, Thor?" Those jet-black obsidian eyes snapped to Astrid. "Are you accusing me of something?"

"Can you deny it?"

The god stood. "Would you believe me even if I did?"

"You have yet to answer me."

Even with Sigyn's hand upon his chest, trying to calm him with her foreign words, Loki snapped around the table, towering over the Prince. "Look at me, boy," he spat.

Thor gazed up, a lazy smirk pulling at his lips.

"What do you think you are compared to me? You are a flicker of light, barely divine, barely a *being*. I am the beginning," he hissed. "I am the end. I have seen things you could never imagine, and I could rip your soul from that shell of a hideous body," the god's hand touched

Thor's chest as his mother did before, "and watch you wither into *dust*. Do not walk into my home, *my home*, as if you own every place the light touches. Look at me, boy, and remember this: *you are not your father*." Loki pushed the Prince back, shoving his finger out accusingly. "Neither I nor Sigyn have to answer you. The jurisdiction you believe you hold is nothing but air. Do you want answers? Then I shall kneel before the Queen, and I shall kneel before the King, I shall rip my heart out from my *chest* before every living thing in Asgard, but *never* shall I bow to you." Loki exhaled. "Never shall I bow to you."

Astrid felt Ullr's eyes upon her. There was nothing for them to do. Thor's rage gathered as quickly as a thunderstorm. Rain began to fall in his eyes, clouds bunching at his hands, and thunder snapped in his chest. And worst of all, lightning, hot and burning, sparked in his hair. Astrid held her breath.

"Do not bow," Thor said. "I don't need you to." And with a movement so fast that Astrid did not catch it, Thor gripped his spear and flung it behind him, whizzing past the silent royal guards and plunging into the innocent cleaning man.

"*You* -!" Loki gasped, lunging forward but unable to stop the death.

The man wheezed and collapsed, a woman screaming behind him.

Thor grabbed a second spear. "For insult upon the crown," he said, "for refusing to follow the King's command, I shall kill every living soul within Sjel." He looked over his shoulder at his company. "Come, warriors."

Astrid was stuck in place. The royal guards behind her unsheathed their swords without a second thought. Ullr, beside her, removed his bow, a shaking hand pulling an arrow from his quiver. He looked faint, an ashy gray taking over his face. Loki was screaming, held back by Sigyn as tears streamed down her cheeks. His black eyes landed on Astrid. He shook his head, pleading. His hands outstretched, beckoning for her to go to him, to drop her sword. Everything grew foggy. The only thing she could see was Thor, his hair around him like a halo, removing the spear from the first of the dead, following a weeping woman as she struggled to run from the longhouse. Astrid looked back towards Loki. He was crying.

She unsheathed her sword.

"I *swear*," Loki screeched, "they are innocent! My people - *my people* - they are innocent!"

Astrid grabbed a handful of hair. It was only a young girl, eyes wide and pleading. Prayers came from her lips, hands pressed against her heart. The girl did not fight, she did not beg, she only raised her eyes, praying her soul might find a better place in death. Astrid slid her blade along the girl's neck. Blood stained her feet.

It did not matter, in the end, whether or not the people of Sjel gathered a rebellion to overthrow the King. After long nights recalling the events, remembering every face of every kill, Loki and Sigyn's screams still echoing in her ears, Astrid concluded that no revolt grew in Sjel. No, it was Thor's pride they defended. It was the gods they killed for. And when the fields were painted red, and the iron, death, and lightning took over the settlement, Thor entered the longhouse again, panting with the lives he stole.

Loki wept. There would be no Valkyrie to spring his people off to a great heaven. There was no battle. The souls were caught by Hel, and carried to her land of the undead. No townspeople received proper burials. Their souls would be forever wandering, forever marching down Hel's icy terrain, searching for a clue as to where their lives went wrong.

"Now," Thor said when it was done, "are you ready to comply?"

There was silence in the longhouse. Then, a whisper. There was a quiet sound, a young boy creeping out from a hidden room, hand wrapped around another. Led by a tall woman, her dress long and colored aqua, a golden circlet wrapped around her head, tangled into wild curls. Astrid knew her immediately.

Thor choked on air. "*Skadi.*"

Goddess from snow and ice, carrying a young boy in her arms, gazed upon the bodies. Her bronze stare raised to Thor. "What have you done?"

The Prince's eyes flickered between his betrothed and the trickster. "You *dare* leave the castle?"

"I am not your prisoner," she said. "These are my *friends*."

"And the boy?"

Loki was suddenly in front of Skadi, grabbing the child from her arms and burying his face in his neck. Sigyn was beside him, her hand holding the boy's. "You stay away from him," Loki hissed.

Astrid sighed. She knew the rumors, the godly pair birthing a son, Halvar. It was odd that the gods had a child who aged at mortal speed. He never stepped foot in the castle nor anywhere beyond Sjel. He was only ten years old, boyish curls framing his face, and eyes colored a deep black, diamond freckles scattered within them. He held his mother's darkness, the curve of Loki's clever lips, a charming look in his eyes. Curiosity overtook her. Even if he did not age like a god, Astrid did not doubt that the power there was unimaginable. The boy struggled against his father's tight hold. He wanted to see the commotion and lay eyes upon the one they called *Prince*.

"Your boy," Thor said. He smiled. It was painful to see. "What is he called?"

Loki breathed heavily. "Halvar."

"A mighty name for the son of gods." Thor walked to them.

Skadi blocked his path. She outstretched her hand, energy trickling from her fingertips. Astrid's hand gripped her sword again. Another life felt like nothing to her, but the Vanir Princess was divine and as ancient as the mountains: no harm could come from Astrid's mortal blade. "You have reached your line, Prince," she snapped. "Take another life, and I will be forced to -"

His hand smashed against her cheek, slamming the goddess across the longhouse. She practically flew, her back creaking as it slapped against the back wall. Sigyn ran, bending down to retrieve the winter goddess.

"You have no power here, Skadi," Thor said, unphased. "Will you bow, Loki? In front of your son?" His lip curled into a cruel smile. "How about kissing my ring? Or rather," he grew deadly serious, "my boot?"

The god held onto his son. He did not speak.

Thor raised his shoulders and laughed at his company behind him. The laughter continued as he turned back to the trickster, head tilted as though they played a game. As swift as lightning, Thor's hand snapped out, and he grabbed Halvar's hair, ripping him from his father's arms. Sigyn screamed, the blade tight in her fist as she ran towards him. Ullr stopped her, wrapping his arms around her torso, holding the goddess as tight as possible. Loki looked shell-shocked, staring at the image before him.

"*Father*!" Halvar screamed, struggling against Thor's hands.

Loki's shaking hands touched his lips. "Do not be afraid, my son."

Astrid could not look away.

"I am here," he whispered, "my soul."

The boy's body snapped in Thor's hands. Loki collapsed to his knees, Sigyn's wails as loud as thunder. Thor was satisfied, looking down at the trickster with a sad smile. "That wasn't so hard," he said softly. "You bow quite easily in grief."

There was silence.

Thor nodded over his shoulder. "Round them up," he commanded. "We bring the Deathbringer to my father." He looked back towards the god. "I hope you can comply as easily before the Bleeding Throne."

* * *

The council was silent as Thor recounted the events in Sjel. Sigyn and Loki were bound by chains and brought before the Bleeding Throne. As the goddess cried, her head bent towards the ceiling, murmurs leaving her lips, her husband stared directly at the King. Astrid stood at Thor's left, Ullr at his right, and the other royal guards lined up behind them. They were silent as Thor continued his story - because that was what it was. The young Prince spun a tale sounding valiant and brave for the company and vile for the bound gods. Astrid listened, her helmet beneath her arm, the blood scrubbed from her armor. She held her tongue. The Prince continued his lies.

"He is the Deathbringer, father," Thor said. "Massacred all Sjel, every last innocent life." He frowned, eyes glossy with rain. "Even a boy, a child from Loki and Sigyn's blood, broken at my feet, *killed* for their dark magic."

"So we were right," Tyr said, eyeing Frigg.

The King stood. "Let the accused speak."

The guards dragged Loki to the King's feet. Loki raised his head, eyes bloodshot, cheeks streaked with dried tears and dirt. "Your son *lies*," he spat. "Look before you, witnesses in your guard." He pointed to Astrid. "Ask her."

Odin gestured. "Young Astrid," he said. "Speak your truth. What did you see?"

Eyes fell upon her. The gods' stares penetrated her skin and burnt her down to the bone. Their divinity leaked into her blood. She swallowed, throat full of knives. "My King," she said, "when we arrived in Sjel for an audience with Loki, there was -"

Thor was watching. And how could she say anything else?

She looked at the King. "There was only death."

"*No*," Loki pleaded. "Astrid, no!"

"Sjel had experienced a genocide," she continued, "from the hands of -"

"*Don't!*"

"Loki," she said. "And Sigyn."

There was commotion from behind. At the throne room's grand doors came Skadi, her dress flying wildly behind her as she stormed in, shoved by protesting guards, ice trailing behind her bare feet. The Princess stopped before the King's throne. She did not bow. "I was there, King of Asgard," she shouted, voice booming, "and unlike your scheming Aesir," she paused, eyes stabbing into Astrid, an unbearable iciness spreading through her, "Loki and Sigyn did not commit that act, it was -"

"Remember where you stand, Princess," Odin said. "Remember, your betrothal to my son ceases a war." He stepped down from the throne. "Look at me, Skadi. You are a foreigner in my court, and if lies spill from between your lips, my hand will remove your *pretty* head, delivering it on a platter to your dear Freyja." The King reached forward, grabbing onto her curls, holding her still even as she jerked away. "I seem to recall you have a land of your own. Hjerte, is it not?"

She paled.

"Choose your next words wisely." He let go.

Skadi clenched her teeth, avoiding looking towards Loki or Sigyn. "Forgive me, King," she forced out. "For I have *misspoken*."

The All-Father smiled and nodded his head. He waved his hand towards the guards as he returned to his throne, using the Gungnir as a walking stick. He did not turn when he said, "For your crimes, I declare Sigyn the sorceress and Loki the *Deathbringer* shall be," he paused, falling into his throne, "exiled."

Guards dragged the bound gods from the throne room.

Loki was shouting. "Take me away now, Odin," he screeched, "but I'll see you all in Ragnarok! Every last one of you!" His eyes landed upon Astrid. "*All of you*!"

And Astrid wished he would.

The longhouse leader in Hjerte no longer gazed at her. Astrid glanced at her ale and pushed the cup away. She felt sick. The memories never felt stronger than in that moment. She looked around. The berserker was gone, as was the Prince. The other dead ones were ahead, still playing and laughing for the first time in days. Kali's stoicism and guarded nature seemed to have fallen. She melted into the music playing within the longhouse, Silas sitting wistfully beside her. She smiled. It felt unnatural for one to be on her lips.

"There's a storm brewing."

Astrid couldn't move. She already knew who it was, the voice sliding into the wooden seats beside her. He wore fur cloaks, no hood above his head, and no paint along his face to make him blend in. Midnight hair was tied up, braids decorating his head. He watched as the dead ones danced to the wild music, hands twisted on the table.

"What do you want?" she whispered.

Loki chuckled. "Is that how you talk to an old friend?"

"We stopped being friends long ago," she replied. She could see something along his face. The clever and playful exterior she had grown used to was nowhere to be found. There was determination in his jaw, an echoing emptiness in his eyes. The firelight cast embers across his skin like he was on fire.

"You say it as though I were to blame."

She went stiff again. She swallowed. A billowing anger rested in her breastbone, a squabbling voice in her mind, screeching it was his fault and his fault alone. The urge to grab him, shake him till his eyes rattled, cry and wail that he should've listened to Thor, was strong. But then, who was she to do such a thing? To feel such a way? Was it not her, a being of free will, who unsheathed her sword and committed the deed? Astrid kept her eyes on the dead ones. They remained oblivious to the god's looming presence.

He did not wait for her to speak. "I need to know."

"Know what?"

"Why did you do it?"

Astrid paused, finally looking at him. The god stared, his eyes lacking the rage and pain she expected. There was no vengeance in his lip, no hatred in his jutting chin. In his face, Astrid saw the boy, Halvar. Just a child searching for answers through smoke, grasping at nothing. What the god failed to notice, though, was that Astrid was in her own fog, clawing her way through the darkness, dragging at her chest, clutching her skull, and screaming *why am I a monster?* And the answer was there, buried beneath the soul, beneath her tainted heart that loved too quickly and hated too late. But she didn't want to see it.

"I don't know."

"No," he said defiantly. "You do. You know *very well* why you killed those people, why you let *him* do what he did. You're just too much of a coward to say it."

"What do you want me to say?"

"The truth."

The lie came out as easy as breathing. "I had to follow Thor. He was my -"

Purple mist rotated around his fingers. "Shut up!" he shouted. "That is the line you have procured for yourself for years, Astrid. It won't work on me. I am not a fool." His hands relaxed. He took a deep breath as if to calm himself, but his words were wobbly, coarse, and fragmented when he spoke next. "You *protected him.* After everything he did, everything you *knew* happened. You swore -"

"Thor was next in line for the throne," she whispered. "If his name was sullied -"

Loki flung around, grabbing at her shoulders, pulling her so close his hot breath fanned against her nose. It was not from anger or reproach. He did not squeeze her or try to bruise her mortal skin. The touch was of familiarity, a brother trying to show how much he loved his sister. A sister lost within herself, forgetting what might have truly mattered in the first place. Centuries of despair filled his eyes. "Where is your heart?" he breathed. "Where is the heart and *morality* of the wounded farmer girl I once knew? *Where is she?* What have you done with my friend?"

When she started to cry, there was no pity in his eyes. She did not expect there to be. He released her and turned back to face the dead ones without another sound. The anger returned. She was nothing more than a shell to him, a face he only recognized from someone in his past. In a crowd of mortals, her soul would be mixed in with the rest, no longer friend of the divine, no longer blessed by the gods, no longer welcomed in an immortal's heart. Astrid held her hands against her chest. She was only mortal.

"Know this, Astrid," Loki said, voice as sharp as her blade, "all the death, destruction, and rage spilled from my hands sits upon *you.*

My soul is not heavy from guilt. My eyes do not cloud with blood. My heart - however empty you might believe it to be - sits upon a mountaintop, unscathed. But it will be you, after it all, that takes the fall. It is you, old friend, who began this, and it is with your last words it will end."

She was suddenly angry. Maybe it was the guilt, the recognition of what she had done, how much her lies and unwavering loyalty to the Aesir had ruined her future. Astrid faced him. "Do you truly believe this is what Halvar would have wanted?"

Loki's hand shot out, a talon grabbing her throat with impeccable speed. His fingertips pressed against her skin, squeezing suddenly and hard, forcing a cough out. He raised her head and brought her close once more. She could see death in his eyes. "You have no right to speak his name," he hissed, "*no right.*" He watched her face. He watched the color rise in her cheeks, the fear burst in her eyes and listened to the air trying to rush down her throat, the pain gurgling in her neck. Her heartbeat thumped against his finger. Mortality, held in the god's hands. He frowned at her and released his hold, standing from the wooden bench. "What happens next is on you."

Commotion came from outside the longhouse. Astrid turned, holding her neck as townspeople rushed through the screaming snowstorm, hands clasping onto their axes and shields. She could hear the dead ones calling her name. There was running, battle cries, spears against gold. *The rebels.* Her eyes jumped back to the god. He stared into the snow.

"What have you done?" she shouted. Her hand shot out, grabbing at his wrist. "*What have you done?*"

But he was already gone.

Hjerte was under attack.

* * *

The eternal blue flame was gone. The obsidian border that once covered Hjerte from prying eyes had fallen and crumbled to the ground like crushed mountains. Soldiers dressed in royal gold rushed into the village, pillaging houses and killing whoever they saw. They fought the same way Astrid remembered: reckless and poorly trained. They held no strategy except to destroy. Astrid wielded Hofond like another arm, sliding through the rebels without thinking, her blade slipping between armors and hearts. The dead ones crowded behind her as though she were their shield, their hands grasping each other, Kali's Laevateinn casting a glow in the rushing winter storm.

Astrid slid the blade through another chest. Received an exhale from the dying body. Blood stained the snow. "Where is your guardian?" she shouted.

"She's gone!" Silas screamed, his arm raised to try and block out the snow. "And Milo -"

Another rebel stormed at them. Astrid twirled her sword, iron clashing upon iron, sparks filling the air. The woman before her moved too slowly, the armor slowing her down. Astrid turned the blade around in her hands and dove its edge through the woman's waist. She watched as another crumbled at her feet. More blood upon the white. "*Find them!*"

The search did not take long. An ax shot through the air, lodging itself into a rebel who loomed over children. Thalia was not far behind, suddenly sprinting before them towards the weeping children, collecting her weapon, and rushing them into hiding. The berserker looked wild in the moonlight, snow catching in her eyelashes and clothes. The paint drawn upon her face by Aegir slipped away, only fragmented red staining her cheeks. Behind her was the Prince, looking incredibly pale amid the low-hanging stench of genocide. He thrashed about, eyes catching onto everybody that fell, every drop of life, every scream, every wail.

Astrid grabbed him. "By the gods, where *were you*?"

"We saw the wall fall," Thalia shouted back. Her normally harsh bronze eyes were filled with a deep sadness, a fear as her shoulders lowered. "The flame -"

"It was Loki."

Thalia gripped onto her axes. She turned. Through the snow, where shadows danced with the trees, where the moon could hardly light up, stood the Deathbringer. He was no longer masking his appearance with cloaks and fur. No, he stood in the darkness with his purple and black leather suit, a cloak flying behind him, midnight hair soaring in the wind. His ebony eyes were stuck on them, lips turned down in a frown. Astrid could not make sense of the expression and could not see the meaning behind his actions. She held onto Milo, placed Hofond in its sheath, and grabbed Thalia.

"We must find the sea god," she said, "before we are trapped here!"

The berserker pulled away. "And leave these people to die?"

"What more can be done?" Astrid winced. It was the same at Sjel. "Cities fall. Mortals die. Our journey is not finished. We must -"

Thalia turned towards her. Tears streaked her cheeks. Her lips parted, and by the look in her eyes, Astrid figured the berserker was gearing up to let secrets tumble out from between her lips. But suddenly, she did not want to hear it. She reached, grabbing the berserker before everything trickled out. Astrid held her and tried to tell her it would be alright even if it wouldn't. Their foreheads touched: a familiar gesture between warriors, an act of binding companionship, where one would do all it took to save the other.

The sea's smell wafted around them. Like a tsunami, Aegir appeared, towering over them in his natural form. Within his hands were weapons, colored gold and unnatural in the moon's light. "Warriors," he said, "it is time for your journey to continue." Quickly, he shoved a shield into Milo's arms. "Take this, young one. It is Svalin, a shield that will guard you well. Use it, for I sense something in your path might aim for your life." He tossed a sword, its blade bound by leather, into Silas's hands. The Valhallian fumbled with it, gripped the hilt, and touched the sheath, his mind ready to release the blade. Aegir's hand shot out to stop him.

"That is Dainsleif, boy of the ocean, once unsheathed it must take a life, as its curse demands. Do not remove it unless you are ready to pay the price." And as Silas slid the sword into his belt, Aegir reached forward, touching his fingertip to Laevateinn. "My power rests in your staff, child. Think of Nifelheim, and it shall take you there." His old divine eyes glazed over them. "Leave now, warriors, and be well." A spear appeared in his hand. "I shall defend this land with all I can. But it is only you who might save us all." His eyes touched Milo. "Be better than us."

And as Kali thrust her staff into the air, light extending around them like Heimdall once did for Astrid, they were transported from a dying world and brought into something much worse.

The last thing Astrid saw was Loki the Deathbringer's eyes.

XXIX. Lys, the Son of Light

The underworld was nothing like Milo expected.

Like Hjerte, it existed in perpetual winter, blankets of snow layering the earth. And yet the trees were full of life, growing emerald-colored leaves and blossoming countless flowers. Even different fruits, however biblical they may seem, grew in the snowfall. The only light came from golden shards escaping through the murky gray sky.

Nifelheim's castle was only a mile away, dark and obsidian, standing up like towers instead of a cohesive building. A path led to its doors, already filled with passersby. Milo watched, eyes squinting against the light to realize they were not people but ghostly figures, slowly taking steps toward the castle. Their faces looked the same: sagged and gray. They melted into each other as a cohesive mob, never noticing the company's presence.

"They are the *Spøgelse*[21]," Astrid said. "Spirits that did not make it to Valhalla are condemned to walk this trail till they arrive in Hel's castle."

Silas cleared his throat. "And then?"

"Then they become her Dragur. An impenetrable army, neither dead nor alive." She pulled her sword back out. "Pray we never cross their paths."

Milo held onto Svalin, his shield. Its golden cover pierced his eyes against the light and bright snow. *I sense something in your path that might aim for your life.* He shuddered. Aegir's final words still rang in his ears. It was a warning, a threat. He looked around. Silas clutched onto his sword's hilt. The hours spent in Valhalla felt so long ago. Waking up in that golden room with a moving ceiling seemed like a fantasy in his mind, a dream he once had as a child.

"So what the hell are we supposed to do now?" Silas blurted.

Thalia looked as harsh as stone. "There's only one way to get something from Nifelheim." She used her ax to point at the distant castle. "Ask the Queen."

Milo watched her. He wasn't quite sure what happened next. Sure, they would travel to the castle, march into the throne room, and demand Hel to deliver what they searched for, and her answer could determine all their fates. He looked at her, *Thalia*, and wondered what would happen now. There was the moment in the snow, a moment where everything else faded, and there was only falling light washing around them like an ocean, and suddenly, the blue flame above them burst with a hissing sound, and a rumble echoed through the quiet Hjerte. They remained oblivious to it for a second till goosebumps riddled Thalia's arms, and she lunged away, shoving him behind her, axes readied in her hands. He touched his lips. The feeling still lingered.

---

[21] Ghost

The berserker turned, squinting at him as if she could hear his thoughts. Her lips curled up.

He smiled. His heart was about to explode.

"Great plan," Astrid muttered.

"It's the *only* plan." Thalia marched alongside the trail, careful not to get in the *Spøgelses'* way.

The company followed silently. There was no bickering or jokes exchanged. They were in the dead lands, where in any other occurrence, their souls would've ended up. Ghosts lazily walked beside them. Milo wondered if they knew where they were going. Did they know their eternity would be spent in an army, previous lives left behind? He hoped something remained. Something to let their world know they were, in fact, once alive, however long ago it might've been. Kára rubbed her nose against his hand, her tongue lolling out her mouth, giving off the impression that she had a broad smile. He scratched her ears.

He feared what was to come.

Hel's castle was, in fact, everything Milo figured it to be. To describe it as dark would be an understatement. The walls were the same as Hjerte's border before they collapsed, obsidian and black. There were no windows, but Milo figured the light would only make the dark more obvious. He held the shield close, Kára creeping at his heels. The oddest part, however, was the Dragur. The undead soldiers looked merely like skeletons, the gaps between bones filled with decaying flesh. Their hollow eyes glew a pale blue, mist dripping out like a river in the morning. They stared silently, not stopping the company as they walked through the castle.

"Hey," Milo called out to Thalia, who still led the group, "how do you know where we're going?"

She shrugged. "All castles work the same. Make your way to the center, and *eventually,* you'll find an egotistical god lounging around in their oversized throne."

And in a few more moments, she swung open elegantly carved doors, warm air spreading out to meet them. They continued into a throne room, and Thalia nailed it on the head. It was built like an oval, with pillars holding up the open skylight. Wolves lurked through the shadows, growling and snapping their jaws, yellow eyes touching upon Kára. The Dragur followed them inside, low sounds coming from their empty mouths. And in the shadows, a throne made from blackened wood and twisted vines, thorns decorating the arms, was occupied by a dangerously beautiful woman.

With hair coiled into braids, barely lifting above the ankle, the goddess's snowy skin shimmered in the darkness, scarlet tinting her fingertips, blood coloring her lips. Light came only from the skylight, and as the oddly gray rays lit up the snakes making up her dress, the company watched with wide eyes. Those swirling Vanir marks, dark and midnight, were upon her skin. The goddess didn't seem to notice their entrance. She stood from the throne and stepped down, her head barely turning. Milo felt his throat close. The goddess was built like a bodybuilder. She could make his high school's football team. A snake curled around her hand.

"The years I have waited for another son of Odin to come to my halls," the goddess drawled. Her portrait was lit up like a marble statue. She turned, golden eyes the same as her wolves. "And finally, after all this time, I have to say," Hel paused, frowning at Milo, "I'm quite disappointed."

He laughed without meaning to. "Well, that's just rude."

"I'm the goddess of death, lovebug." She shrugged and fell back into her throne, a bored look on her face as she watched her snake. "What more can you expect?"

Milo swallowed. "Then you know why we've come."

"*Why* doesn't matter." Hel melted into her seat. The wolves draped themselves at her bare feet. "I couldn't care less about Asgard, about Odin, about the Gungnir. The reason I've waited this long is not for the discovery of the spear in my possession, but instead, you."

"That's original," Milo said. "Lot's have wanted me, lady, and most get tired after a few minutes of hearing me jab."

The company snickered.

"You joke as though you are not in the land of the dead." Hel's voice became serious, however lazy her eyes remained. "You are only a soul, Milo Odinson. You and your mighty Warriors of Thunder are souls without bodies in my Kingdom of Spirits. If you make one wrong move, you might never find the treasure you seek. And I don't mean the spear."

Milo stared at her, his mind blank. The growing cold enveloped them, not a frosty cold, but the chill after death slipped into their minds like a disease. He shook his head, trying to clear the fogginess of her magical divine sway. He lifted his chin, remembering his mother staring at the sun through the leaves in their backyard tree. "My mother."

She smiled. Her mouth looked like an open wound. "I could bring her here, you know. Nothing can hide from Death's eyes."

"Where is she?"

"Oh, lovebug," she said, "it takes a lot more than pleading to get answers from me."

Thalia came up beside him, her breath fanning his chin. She smelt like lavender. "Give her nothing, Bohr."

"My, my, this just got *fun*," Hel said. "What a company you have here, son of Odin. If I remember correctly, your brother had his own."

"Don't." Astrid was behind him, but her voice was as loud as the gods themselves.

Hel's grin grew. "Do you remember, Astrid?" Her lips puckered. "Tora? Yrsa? Whatever name it is you go by these days."

"What the hell is she talking about?" Milo blurted.

"Tsk, tsk, Odinson," the goddess said, raising her eyebrows, "didn't your mother teach you not to take your Lord's name in vain?" She laughed again. "Thor had his company of warriors who followed him into battle. My, it was so long ago. There was Thor, of course, little Astrid running at his heels like a lovesick *dog*. The war god, Ullr. Correct me if I'm wrong, but wasn't it Sigyn and her husband, Loki, that joined? Were you not the group of legends?"

She pressed her lips together. "Yes."

The goddess continued. "And was it not *your* company, minus the happy couple, that pillaged Sjel? Committed genocide? Filled my halls with hundreds more Dragur? Was it not Thor who killed that poor, innocent child? Yes, Halvar, whose face stamped with fear haunts my halls. You, Astrid of Herjan, reek of death. You'd fit right in here."

"Enough!" Milo boiled with rage. "We didn't come here to play games. Tell us where you have the Gungnir."

"Or what? You'll badger me to death with your airy Midgardian voice? You'll get angry enough to spout some godly Aesir spitfire at me? Give it a rest, Odinson. Your mortality is showing." Hel laughed, the sound like swords clashing against each other. "It's time you learn something: gods only play games. What fun would eternal life be if everyone was so *serious*? I'll tell you what. I want two things from you, son of Odin, and only you. With it, I shall deliver what you seek:

the path to Odin's almighty spear." The smile grew. "Is that what you wish?"

Thalia grabbed him. "Milo," she pleaded, "you cannot trust her. Anything she says is a trick!"

He turned to her. His shadow covered her. Without a thought in his mind, his hand rose, and he touched her chin. "Then let her trick me." Milo moved away, looking back to the goddess. "All right, Hel. You've got yourself a deal. What do you want?"

The goddess stood, an eagerness in her eyes. The room seemed to grow darker. "Like many Vanir, my power is strung from words, you hear?" The wolves lifted their heads at her. "Not names or follies, but rather secrets and *mysteries*. From you, boy with eyes of lightning, I have seen how your words might benefit me the most. Deliver your darkest fear and brightest desire to me, and I will fulfill my end of the bargain."

"You-you want what?"

"I believe you heard me, lovebug. Times ticking."

Astrid grabbed Milo, pulling him back near the throne room's doors. Together, the company stood in a circle, each vibrating with fear and anxiety.

"I say we give her nothing," Thalia began in a rushed whisper. She gripped her ax. "Astrid and I, we can -"

"Take out an undead army?" Milo scoffed. "Just the two of you?"

Thalia eyed him. "Is that *doubt* I hear?"

"No," he said. "Never doubt, not with you. Any of you. But Hel doesn't want all of you. She wants me. Let me do this, okay? You really can't tell me any of you have a better plan!"

Kali raised her hand. "How-how about I do that magic thing again? You know -" she raised her staff above her head " - the thing."

Silas, holding the Dainsleif, chuckled. "I'll do you losers one better: I've got my badass cursed sword."

"Hence: *cursed*." Kali bonked him with the Laevateinn.

Milo smiled. "My mind is set."

Thalia shoved him. "Milo Bohr, stop acting like you're alone! We are a team, a company. You want to do this, fine, but stop treating us like we're just going to abandon you on the side of the road."

Milo turned back to the goddess. She paid them no attention but rubbed the fur along her wolf's chins, an oddly stern look on her face. The fear pooled into him as he looked back towards his company. "I'm afraid."

"You're not alone," Silas said. "You can't say anything that'll make us not love you anymore."

Milo sucked in a breath and stared at his feet, and swallowed the tears rising.

"We do love you, Milo," Silas added.

Kali sighed dramatically. "If we're being lovey all of a sudden," she pinched Milo along his elbow, "we wouldn't still be here if we didn't trust you. You can answer her. We won't leave you."

Warmth surged into his veins as though he bathed in the sun. The cold dreariness Hel pumped through her realm to force people to succumb trickled out of him. The Warriors of Thunder had a magic of their own, he realized, a connection binding their hearts together as one. When united, they were an unbreakable pillar. Milo raised his eyes and never felt more alive.

He cleared his throat. "Darkest fear, huh?"

The goddess smiled.

He shrugged. "Spiders freak me out."

"Do not play games with me, son of Odin. I can see through you like glass. The answer is already clear in your eyes."

"Why ask if you already know?"

Hel laughed. "Where's the fun in that? I need to hear you say it."

Milo bit his tongue. The presence behind him felt like burning heat on his back. Hel's eyes were like the sun on him, prying and burning his skin off. The silence continued until the voice echoed in his ears, subconsciously nipping at him. He knew the truth as simply as he knew the lie. "I'm afraid of hurting someone."

"More, Odinson."

"*Killing,*" he forced between clenched teeth. "Okay, fine. I'm afraid of killing someone, of taking a life." He stretched out his arms. "Happy?"

"Ecstatic," she said. "And for the revelation of such, I'll grant you a gift. Son of Odin, it has been foretold that you will have taken a life before the next sunrise." Her head tilted. "The first of many."

His heart cracked in half. Years ago, if the goddess had come to him and said such a thing, he would've laughed in her face, ran to his mother, and wrapped her tight in his arms, a lingering fear still existing in his mind. He stood in Hel's throne room, surrounded by death, and only wanted his mother. His lips parted: nothing came out, not even air.

"But you're not done."

"Right," Milo muttered. "Brightest desire." He could only imagine Natalie's smile. "I want my Mom back. Good?"

She frowned and looked ageless. "Not even close."

Milo shook his head. Once again, he knew the truth and sat quietly on his tongue. But his eyes spoke for him. He turned, glancing at Thalia. She already stared, the bronze in her cheeks glowing a deep red. They stepped away.

Kali released a loud sigh. She whispered something beneath her breath, sounding like "typical."

The goddess laughed harshly. "Oh, out with it, lovers. Glances are cute, but I need something more."

He avoided looking at Thalia, but her stare remained. "It's Thalia," he said. "I-I...she's my - you know. It's her."

Hel's eyebrows piqued up. Her hand raised, urging him to continue.

"I can't look at her without feeling like my heart is gonna fall outta my chest."

"Love is a silly thing, isn't it?" She traced the vines that twisted along her throne. "It sees through masks and lies." She turned to them. "Wonder how that can be."

Milo huffed. "What's that supposed to mean?"

"Hel," Thalia said, her voice deep and threatening. "Watch where you step."

The goddess stood. The light from above was dimming. "You, *berserker*, threaten me?" She took a few steps, the floor trembling. Her lips curled up like scars. "Unless it is not the berserker who threatens me, but your soul behind the mask?"

"I said what I said. My warning remains the same."

Hel shrugged, walking till she was at the second step leading up to her throne, casting an unbelievable shadow, growling wolves following close behind. "Fine, berserker, let us do this the hard way." Her head moved down an inch.

There was a screech. Thalia shot forward, feet sliding across the marble floor. Invisible magic gripped her ankles till she knelt before the throne, chin jutted upwards.

"Don't you dare -" Milo shouted, gripping his shield and running, feet slamming against the floor behind him. The goddess raised her hand, and they all froze, suddenly stuck in place.

Hel touched Thalia's forehead, light traveling through her Vanir marks till it reached her fingertips. "Come out, old friend." She shoved the berserker. The light erupted from where Thalia knelt. The throne room grew painfully cold, a sound like cracking ice echoing from the stairs. As the light faded, the company could see Thalia was no longer herself, transformed into something otherworldly.

The woman stood. Her skin was as deep as molten bronze, eyes shaped like almonds, and colored amber harvested from honey pits. Midnight scored her arms and neck, the strike of her collarbone, the curve of her elbow, and the muscles on her stomach. Marks of the Vanir tribe. The casual Midgardian clothes Thalia wore were gone, replaced with a silk aqua dress crossed at her breast, showing the stomach, and long skirts grazing her ankles. She was barefoot, ice cracking into the floors. She turned at a crawling speed. Fear laced her eyes, lips strawberry, and cherry, drawn down in a frown. Even then, with everything changed, with the marks along her skin, and with the divinity so obvious upon her that it hurt, she was Thalia.

Hel smiled. "Welcome back," she said, "Skadi."

There was a clang. Astrid had fallen to her knees, hands pressed against the floor. "By Ymir." She pressed her face against the marble. "Forgive me, Princess, forgive me, forgive -"

"Get up, *kriger*," Thalia said.

Her accent was heavy, loud, and ringing. It sounded like fallen snow, the first snow, old shoes crunching against it. Milo stared. She was otherworldly, dangerous, immortal, and eternal, a forgotten star standing before him. He was frightened, forgetting why he was there, staring and wondering what he got into. He was in love, irrevocably and inevitably, watching his future and wanting to fall into her and never come out.

"Do you see a crown on my head?" she said. "There are no more monarchies, crowns, or gods. I am no different than you. Do not bow." Her chin was raised. "I am not Thor."

Milo's mouth opened and closed like a fish.

Thalia - Skadi - stared at him. "I'm sorry." Her attention averted to the goddess. "You think you're so clever, Hel, but all you've done is expose my power. What good does that do you?"

"Well, you remember the game, Princess." She lounged on her throne again. "You've lived it for centuries."

"You're right." Thalia rolled her shoulders. Light fragmented and scattered, growing and burning like a piece of paper till her dress was gone, replaced with a thick silver armor. It fit her nicely, down to the gloves and shinned helmet. He tried to stop himself from being shocked. She was a goddess. A Vanir. What more could he expect? "I practically *built* the game you wield about like your own toy. Do you forget who has lived longer than you? Do you forget who holds more power?" She removed an ax from the belt. "Deliver your end of the deal, Hel. Where is the Gungnir?"

Hel smiled, eyes grazing over the company. "Lake Minde. It is frozen over to the northeast. What you seek," her eyes stabbed into Milo, "sits at its pit."

Thalia lowered her ax. She spun around, armor glowing like a star in the surrounding darkness. Her hands extended, rushing them quickly towards the door. There was a feverish look in her eyes. And as Silas's hand grazed the door handle, the goddess decided otherwise.

"But you see, dead ones," Hel said, "I am not a goddess of justice. I am not the Aesir. I do not care for your mortality, for your mortal quest. I have tasted your souls and believe they will find a home in my army."

Looking over her shoulder, Thalia whispered, "You're going to have to run."

Milo blinked. "What -"

Quickly, she shoved them towards the door. As they turned, the Dragur already catapulted forward, empty eyes cold and lifeless. Hel remained on her throne, watching with a painful silence, blood-stained fingers tracing her lips. Thalia moved away from the company, dropping her axes and stretching her arms. As cold air brewed within the still throne room, Thalia slammed her hands together, and power burst from the Vanir marks beneath her armor.

Ice began to climb up from the floor a few feet away, reaching towards the ceiling. A wall grew between Thalia and the company, sliding up within seconds. The cold, however strong it suddenly became, did not touch Milo. He could only stare through the ice's reflection at Thalia.

She was on the other side.

Seething rage rushed back to him, a burning erupting in his chest, rippling down to his arms. Immediately, he slammed his fists against the ice, wishing the anger he felt could melt it all away, could take him back in time to stop her from doing such a thing, to shout *do not sacrifice yourself. I need you to be selfish*. Words rippled from his lips. It was incoherent, unrecognizable - the only thing ringing important in his ears was the woman he loved trapped in death's grasp.

He heard himself: "You'll *die*!"

"I am Skadi," she said, hand pressed over his own, voice muffled, "daughter of Queen Freyja, Woman of the Hunt, goddess of Hjerte." That smirk, confident and witty, formed on her lips. "Hel and her dead army have nothing on me."

He could not smile back. "I-I can't say goodbye. Not yet."

"Don't say goodbye. Just say you'll see me again." Her eyes grew dark. "Around the corner."

"I will see you again," Milo said. "I swear."

Arms grabbed him, twisted around his waist, lifting him off the ground, forcing him out the double doors. His eyes remained upon her, the last humanity he believed he had. Upon her, the girl from the bar. A wail echoed from his lips. The ocean between them was like a stab to the stomach, his insides ripping, heart snapping in half. Nothing was left.

The last thing he saw was Skadi raising her axes above her head, her battle cry as loud and unrelenting even beyond the ice wall.

"*For Valhalla!*"

* * *

Lake Minde was where Hel said it would be. Death, as Milo came to figure out, did not lie. It was frozen over, and snow delicately spread to leave the water beneath unrecognizable. Milo tossed his shield into the snow before the lake and pressed his foot against the ice, testing his weight. The vision from his drowning experience within the chasm came back to him: standing upon a frozen lake, cracks forming around his toes, snapping in half till he dropped into the ice-cold water. He wasn't afraid. He'd rather freeze to death than remember the last moments of seeing Thalia than face the realization he might never rest his eyes upon her, hear her laugh, watch her get angry.

The company stood behind him, almost afraid to breathe too loud. Astrid approached after a long silence, resting her calloused hand on his shoulder.

"Let me, Prince," she said. "I can find the spear."

"No. You're still alive."

"As are you."

He faced her. "No, Astrid. None of us are." The other Valhallians were not offended by his words but eerily calm, standing in the pristine snow and aware of their lacking mortality. "Out of us all, you're the only one left with a chance." He looked back over the lake. "Hel was talking to me."

She blinked. "When?"

"She said," he began, and the ease he felt was unnerving, "that I would find what I seek in the lake's pit."

Kali tossed her staff from hand to hand. "Pretty sure she didn't say you exactly."

"You're right," he agreed. "But she meant me." He stepped onto the ice. "She knew what I was looking for."

"The spear," Silas said.

Milo could only smile.

"Your mother." Astrid breathed deeply. "You think she's down there."

"Even if she isn't," he kept moving over the lake, "whatever's down there will bring me to her." Milo watched them as he backed up. "Whatever happens, you three stay here and wait for me. Kali," he pointed, "be ready to open that portal. No matter what, we go back to Valhalla tonight."

Kára howled and whined, pacing the shore where the lake would've met the ground, her paws scratching against the ice.

"No, Kára," he called. "Stay."

Silas wrapped his arms around the wolf, holding her close to his chest as she stared with harsh red eyes.

Milo peeled his gaze away, moving till he stood within the frozen Lake Minde, imagining it cracking beneath him and seeing Thalia's face staring back at him. His eyes raised. The castle was on the horizon and looked like paint on his mother's untouched canvas. And as he stared, wondering what the goddess was doing, the ice finally began to break. He fell into the water within the same second.

Milo sliced his hands through the water, diving deeper and deeper till the light was no longer visible, only the murky darkness, silent fish, and an ever-approaching bottom. And as Death promised, within the mud and shells was the Gungnir, an ebony spear riddled with Nordic runes on its shaft, a complex sculpture of ravens upon its top, a jewel he could not make out fastened within. Milo reached, the ring he wore suddenly heavy, pulling him down. His hand curled around the spear.

As soon as he touched it, he was sucked into the lake's bottom, sliding through mud and earth, darkness swallowing him whole. When it stopped, Milo rolled through ocean waves, immediately noticing how warm the water became, the saltiness pricking at scratches and cuts along his fingertips. Gripping onto the spear, he clawed to the surface, crashing up and feeling the sun's gaze on his back.

There was a beach, the bright white sand, clear waves barely tinted blue rolling on the surface, pushing and pulling the sand with it. Trees stood in the distance, a low breeze brushing through leaves and branches. In the distance, so far off Milo barely caught it, were golden spires, the castle stabbing the floating clouds.

Asgard.

A figure stood on the beach. They raised an arm, blocking the sun with one hand, waving with the other. He was too far, moved by the rolling waves, to recognize them at first. Using the spear to steady himself, Milo waded through the ocean, slowly getting closer till the shock rocked his body.

"Mom!"

And then he ran, sprinted through the water, fell, picked himself back up again, shoved waves aside, stabbed the spear into the ground, and pushed himself off. She laughed, waved her arms frantically, shouted and screamed his name, and rushed into the water, her pale blue dress soaking up the ocean. They collided like galaxies, bursting at the seams, arms eagerly grasping the other, holding each other so close the other might swallow them whole. She grabbed his hair, pressed his cheek against hers, and kissed his nose, eyelids, forehead, and chin. All he could do was hold her, hold his mother and carry her out the water, cry into her neck, and remember the nights she sang him to sleep. He promised never to let go. She promised to watch him grow old. They stepped onto Asgard's beach and forgot what happened in the sky when galaxies collided.

"You know," she said in his ear. Natalie pulled back, thin hair flat against her face. "You know."

He smiled. "It's okay," he said. "I know why you did what you did. Not telling me."

"My boy." She twisted his curls around her finger. "You are nothing like him." Her hand touched the spear. Her mortality did not matter. The spear's divine energy ricocheted off her.

Milo jerked the spear away from her. "How can you touch it?"

"Your father wouldn't hurt me," she said. "I don't know the things he did, the whispers he said under his breath that made his eyes glow with an alien power." Natalie smiled wistfully, reaching for the spear again. "I could always touch it."

Milo watched her thin fingertips graze the engravings on the weapon. Her skin held an armor of its own, something bestowed upon her by his absent father. He fought the urge to protect her from it.

"You do not know how proud I am."

He grinned. "I've got *some* ideas."

"Got that humor from me," she said, smacking his cheek. "Your father was a rich kid with a fat spoon up his butt."

"Mom!"

"Tell me I'm wrong," she laughed. "All those gods act like jokes are offensive. How can immortal people not crack jokes? C'mon? What's that about?"

Milo slung his arm around her shoulders, laughing without a care. "God," he said, "I've missed you."

"Hate to break this up." Loki walked towards them across the beach. His hands were twisted behind him, a smile on his lips. In any other case, Milo would've believed his smile was true and sentimental, and he was happy to see such a reunion. But he was now aware of who the god was. Deathbringer. Destroyer of Hjerte.

The god paused a few feet away. "I told you you'd see your son, Natalie."

She scowled. "Am I supposed to thank you?"

"It's the least you could do."

Milo extended his arm, Gungnir's point aimed at the god's chest. "You just keep comin', don't you?"

"My job isn't finished," Loki said, "till you have delivered what I was promised."

"Promised?"

"The spear, Odinson. I did not send you on this journey for nothing."

Milo lowered Gungnir. "You think I'm an idiot or something?"

Loki shrugged. "Depends on the time of day."

"I can't."

"Odinson," Loki said, nervously laughing, "I can give you all you want. Your mother, divinity, sanctuary -"

"I *can't*."

The god stared blankly. "What?"

Milo held the spear closer to him and his mother. "I can't give you the Gungnir," he said. "And everyone's probably hoping I'll say it's because I'm the son of Odin. That I'm the brother of Thor, brother of Baldur, a Prince, an Aesir. But-but that's not it. I can't give this to you because I am Milo James Bohr, son of Natalie Bohr, a Warrior of Thunder, a dead one, a Valhallian. I am humankind, I am earth, I am humanity, I am Midgardian. This is my soul and my everything unwinding: this has shown me what I am, who I will be." With his right hand holding onto his mother, his left gripping Gungnir, what he said next rang like a distant memory, something he had heard before. A name given to him by Yggdrasil was already carved into the tree's branches before he was born. "I am Lys, the son of Light, and you wish to use this for evil, for *vengeance*. And this spear has seen enough death at its hand, with or without you."

Loki looked sad, almost guilty. "Then take my apologies, Lys, for I was once a good man."

"What -"

"But they stole my soul," Loki said, "and your rage is the strongest weapon I have."

The god moved with divine speed. He was behind them, a blade pulled from his belt and driven through Natalie's back, the tip extending through her stomach. She released a gasp, a final exhale, as she fell to her knees, hands shaking as she touched the blood staining her dress. Milo fell alongside her, grabbing her head before she collided with the sand, eyes foggy and displaced. Her hand raised and touched his face.

Natalie Bohr died in seconds.

* * *

"What was first?"

"Love," she said.

"And then?"

"Then the emptiness was filled, and our souls didn't have to search anymore. Then, there was a home, and no one was lost ever again. There was light and darkness and rain and thunder. There was everything, my love, and nothing. The cycle of life. Immortality. Eternity."

Milo Bohr lay on his back that afternoon, staring at the pastel-colored sky speckled with pigeons and crows. Trees wept with branches, building this canopy with natural arches and reaching vines above them. It reminded him of a time beyond human existence, how the world might look without people, technology, or modernity. He closed his eyes, imagining *A Midsummer Night's Dream* stage. He was fourteen. He and Natalie Bohr just moved to Manhattan. There were flowers in his hair.

"Is that what Aunt Ilya said in church?" His eyes transfixed on bickering squirrels. He wondered: *why are they there?* After a moment came: *and why am I here?*

Natalie lounged beside him in the grass. Five years before the end, she rarely thought about death. She remembered Easter when the purple cloak was ripped from Jesus' statuette figure above her childhood church's altar. A blink, a quick fragmented darkness before the light kicked back in. The color violet flashed across her gaze. A blink. She fluttered her eyelashes. The sun mumbled above them. Slowly, her head turned towards her light, and she watched as Milo's frown deepened. She reached, fingertips brushing curls from his eyes. She didn't have to look to know where his jaw curved, where the boyish bounce in his cheeks was dying out, or how heavy the bags were beneath his crystal eyes. Her eyes closed. He flashed behind her eyelids like photographs.

"Ilya would never say that in church," she had said.

"What happened next?"

"History."

"That can't just be it." He huffed in annoyance.

"Why not?"

He sat up on his elbows. "What about us? Humans, women and men, and everything in between. Animals and bugs and trees and flowers. How is mortality placed within eternity?"

"I don't know."

"Why are we here?"

She blocked the sun with her hand. "You said the first thing you wanted to do was go to Central Park."

"Not here, I mean *here*. We're alive, you know, and for what? What's the purpose of putting people on earth if we're just gonna leave years later?"

"Purpose?" she repeated.

Natalie looked away from him. The weeping willows cascaded down around them like rain. She stared into the sky, noticing the crickets' and cicadas' dull songs, wings fluttering, and quiet rabbits jumping through the low grass. A monarch butterfly flew over them. She wondered why. Why does all that exist? No matter how happy he made her, why did she have her boy? Why did she fall in love? Why did *he* choose her? Why did *he* leave? And, most of all, why did she not feel angry anymore? Natalie closed her eyes. She wasn't angry.

"I don't think I have one." He sounded older.

"One what?"

"A purpose."

Natalie blinked. The world flashed into darkness, like Easter. Five years before the end, Natalie began to fear for her son's life. "Who cares?"

His head shot towards her. "Huh?"

"Why do you need a purpose? Who are you looking to please?"

"I'm not -"

"Milo," she said, "the point of living isn't to fulfill some faraway hope pressed upon you by others. The point of living isn't to know that you'll eventually die. Why do we have the ability to love if it wasn't the point? Or laugh, smile, cry, get angry?" Natalie grabbed his hand. "People will tell you what your destiny should be. They'll force you into it, but, my love, my beautiful boy," she touched his face, and in a fractured moment, sunlight displaying across him like glass, she saw the man she once loved, "you are more than any of them might say."

"How?"

"You are *my* son. There is nothing in the world that you cannot do. My greatest success was having you, my sun, my light. For you, I'd give up my soul. You understand that, don't you? You *saved* me. You were my guardian angel, and I'd give it all up for you. All of it."

As if stuck in a trance, Milo slowly took a flower from his hair, reaching towards her to tuck it behind her ear. He smiled and tilted his head. "Do you regret it? Meeting him? Having me?"

"I regret nothing."

In five years, Natalie Bohr would remember that moment. Natalie would look upon her son in five years and only see an angel.

In five years, she would have no regrets.

And there would be flowers in her hair.

Milo couldn't remember what happened afterward. He held her body. He cried into her hair. He held her hands, stared at her nimble fingertips, and remembered what a paintbrush looked like around them. He pressed his hand over her wound, trying to stop the blood. He listened to Loki walking away. He dropped the spear. He picked it back up. The ocean sloshed onto the shore, pulling the blood, pulling the death, pulling all he had left. It called for him. It wanted him to fall into its waves, slide back through the invisible portal, and make the journey back to Nifelheim.

But he couldn't. Not with the thought of her soul walking the path towards Hel's castle. Not with the realization that he would have to continue without her. Maybe it was selfish, but he was willing to let all the world burn to lay there on the beach, holding his mother, praying life would come back to her eyes, hoping for the universe to give them a second chance. It was wishful thinking. It was selfish.

He pulled his arms out from underneath her, relaxed her arms across her chest, and dusted sand from her eyelashes. Milo leaned down and said, "I love you." The sob stopped in his throat. "I love you more than my life," he cried. "I'd trade places with you. I would trade places with you if I could."

She didn't wake up.

He left his mother there and walked into the ocean. It was there, swimming and surrounded by the warm liquid. Everything else hit all at once. The anger, the betrayal, the pain, the sorrow.

His rage was, then, universal. There weren't words strong enough, tears heavy enough, to mimic the hole that blew through his chest. Like a divine arrow, the grief caught onto him suddenly and chaotically - all at once. In a way, it was the same as love: invisible hands shoving him down a cliff, excitement, and exhilaration, up until the fear kicked in, the growing impact. He fell through the portal.

I am not my own. No choice he had made helped himself, built him into something he wanted. Something else, hidden and soft, catching on his hair and eyelashes and clothes like the first snow, held onto him. Milo Bohr was not his own. He was Odinson, he was Prince, he was Heir, he was Son, he was Bastard; forgotten, alone, and remade. Yes, alone and remade. And that was when he, whoever he was, indeed lost something in death. His mind reached, clawing and searching desperately for his soul.

In the end, it didn't matter.

His soul was gone the moment his heart stopped.

* * *

Milo broke through the ice for a second time. The company was already there, snapping him up like a shark's jaw, yanking him from the water, and draping themselves over him.

"You're safe," they said.

"You found the spear," they rioted.

"We can go home," they shouted, as though they had always been dead, always just a soul, always of the Nordic heaven.

At that moment, he hated them.

Astrid touched his elbow. "What is it?"

"He killed her."

"Your mother." She paused. "Loki."

Kali reached for him. "Milo -"

He flinched away from her. Kali's slim fingers reminded him of his mother. Pulling her face down as though she had melted, her frown forced the sadness to rush through him like a tidal wave. Kali watched him, her face contorted, and a whisper trapped on her parted lips.

"It'll be okay," Silas said. He tried to push Kára towards Milo. "Go on," he muttered, "comfort your papa."

The wolf whined impatiently, licking Milo's stained fingertips.

Silas reached and snagged onto Milo's shoulder. "What can we do?"

"This doesn't change anything, Si," Milo muttered.

"It *can* change things if that's what you need."

Milo's eyes raised. "It changes nothing."

In the beyond, near the diminishing foggy figure of Hel's castle, a group resembling marching ants stormed towards them. It was the Dragur army, somehow past Thalia's defenses, making their way towards the frozen lake. Milo felt no fear. He gripped his spear. Everything upon his body felt like fire, heat prickling beneath his skin, blood boiling and turning within his veins. He stared and remembered Hel's promise. *You will take a life before the next sunrise.* The following sunrise felt like a distant future, something he might never reach. He swooped down to retrieve the shield, Svalin, from beneath the snow. Kára already growled beside him, shoulders hunched and hairs raised as if lightning struck her.

"Open the portal," he commanded. "I'll handle that."

Astrid scoffed. "You're not even trained!"

"No," he said. "I'm not."

He started to run, snow flying up his legs and catching in his hair, Kára howling behind him, the noise carrying like music across the wind. As the army grew more prominent, the Dragur becoming clearer in his eyes, he saw Hel at their head, her armor made of rattlesnakes curving around her figure. The helmet she wore looked like her Dragur. He was not afraid.

I regret nothing.

XXX. Kali Rips a Hole through the Space-Time Continuum

There were many things Milo always wanted to do in life. He never called it a bucket list, but rather moments, strings tied together to form this extending band of memories. It came down to realizing that, in life, the little moments were lacking, fading, too distant for him to remember they even existed. Death made it sharper. Death revealed who he was, bringing forth his lineage. Death gave him Thalia. Death gave him his company, and Death even gave him a wolf. But the moments were there. They were there, and he could close his eyes and see them without thinking about it.

Thalia, sitting at the bar table, hair cascading like a curtain across her shoulder, bronzed skin shining with sweat, eyes transfixed on her black pen—the dim lights. Kids partying, underage drinking, fake IDs, Oba.

Natalie Bohr surrounded by grass. Flowers in her hair. A whisper. *I regret nothing.*

He was lying on his bed. Kali was dressed in his mother's old clothes, with cups juggling in her hands and a photograph in her left hand. Diamond tears fell down her cheeks with a majesty he had never seen before.

Asgard's golden castle was visible from a hill and through a valley. Astrid at his side.

Silas. *Time, order, and faith always mean something, even when it doesn't.*

Snow cascading across a village.

Loki's black eyes.

Milo ran across the snow. Svalin felt like a feather in his hand, the Gungnir like iron. He moved through the cold with a silence he never had in life: no panting, no burn in his claves, no crunching snow. It was like he wasn't human. The spear stretched out from him like a snake, slithering and sliding through the air. And it wasn't *'like.'* He was not human. He didn't mind that his blood would shine if it fell upon the snow. He didn't mind that his father was a god and a king. He didn't mind his hands burnt when he was angry. He didn't mind.

He minded that his mother was dead. He minded that Thalia was someplace else, not by his side. He minded that he ran towards immediate danger, towards death personified. He remembered Loki's words. *Death is a woman, and I fear her the most.*

I have to do this. Then, *even if I can't, I have to.*

He didn't have the time to rethink it all. There wasn't any time to turn around, to sprint back towards his company and leap into the portal. He stole a look over his shoulder. Kali waved her staff frantically above her. With her gigantic sword stuck in the snow, Astrid grabbed Kali from behind, shouting to calm down. Behind them, Silas sat in the snow, his head buried between his knees. Their fear radiated like heat waves.

Kára nipped at his feet, running ahead. The Dragurs were not far away now. He raised the spear over his head and pulled it back like a fishing pole. With a quick motion, the spear flew from his hands, soaring through the air like a raven, puncturing a Dragur's neck. Kára let out a rolling howl. The undead soldier collapsed. Like he had been doing this his entire life, Milo extended his hand again, and the Gungnir whistled. It shot back, landing in his hand with the same force as a bowling ball. He staggered, regaining himself as the Dragurs came upon him, smashing their swords against shields, wispy cries wailing from their empty mouths.

Milo closed his eyes. *They're not Mom.*

And somehow, the thought broke something within him. Fire sprouted at his heart, stinging heat nipping below his skin. Whatever color Nifelheim held faded into blood; red scarlet tainted the snow, filling the ashy gray sky and pooling into the castle. Every Dragur looked like Hel, with her moon-lit skin, hair so black it gleamed like the midnight ocean, and hands stained with death. And so he threw the spear, and it stuck the soldiers, over and over. The heat stung in his hands. It was overwhelming: the rage, the fire trapped beneath him, calling for release. Milo thrust his hands forward.

Chills rolled down his spine. Golden light snapped from his fingertips, feeling cool against him rather than the exploding heat he expected. The light soared through the air, scattering and cracking like fragmented glass, rainbows falling on the snow, ice melting and freezing in the same second. The energy shot through the Dragur, exploding through their chests, disintegrating their bodies until only ash was left. The goddess stalked him; her head lowered as she watched the power retract, disappearing like it never existed.

Milo was breathing for the first time. He looked down. His veins glowed and pulsed golden beneath his skin. The Gungnir snapped back. He grabbed it in midair. The spear vibrated, the same light from his hands seeping into the ebony weapon, rising till it funneled into the jewel at the top, lighting till it burnt his eyelids.

"Nice to see you've grown into yourself, lovebug," Hel said. She crept around him. Her hands held matching swords, the blade so bright from the snow's reflection it made her difficult to look at. Up close, the goddess's dress was made from snakes; every barefoot step into the snow received a hiss and snap. "A King without a crown." Her wolves were suddenly there, yellow eyes angled at Kára. The goddess smiled. "Charming."

"Where's Thalia?"

Hel blinked. "Who?"

"Skadi."

"The Princess has found a home here before," she said, twirling the swords around her like helicopter blades. "She'll be fine."

He tried not to imagine what Thalia looked like in those empty black halls. Her perpetual shining, a radiating glow from her bronze skin, a single star in space's vast reaches. The heat rose. "And *my...my....*" His eyes were raised to see the goddess. She was smiling. "She's here, isn't she?"

"Your mother?" She stopped pacing. His back was to the company. "Yes, her soul walks the path of solace to my halls. One day, seconds for me and centuries for you, she will be one of my Dragur."

Milo swallowed. His throat was on fire.

"How about a deal, son of Odin? Hand over the Gungnir, and I'll give your mother back."

"Why the hell would you -" He cut himself off. The goddess stared like she knew everything before he did. And it was true, wasn't it? She *knew* the world, while he only experienced it for seconds, unaware of where he stood and what lay ahead. He frowned. It was like they played into her hands, Lake Minde's reveal, the desertion of Thalia. A goddess like Hel would have probably snapped her fingers and changed them into frogs. But she didn't. She led them to the spear. His eyes raised, and he looked into the goddess's staggeringly intense eyes. *It's all a game.* That's what the gods did. They clasped these chains upon mortal's heels and told them they were free but always hung onto the ropes. He gritted his teeth. "You wanted this."

Hel shrugged. The blades rested on her shoulders. "No matter how strong, we gods have our restrictions." Her eyes stuck on the spear. "There was no way I could ever get my hands upon the weapon myself."

"You're not gettin' it."

"What makes you so sure?"

"'Cause I'm half a god now," he shouted, the confidence not sounding right on his tongue. "There's no way in hell I'm letting another god underestimate me. Not again."

She smiled. "Over your dead body, then."

"Over my dead body."

Milo had no idea how old the goddess might've been. How long had death been around? He supposed that, maybe, there was a time when no one died, when everyone was safe from Nifelheim, from Valhalla, from their souls leaving their bodies. Until one day, death arrived, and everything changed. If killing shook him before, fighting Death herself seemed impossible. How could death become dead?

She sprinted towards him, her head ducking down and hunched as she became the snakes upon her arms, the swords loose and wobbly. Her sword smacked against his nose. He swung the spear. She was gone. He gripped the Gungnir. Hel snapped the sword behind his knees. He fell, the stinging vibrating through him, different from the euphoric heat from his fingertips. The light rays shot out sporadically and disappeared into the sky. There was a laugh. He swung the spear. Hel was nowhere near him and then suddenly behind him. Her foot slammed against the soft spot between his shoulder blades. Milo collapsed into the snow with a yell.

He lay there, imagining he was dead for a second time. With the cold against his cheeks, the simmering pain behind his knees a faded numb, blood tricking against the ice, he felt eerily calm. For the first time, the darkness did not show him those he lost. It was just still. This, he thought, is what death was supposed to be. Something grabbed his hair, raising him from the ice. The blood, heavy with the thick gold, trickled around his cheeks and stained his lips.

The only thing Milo could see was the company. Kali slammed her staff into the ice. A crack rippled through the air. Before her, the world snapped, the ashy sky and snow ripping in half, peeling back as though hands were ripping through the atmosphere. This tear revealed a portal, fizzing and popping with electricity, exposing a new scene. Through this oval portal, wide and berthy, the company could see Valhalla's tower, the surrounding ocean, the dull green ground, grass swaying slightly with the gentle breeze. Snow drifted through the portal. Kali screamed with glee, jumping and waving her arms, pointing at the shadows passing by the windows.

The elation was gone in a second. Dragur ran towards the portal, their attention moving away from Milo and his wolf, their swords and spears dragging in the snow. Astrid saw them quickly but never moved. It was an army, an onslaught of the undead, sprinting towards her at full speed.

"*No,*" he breathed.

Astrid extended her arms, backing away and holding the Warriors of Thunder behind her. Silas tried to run towards the undead, a sword in his hands. Kali hadn't stopped screaming. She was fighting the Asgardian, smacking her hands against her, thrusting the staff towards the portal - empty efforts to try and close it. The Dragur pooled in like ants, toppling over each other and dropping their swords. They wouldn't need them to destroy the tower.

Hel's hot breath fanned against his ear. A snake pulled at his hair. Another twisted towards the spear. He could hear her smile. "Thank you, *half-god*, for finally giving me Valhalla," she said. "Did you know," she paused, turning him to look her in the eyes, "once you kill a soul, it just...disappears? No one knows where it ends up." The smile grew. "Freyja used to say they returned to Yggdrasil. Seeps back into its leaves, stretching through the branches." She dropped him. "Time for a long, mind-numbing conversation with the Master." And without another word, Hel stalked towards the portal, her wolves running ahead.

Milo groaned, Kára's head sliding beneath his chest to lift him. He slung his arm around the wolf's neck, swaying till he wobbled to his feet, the Gungnir sliding through the snow. The wolf released a low whine. As they ran to the portal, all the Dragur stragglers entered Valhalla, Hel out of sight. He collapsed into Silas. He let him lean on him till Milo could stand on his own.

"I-I couldn't stop her," he breathed.

Astrid frowned. "You seriously thought you could beat the goddess of Death?"

He glared.

"It's fine," she added. "We should follow."

Kali rubbed her nose, sniffing loudly. "I should've closed it. I mean, what have we done? Like *really*?"

"It doesn't matter," Milo said. He pushed himself off Silas, resting the spear like a walking stick on the ground. Kára leaned towards the portal, her nose flaring as she sniffed the opening. He walked towards the portal. "There's only one thing left to do now. We stop them from destroying the tower."

"It's gonna happen," Silas muttered.

"How could you know?"

Silas turned. "The prophecy."

And though those words sparked a bubbling in his stomach, Milo looked away. None of it mattered. He smiled. "Changes nothing."

The Warriors of Thunder walked through the portal.

XXXI. And the Sun was Rising

"Holy shit," Kali drawled as they passed through the portal. "Everything's going to hell."

Valhalla was abuzz with energy. While the thought would've meant nothing with Milo's mind on the ordinary, he bristled with fear. It was indescribable. The tower seemed shorter then, with glass windows exploding, warriors falling through the walls, and randomly placed doors. The tower from the outside was something he had never seen before. Grass burnt down to a whittled brown from the overhead sun, a shadow so large Milo could've sworn it was a blimp coming from whatever was at its top, an ocean colored such an enchanting blue it hurt to look at. But there was one thing that was immediately recognizable as different.

There was no sun.

Milo clearly remembered the bright sky and forever hanging daylight as though he had lived there all his life. And yet, after stepping through the portal and watching a war around the minuscule island, Valhalla journeyed into darkness. There was no moon. No stars. Only light upon the horizon, where the midnight sky touched the lifeless sea, existed, catching fire upon the tower. It was a rustic orange, barely peeking from the night's cover, casting its light upon the battle. Milo squinted in the darkness: fires burnt within the tower, red glow catching onto the already dying grass. It was all unrecognizable. His hand shot around, searching and snatching onto Kali's. She flinched and squeezed his hand back.

"That's ironic." Silas's voice was quiet. "You know, considering."

She blinked. "Considering?"

"He means the hell thing," Milo muttered. "You said it's going to hell, but...well, Hel's already here."

It was silent between the fractured company. He missed Thalia. The spear was uncomfortable in his hand, and Svalin was so heavy that he practically threw it into the portal, now lost in the surrounding darkness. He listened to Astrid stepping around them till she blocked the battle from their view.

"Dead ones," she said, "remain here, by the shore. Promise me you won't fight."

They nodded at her, giving mumbles of agreement.

She looked over her shoulder towards the tower's entrance. The doors flung off the hinges, and a woman taller than the Dragur army stalked into the building. Light landed on her stomach. It was made from snakes. Astrid's fists clenched around her sword. When she looked back at the warriors, she was not herself. "Leave the goddess to *me*."

Milo wanted to scream at her, to beg her not to go. Without Thalia, Astrid was the next best thing they had for a leader. But before he shouted his protests, the Asgardian was gone, sprinting towards the tower, sliding around the battling Valhallians and Dragur. The ground was already scattered with dead souls. Dead Valhallians. Too many dead. He turned around. The portal was gone, with no trace of it, as though it had never existed in the first place.

Kali's hand was still holding onto him. "What happens now?"

The spear hummed. Before he even spoke, Milo already knew his answer. "There's no way we're just gonna stand here," he said. "We protect our home.".

"Then we stay together." Kali pulled her hand free. From the ground, she grabbed a fallen sword no longer than her calf, the Laevateinn quiet and still. "No matter what happens, we do this together." She sighed heavily. "Things usually work out in the end for people like us."

Milo sighed. "Don't be naive."

He pressed his lips together. He wanted to agree. But she was wrong. After everything, she was wrong. He didn't look at her. For some reason that he couldn't pinpoint, he felt ashamed. "Not for people like us."

A sound like nails against a chalkboard came from Silas to their left. It was the Dainsleif leaving its sheath. He had been silent, practically nonexistent, while chaos raged around him. Suddenly, he was stepping towards the light, the crawling fire upon the horizon casting itself across his eyes.

"Whoa, man," Milo called out, pointing his spear, "what the hell are you doing? The curse -"

Silas lifted his head. The light scattered across his eyes. They were purple, this inky mist dripping from his tear ducts, sliding down his nose's bridge, falling like a sticky mess. He looked directly at Milo, the Dainsleif shaking in his left hand. It was not a regal blade but like rough iron angled to have a sharp tip, leather binding the hilt. There was a darkness, though, radiating from it. That cold energy reminded

Milo of the moments after death, that rope tied around him, yanking him and yanking him away. His mouth opened like a door. "There's only one way this night ends."

"Shit," Milo breathed. *Loki.* "Remember who you are, Silas." The spear shook in his hand. "You're not Loki, you're not -"

He was running. There wasn't much space between them, only a few feet, and with barely two strides, Silas was upon him, the Dainsleif raised above his head like a baseball bat. Milo shoved Kali into the water, hearing her yelp and clash into the gentle waves, shouting obscenities and pleas to her fighting friends. Milo raised the Gungnir. Dainsleif ricocheted off the ebony material, sparks flying like bugs into the grass. Smoke trickled up. Milo's fake heart hammered against his chest like a hummingbird. He wondered how fast their hearts beat. He wondered what would happen if their hearts slowed. Milo held the spear close to his chest like a dying bird, Silas's hammering sword smashing and crashing over and over against him.

Milo's arms were as heavy as lead. Silas slid through the atmosphere like the ocean's tides, pulling and pushing the air. With every strike, he carried away rocks and sand, and as he fell back, his unbelievable strength returned for him to jump back again. It was a constant cycle Milo was victim to: nothing to defend himself against the attacks, nothing against the rage, nothing against the enchantment Loki placed upon his friend. All he could think about was the Dainsleif. The curse. The life it had to take. Milo's chest at its point. The inevitable end was written out for him, so clearly he never realized it. He tripped over his feet. Svalin was there, glittering against the light.

The other Warriors of Thunder were screaming. Dragur approached, moving past the falling Valhallian souls and sensing the remaining warriors. Milo scooped up the shield, sliding his left arm through its loops and raising it towards his chest as he rose. Silas came again with the Dainsleif. It clashed against Svalin, and Silas went skidding back, surprise taking over his features before the emotion was quickly gone again, and he ran at full speed.

Once, there were flowers in his hair. He was confused as to why the thought came to him but not upset. It brought back the grass, blossoming flowers, moss, and a rippling lake. He could hear children laughing, ducks quacking, wind rustling the tree branches. A woman would be by his side. She was an angel, now poised and crystal, brown curls framing her head like a crown. Flowers twisted behind her ears. There was no bloodstain, no impending sword, no gods, no spear, no beach. It was only them, with flowers in their hair, laying in the park on a spring day.

The spear shot out before Silas got too close. The ends nipped at his wrists, sliced at his arm till the Dainsleif clattered to the ground. The Gungnir flung around, and its butt knocked into Silas's temple with a shattering crack. Svalin snapped out to his nose, and Silas toppled backward, falling to his back.

Milo blinked. The world did not go black at that time. Nothing faded. He knew what he was doing and how steady his heart was. His mother and the park were gone. They did him no good. Milo dropped the shield, replacing it with the Dainsleif. His arm went cold as he grabbed it, the heaviness draping over Milo like a weighted blanket. He wanted to drop it, to bury it under the earth, but could find that once his fingers wrapped around its hilt, there was no sign of letting go.

He looked down at Silas. There was blood trailing down his temple, gliding to his chin. His dominant arm held cuts, dirtied with mud, grass, and ocean water. The light felt against his face. His blood, for a second, shimmered with gold.

"Silas," Milo said, the wind suddenly rushing around them. The ocean was riled up, waves splashing against the shore with loud bangs. The battle grew quieter. The Dragur entered the tower. "We can stop this! Let me help you, let me -"

Silas's lips parted to show teeth clenched so hard together that blood trickled from his gums, red staining his mouth. The purple flashed against his eyes. "Use...the....sword!"

"Wh-what?"

He fought himself, fists digging up dirt to stop himself from battering his own hands into his throat. He got to his knees, bent down till his nose dragged against the earth, and released the most painful scream anyone ever heard. When his eyes raised, the blood mixed with his tears, and the purple gone, the curves and lines in his lumber-colored cheeks familiar. "*Kill me!*" he screamed. "*Please!*"

Milo tried to remember the first time he saw Silas. It was in the tower, that much he knew. But it felt like centuries ago, a long friendship just beginning. As time went on, Milo believed he'd spend eternity with his company, living out their days in a never-ending tower with the only hope for a future being the world's end. And yet, right there, it felt like he already reached that future. The Gungnir fell from his hand. He didn't care where it ended up. He couldn't care less if the thing rolled into the ocean, snatched up by whatever sea god that caused the waves to snap so violently at their feet. His heart was breaking.

He didn't argue. The boy died a long time ago. Not when he was stabbed back in his old life, but rather, the moment Loki did his deal upon him. The second they lost Silas was the second he lost control of *himself*. There was no more arguing about God or the aspect of faith. There were no pointed stares or heavy words laced with malice. There was only them on that beach - it was always the beach - victims of a god's war. Milo walked towards him. Silas had already gone. The purple was back. The blood-stained his shirt.

Milo wrapped his arms around him, resting his chin upon Silas's shoulder before plunging Dainsleif through his stomach. It slunk like butter, the tip slicing through to the other side, ripping his clothes and skin apart. Immediately, he went loose in Milo's arms, breathing rugged and staggered as a cry left his lips. Milo dropped the sword, cradling Silas as they fell to the ground. The enchantment was gone. There was only Silas there, his brown eyes staring toward the horizon. The waves still crawled onto the shore, eager to grab Silas's limp hands. Milo looked out to sea.

And the sun was rising.

* * *

The great hall in Valhalla was filled with dead bodies. Or dead souls. The resurrected warriors found their last moments in the hall, weapons scattered across the floor, fire chomping up the tables and rotting wood, goblets toppled over, and food thrown. Down from the walls, shields clattered, spears and swords tainted with Hel's dead army, their bloodied footprints leading a trail across the floor. At the room's center stood Hel. Her double swords dripped with blood. The helmet was lost from her head. The snakes that made up her armor hissed and looked upon her conquest with beady eyes.

Astrid stepped into the hall. There was no need to hide her presence, try to silence her entrance with hushed steps. The goddess would have known her by scent alone, the familiar crawl of her soul, the constant snap in her heart. Her mother would whisper before bed that Hel stitched their bodies together from our fallen ancestors and built humankind from her wolves' fur. Eventually, it would be in her hands that they would return, ready to be pulled apart and remade for their legacy. Astrid once prayed to Hel, though she would never admit to it.

The goddess raised her blade, looking at the blood trickle. "I have heard much about you, little warrior." Hel turned, the snakes chomping at the air. Her eyes, filled with venom, landed upon Astrid with a smile. "Your lover is one to boast."

Everything became cold. Astrid stood rigid, forcing her face to remain still in the sudden awareness. "You've seen him."

"Seen him, hated him, thought about whether or not I should kill him." Hel shrugged, kicking a plate aside. "All of life in one moment."

"Where is he?"

She laughed. "I don't give away knowledge that easily, little warrior."

"I am not clueless," Astrid said. "I will not make deals with you."

The goddess moved closer. "Oh, look at you! Acting all big and bad." She rested the swords upon her shoulders. "Did you forget that you are a slave to the Aesir?"

"I am stronger than you think."

Hel tilted her head, her lip poking up. "Do not worry, little one. I have tasted your soul and felt its strength." Her diamond face grew uncharacteristically soft. "I do not underestimate you."

Astrid breathed deeply, holding Hofond up. "Then you know I cannot let you pass."

"You cannot *let me*?" Hel's laugh was different that time, loud and clanging like metal upon metal. The air went cold. "Your lack of understanding of your mortality is astounding."

Her smile was genuine. "It is my mortality that makes me bigger than you."

"Is that truly what you believe?" Hel asked. "What would your little Frey think?"

At any other moment in her life, Astrid would have screamed. She would have had to hold herself back from sprinting at the goddess, slamming her fists against her armor, hot, angry tears streaming down her face. She would have tried to stick her finger through her palm, asking herself the magnitude of reality. That day in Herjan. Instead, she stared Hel in the eyes and found nothing short of assurance. *I am alive,* she thought. *I am no longer dreaming.* "The dead don't think," she said. "It's one of the benefits of being dead."

Hel grinned. Something like pride settled in her gaze. "So be it, warrior." She bowed her head, and the swords extended. "I would be honored to have your soul in my army."

And the dance began.

The goddess was nothing less than a snake slithering through the air. Her arms snapped out, and the swords made no sound, cutting across the air and slicing along her skin like butter. Hofond did the work. It moved like a hammer, crushing the snakes and dividing Hel's armor. They worked around each other as though they carved a statue from marble, building a beautiful work with every stroke, every hit, every chip to fall away. And when the first strike had been made - Hel's sword dragging against Astrid's side - the blood scattered against the marble-like paint.

Whatever it was they built, it was magnificent. It was not death, it was not war, it was not the outside battle. It was like the beings Hel sewed together with bones, the Dragur she reanimated after faceless souls made their journeys to her castle. It was the same as a ripple along Herjan's creek. A butterfly coaxed the water to follow as it swooped up and down, up and down. Astrid struck with Hofond, and Hel diverted. Hel snapped her swords down upon Astrid's wrists, and the sword clattered.

It was a melody. One becoming sharper and grotesque, one that filled Astrid with exhaustion. She struggled to lift Hofond for the second time, raising it over her head and bringing it down upon the goddess. When the blade landed, Hel disappeared as though she had never been there in the first place. In reality, the warrior moved so slowly that the goddess only needed to walk to relieve herself from danger. The goddess stalked, circling Astrid as she wobbled around. Pain struck her leg. Needles danced upon her arms. An ache grew on her neck. Her eyes watered. She wanted to sleep.

In the end, Astrid was always a mortal. She was temporal and mutable. She was the grass. She was the sand. She was the fading star. Hel was the sky. Hel was the ocean and the galaxies, and the universe. In between, there was only space. The divine sat upon a pedestal, and the mortal was closest to the earth, for it was the only place they truly belonged.

Astrid blinked, and suddenly, she was on her knees. Her shirt was drenched in sweat and blood, her back torn apart, her legs shaking and scored from Hel. Hofond fell from her hands.

The goddess appeared. "You don't *get* to surrender, warrior. You lose when I say you lose, you win when I say you win, you die when I say you die. I haven't said you can die yet." She kicked Hofond forward. "Pick your sword up."

Astrid wasn't sure why she bothered. Already, she came to terms with her death. Why prolong it? She told herself it was for respect. Slowly, she reached for the sword, using both hands to steady it as she rose, blood dripping loudly in her ears. A groan rippled from her lips as she held the sword above her head, slamming it down upon the goddess. Hel looked irritated as she shoved Astrid's arm away. The sword fell once more, skidding to the far wall. The anger in her eyes was as bright as fire. The goddess grabbed Astrid's right arm and snapped it like a twig. The *crack* echoed.

The scream erupting from her lips could've shattered glass. It was pain she never felt, an intensity soaring through her entire body, forcing her to gag and spit as she fell to her back. Astrid held her broken arm to her chest, gritting her teeth. It was finally happening. She raised her head to face the goddess.

"Now, little warrior," Hel said, "I say your time has come."

The blades were angled around Astrid's neck, raising and falling with a grand swoop. Astrid did not close her eyes.

"Touch one hair on her head, Hel," a familiar voice called out, "and I'll make you wish you were never born."

A hand, colored pale blue and filled with silver tattoos, held onto the blade just inches from Astrid's neck. She turned. There in Valhalla's great hall stood Rundi, the Vanir Fae. No more did she cower beneath a hood. Instead, the Fae dressed in armor, colored midnight and raven feathers, hair falling like a cloak behind her. There was a sword on her belt, lined silver and emerald. Elation filled Astrid's chest.

"Look at you, little Fae!" Hel shouted. "All confident in the power granted to you from the Vanir you come from. While I like the idea of killing you, I have to say, quite unlike you to come alone." She touched her chin. "Quite foolish."

Rundi smiled, showing off those pointed teeth. "Who said I was alone?"

A loud crash came from the room's back wall as if on cue. It was a window imploding, the cool night breeze wafting through the hall. From the window came a tumbling figure, one dressed in rags and hoods, long hair scraggly and unwashed, coal-colored fingertips and runes drawn upon arms. Astrid couldn't stop the laugh from falling out.

Ullr brandished axes, jumping beside Rundi with a hysteric stare. He laughed, waving his weapons about. "Thought I'd miss all the fun, didn't ye?" He leaned down to Astrid, swiping his finger below her chin. "Don' you worry there, love. We've got you now."

"Ullr," Hel said. "A boy that is barely a god. At least give me a challenge, Aesir!"

He nodded. "That's why we brough' *him*."

Out from the doors came the god of guardians. With obsidian skin, eyes as wide as diamonds, dressed in armor forged from gold, and a helm resting beneath his arm, he moved with tentative steps, eyes never leaving Hel. She stared, lips parted, the snakes ceasing in their hissing and angry snaps. Her blades lowered.

Astrid sucked in a deep breath. "Heimdall."

His arm shot out. Hofond soared through the air, landing in his hand with a *thud*. "Greetings, goddess." Heimdall bowed. "You have overstepped your boundaries."

Hel held her head high. "You have no power here, guardian."

"Truly, Hel, it looks like I have *all* the power." Heimdall turned to Rundi. "Take the warrior to safety, Fae. We can handle this."

Astrid wrapped an arm around Rundi's neck and peered over her shoulder as the Fae lifted her off the ground. The last thing she saw was Heimdall and Ullr shooting toward the goddess, the move as silent as a moth's fluttering wings. No sound came from the battle, movements as right as air, gliding across the hall to clang swords, slice skin, and battle immortals. Rundi took only a few moments to make her way to the tower's bottom, knocking doors open with a kick, wielding her blade with one arm, and juggling Astrid in the other. When they reached the outside, where a sun crawled above the sea, making its way over the sky, Astrid gulped down the air with much relief. The pain drifted from her arm, becoming a steady numbness across her chest.

Kali stood near the shore, where the ocean lapped against the rocks. She was not holding her staff; it sat against the grass alongside the Gungnir. Even from a distance, Astrid saw the darkness in her eyes, the new light glinting against her crystallized tears. At their feet were the other Valhallians. Her heart jumped to her throat. All she could imagine was Milo Bohr's lightning-colored eyes.

Don't be dead.

Rolling out from Rundi's arms, Astrid tumbled, ignoring how her arm bent and the startled shout from the Fae. She clawed across the ground, getting closer and closer till she felt her breath get stolen from her throat.

Milo looked at her. In his arms was Silas. His chest heaved sporadically, hand covering the gaping flesh wound the same color as Hel's mouth against his stomach. His eyes were dull but his own, watching the sky turn blue.

Astrid collapsed. Her heart shattered, crumbling at her feet with a soft exhale. She touched her chest, shoved her hands against her skin, pressed till there was a dull pain echoing through her bones and muscles and blood. Her head dropped to the ground. A hand touched her cheek, fingers tying into her hair and lifting her to see.

"Don't cry," Silas breathed. "Not for me."

She wished the world would burn.

XXXII. Silas

Is it possible to be good and evil?

Milo could be good when the moment arose. But he realized he was evil more times than not. There he was, holding Silas in his arms, and could only think himself to be a bad person. It was he, in the end, who drove the sword through his stomach. It was him. He watched him struggle to breathe. There was a pain spreading in his chest, enveloping his arms, crawling down his legs, and swallowing him whole. He pressed his nose to Silas's forehead. The dying boy felt warm.

How many dead, he thought, *how many bodies will I bury?*

There was death on the floor, death in his arms, death lingering in his fingertips and filling his eyes. How different was he from Hel? He wanted to pull out his soul and heart and shove it into Silas, bringing back the glow in his eyes. Why should he have life with Silas fading in his lap? What was the point? A tear slid down his cheek, dropping onto Silas's nose. He prayed God listened. He prayed Silas could find his way to his God. He fought the urge to scream, to raise his eyes to the sky and scream as loud as he could, just to wait for a response. He needed a response. What would be the point if there wasn't?

Twice in the nineteen-year-old's existence, he would die. First, the bodily death, separating his soul from his mortal body. And now the second, when Silas's soul could no longer glow with life. What happened to souls that died?

He watched Silas. It was his fault. From Silas's eyes, which might've come from his mother. The curve in his cheeks might have come from his father. The bump on his nose. His full bottom lip and the dimples. Maybe even siblings. What would they have that Silas also did? The strength in his hands? The way his skin was the same shade as a forest? Milo hooked his arms around him.

Shadows danced around them. There was low chattering; unfamiliar voices tossed his name around a few times. He raised his head. There was a circle around him: a freakishly tall man dressed in golden armor too bright for him to stare, a surfer guy with shaggy hair and a bare chest, skin filled with thickly drawn runes, and a woman whose skin looked like his mother's blue dress. They spoke in hushed tones, eyes glancing down at him.

"...needs to leave the body."

"You will only upset the Prince."

"Oi, are we callin' 'im that now? Prince 'n all?"

There was a huff. "What we call him matters not. The body -"

Milo gripped on the Gungnir. Quickly, he raised it, pointing towards the trio. They looked down with blank stares, no fear or surprise. The realization hit him. Gods. The anger funneled into his chest. Hands touched his shoulders.

"Milo," Kali whispered, "lower the spear."

He didn't move.

Kali made a noise like a growl. "Somebody *do* something!"

Astrid stood in his way. "You cannot raise that to the gods, Milo. Please, just -"

"The *gods*," he mocked. The anger pooled into him. His arm gripped harsher around Silas's torso. The boy exhaled, wincing at the contact. "The *gods did this to him*! Look around. All this has happened because of them," he shouted, thrusting the spear.

The blue-skinned woman took a step away. "I'm no god."

"There's no way I'm letting them near him."

Astrid nodded. "If there's anyone who could agree, it's me, Milo. But look at me."

Nothing pulled his eyes away from them. The tall one who wore gold, radiating like the sun. He wielded eyes so deep they shocked him as though he could see everything within him, down to his blackened soul.

"Look at me, Odinson."

His eyes flickered over. She looked gaunt in the light, her cheekbones standing out like sharpened knives. Her hair was pulled away from her face, dried blood painted on her temples, staining her neck, dirtying her hands. But it was her arm that caught his breath. It was bent oddly, colored purple and red instead of her olive skin. There was an emptiness in her eyes mirroring his own. He lowered the spear.

"I'm sorry," he said.

"I know."

"He's -" he stopped, choking on his words. He looked down to see Silas watching him, tears welling in his eyes. His clammy hand fell into Milo's. "I didn't mean to."

Astrid touched his face. "I know."

Hands gripped onto his shoulders. Silas squeezed his hand. "Milo," he whispered.

The tears had already fallen. He couldn't look at him.

"*Milo.*"

And when he finally did, Silas smiled.

"It's okay," he said. "I'm okay." He swallowed, the movement slow and methodical. "Whatever happens next," he continued in a breath, stomach rising even slower than before, "I'll be okay."

"It was supposed to be *together*. Whatever happens next *together*."

"No, buddy," Silas whispered. "I'm-I'm-" he sucked in a sharp breath. "I'm sorry, but I think I've gotta do this alone."

Milo's raised his eyes to the gods. They watched silently, those blank looks boiling his rage. It hurt how much they didn't know about mortality, how easy it was for someone like Silas to die again. To die over and over again. "*Save* him," he demanded.

The one with golden armor stepped closer, kneeling in an attempt to reach his eye level but still managing to tower over him. "Young Prince," he said, "I am Heimdall, guardian of Asgard. Accept my condolences for your companion."

He glared. "Does he look dead to you?"

The other god scoffed. "Look at 'im, mate. Boys damn close to it."

Light funneled into Milo's fingertips. He glared at the surfer-looking god so hard he could've sworn he would burn him alive. The god narrowed his eyes, glancing towards Milo's hands. "I don't want your condolences."

Heimdall nodded. "But we gods have our limits. The Dainsleif demands payment, and it has found it within him."

"You're just gonna let him die? It was a *god* who gave him the sword! Whose fault is it?"

"Fate does things for reasons we can never truly understand."

Milo chewed on his lips.

The other god stepped closer, kneeling beside Heimdall. "My name is Ullr, Prince," he said, "and I think I can offer ye somethin'."

"What?"

"I can take him to where he'd like to die," Ullr said.

Silas's eyes opened. "You-you can take me home?"

"Where is home?"

The smile crawled onto Silas's lips. "The beach," he whispered. "In Virginia."

And Valhalla's island disappeared.

* * *

The beach looked a lot like Asgard's. Milo believed it wasn't Virginia Beach, but something else, like a widespread illusion. It looked too good to be true. The water was calm, barely creating waves to claw at the shore. Even the sand was a pearly white, untouched by humans. There was a singular tree beside the sea, a light breeze running through its leaves. When Milo opened his eyes, Silas was upright, leaning against the tree trunk. Around him was the company, kneeling in the sand and taking in the warm light. Milo looked over his shoulder. The gods stood at a distance, whispering to each other with their eyes still hanging onto them. They did something to Silas: the air did not catch in his throat, and the blood steadied from his stomach.

Silas's breathing picked up. He stared into the ocean, his lips curling up in an exhausted smile. "I-I used to imagine death so much I thought it already happened," he said. There was a faded look on his cheeks, an ashy gray taking over his lips. "Early mornings, the sky looked so perfect I could've sworn I had to be dead to see it." His voice rose. "And as more people died in my life, it-it-it became easier to swallow. But I'm scared. I'm scared because I don't think I'll open my eyes this time. I don't think I'll wake up in a tower as a hero." He glanced between them, his breath rising with sudden hysterics. "This is it, isn't it? Like what the Master said, right? Since there's no tower. I'm scared. I'm-I'm-I'm -"

Milo grabbed his hand.

His eyes flicked over to him. Silas started to cry, lip quivering as he spoke. "You-you tell them I died a hero," he cried. "You *swear* it. I died a hero. You tell them-tell them-tell-tell-"

"I swear, Si," Milo said. He leaned forward, touching his forehead to Silas's, "I swear."

He died not long after that. There was an enveloping silence, calm and still, wrapping them together in a singular embrace. They breathed the same air, watched the same sun, counted the same waves, and listened to the same birds. They stared at Silas as he inhaled for the final time, that final exhale rippling through them, carried over the sun and dissipating into the atmosphere. He was silent, facing the ocean with eyes as bright as the sky. Milo felt stunned. What would happen next? Who would there be to call? Who was left to tell that Silas was, indeed, a hero? There were no parents in the afterlife, no relatives thinking he still lived somewhere. It wasn't like he hadn't died before, already buried, already mourned, already given that stale reception with cheese plates and flat sodas.

It reminded him of the audiobook that played after their fight. The chilling voice echoed something about going into the garden through the room. There was no idea of its origin or how the company got its hands on it, but it didn't matter. He took it as a sign, words presented to him foretelling his future. A better prophecy than what was presented by the Norn.

I was mad that I might be whole and dying, that I might have life, knowing what evil thing I was but not knowing what good thing I was shortly to become.

He held Silas's hand. It was cold. He frowned. It wasn't supposed to be cold. It was *never* supposed to be cold. The gods' whispers grew louder till he could've sworn they were upon him.

And suddenly, Kali was holding Silas's other hand. Astrid touched his knee. They were broken but whole, fractured, and mended. Heartbroken and alive. Painstakingly and undeservedly alive.

Milo frowned. He shouldn't be alive.

* * *

The gods took them back to Valhalla. Astrid lingered behind, knowing what came next in the Nordic burial tradition. It was a peaceful ceremony, open to the remaining survivors. As the dead ones pooled out from the tower, limping and bandaged, huddling close together in need of emotional support, Astrid realized war did not point out victors but rather made certain to emphasize those who were *left*. Indeed Dragur still sulked through the halls, no one strong enough to banish the living dead back to Nifelheim, abandoned by their goddess. Odin's population of chosen warriors lost in battle faded to the ash tree. Even the Valkyrie, finally choosing sides in the billowing civil war, left the tower through the portals in a rush to escape Death's wrath.

What remained were survivors, century-old souls waiting for the end, hoping their god might appear, praying the tower would tighten, using old magic to repair itself. They watched the doors expectantly for the Master. The mourning Warriors of Thunder paid no attention to them. Astrid, who reveled at a distance, watched it unfold. She could see the disdain on the Valhallian warriors, their hushed whispers not quiet enough.

"Quite the party, ain't it, love?" Ullr stood at her left. There were new runes along his hands, scaling up his arms and scoring the collarbones. Newfound energy rippled through him, powered by runes and magic.

She stared at the wooden casket Silas laid in. "How are you here, Ullr?"

"Gratitude sounds nice on ye."

"I'm serious."

He sighed. "The guardian has his ways." He nodded towards Heimdall. "He doesn' talk much." Ullr turned, resting his hand against her shoulder. "Sorry about your friend."

"Just another name to cross off."

"How'd you end up with this lot anyway? What happened to findin' the big man?"

Astrid wasn't paying attention. There was an emptiness in her hands from Hofond's absence. Her heart burned, and they were getting ready to push Silas's casket into the water. Heimdall showed Kali how to hold a bow and arrow. The dead one wanted to fire the flaming arrow to finish the ceremony.

"Astrid," Ullr said. "Where's your amulet?"

Her hand shot up. The chunky amulet wasn't around her neck or on the ground beside her feet. She checked the oddly shaped pockets in her Midgardian pants. Empty. It was gone. And for some reason, it didn't bother her. She only felt lighter, thinner, and skeletal and nothing more. Ullr watched.

"I don't mind," she whispered. "I don't need it."

Ullr's eyebrows scrunched. "What about Thor?"

"He'll be found." Astrid's hands dropped. "I'm just tired." She eyed him. "Do you *know* what that feels like, Ullr? Being tired?"

If he was offended, he didn't show it. Ullr only tilted his head, watching Kali pull back an arrow in practice. "You have no idea." He kept staring as the arrow dropped into the waves and swallowed immediately. "Tired of what?"

She frowned. "Fighting."

"You were born to do it, love," he said. "Can't get tired of your purpose."

"Watching people I love die is my purpose?"

"Look." He swiveled around to face her. "All ye lot are fighters. And I don' mean ye were born brave. Ye were born with fire and steel in yer blood. And aye, the universe will test ye because what else are they bloody goin' to do?" He chuckled. "No one chose this life, love. Who knows, maybe yer dream is to lay down yer arms, never to raise a damn sword ever again. But ye were *born to fight*. It's what ye know. It's what ye do best." Ullr turned back to the ocean. His eyes looked empty. "It's all we can do."

Astrid couldn't deny it. Her urge to reach to her back to grasp Hofond was undeniable. And the stillness, the hovering Valhallians staring at the Warriors of Thunder like meat, triggered this nervousness that crawled down her spine. She was trapped in the calm, in the drag within peace. There was an anticipation for a Dragur to exit the tower, to give her the need to snatch up a sword.

"Do you think he was in love?"

Ullr shrugged. "Ye knew him, I didn'.￼" He turned towards her. "Why are ye crying, love?"

"So many people fall in love, and now they are dead," she said. "*I* have been in love, and maybe one day I will be again or won't." She shook her head. "Either way, I will be dead eventually, and all the love that swells up in my chest will be dead with me. Where will it go?"

"Back to the ash tree." He smiled. "If the boy had love, it would only strengthen its branches. Don't cry for it, love."

The god touched her cheek and turned her towards the ceremony.

Heimdall knelt before the sea, pushing the casket into the water with a sweeping motion. Inside, Silas lay peacefully, arms crossed over his chest with axes clenched within his fists. From a distance, with the light cascading upon him, the blood dried and cleaned off, Silas looked alive as he ever would be, about to sit up at any second. The casket slid onto the water. Kali took her place at the shore, pulling the arrow back as Milo lit its point with a match. She stood there momentarily, arms stiff and tense with beautiful piety, poise, and statuesque. Once the casket moved a little into the sea, she released the arrow, which soared through the air, landing in the wooden boat with a small thud. It caught on fire within a second. Ullr's arm wrapped around her. Milo, his face pale and eyes deadly with anger, turned to look upon her. He softened when their eyes met.

The ocean in Valhalla did not stretch on forever. It reached an end at its horizon, snapping into a waterfall that led into an emptiness Astrid did not want to see. Where Silas's body would end up was unknown to them, a chasm much like the one that swallowed up the Bifrost. And in a way, it was freeing, an inevitable death from death, an end to the end. Astrid knew not where Silas's soul traveled, but it served better that way. His soul is free, gone and flying, swimming through oceans, lakes, and rivers. Astrid raised her eyes to the sky. Rain fell for the first time in the fallen Heaven of Valhalla. She smiled. His soul flew indeed.

"An end to the end," Astrid mused. "Sounds nice."

Ullr did not speak. He did not need to.

They were, indeed, tired.

XXXIII. We are Dying Stars

Milo watched the casket till it cascaded into nothing.

The water picked up after it disappeared, waves crashing against the shore, mixing with the bloody sand. More caskets were made, and more bodies dropped into the wood, dressed with axes and shields, cleaned and scrubbed for their after-afterlife. He knew the other survivors watched with laser gazes, this impenetrable darkness so heavy it weighed upon his shoulders. Who else was to blame for the invasion of their sanctuary? Who else to point the finger, with the Master still missing? Who could they whisper about with Dragur still lurking through the halls?

Valhalla was in ruins, and Milo knew it was his fault. He wanted to grab them, rip out his heart, and drop it in their hands. Milo wanted to fall, raise his eyes to the sky, and let cold rain stain his face. He wanted the ghosts to haunt him. Milo watched the suffering that came with his death those few days ago, one night in a bar; effervescent pain and longing took over his entire being the moment his heart stopped beating. As he stood there, watching the caskets wade through the water, each catching flames and dropping into nothing, Milo realized suffering, pain, longing, and hate were the consequences of being around.

And yet, when he was *truly* alive, everything was colored black and white. Emotions were dull, moments scattered, movements slow and heavy. He searched for himself during life, wondered what lay beyond the atmosphere, stared into his mother's eyes, and yearned to ask what came *before*. He dreamt of his father and prayed one day he might meet him. He met his only friend but knew a wall stood between them years before his death. He only felt alive in the rain when the world rested on his shoulders, and thunder broke the sky in half and resonated in his chest. He only felt alive when his mother smiled when her face lit up like a neon sign. He felt alive when the sun rose, the moment when it crashed against the horizon, light shooting across the plains like faraway boats, carrying shipments to and fro, filled with passengers he might never know, whispers in different languages, all heading in different directions and never noticing the paths they missed.

The first time Milo saw color was in *her*. At the bar, everything faded into a dull blue, the atmosphere hot and heavy with sweat and alcohol, Thalia there like the sunrise. His eyes fell upon her, and it felt like he was staring into the sun. To look at her through a reflection would be an insult; to do anything besides take her straight on and bask in the light she presented would taint her name. And maybe it was because her blood gleamed gold, but he didn't care, for he fell in love with a goddess who showed him light in its purest form. He found himself alive in death. Even though his heart was merely a shell within, a vessel of once was, Milo never felt it beat stronger. He was *alive* in every way possible.

✳ ✳ ✳

Milo watched the water slosh and sway by the shore. There were no more caskets. Valhallians burnt the other bodies in a triangular pyre, the burning souls and spirits hanging like smog around the island. No one tried to rebuild the tower. There was no point.

"Yggdrasil will remain," Heimdall said to the remaining Valhallians, his godly voice booming through slightly parted lips, "but its connection to the tower has been severed. Nothing is connecting your souls to their eternal life." There was confusion. The Warriors held hands. Children, still alive despite the invasion, held onto each other, crowding around the century-old war heroes, clutching their legs. Heimdall's face did not change. "Death can even take you, Valhallians. It is time to pray that your souls might remain till Ragnarok." The god walked away.

The Warriors of Thunder knelt by the shore. None spoke in a while. They would have if they could, but there was a gap between them. Someone was missing. Astrid approached with the other god, Ullr, her hand gripping her belt as though a sword should've been there. They whispered in a different language, one Milo recognized from his moments with Loki. He didn't bother to try to translate.

"Young ones." In the water stood Aegir. He looked as he did in Manhattan, half surrounded by the drifting sea, beard grazing against the surface. He wore a necklace with an amulet at the end, curled from steel to make an elongated *S*.

Milo didn't look at him. "Leave."

"Hey," Astrid snapped. "Show some -"

"*Respect*?" He pushed himself up. The other survivors did not notice the god's presence, chatting about who would take a party into the tower to recover the Master. He faced the sea god and saw nothing but rage reflecting on him. The god's eyes were like two snowglobes, trapping an ocean storm within silver. Milo saw his anger raging in them, lightning strikes and thunder booms echoing in his eyes. "Why the hell should I give gods respect? What have they done for me?"

Aegir frowned. "You are angry."

"You can see," he said. "That's good."

"I will not offer condolences."

Milo waded into the water. "Are you kidding me?" he screamed. "You-you *gave him* that sword!"

"And told him of its curse."

"What did you expect him to do," he said, "ignore it? I'm not an idiot. You gave him that damn sword for a reason! What was it, huh? You wanted him to die? You wanted to *force me* to kill him?" He was getting closer to the towering god, feet sliding against the seafloor. "You wanted him -"

Aegir swooped down, the water echoing around him like a tidal wave, latching onto Milo by the shoulders. His hands were slimy and mossy; seaweed twirled through his beard and caught in his teeth. The god leaned down and said, "I washed waves taller than anything you might conjure up in that *mortal* brain upon the Norn for doing this. I have slaughtered the Norn repeatedly, only for them to be reborn by the ash tree and do it all over again. I watched over Silas's mother as she mourned and helped his sisters play in the water during his funeral. I pleaded and traded to the Norn to spare him," his voice was heavy, "and I watched him die from afar. I guided his body to my seas. Even you, son of Odin, I saw and stopped your tears. I did not offer my condolences because," his head lowered in a bow, "it was me who took him away from you."

Milo stood in the water, listening to shuddering breaths echo from the god, watching as tears colored the same as the ocean crawled down his cheeks, dropping back into the water. Aegir did not remove his hands but held him tighter. His arms exploded with fire, like when Thalia got too close when her hands grazed his skin. Milo sighed.

"He...he was your son, wasn't he?"

Aegir released him. "Years ago, the Norn said my firstborn would be my last, to perish by my hand." He waded further into the water. "So I stayed away till I was called upon. I did not wish for him to die, young ones. He-he was my son."

And Milo no longer saw a god. There was only a person, a father, who held the world's regret on his lips. He mourned as much as them. "I'm sorry," he whispered.

The god slunk into the water. "The Norn have made me a promise."

"Those witches made a Vanir a promise?" Ullr squawked. He huffed. "Bloody 'ell, 'course they did."

Aegir rolled his eyes. "The fact you believe the Norn only lives to declare prophecies for the Aesir merely proves your ignorance, war god," he said. "They said since the era of the Warriors of Thunder is not yet over, Silas's soul would find itself in another, a child whose heart still beats, to replace the hole he left within your future."

Kali sighed. "Replace."

"No one's replacing Silas," Milo said.

The sea god was disappearing in the water. All they could see were his echoing eyes. His hand rose, and through the waves came a chain link, sliding upon the surface till it landed in Milo's palm. "Thalia is doing well," he said, voice muffled by the water. "Give her Gleipnir for me, young one, when she is returned. Tell her...tell her Hjerte still stands, and I will protect it with my life till her return."

Milo pulled his hand from the waves. Gleipnir was no longer a single link. It was a full-length chain, the piece the Master gave obvious in the center with its light silver glow. He wrapped it around his arm as he left the sea, helped to his feet by the company. The god was gone with a glance behind him, and Milo felt alone. He sensed they were like dying stars, rotating in faraway space as light expanded from their chests, swallowing everything in its path before they disappeared. His chest already exploded, and he was disappearing.

"Do you think we're born unlucky?" Kali asked.

If Silas were there, he'd answer with all the divine hope they wished they had. He'd say it was in God's hands. He would say it was up to them to be lucky or unlucky. He would lean back against the grass, staring at the sky with his feet dipped into the water. There would be a smile pulling back his lips. His skin, the same shade as a forest, would glow like a bronze statue beneath the rising sun. And he'd not doubt his words. His faith would grab onto them, spreading warmth throughout. But Silas was gone, and there was a silence answering Kali. She looked deflated.

Milo already knew his answer. *Yes*, he would say, *we are born with our mistakes in our blood, daggers in our veins, and darkness in our hearts*. And then: *but maybe it doesn't have to be that way*. But it wasn't what he would say. Instead, he turned and grabbed her hand. "No," he lied. "I think we're born with a clean slate, and it's the outside that makes us unlucky."

The sun was still rising. The company stood side-by-side at the ocean's shore, the waves running over their feet, pushing and pulling the earth beneath them into the sea. The horizon was smooth. They were stars and death, galaxies and life. Their blood held gold and magic, stories from realms far away and homes so familiar it drew tears. Whatever came next would come, and they would remain together, souls intertwined and forever attached. Wherever one went, the rest would follow. It had already been written in the stars.

It was morning, the bruise once upon his lip was a foggy memory, and Milo Bohr might've been terrified, but the sun - *the rising sun right over there* - was hope.

Real hope.

XXXIV. The Last Word is Always from the Villain

The Master of Valhalla walked through his ruins and burned down halls. He was practically unscathed from the invasion, considering the Dragur army making their merry way through the sanctuary. Instead, his cloaks were lightly dusted with ash, his beard scraggly and unbraided. His cane was lost in the chaos, and his swinney legs shook and creaked with each step. Gripping onto the wall, the Master crept towards his chambers, the hinges swung off the wall, bookcases ransacked and turned over. Not like it mattered. It was not what he came for. The Master slunk through the threshold and purple smoke engulfed him.

Loki stretched out from the Master's short figure, cracking his back in a single motion before bending down to touch his toes. The body was a scrunched one, old with scars and trauma, made eternal by the ash tree sitting miles above his head. Loki found the Master's body in the great hall after Hel's battle with the guardian and war god, snakeheads decorating the floor. After he jumped over the golden blood puddles, Loki changed into the dead old man and made his slow, illusionary way toward the rustic chambers.

While he hadn't anticipated the invasion, he made sure to leave a bouquet at Hel's doorstep. She played her role well. Loki moved around the fallen books and overturned tables, pushing aside scrolls and papers till he stood before the window overlooking the surrounding sea. By the shore were the Warriors of Thunder and Astrid, minus the handsome one. He frowned. There was something stinging in his chest. The boy died due to the enchantment. But Hel, for her compliance, demanded something in return, and her reward was fulfilling Milo Odinson's greatest fear. He had no power to deny her. And in the end, as he watched them stand together and mourn, watched over by the Aesir gods behind them, Loki could not help but let the regret swell in his heart.

But then there was Halvar. His eyes hung onto Astrid.

There was no more regret.

Gentle wind chimes came from behind him. Golden light fanned against the walls. He smiled but did not turn around. He had been expecting her.

"You killed the wrong warrior." Sigyn's voice always held steel at its end. That hardness, the sharp cut in her words, was something he found himself loving more than fear. It was Halvar's birth that softened it, even when her gaze would fall upon Loki, the words lightened, and her anger was not so obvious. The fear was that it would never come back. Even realms away in Asgard, her appearance brought through her magic, Sigyn's voice kept its iron edge.

Loki watched the company. "That's your one flaw, my Queen," he said. "Constantly doubting me."

"Doubt is different from skepticism."

"Everything is going according to plan." Loki looked over his shoulder at her. She was beautiful even through the hologram. "There's nothing for you to be skeptical about." He crossed his arms behind him and hoped she could not hear the lie in his voice.

Sigyn huffed. "*Plan*?" Her image flickered and fluttered as she sat upon the Bleeding Throne. She looked like a steel sword. "You gave the Aesir a King! They'll put the boy on the throne and retake the realm."

Loki smiled. From behind, Odinson looked nothing like his family. No, he looked like Natalie Bohr. He felt himself chip away. *It was fine*, he told himself, let the Midgardian haunt him. "It was never about taking the realm, Siygn," he muttered. "Give the throne to Freyja, and let the Vanir handle their war affairs. That'll keep them off our backs."

"It'll never work." She was becoming angry. "The bastard will take the throne and we'll never find Thor."

The sky echoed at his name. Loki turned away from the window. Her image flickered, scattering and falling into the air as though she was never there. He smiled at her, the same look that used to calm her down within the second. Instead, he feigned the smile to relax himself - it was a wistful reminder, and Sigyn used to remark that Halvar held the same grin as he. Loki shoved the guilt away. He shoved away Silas and Natalie. Only one thing mattered.

"No, my love," he said. "The Aesir are traditionalists to their very core. They'll see the accords, and recognize them, but in the end, they'll do what they do best and make him quit before the crown ever touches his head. And if they don't," he shrugged, "we'll handle that ourselves." Loki stopped himself from looking out the window. He could smell the rain and fragmented lightning even from within the broken tower. When he looked back to Sigyn, she was already half gone, her gaze doubtful but at his side. Loki smiled. This time, it did not help.

"He will give us Thor, and I'll have my revenge."

THE WARRIORS OF THUNDER
WILL RETURN

Index

<u>The Aesir</u>

Known as the ruling gods of the Norse Pantheon, the Aesir have resided in Asgard since the creation of all realms. They are the sky gods of justice and iron, filled with the self-inflicted responsibility of governing all creatures.

Odin: The All-Father, King of Gods, and Lord of the Hanged. Once king of Asgard, Odin ruled over the Aesir with stoicism and intimidation. Beloved by some and feared by all, Odin's battle-ready mind pulled the royal gods into many wars. He is normally seen with a pair of ravens circling above his head.

Thor: the fiery-tempered defender of Asgard, Thor, was once the crowned prince, set to rule the realms once the time came. Known across the battlefields for his thunderous strike, Thor won almost everything in his father's name, the All-Father. When a war swept through Asgard, the prince disappeared within the year.

Tyr: God of justice and law, Tyr resides within Asgard's golden halls, diligently working as the All-Father's right hand. As the mouthpiece of the realm, Tyr could turn a hall of Jotunn into friends instead of enemies.

Frigg: As the Queen of Asgard, Frigg blessed the land as a goddess of fertility and new growth. Her annual festival marked the beginning of the farming season, and the number of tributes offered dictated the upcoming harvest. Frigg's marriage to the King allows her to be the light of the land, the life left behind during war.

Baldur: Originally the heir to the throne, Baldur is the eldest son of Odin and the most beloved across Asgard. When visions came to the All-Father surrounding the death of Baldur, the prince was sent away for his safety, and any hope for him to one day be named king, disappeared.

Ullr: Ullr, the archer god, lurks in Asgard's castle halls as a carefree spirit, leaving magical runes in his path.

Heimdall: Known as the Eyes of the Aesir, the watcher god Heimdall protects the realm through his extraordinary sight ability. He reports to the Pantheon on the ongoings of all the realms.

Loki: Once the trickster, Loki was a teacher and guide, a master in illusionary magic who relied on years of study and natural talent. When a tragedy befalls his settlement, Sjel, Loki is banished from the Aesir, alongside his wife, Sigyn.

Sigyn: As the most skilled sorceress in Asgard, Sigyn was a formidable ally to all in any battle. Married to the illusionist Loki, the pair lived peacefully in Sjel till a violent tragedy.

Hodr: The blind Aesir god, Hodr, is a quiet clan member, mainly due to his ignorance of their affairs. He is one day fated by the Norn to take the life of Baldur, after being convinced by Loki.

<u>**The Vanir**</u>

The second godly clan residing in Vanaheim strives for the powers of nature and magic, identified by the mystical runes permanently lining their skin. Juxtaposing the battle-hungry Aesir, the Vanir revels in the strength of earthly abundance.

Skadi: Secluded in the snowy peaks of Hjerte, a covered settlement in Vanaheim, Skadi is the Vanir's beloved princess. Having removed herself from the violent conflict between the godly clans, Skadi devotes her life to protecting her small home, known as the Woman of the Hunt.

Hel: Ruler of Nifelheim, collector of the dead and mother of the Dragur, Hel is the most feared Vanir goddess. The dead, unclaimed by Valkyrie, find themselves in her land, allowing her to grow in numbers and strength every second of the day.

Aegir: Keeper of all seas, Aegir remained a voice of solid reason within the Vanir clan. He values protection and believes in following fate. Once captured by the Aesir, he was held underneath the great golden statue of Odin in Asgard.

Freyja: The beautiful and esteemed Queen Freya rules over the Vanir clan from the mystical world, Vanaheim. Once known as a reserved Queen, this goddess of magic had a great bloodlust for war when the All-Father tried to murder her for jewels during peace talks.

Frey: Twin brother to the Queen, the Vanir god Freyr is a master healer, and is fabled to have helped the cursed Mimir brew Yggdrasil's elixir. During wartime, Freyr stands in as the Queen's right hand.

Hraesvelgr: Known as the Eagle, Hraesvelgr can be neither identified as Aesir nor Vanir. One of the oldest gods in existence, a child of the goddess Hel, looks more like a bird than a human to the mortal eye. Whether he stands with his relative clan or the rival Aesirs during the war is unknown.

Realms and Beings of Yggdrasil

Asgard: Known as the center of all realms, Asgard is the realm of peace, where its rainbow bridge symbolizes the union between worlds. Whoever sits upon the Bleeding Throne of Asgard is the Guardian of Peace, burdened with the responsibility of keeping the people of Yggdrasil united.

Vanaheim: Homeland to the Vanir clan, it is covered with forests and green fields of exotic flowers surrounding his ancient castle. Magic exists in every crevice and its natives, the Fae creatures, are connected spiritually to the realm's natural world.

Midgard: A realm full of mortals, the realm of Midgard changes faster than any of the other realms tied to Yggdrasil. Though its inhabitants remain oblivious to the magic within their own world, hundreds of beasts and monsters cast off by the godly clans take sanctuary in Midgard's naivety.

Valhalla: The All-Father's forever-growing heaven for his chosen warriors sits on an island in the middle of an ocean, the only building being a skyscraping tower. At Valhalla's peak is where Yggdrasil rests and the Norn circle its roots.

Alfheim: The magical world of Alfheim is known as both hauntingly beautiful and terrifyingly dangerous. The elves native to the land can brew heinous illnesses, as well as the cures for them.

Svartalfheim: A world built within volcanic tunnels, Svartalfheim is uninhabitable above the surface. The dwarves, native to Svartalfheim, work in the always-growing and changing labyrinths, searching for materials to forge everything and anything. Four dwarves, the first of them as the legends say, hold up the corners of Svartalfheim's sky.

Nifelheim: The Norse underworld Nifelheim is ruled by the devious Vanir goddess, Hel. Her wolves roam the icy wasteland searching for trespassers, and her Dragur march towards her castle, awaiting her command. The undead left behind by the Valkyrie find their way to her halls, and will one day join her Dragur army.

Jotunnheim: A land of snow and ice, Jotunheim houses its blue-skinned giants, and has a peaceful society when left alone.

Hjerte: A small settlement in Vanaheim, hidden by mountainous walls, the only entrance being a hole at the top. Built by the mountain goddess Skadi, Hjerte remains untouched by the feuding clans' conflicts, making it the perfect sanctuary for its inhabitants.

Herjan and Valdorf: Originally known as Herjan, the merchant town sat at a valley's entrance, the first blockade between the outside world and Asgard's city. After the Aesir raided the town due to rumors of an uprising, it was renamed Valfodr, symbolizing its destruction.

The Norn: Urd, Skuld, and Verdandi are three women-like creatures known as the Norn who control all strings of Fate.

Well of Urðr: Used by the Norn, the Well of Urðr is filled with *Mótefni*, a medicine brewed by Mimir. The Norn uses the elixir inside the well to care for Yggdrasil.

Valkyrie: Winged women who can travel between realms to collect warrior souls for Valhalla, normally dressed in sterling silver armor.

Fafnir and Sigurd: Once the son of a mighty Dwarf King, Fafnir became cursed with greed and transformed into a monstrous dragon after being tricked by Loki into wearing Andvari's cursed ring, Andvaranaut. He was fated to be slain by the great warrior, Sigurd.

Sigrdrífa, Olrun, and Svava: A trio of Valkyrie, known for their corrupted views of justice. Once a name sung in praises, Sigrdrífa rose to notability by guiding one of the All-Father's favorite legends, Sigurd.

Andvari's Ring Andvaranaut: When Loki was only a trickster, he stole a ring called Andvaranaut from Andvari, a dwarf, whose ring could collect riches. When the dwarf realized his treasure was missing, he cursed it, that the wearer might succumb to greed, and transform into a gruesome beast.

Jotunn: As the natives of Jotunheim, the blue-skinned giants are used to being visited by their godly neighbors from Vanaheim, the clan never failing to take advantage of their growing numbers and immeasurable strength. While they are harmless in their homes, their great stature and impressive horns strike fear in many mortal creatures' hearts.

Fae: Natives to Vanaheim, these creatures normally have pale blue skin, and share the same lines across their skin like their creators, the Vanir. The Fae are skilled in magic, especially verbal magic, coaxing things from their victims to grow their strength.

Yggdrasil: The tree of life and death, always growing and decaying, connects all realms and peoples. Yggdrasil remains an enigma towards all living creatures, god or not.

Laevateinn: Forged by Loki, Laevateinn is a magical staff embedded with the trickster god's power. After his exile, the tool was removed from his possession.

Gleipnir: As the most coveted and dangerous weapon within the nine realms, Gleipnir can only be rightfully wielded by anyone with the All-Father Odin's blood. It was forged in Svartalfheim specifically for Odin's use, and blessed with unimaginable power. Any mortal struck by Gleipnir is doomed to fall.

Dainsleif: A cursed sword, fated always to take life whenever it is removed from its scabbard.

Svalin: A legendary shield, said to have been used to keep back the heat from the sun, built by the Aesir sun god, Sol.

Warriors of Thunder: A band of heroes the Norn chose to be the Guardian of Peace's advisors and warriors.

Acknowledgments

Thank you to Caitlin, whose aspirations to be a freelance editor allowed her to spend some time on my unpolished manuscript. You're my best friend, and having you by my side has kept the dream afloat through all the hardships we've gone through. I feel like I can achieve anything with you around.

Thank you to George Jreije, the wonderful editor and author of *The Shad Hadid Series*. Without his edits, I would have never gathered the confidence to publish.

Thank you to my family for being there from day one: when I was 13 and self-publishing a 90-page novella about a girl named Alice, when I was 15 and publishing more and more.

And thank you to Kyle, who taught me what it means to love relentlessly in the last three years. Finding you was like finding a home. Without you, the characters in *Valhalla* would not know how to love each other without bounds.

About the Author

Born and raised in central Florida, Gabriella Dennany now resides in a small Virginia town, surrounded by mountains and valleys. After spending almost ten years researching Norse Mythology and planning a series surrounding undead young adults, *The Halls of Valhalla* is the first in a projected chronicle of four books. She spends her days gawking over her cat and watching birds at the feeder from her window.